T0279161

# SERPENT SEA

# SERPENT SEA

MAIYA IBRAHIM

DELACORTE PRESS

Visit us on the Web! GetUnderlined.com

Educators and librarians, for a variety of teaching tools, visit us at RHTeachersLibrarians.com

Library of Congress Cataloging-in-Publication Data is available upon request.
ISBN 978-0-593-12700-1 (trade) — ISBN 978-0-593-12701-8 (ebook) —
ISBN 978-0-593-90263-9 (international ed.)

The text of this book is set in 11.25-point Adobe Garamond Pro.
Interior design by Michelle Crowe

Printed in the United States of America
10 9 8 7 6 5 4 3 2 1
First Edition

For Mum and Dad,
who showed me the true magic of love

Darkcliff
The Garden of the Huntsman
The Dark
The Swan of Shorehill
Lift Street
River Waden

The Cliff
Observation Tower
Royal Citadel
The Lifts
Lift to the Citadel
North
The Filthy Bilge Tavern

# 1

# IMANI

IN LONG GRASS, THE SERPENT IS KING. IF THE LION IS *wise, he will take care where he steps. This is how you become strong: by knowing where you are weak first.*

"Imani, it's time."

I rouse with a gasp, Baba's lesson fading to memory. The shadow of my twenty-two-year-old brother, Atheer, leans over me. Abovedeck, sailors call, ropes and canvas shift, the ship rocks, and long, ominous bellows reverberate across the Bay of Glass. I lay a hand over my thrumming heart and inspect the bunk below me. Our sister, Amira, two years younger than me at fifteen, is snoring in it.

I sit up. "How long have I been asleep?"

"A few hours. Horns are blowing in the city." Atheer gives me room to slide down from my bunk. "We'll find out why on the way to the stables. We need to fetch the horses."

"Is it wise for you to leave the ship when you're the most wanted man in Taeel-Sa?" I ask him. "Glaedric's men will be searching for you." I sling my cloak over my shoulders, thinking of how we sprang King Glaedric's prize prisoner from captivity last night and sank the royal ship in a blaze. But I should know my brother better by now. Brave to a fault.

"We'll be cautious." He waits for me to pull boots onto my aching feet and check that the bandage on my neck isn't blood-soaked. We retreat through the cramped crew quarters.

"How about a tea ceremony to replenish our magic?" I suggest, sidestepping a tipped-over clay jug that smells of wine.

"Better not to risk the temptation of using it in Glaedric's city." He glances at me sideways. "I already made that mistake."

And it got him arrested, imprisoned, and tortured. As we near the hatch leading abovedeck, the red afternoon light confirms that this Atheer is not the brother of my happy memories, in which we spar with wooden swords in the courtyard at home and later take our horses for a ride beyond Qalia's walls. Neither is he like the warrior-heroes of folklore I've admired since childhood, immense figures who move mountains and swallow dust storms whole and never look the worse for wear. This Atheer is marked by bruises, scratches, and burns; he's gaunt from starvation, his jaw sharp enough to cut steel, his brown eyes unduly large and framed by limp caramel-colored curls. This is my new brother in my new world.

Qayn waits for us by the mainmast, portrait-still in odd contrast to the sailors working the rigging around him and those extending the ribbed bridge from the ship to the pier. The *Lion's Prize* has been moved from where it was anchored this morning into an isolated berth on the Bay's edge, inhabited by barnacled fishing boats and tired, worm-eaten merchant dhows. A place no one willingly comes except to be forgotten.

The sailors repay Qayn's attention with bashful glances.

Though I'm more familiar with the djinni, I'm equally captivated by the symmetry of his angular features, and the way he comports his slender frame with both serious, regal grace and a casual, boyish ease. At dawn, he promised to save my people if I returned his stolen magic. Now I regard him as if he's an oasis. Beneath my relief at finding a life-saving refuge, I feel the primal fear that I am being lured by a mirage to my death.

He greets us with a nod before glancing wryly over my shoulder. "Quite the motley company you've assembled, Atheer."

Taha and Reza lurk in the recessed shelter under the gangway behind me, but the ropes that the sailors used to bind their wrists after they tried to kill us are nowhere to be seen. Sunlight touches Taha's eyes, their color the pale green of drought-stricken fields; it finds the wounds I gave him last night, his split bottom lip and the welt on his cheekbone. How could I have ever craved his kiss? I was a trusting, foolish girl who cared too much what he thought of me. It's clear now that during our entire journey here, he was only manipulating me to make his mission easier. In the prison, I even confessed that I wanted his kisses to mean something. And he was surprised, not because he'd assumed I'd been pretending to like him all along and was moved to discover that the opposite was true. No; it was because the thought of how I felt had never crossed his mind before.

I turn to Atheer. "What are you thinking, letting them go free? They tried to kill you barely ten hours ago!"

They also nearly buried me alive in the prison. I only escaped that place by falling down a chute onto . . . *Don't go there,* I order myself, but I'm already seeing and feeling—*smelling*—the mountain of decaying bodies and polished skeletons I tumbled down in my own fight for life.

Atheer is frustratingly undeterred. "They won't try again. Their mission orders no longer apply."

"No!" I'd be embarrassed to air my outrage before the crew if bottling it up weren't corroding my insides. "The only reason they didn't kill you last night is because they were cornered! It was never about mission orders!"

"What was it, then?" Taha demands.

"Old-fashioned clan warfare against the 'elitists' and 'parasites' you despise," I reply, echoing the hate-filled words he uttered in the prison. "The wellbeing of our nation is nothing more than a shield for you to hide your sordid truth behind."

The light gutters in his eyes, giving rein to some waiting inner darkness. "You're wrong. If I'd intended to kill your brother for any other reason, he wouldn't be standing here now. I've only ever acted in our people's best interest."

"Is *that* why you ordered us to leave that defenseless woman to her fate back in Bashtal? I suppose innocent Safiya posed a threat to the Sahir too?" I push my cloak away from the dagger on my thigh. "Drop this embarrassing pretense and admit you don't care about anyone or anything that doesn't further your vile father's ambitions."

Taha's nostrils flare. "I ordered you to leave that woman in Bashtal because I didn't want to endanger our lives by alerting the soldiers. Remember Fey?"

My gut suspends at her mention, as if I've been thrown from a great height. "You mean my brother's third assassin."

"Fey didn't know about Taha's orders and was never going to," Reza interjects angrily.

He startles me; I'm almost unaccustomed to hearing his voice. When I first met Taha's cousin—older than Taha by six years at twenty-four—he couldn't survive ten minutes without telling a crass joke to amuse their squadmate Feyrouz. He all but stopped talking after she was captured by the Harrowlanders in Bashtal.

I feign indifference, pulling my dagger from its sheath to inspect its polished blade. But while I do, I think of my promise that we'd find Fey after we found Atheer. An empty promise now, and I'm the liar who made it. "I remember that Taha forced us to leave her behind too," I say.

"After *you* got her captured by refusing to follow my orders," Taha retorts. "It's easy now for you to criticize me and my decisions. You weren't responsible for our safety, the mission, or any of the consequences. Not like you care about those. You only care about playing the hero."

"And you only care to *talk* about fighting injustice," I snap. "You see Alqibahi people suffering right in front of you and you try to punish my brother for helping them." I use the dagger to point at him. "You, of all people, should see why that's hypocritical."

"Oh, why? Because I grew up poor and scorned?" He leaves the shadow of the gangway, sneering; the daylight burnishes his ebony hair in a fiery crown. "What's hypocritical is how you've ignored the suffering of other Sahirans your entire life. You're from a powerful, wealthy clan, Imani. Why didn't you ever help them? They were right in front of you."

My ears burn; I feel the eyes of the crew on the back of my head. "We donate generously to the needy on festival days," I respond woodenly, the heat of humiliation seeping down my neck.

Taha grants me slow applause. "Well done. You applied a bandage to a mortal wound and then praised yourself for being virtuous. The Beya clan has almost never gone unrepresented on the Council of Al-Zahim. Why didn't they do something more substantial to help? I'll tell you." He steps up to me, striking in his fearsomeness and undaunted by the dagger now hanging limply in my hand. "The real sordid truth is that wealthy clans like yours benefit in every way from the power structure that rules the Sahir. Why would they change it, and why would you ever protest their inaction? It's easier to question my conscience and demand that I risk my Scouts' lives and our people's security to relieve your own raging guilt, now that you've realized you've been molded into the very person you denounce: someone selfish, ignorant, and privileged. But you'll never admit that, because it hurts too much to look in the mirror and see the real you staring back."

I suddenly remember something Qayn told me: *You only use others to get what you want, and you are outraged when they refuse. You're like the rest of your kind. Selfish.*

"You've said enough, Taha," Atheer warns.

But he could've said much less and I still wouldn't have a retort for the most shameful dressing-down of my life. His razor-sharp words have skinned me, pared the gristle back, and bared my humiliated innards for all to see. Earlier I wondered how I could've craved Taha's kiss. Now I wonder how he could've tolerated mine.

"You had your orders in the prison," Taha says with less vehemence. "You shouldn't have gotten Safiya involved."

My heart is heavy; my eyes ache. "I was supposed to die alone."

"As you said, Safiya was innocent." Taha sighs, his stony expression softening. "Can we speak privately for a moment?"

I pretend my pulse hasn't sped up at his request. I'm curious to know what he wants from me, but I refuse to reveal that I care or that I'm nervous. I gesture with my blade at the hatch. "Fine. You go first."

I follow him with my fist wrapped tightly around my dagger. Atheer looks as if he wants to intervene in whatever's about to happen, but he can't. That would only contradict his earlier stance that the cousins no longer pose a danger to us. Instead, he tensely watches as we descend through the hatch into the gloom belowdecks.

I stare at Taha's exposed neck as he goes down the steps. "You got your privacy. Say what you want, unless this was an uninspired attempt to lure me somewhere where you could finish what you started in the prison."

He reaches the deck and twists to look back up at me. "I had to stop you, Imani, or you would've stopped me."

I falter on the second-to-last step, imagining what I would've done if Taha hadn't trapped me in the prison and I'd uncovered his intention to kill my brother. I would've driven this dagger into his chest to stop him, right through his duplicitous heart and out the other side, and I would've hesitated for such a brief moment beforehand that it wouldn't even be worth mentioning.

"Don't lie and say otherwise," he starts, but I shake my head.

"I won't," I say quietly, because no truer words were ever spoken, and that's what makes them so painful. We're two people stuck on opposite shores of an impassable sea. Who put us here? Was it the Great Spirit? Taha's father or mine? Our ancestors? Just us, perhaps? The answer doesn't really change things. Taha accepted his fate regardless of who orchestrated it, and I would've too if Atheer's life had demanded it.

Taha rises onto the step below mine, the sunlight restoring the familiar, arresting brightness of his gaze. "You said you wouldn't accept my apology, but I'll give it anyway. I'm sorry. I wasn't happy about what I did to you or your brother. I was only trying to shield our people from the invader."

It's an apology I didn't think I'd receive and don't know what to do with. An apology that doesn't triumph over those treacherous waters to reach me; it sinks below the surface just offshore, and that hurts so much worse than if it hadn't tried at all. This is only an acknowledgment of the heartbreaking truth that Taha and I will never find peace together. The battle that raged between us last night will always be only a small twist of circumstance away.

My hand trembles as I stash my dagger. I try to do the same with my feelings as I silently rejoin my brother. Protecting our people is what matters most, isn't it? The fate of the Sahir hangs in the balance while Taha and I stand around arguing. Suddenly a thick fog of fear rises in me. How do I distinguish the truth from the lie, my enemy from my ally? How do I know who or what to trust? Whether I can even trust myself? The fog seeks to enshroud the future completely. I'll have to wade through it, and there's no telling whether what lies ahead of me is the precipice of a sheer cliff or the threshold of home.

A horn interrupts the tense silence. Perhaps Atheer knows that no explanation of what just happened between me and Taha will be given, because he doesn't ask. He shares a kiss goodbye with Farida, the mid-twenties captain of the *Prize* and his sweetheart, and goes to the bridge. "Let's head out," he says. "We can't leave Taeel-Sa without our horses."

"After what I did to you, why not send others?" Taha calls after him.

Atheer pauses to contemplate the boats moored across the pier. "I think you and Reza must see things for yourselves," he answers pensively. "Hurry now, and keep quiet."

And then he's gone, and such has always been Atheer's power that people want to follow him. We leave the ship armed with only our wits, except for the ancient dagger hidden again under my cloak, though I pray I have no occasion to use it. After minutes of swift, silent walking, we reach the port of Taeel-Sa. It's heaving with Harrowlander soldiers, sailors, and officials racing around in the dry heat to a cacophony of horns, harried by the burden of some urgent task.

Atheer navigates between them with the hood of his vine-green cloak pulled low. Back home he could go anywhere with his head held high. Sahirans called him the Lion of Qalia and shared tales of his skin-changing magic, his bravery in defending remote Sahiran settlements against monsters. But Atheer is no lion here; he's a mouse scampering between pipe-smoking Taeel-Sani stevedores muttering about the mysterious blaze that took King Glaedric's ship in the night, and soldiers who've descended upon the port like clouds of locusts on a wheat crop.

At a row of warehouses, the soldiers hastily load boxes onto wagons, supervised by heat-flushed officials in staid brown robes too heavy for the climate. Only when each wagon is sitting low on its axles does the line trundle on, clearing the road for another convoy. These wagons too are promptly filled in a well-ordered procession, and it seems there's no end to the boxes stored within the warehouses.

In the war-scarred streets behind the port, palisades persist, ditches remain half-filled, and the skeletons of wrecked wagons rest under mounds of sand. Many buildings in this area were never rebuilt after the war, the hurled boulders that ruined them still crowning the rubble like gravestones, between which children dig for arrowheads and shattered swords to smelt for coin. Though the ordinarily loud city is quiet, it is the busiest I've ever seen it. Every person in Taeel-Sa must've been lured to the streets by the rumors rippling out from the port; they meander about on false business, gathering to converse in murmurs while absently perusing linen dresses, colorful clayware, and boxes of fruits, never seeming to purchase anything. Wary eyes peep from beneath draped veils and wrapped keffiyehs. I catch a snippet of whispered speculation at a grocer: "—the fire started in more than one place. This was either the work of our rebels or *their* traitors."

It's conspiratorial talk that could get one arrested, but few soldiers are patrolling. Pairs of them, shouldering backpacks, march past to elsewhere, and the rest are busy erecting cordons to redirect traffic into narrower side streets. Since we left the *Prize,* I haven't seen anyone pulled aside to be interrogated or searched. Nobody has been told to move on; no additional checkpoints have been established to sort through citizens in the king's hunt for Atheer. I expected to see gangs of soldiers separating young men from the crowds and forcing them to remove their head and face coverings. But it's as if King Glaedric has forgotten about us.

More troubling is the veritable army of workers putting up decorations. As we walk, brown-and-maroon banners depicting golden stag heads unfurl over us, and green cords embroidered in white flowers made of linen are carefully wrapped around lampposts and the beams of grapevine lattices. Whoever commanded the city workers to perform this task would be aware of last night's incident on the Bay, so why does King Glaedric care more about decorating the city than about recovering his prisoner?

Suddenly a series of strident horn blasts echoes up the street. Carriages and riders shrink to the left, and the foot travelers around us withdraw to the sandstone frontages of the buildings, where they stop to look down toward the port. The ground trembles under my boots as I jog after Atheer into an alleyway and huddle there with several others, who squeeze their eyes shut and shield their airways with their head coverings. I decipher the galloping of horses and the clattering of wheels only a few seconds before the convoy of wagons roars around the bend, so loud that it muzzles all else. It thunders past in an explosion of dust, steered with a single-minded fury that demands that any obstacle in its path be summarily cleared.

It's gone just as quickly, leaving a vacuous silence and crushed doves in its wake. With watery eyes, I watch it wind up the incline between the tall buildings like a serpent belly-down through yellowed grass. It's left several things behind on the street. Reza darts in front of the resuming traffic, snatches up one of the cylindrical objects, and brings it back to our group. We gather outside a coffeehouse with pale-lime shutters coated in dust.

"What is it?" Taha asks.

"A vambrace," I answer.

Reza nods, handing the object to me. The hard, boiled leather is a piece of armor that a soldier would wear on their forearm for protection. It's not as well-made as a Sahiran vambrace, which is specially crafted for the warrior who will wear it, but the construction is sturdy enough.

Taha takes it from me, frowning. "Strange," he murmurs. "This fell from the wagons. *This* was in those boxes at the warehouses."

"Better not to hold on to it," says Atheer, starting up the street again.

Taha tosses the vambrace to the ground, and we continue on.

A few hundred yards past the Grand Bazaar, Atheer stops us in a lane behind a tapered correspondence tower announcing itself far and wide with its unique blend of burning spices. It surpasses the city's defensive walls in height; I have to crane my neck to peer at the balcony encircling its peak, where messenger falcons with scrolls fastened to their ankles sweep in, their broad wings fanning curtains of aromatic smoke escaping the large urns fixed into the stone. Yet for all the falcons arriving, none are leaving, and the tower's front doors are closed.

"I need to check something here before we go to the stables," Atheer says. He knocks on the narrow door in the wall enclosing the tower's back courtyard, thudding his fist several times in a deliberate rhythm. It opens, and a curly-haired young man pokes his head out. His eyes widen.

"Brother! I thought you'd been—" He halts, warily glancing at the lane behind us, and continues in a lower voice. "It's been a long time, Atheer."

"Too long, Basel," Atheer replies. "Could we sneak up to the balcony for a minute?"

"Just for a minute." Basel stands aside, palm pressed to his chest in greeting as we filter into the courtyard. "Officials came past this morning and forbade us to send out correspondence; said if we did, our falcons would be hunted down and shot. Didn't give a reason why, only said they'd be back to make sure we're complying."

I suspect the reason has to do with us, but like Atheer, I don't say anything. We pass the wooden mews and step into a large administration room partitioned in two. One section is a maze of shelves stacked with labeled jars of messenger spices for various towers across Alqibah. Depending on where a departing falcon is destined, the spice blend of its destination tower will be burned in small quantities to allow the falcon to catch the scent. The room's other section is full of cabinets and desks laden with paperwork. On our right, a wide stairwell curls up into the tower.

Basel hands Atheer a lit lantern. "Don't draw attention to yourselves up there," he says. "I noticed soldiers lurking on the roofs of nearby buildings. They all had some sort of buzzard with them. If I were to guess, that's how they mean to hunt down outgoing falcons."

"Appreciate the warning," Atheer says, and Basel returns to his task of sifting through a bucket of scrolls.

Atheer leads us up the stairwell to the breezy top level, cross-hatched with deep shadows and rosy afternoon light, scented strongly of hay, seeds, falcon droppings, and the heady heat of the burning spices. Atheer sets the lantern down on a table by the landing, pulls a bronze spyglass from his jacket pocket, and continues to the balcony railing, where he stops and peers out.

I tentatively join him. Majestic Taeel-Sa sprawls around us in squares of sandstone, columns of marble, triangles of green and tangerine canvas, and domes of glittering tooled gold. Its beauty is protected from the green-speckled wilderness beyond by the defensive walls, and at this angle, from this height, I can see directly over them to the outer fields, where the Harrowlander military camp is erected around stone debris left behind from Glaedric's assault on the city. When I arrived in Taeel-Sa, the camp was an intimidating arrangement of hundreds of tents in orderly rows. Not anymore.

"The camp's being packed up," Taha says beside me.

I accept the spyglass from Atheer and use it to locate the camp again. A toppling tent swings into view, pulled down by soldiers.

Elsewhere, campfires are snuffed, and piles of stone, wood, and hay bales are loaded onto wagons that roll out onto the Spice Road. There, they compete with convoys speeding into dusk and the long, dense ribbon made up of thousands of marching soldiers.

I lower the spyglass and stare into the horizon, distantly mindful of Taha taking the instrument from me. "They're all leaving," I say. "They're going south . . . to the Sahir."

"Y-you don't know that," Reza stammers. "They're probably heading to another city."

"They've already conquered every city in Alqibah," Taha says, pulling the spyglass away from his wet eyes. "There's only one place left for them to go."

"Our home." I turn my head to Atheer, expecting shock and exclamations of disbelief. But my brother isn't at the railing anymore. He's gone to lean against a thick wooden beam in the middle of the balcony with his back to us.

"This is what you brought us to see." I walk toward him, my heart pounding. "You already knew when we left the ship this morning that Glaedric's invasion had begun."

"I knew when you broke me out of captivity." His voice echoes in the eaves, disembodied. "Apart from the soldiers guarding the gates, I suspected that no one would be looking for me today. No checkpoints, no resources or time unnecessarily spent trying to recapture me. This is a race to reach Qalia, and Glaedric understood that the race had begun the moment you freed me."

"What did you do, Atheer?" Taha mumbles, his shoulders heaving. He pushes away from the railing and shambles forward. "What did you *do*?"

"No," comes a voice from behind us, "the question now is what will *you* do?"

We look back to see Qayn perched on the railing beside a newly arrived tawny falcon. I meet the djinni's burning-coal gaze, recalling the offer he made me at dawn: help him get his magic back in exchange for a magical army to defeat the Harrow-landers.

"We'll fetch the horses and discuss the rest on the ship," says Atheer. "Take one last look if you must." He collects the lantern and descends the stairs.

Taha and Reza eagerly return to the railing, as if to find that the vision was a mirage. But once they are there, their faces fall, and any remaining hope is erased from them. They go after Atheer, leaving me alone with Qayn, now reaching into an urn of burning messenger spices.

"Don't give me your answer yet." He saunters over to me with something black pinched between his fingers, raises his hand, and blows on the ash. It plumes between us, lifted on a breeze wafting over the balcony. My eyes water; the back of my throat tickles.

"Do you know what that is?" he asks me. "It's the bitter taste of regret. From now on, think of it before every decision you make."

He watches the ash fall. Fear slips down my spine, an old struggle erupting inside me. We're alone. Nobody could stop me from killing the monster I am oath-bound to destroy. But if I uphold my oath, I may doom my people and kill my unlikely ally and my brother's trusted friend. He saved Atheer from torture and death; this time, he's offering to save my entire nation and the people of Alqibah.

The air between us clears. Qayn starts toward the stairwell, speaking to me over his shoulder. "As I said, don't give me your answer yet. But I suspect you already know in your heart what it must be."

My lifeblood thuds in my ears. For a long moment, I stare at the soldiers marching under the blood-red sunset, and then I follow Qayn down into the darkness.

# 2

# TAHA

NOT EVEN REUNITING WITH HIS WHITE COLT, AESIF, is enough to comfort Taha. The city workers come too late to light the lampposts, and the journey back to the *Prize* is made on the edge of dusk.

He and Reza are riding through a lonely laneway when Reza suddenly breaks the silence between them. "I understand why you left Fey behind. You were right to chase the mission. I forgive you for that."

Taha glances at his cousin, brows raised. This is the first substantial thing Reza has said to him since Bashtal. Still, he's careful not to feel relief at this tentative reunion. He senses that Reza isn't done with him yet.

"There's something else for which you don't forgive me," he says.

Reza nods at the shadows on the walls around them. "It wasn't easy, but I understood why we had to stop Atheer. But what I did in the prison and then on the ship, what you wanted me to help you do to Farida and her crew afterward . . . That's not who I am, Taha, and that's not you either. We want to protect our home, but not at the expense of innocent lives. The rebels didn't choose to learn about our magic; they shouldn't die for a decision made for them."

Taha stares at Imani and Atheer riding about a hundred feet ahead, his fingers tightening around the reins. "I'm sorry, Reza. Sometimes I don't know what comes over me."

He knows perfectly well. It's the "other" Taha, the hard-hearted warrior shaped by Bayek, his father, who assumes control when unspeakable things must be done. After last night, it's a man Taha fears encountering again.

Reza leans over to squeeze his cousin's shoulder. "You were trying your best."

Bayek would say that Taha's best wasn't good enough. At the thought of it, something scared skitters along the back wall of his mind, casting a too-big shadow that looks like frustrated fists and wounding words.

Reza distracts him from it with an offhand remark. "You never told me that Atheer was your mentor."

Taha says nothing, but the falcon pendant Atheer gifted him for his birthday sits heavily against his chest.

"Were you afraid of word reaching your father?" Reza asks. "Didn't want a repeat of what happened with Fadi?"

Taha blinks. "Nothing happened with Fadi."

"No? Your father told mine that he was worried Fadi was going to make us soft because he saw Fadi crying in public, Spirits forbid."

An old, dull hurt unearths in Taha. "We grew apart, that was all."

"In one night after years of friendship, sure," Reza says dryly. "I dread to think what your father would've said about Atheer had he found out. That's why you kissed Imani in secret too, isn't it?"

Taha flinches as if he's been struck by a stone, then cranes forward in his saddle to anxiously study the distance between him and Imani, just to be sure there's no chance she could overhear Reza.

"No," he says, leaning back, "I didn't want you getting the wrong idea."

"You were manipulating her?"

Taha jumps at the excuse, nodding. "I hoped that if she thought I was interested in her, she'd agree to stand aside. I should've known better—someone like her would never be interested in someone like me." He bites his tongue; heat collars his neck. He sounds as bitter as ash, and he hates it.

"I would've agreed with you a little while ago, but I think there might be hope for Imani," says Reza. "You said some harsh things to her this morning, and she actually seemed to listen."

Taha ignores the maddening spark of hope fizzing in his chest. "Wouldn't matter to me if she denounced her birthright and devoted her life to the charitable care of orphans."

"Ah. She'll always be from the Beya clan, right?" There's an edge to Reza's tone. "You must've enjoyed kissing her to do it more than once."

"Sure." He shrugs. "Didn't have to care about her to enjoy it. Is there a reason we're talking about this?" He adjusts his sweaty palms around the reins and glances up at Sinan, his falcon mind-beast flying overhead with whom he shares a magical bond. The falcon has been tracking them since they left the *Prize.*

Reza sighs. "You know your secrets are safe with me, Taha. I'd never tell your father anything unless you asked me to."

The collar of heat feels more like a noose now. Why does

Taha have to desire someone he hates anyway? It was purely physical at first, even though he knew Imani was from *that* clan and condescendingly proud. He was still drawn to her. Then he began hearing stories, like how she single-handedly defended three children from a clan of djinn before her squad arrived. He began noticing how hard she tried in lessons, always the first to raise her hand to answer a question or volunteer for a task, never one to engage in idle gossip or waste time. He appreciated how seriously she took being a Shield, and her accomplishments were only made more attractive because he knew she didn't have to put so much effort in. Like plenty of other Shields from famed clans, she could've skipped lessons and training sessions and stayed safely behind at camp whenever her squad went out on a mission, and she *still* would've been praised, thanks to her clan's reputation. But Imani didn't choose the easy path. She devoted herself to their dangerous duty of defending their people from the monsters that plague the Sahir. His opinions on her many privileges aside, Taha respected that.

Now it's Imani or nobody, and he accepts her however she arrives in his fantasies. Sometimes she's warm, inviting, aware of her fortunes; she doesn't belittle his clan or laugh at him for thinking he could ever have a chance with her. But sometimes when the mood strikes him, she's as mean as they come, and his pleasure hinges entirely on her derisive laughter. . . .

"Can I ask you something else?" Reza says suddenly in a careful tone. "What did Atheer mean when he said you'd acted as your father's assassin?"

Taha realizes he's been watching Imani this entire time, and now they've reached the port. He shifts his gaze to the water, stained crimson under the setting sun as if by bodies sacrificed to the bay. "Slander," he says flatly.

It's a moment before Reza speaks again. "Was Atheer referring to Uncle's election, or—"

"Don't," Taha interrupts, looking at his cousin. "Please, Reza, for your own sake, don't ask me about this. If you must know something, know that everything I've ever done has been for the greater good."

*Some lives for many others,* as his father once said.

Taha returns his gaze to the water, and an uneasy quiet occupies the space between them. Eventually his focus drifts, and the memories he consciously keeps locked away seep out, as sly as mist. He remembers things from moments he wishes he hadn't lived: a carriage burning on the long, shadowy road back to Qalia; a motionless figure spread-eagled in bent rosebushes under sheeting rain; bloody knuckles and a cracked mirror, his own broken reflection staring back at him—

A horn blares from deep in the city and chases the memories back to their cage. The bosun, Muhab, meets them at the bridge to the *Lion's Prize* and orders his sailors to bring the horses across. Taha leaves Aesif and follows Reza to the deck. It's been adjusted to accommodate the beasts, crude fences having been lashed to the rails and masts to create provisional stalls, and hay and jars of water stacked in the recess under the gangway.

"Join us in the captain's cabin," Atheer tells them before going up the steps.

His civility is vexing. Several times today, Taha wished for Atheer to lash out at him and prove he's not the warrior Taha admired for years. He's not the generous mentor who became a friend; he's a reckless zealot who'll charge through anyone daring to challenge his ideology, if he can't convince them with his veneer of decency first.

Taha and Reza go up to the captain's cabin after Imani,

Muhab, Farida, and the quartermaster, Makeen. Small and tired, the cabin at least smells nicely of the sea and faded frankincense.

"What are *they* doing here?" Amira scowls at Taha and Reza from beside the desk.

"We must all work together," Atheer replies, closing the door.

Briefly, Taha's eyes meet Qayn's, though he didn't hear the djinni enter the cabin. He's convinced that he's never feared Qayn, but a shiver traces his shoulders regardless.

"They don't want to work together," Amira protests shrilly. "They want to kill us!"

"King Glaedric wants to kill us. His men are marching south to the Sahir." Atheer gently seats her in a chair by the scratched desk littered with scrolls, seafaring instruments, and a lifelike lion carved from wood.

Amira's chin wobbles. "Already?"

"Unfortunately." Atheer goes to the curved window in the alcove behind the desk and peers out. "I suspect that Glaedric fears losing the element of surprise if we get a chance to alert the Council to the invasion."

"Glaedric is doomed to fail," says Taha. "Every path across the Swallowing Sands is narrow. It'll take him at least several days to move his soldiers across through a single column three bodies wide. And that doesn't factor in supplies."

Atheer studies the ships moored out on the bay, their shapes fading in the growing dark. "Glaedric knows every path that I know through the Swallowing Sands, and he has my map of the Sahir. He can get into and around our land faster than you think."

Taha stares, aghast, at the man he once hoped might convince his father that not everyone from a powerful clan is untrustworthy. Even the word *traitor* feels insufficient.

"We must warn the Council immediately," says Amira. "No army can outpace a messenger falcon."

"It's too risky," says Atheer. "Glaedric is already putting measures in place to stop messenger falcons from flying south."

"Then get us back to the Swallowing Sands," says Taha. "Once we cross into the Sahir, I can send Sinan ahead to Qalia with a warning. The Council need as much time as we can give them to prepare their defense."

"We mustn't encourage them to fight Glaedric," says Atheer, still gazing out the window. "He seized my caches of *misra*."

Their people's sacred Spice. Made from the bark of the ancient misra tree growing in Qalia's Sanctuary, the Spice grants temporary magical ability to anyone who consumes it in tea. And now, after being a secret to everyone but their people for a thousand years, it's in the invader's hands.

"How much misra?" Taha asks gravely.

"Enough to be a problem. Glaedric has magic, and his army in Alqibah outnumbers our forces ten to one. Abroad?"

"A million strong," Farida supplies. "Your warriors are better trained in magic, but Glaedric has the numbers to overwhelm them."

"And once Glaedric has dealt with them, there'll be nothing left to stand between him and the misra tree," says Atheer.

"Are you forgetting Qalia's walls?" Taha approaches the desk. "We'll warn the Council to prepare for a siege: gather resources and order everyone from outlying settlements to retreat inside Qalia. The walls will protect them, and the magic of the misra tree will sustain them."

"For a short while," Atheer says quietly.

Taha furrows his brow. "No city in Alqibah has walls that rival the height and width of Qalia's. They can't be breached without siege engines—trebuchets or at the very least catapults, and a significant number of them—which Glaedric has to either transport finished across the Swallowing Sands or assemble in the Sahir. Neither option is easy or fast."

Atheer finally turns from the window. The leaping lantern light exposes the harsh ridges of his skull straining through his skin, the dark hollows where his eyes should be. "Do you know what Glaedric said when I warned him that he would never breach Qalia's walls?" he asks. " 'I don't need to topple Qalia's walls. I only need to topple the people who hide within them.' You don't understand this man yet, Taha, his wealth, his influence, and, most important, his *ambition.* There is no defense that can meet Glaedric's threat."

"Then you've ruined us with your treason," Taha says in disbelief. "No defense and no attack? Nothing to do but to wait for death, is that it?"

"Watch your mouth," says Farida, glaring down her nose at him. "What you call treason was Atheer helping us in our time of need. It was an act of humanity that your Council refused."

"Do you feel 'helped'?" he asks her. "Or is this more of the same? Worse. Much worse if Glaedric takes the misra tree and has its magic at his disposal. Then you'll know the true meaning of oppression, and your regret over your blunders will haunt you for the few short years you have left. Make no mistake, Captain. King Glaedric in possession of the misra tree is the end of everything."

"Only if you do nothing." Qayn surfaces from the shadows in the corner, fingers interlinked. Taha instinctively tenses. It takes everything he has not to lay hands on the djinni. He couldn't kill Qayn with his fists alone—he'd need the steel of a sword for that—but he'd be satisfied to break something in the slight body that Qayn presents as his own.

"Is there a reason you're still here, devil?" Taha asks.

"The same reason you are, boy: I've not yet outlived my usefulness." Qayn gives him an infuriatingly attractive smirk. "Tell me, Taha, what would you say if I promised that I could save the Sahir and Alqibah from King Glaedric?"

"I'd say you're doing what your kind does best."

"Lying?" Qayn chuckles. "Fortunately for you, I am being very honest. You see, a long time ago, a cunning thief stole my magic and hid it from me—"

*"Oh."* Taha cuts him off, grinning meanly. "*That* explains why you're so useless."

"For now. But if you help me find my magic, I will gladly repay the favor by summoning an army for you to fight King Glaedric."

Taha's grin evaporates. Muhab, Makeen, and Amira murmur in shock, and Farida turns to Atheer, saying, "*This* is the plan you mentioned before you were arrested."

"Hold on." Taha turns to Atheer too. "Imani made it seem like you were barely friends with Qayn, but you've actually been working together on *this*? How could you have been so deceived, Atheer? Magic of this scale isn't possible for a djinni."

Qayn dons a withering sneer, crossing his slender arms. "And you know this because you've interrogated every type of djinni during your short, dreary existence, have you?"

Taha sighs. "Really, Qayn? You're implying that you're an *ifrit*?"

"Am I?" Qayn replies, smirking again.

He's trying to. Though little is known about ifrit, the consensus is that they're flying monsters made of black smoke with fire for hair and are rumored to be capable of unbelievable magical feats—cleaving mountains, ending drought, raising the sun during the night. But the scant accounts of Sahirans' encounters with ifrit date back to before Shields existed. Most modern scholars classify them as myths, with only a handful positing that they were real monsters now extinct in the Sahir.

"Well, are you? An ifrit?" Amira asks, nervously tapping her pointed slipper.

"*No,* he isn't," Taha says, exasperated. "Ifrit don't exist, and neither does Qayn's ability to conjure us an army. I can't believe we're using the little time we have left to protect our people discussing this charlatan's lies instead."

"Careful, Taha," Qayn drawls. "Hasty decisions hasten ruin."

Taha glares at him. "Clever. But I know your true nature, devil. Even with that pretty face and silver tongue, you can't deceive me."

Groaning, Qayn rolls his eyes. "Aren't you *dull*! At least *consider* my offer. My magic takes the form of three jewels. Find and return them to me—"

"I thought you said your magic was your crown," Imani interrupts.

"I *access* my magic through my crown," Qayn clarifies. "Once the jewels are mine again, I will reforge it."

Amira leaves her chair in a flutter of peach silk, addressing Imani with a deep frown. "I wasn't aware that djinn relied on external sources for their magic. I thought it was innate."

"Not for all of them." Taha scoffs. "Inferior djinn don't possess any magic of their own. They have to steal scraps of it from their kin and contain it within talismans because their weak constitutions can't tolerate using magic directly. Isn't that right, Qayn?"

If the underworld possessed eyes, they would be Qayn's, as spiteful as thwarted Death. They don't even blink when Imani raises her voice to defend him.

"Stop playing dumb, Taha," she says before turning to Amira. "A talisman of stolen magic is just *one* kind of external source, and the word *external* itself is misleading. Magic can manifest in an implement yet still have originated from the monster, and it has nothing to do with the monster's strength. Matriarchs of werehyena clans are especially powerful, and they wield staves containing their own magic."

That, Taha knows. A matriarch almost killed him last year, and he breaks out in a cold sweat just thinking about it. The planks start to drum under his boots, as the fractured stone of the ruins did; the rotting stink of the loping werehyenas fills the cabin; so too do their snarls, laughter, and twisted pleas. He had scouted the crumbling ruins ahead of his squad in search of the matriarch, a towering, sinewy, yellow-eyed monster too human to be beast, too beastly to be the human she once was. But by the time he found her, Taha had run out of arrows, and she had him cornered. He remembers most vividly the glow of her bone-staff as she tried to join his soul to her clan. The actual rending of his soul was agony; he screamed at every severed seam, at every happy memory sucked away and trapped inside the mysterious crystal fixed into her staff.

It was Spirits' luck that Reza showed up and used his magic to bury the matriarch under a pile of stone. The blinding light snuffed; the seams mended, and the memories settled back in place. At least, they were supposed to. But that evening back at camp, Taha couldn't sleep. He didn't feel like himself, and he couldn't decide whether the matriarch had succeeded in stealing something from him, or if she'd simply alerted him that something was already missing. . . .

"Just because we haven't documented the use of an implement in a djinni doesn't necessarily mean it can't happen, nor does relying on a magical implement have any bearing on the degree of a monster's power." Imani's matter-of-fact voice draws him back to the present.

Amira is still frowning. "Fine, but why is Qayn's magical implement a crown?"

"I was a king." Qayn smiles. "Your sister didn't tell you? I ruled the First City in what you now call the Vale of Bones. I *built* the First City."

"Each lie is more ridiculous than the last," Reza mutters from the corner.

Amira goes cross-eyed staring at Qayn. "You built . . . But . . . That was a thousand years ago."

"I am rather long-lived."

"And Hubaal the Terrible—"

Her mention of the monstrous giant that almost killed their group, and that devastated the Vale of Bones and slaughtered the tribes who lived there a millennium ago, elicits no unease in Qayn.

"Mine to command, and I commanded Hubaal to let us pass from the First City," he says.

Taha can't endure this farce any longer. "Tell me," he growls, roughly dragging Qayn over by the arm, "did you also command Hubaal to aid the Desert's Bane?"

The most destructive monster to have ever threatened the Sahir. It was the Desert's Bane who urged Hubaal to rampage through the Vale as part of the Bane's campaign of terror against the Sahir. And if the Great Spirit hadn't gifted Taha's people the magic of the misra tree to defeat the Bane, it would've destroyed them before turning its aggression on the world.

*"No,* I did not." Qayn blows away a lock of black hair that dangled over his eye. "But I regrettably permitted it."

Taha yanks the djinni close. "Then you're an even greater enemy to our people than I first thought."

"Let him go, Taha," says Imani, practically leaping off the wall.

He looks up at her. "How could you bind one of the Bane's allies to your dagger and seek his service?"

Her face reddens. "Qayn was *not* an ally."

"No? According to him, he let Hubaal rampage through the Vale."

"A rash act of revenge." Qayn peers up at Taha coolly. "The thief who stole my magic was the same person for whom I built the First City as a gift. Her name was Nahla. One of your kind."

*"Ohhh."* Taha raises his brows. "So I was right. The beast has an appetite for human females."

Imani flits a nervous glance at Qayn. Resentment twists Taha's guts; self-loathing mocks him. *See?* it whispers. *She never truly wanted you. Even a monster appeals to her more than a poor man of no repute.*

Qayn laughs low and deep in his chest. "Or is it that they have an appetite for *me*? You know, Taha, I'd happily furnish you with advice on how to win a woman's favor if you want." His smirk widens. "You do seem woefully inexperienced."

Taha crushes the djinni's arm, leaning over him. "How about I rip that silver tongue out and spare us more of your lies and empty promises? Then you'll truly be powerless."

Ill will simmers in Qayn's black gaze, his sharp smirk twitching.

"Release him, Taha. I won't ask twice." Atheer palms a knife on the captain's desk to illustrate his meaning, and Taha finally understands *who,* not *what,* Atheer is devoted to.

He opens his fist. Qayn saunters to safety behind the desk, straightening the creases from his black tunic as he goes.

Satisfied, Atheer pulls his hand off the knife. "Let's get back on topic."

"Gladly," Imani mutters. "Nahla robbed Qayn of his fortune, and to stop him seeking its return, she stole his magic too."

"Must have been quite the fortune," says Amira, watching Qayn unfurl a map of Alqibah across the desk.

"Wealth of the kind you could not imagine." He taps a spot on the map. "Some time ago, I sensed my magic in this region, north of Brooma."

"But your magic was stolen during the period of the Desert's Bane," she says. "Why has it taken you so long to locate it?"

"A better question is why didn't you just steal some more magic from other djinn and create a new talisman?" Taha interjects. "You had plenty of time to do it."

"My crown *isn't* a talisman," Qayn snarls, not looking up from the map, "and I am no thief." He sits silently for a moment, as if waiting to regain his composure. Then he begins tracing a band of dunes to the south. "Once I decided to search for my crown in Alqibah, I discovered that a protective enchantment had been cast over the Swallowing Sands that prevented me and every other so-called monster from leaving the Sahir. I was imprisoned."

"Then how did you . . ." Amira drifts off, glancing at her brother. The answer occurs to Taha too: Qayn must've been bound to Atheer before he was bound to Imani's dagger. There's no other way but with Atheer's help that Qayn could've defied the enchantment to cross the Sands, reach Alqibah, and sense his stolen magic. The roots of this scheme run deep.

"Hmm." Amira stops at the desk, studying Qayn rather than the map. "And if the thief, Nahla, wanted to keep your magic from you, why did she go to the trouble of hiding the jewels? Why not destroy them instead?"

"I think that's enough questions for now, Amira," says Atheer, quiet but stern.

"I'm only curious," she says defensively.

"No harm in it." Qayn levels a calm gaze at her. "The jewels cannot be destroyed by one of your kind, only pulled from the crown and rendered useless."

"Oh. Does that mean a person could use your crown?" she asks.

Qayn's hollow smile would be more convincing if he had painted it on. "If they were so inclined, but as with using a monster's talisman or magical implement, doing so marks one for death. That's aside from the very unpleasant physical effects that come first. But if none of that turns you away, entertain the temptation, certainly. Just know that only I have the power to reforge the crown."

He looks at Atheer, who nods and says, "We need to discuss the particulars of the plan—"

"Not so fast," Taha cuts in. "Are you mad? Qayn is a malevolent being from the time of the Desert's Bane. We shouldn't be helping him do anything."

Atheer sighs. "Qayn is our trusted ally, and we need his help whether you like it or not."

"He *can't* help us. Imani"—Taha catches her eye—"destroy Qayn as you promised me you would. Do it for our people. It's your sworn Shield duty."

"I know my Shield duty," she snaps, looking away again.

"Then see it through! Qayn is deceiving you about his power, all of you! He can't conjure you an army! The moment his magic is returned, he'll abandon this cause."

"You're wrong," says Atheer. "Qayn has been committed to defeating the Harrowland Empire since the beginning of our friendship."

Taha has an unsettling thought. "When *was* the beginning of your friendship? Before or after you began stealing misra?"

Atheer is suddenly tight-lipped. Taha edges closer to him. "Was it Qayn's idea to smuggle our magic to the people here? It must've been. This was his plan all along, to use the Harrowland Empire as a means to an end. Don't you see it, Atheer? He's promising to save us from the very problem that *he* created if we find his magic, and he's lying."

"Tell us, Taha, did Qayn create the Harrowland Empire?" Imani asks in a tone of derision. "Did he bring King Glaedric down the Spice Road? Did he encourage your father to deny aid to Alqibah?"

"No, but he *is* taking advantage of the situation." Taha sighs. This is pointless; he may as well be speaking a different language.

"It's exceptionally impolite to discuss someone as if they're not in the same room as you," says Qayn, replacing the compass he was examining on the desk. "My word is my bond, Taha, and I have never gone back on it. Find me my magic and you will have your army. Or don't, and prepare for—how did you phrase it?—'the end of everything.'" He smirks, tilting his head to view Taha at a new, more amusing angle. "You have no reason to fear me. I'm monstrous only to my enemies."

"Horseshit," Taha mutters, pacing to the cabin door.

"We have only a short time to act," Atheer says to him. "We

make for Brooma at first light. It won't be as busy as Bashtal, and it's closer to both our destinations. We'll get you near enough to the Sands for you to send Sinan across with a warning to Qalia. Once he's safely in the Sahir, we can begin our search for Qayn's magic."

Taha stops in his tracks. "Sinan can't go alone. If something happens to him, Reza and I have to be there to deliver the warning to Qalia ourselves."

"It's highly unlikely that something will happen to him, and if you go with him, you'll be trapped in the Sahir once the Harrowlanders cross over." Atheer makes a show of pushing away the knife on the desk. "But if you stay here to help in our search, well . . . many hands make light work."

Taha's lips part. This whole discussion feels like something out of a bizarre dream. "Atheer, is this truly about saving the Sahir and Alqibah?" he asks. "Or has the djinni charmed your mind and made you a servant to his selfish cause?"

"I take that as your refusal to help us in our quest," Atheer replies.

Taha makes his own show of cracking his knuckles. "That's right. Now speak plainly: Do you intend to keep us as your prisoners while you wander off on your fool's errand, or will you let us return home?"

There's no mistaking the threat, but Atheer's manner is easy. "Once we reach Brooma, your weapons, horses, and belongings will be returned to both of you and you'll be free to leave for Qalia. I hope you'll reconsider before then, for your own welfare and the good of us all."

"If only you'd thought of our welfare before you revealed our magic." Reza storms out of the cabin.

Atheer's temple pulses. "Very well. The meeting is concluded."

Unkind words mass on Taha's tongue, but after the arduous journey here, the mental and emotional preparation required to accept the task of executing Atheer, he lacks the wrath to utter them. For years, Atheer risked his life battling monsters across the Sahir, only to succumb to the influence of the feeblest monster that has ever existed: Qayn. It's an end unbefitting a great warrior, and Taha must admit, at least to himself, that it saddens him deeply.

Taha leaves the stuffy cabin. Night has fallen now, and he's cloaked in it as he descends the gangway, lost in that abyss between lanterns that goes on so long, he begins to wonder if the light will ever return.

# 3

# IMANI

WE SAIL THE AZURITE RIVER BY DAY AND SHELTER in its inlets by night. On the morning of the third day, Farida announces our approach to Brooma, and Atheer interrupts my breakfast with Amira for help preparing a tea ceremony.

"Our real mission is about to begin," he says, holding out a tray of ceremonial tools. "The Sahir and Alqibah depend on what we do next. If magic is our only way through an obstacle, we use it."

I take the tray, placing my pouch of misra on it. We part at the shelter under the gangway; he goes to boil a pot of water on the open-top stove, and I continue to the captain's cabin and edge the tray onto the corner of Farida's cluttered desk. The curtains on the window are parted, giving me full view of the river upon which everything and everyone here seems to rely. Over the last few days, I've seen shepherds bring their flocks of thirsty cattle to its banks, locals fill jars and carry them away on their heads, and trading caravans replenish their camels while the riders peel away their scarves to splash cool water over their faces. On the choppy waters in our wake, local fishers push off in boats and cast tangles of nets; a young woman leaves a basket on some rocks and dives below the surface, presumably in search of pearls and prizes. All manner of vessels flow along the river: boats loaded with fresh produce; a big-bellied merchant dhow, marked as a spice trader by its red flag; a few small feluccas, made tall by their white sails, ferrying wealthy Harrowlanders reclined on cushions on deck. But the most numerous vessels are the long barges sailing parallel to us, manned by dour Empire soldiers transporting mysterious-shaped cargo under brown canvas.

I do my best to ignore them while I prepare the ceremony. Clearing the clutter, I place a brass teapot in the center of the desk, with a collection of variously sized brass spoons. I give thanks to the Great Spirit as I remove a glimmering strip of misra bark from the pouch and tuck it into a lightweight brass mortar alongside its matching pestle. The ceremonial set was a gift to Atheer from Auntie Aziza on his initiation into the Order of Sorcerers; it's a reminder now of an uncomfortable accusation that Taha leveled against my family.

Atheer enters the cabin, startling me from my thoughts. I compose myself and separate two teacups from the stack.

"We need two more, for Taha and Reza," he says, placing the lidless pot of boiled water on the desk. He doesn't give me time to protest. "They may disagree with our approach, Imani, but a warning must reach the Council, and they're the ones to make sure it does."

Irritated, I pluck two more cups from the stack. "You know, Taha said there were rumors about Auntie. That she knew you were stealing misra from the Sanctuary and she looked the other way, or even helped you get it out."

"Would it upset you if I said that she did help me?"

I shrug, examining the cups. I'd rather look at them than Atheer.

"You're conflicted," he says. "You think it was an abuse of her position as Master of the Misra."

"Did she manipulate the reports of how much misra was missing?" I ask.

"She underreported, yes, to protect me," he says.

I shut my eyes. Taha, Reza, and Fey were right. I indignantly disputed their accusations; I accused them of defaming our clan and hurled thoughtless insults. And they were right.

"In your heart, you know it was the just thing to do," says Atheer.

"Was it?" I ask. "The people of Alqibah need our help, but to deceive our own people to achieve that—wasn't there some other way?"

"What other way?" he asks, filling the teapot with water. "I told the Council about what I'd seen here and argued my case until I was hoarse. Nothing changed. It was Qayn who showed me that I could still do something, and when Auntie found out, she offered to help me, because she believes that we can use our magic to help people outside the Sahir and still protect it as the Great Spirit commanded us." He considers me curiously. "Why does this bother you so much?"

"You decided to do something that impacted everyone at home without consulting anyone but yourself."

"I consulted the Council several times," he says. "I begged them to intervene—at the very least, send essential supplies, medicines, *anything.* I was rejected, over and over and over again."

I sigh. "I understand, Atheer. It was an impossible position the Council put you in. But did you ever fear you were making a mistake?"

"Always," he says seriously. "But being afraid to make mistakes is petrifying. If you obey that fear, you never get anything done. Like Baba says, *Move your stone—*"

"*—or forfeit the board,*" I finish. It's one of Baba's many surprisingly wise maxims, uttered during heated matches of Table in the gardens near home.

Atheer smiles. "That's it. And once you've decided to move your stone, stop worrying about the other moves that you could've made. Focus on what you'll do now to win with the stones and squares you have left, right?" He takes the lidless pot with him to the door. "I'll go get Taha and Reza."

"There's something else I've been meaning to ask you," I blurt out, even though I never consciously decided to raise this subject with him. But it's too late to turn back now. "Was it true what you said about Taha . . . that he was his father's assassin?"

Atheer stops out of the sunlight's reach. "Yes. He was sent after certain powerful individuals who were opposed to Bayek becoming Grand Zahim and were pressuring to have the Elders' decision reversed."

I think back on the turbulent events surrounding Bayek's election and recall his most outspoken critics, now dead. "The merchant Farhat of the Azhar clan—"

"Sayf of the Hadid, and Nasir of the Gallib." Atheer nods. "Taha was responsible for all three."

My stomach turns. "But Nasir was very old. His heart failed him."

"He was poisoned."

"Farhat fell to his death—"

"He was pushed. And Sayf and his carriage drivers weren't robbed and killed by a gang of marauders on the way to Sayf's gold quarry. They were set upon by a boy who staged the scene to conceal the true motive."

"Great Spirit," I whisper. "How do you know this?"

"I ran into Taha late one evening in the barracks. He was training alone at the archery range by torchlight. We were already friends by then, so we spoke a while and then he asked if I'd join him at a *shisha* lounge. I accepted."

My face contorts. "Why would you?"

"It seemed like he didn't want to be alone." Atheer pauses to consider my expression. "It was just a nice thing to do, Imani."

I cross my arms over my racing heart. "And then?"

Atheer sighs. "He took us to this place in Baraket. We ended up smoking hashish, too much of it, and he volunteered the truth to me. He was shaken by what he'd done; he kept saying that his reflection in the mirror has never been the same since the killings. It must've become an unbearable secret to keep, and I was there, his secret friend. Probably the only friend he had left outside his father's control." Atheer shrugs. "The next time we saw each other, I didn't mention his confession, and neither did he. I suppose he hoped I didn't remember any of it."

"And you didn't alert anybody."

"No. I kept the secret as a friend would." Atheer's sad gaze drifts to the window and the water frothing at our stern. "Do you know who Bayek's first victim was, Imani? His eldest son. Taha doesn't realize it yet, but it was his life consumed first by his father's rage."

I shake my head, desperate to stop this ache that's building up inside of me. "No, I think it's time we accepted that Taha agrees with his father's beliefs."

"That doesn't mean he wants to kill for them."

*"Yet he did,"* I hiss, rounding the desk. "And he tried with you! He almost buried me alive in the prison in Taeel-Sa! If Taha had any moral fiber in his body, he would've refused his father's orders."

"Even if he disagreed with them, someone in his situation can't simply refuse."

"What situation?" I demand hotly. "Being a popular Shield? The son of the Grand Zahim? I think the matter *is* simple, Atheer, and we'd do ourselves a great service by facing the truth."

"The truth . . . the truth is the thorn." Atheer sounds tired now, and that angers me. *I'm tired too,* I want to say, tired of this new existence where I'm left hanging on the complex spider's web I was sprung onto without my consent and told to navigate if I want to survive. Before all of these troubles, things were straightforward. I knew what I was doing, who I was and what I believed in. Now my world is as clear as mud.

Atheer's gaze regains its sharpness. "I want you to remember something as we venture into this war, Imani. It's easier to dismiss those who hurt us as being senselessly evil than it is to accept that all our actions are trees, and all trees stem from roots, and all roots stem from seeds. No living being in any land develops in total isolation." He goes to the door. "I'll get Taha and Reza."

I don't cry until he's closed the door behind him, and I despise every tear. I should know better by now that feeling anything for Taha beyond hatred is dangerous. So I dry my tears and recount in my head every cruel thing he ever said and did to me. I stoke the fires of my fury right until the cabin door opens again, and the young man who set my heart alight stands in the frame.

Atheer prefaces our tea ceremony with a lecture on the risks of developing magical obsession if we are continuously exposed to misra. I don't listen closely; I have to concentrate on ignoring Taha. Every time I look at him, I see him stitching my wound in the First City while my heart fluttered like a songbird. I see him pointing an arrow down at me from behind the railing of the *Lion's Prize,* lamenting my refusal to go compliantly into the dark. I imagine him murdering Sayf of the Hadid with the same hands that held me, and I feel torn up inside.

At the end of his lecture, Atheer grinds the bark into Spice and scoops it into the teapot. The cabin blooms with magic, and I'm relieved that the scent is no longer bitter, as it was while my brother was missing. This magic is hot, earthen, and bold.

While the tea steeps, I follow tradition and meditate on the Great Spirit's gift of magic. The misra tree was granted to the Sahiran people a millennium ago to help us fight the Great Spirit's archenemy, the Desert's Bane, a monster with no counterpart from any other time in history. After we defeated the Bane, we were permitted to keep the misra tree as a reward for our sacrifices, so long as we promised to use it to protect the sacred Sahir from monsters and outsiders. At least, that's what the accounts that Taha staunchly believes in tell us, but I don't know if I trust them anymore. Perhaps there was truth in what Qayn said to me back in the First City: *Your mother knows falsehoods, so you know falsehoods.*

Atheer pours the hot tea and brings the tray around the cabin. The misra is vigorous and full-bodied, and as we pack up the cabin after the ceremony, magic blazes in my veins. It's just in time too. The bell on the mainmast tolls to signal our final approach to Brooma, and Atheer unlocks a wooden trunk at the foot of the captain's bed. Inside are two bags, a tangle of leather armor, and the same weapons that were used against us only days ago: swords, daggers, and Taha's bow and quiver.

# 4

# TAHA

"DON'T DON YOUR GEAR UNTIL WE'RE OUTSIDE THE city's bounds," says Atheer, going to the cabin door. "Do you have the warning for the Council?"

Taha holds up the scroll he inked by candlelight yesterday.

Atheer nods. "The Great Spirit willing, it'll reach the Council in a few days."

Taha tucks the scroll into his *sirwal* pocket, clearing his throat. "You need to come back with us. Do your Shield duty and help us protect our home from these monsters."

Atheer pauses in the doorway, thoughtful. "All defenses fail, Taha. You know the parable: 'Only the shield served by the sword does not shatter.' Qayn is our sword. Finding and restoring his magic is what will protect our home. I wish you would trust me on this."

When Taha says nothing, Atheer leaves, taking Imani with him.

For a while, Taha and Reza check their belongings in silence. Suddenly Reza gasps and pulls a scroll from the bottom of his bag.

"Oh, *man,* do you remember this?"

He crosses the cabin, giggling and holding up the unfurled scroll. Taha grins, recognizing the comical sketches scribbled on it. There's a donkey dressed in robes lecturing a hall of bewildered students; and a frightened ghoul, djinni, and werehyena hiding inside a farmstead from maniacal caricatures of Taha and Reza leering through the window. Reza used to draw the pictures when their squad made camp for the night and there was nothing else to do. Their squadmates would turn in, but Taha, Reza, and later Fey would stay up, snickering over the scroll as Reza illustrated his imaginary characters in outlandish scenarios, narrating the stories as he went. Now he comes to stand beside Taha so that they can both examine the sketches.

"I almost forgot about 'The Tale of the Donkey Scholar,'" says Taha, laughing at the erudite donkey in academic garb. "I think it's your best work."

Reza's chuckle falters. "It was Fey's favorite. Nothing made her laugh more." He drifts back to his bag, furling the scroll.

Taha follows him. "We'll come back here and find her, Reza. I promise." He squeezes his cousin's shoulder, but Reza only nods at that.

By the time they finish saddling their horses on deck, the Azurite River is pouring into a wide bay shrouded in slow-moving mist, from which arises the incessant bellow of horns. Anchored ships, many of them warships, momentarily appear deep in the harbor only to vanish behind the mist again. Brooma's long wharf materializes soon after, busy with stevedores, clerks, and Harrowlander soldiers attending to the army barges taking up the majority of the berths.

The *Lion's Prize* lands without incident, and the crew begins transporting the horses to the sunbaked pier. Farida meets a brown-skinned clerk, who's waiting for her in a basil-green vest over a thin beige tunic that reaches the knees of his fitted brown sirwal. Since Brooma is a major city, Taha expects its skies to be dotted with messenger falcons, but Glaedric's measures have ensured they're ominously vacant, and Taha decides that it'll be safer for Sinan if he manually carries the falcon. While their group waits out of sight under the gangway for Farida to finish with the clerk, Taha puts on his leather falconry gauntlet, though much of the time is spent sneaking glances at Imani in her pale-blue belted tunic, over which she's slung a sea-colored cloak with a fish-shaped silver clasp. But Taha can't look at her for too long before the frustrating embers of desire flicker to life. He's spent years avoiding Imani, unwilling to make the first attempt at acquaintance solely because she and everyone else expected it. When he had to say something about her in front of others, he made sly mockery or pretended he didn't know who she was at all—something he hoped would infuriate her if she ever noticed it. But this might be the last time he ever sees her again, brazenly beautiful in the light, and still so much of what he really thinks of her remains unsaid.

The clerk burdens Farida with a stack of papers and finally leaves, allowing them to disembark from the *Prize* in private. She tucks the wadded papers into her pocket and ruefully limps back to Atheer.

"I wish we could spend more time together, *habibi,* but I have forms to lodge and dues to pay and it's not wise for you to wait." They embrace, sharing a lingering kiss. "Remind me, did I ever mention Maysoon to you?" Farida asks when they part.

"Wasn't she a good friend of your father's?" Atheer replies. "In the same 'business.' You called her . . . the Whisperer."

Farida nods. "Works alone, trades in valuable information.

The crew and I will stay in her teahouse while you go north. If you need to find us here, check Maysoon's, not far from the eastern correspondence tower. Ask any of the waiters to have your tea leaves read by Yara, Maysoon's wife; they'll let you into the private space upstairs."

She and Atheer hug again, trading kisses and well-wishes, and the captain finally turns to Reza and Taha, who is holding Sinan on his forearm.

"I hope you two receive what you've earned, in as violent a fashion as the gods deem fair, but only after you warn your people that they're in danger."

Reza taps a finger to his brow in salute. "Good fortunes to you too, Captain."

She leaves them with a cold smile.

A group of sailors led by Makeen heads down the pier first, escorting the horses toward the maze of stalls of an outdoor souq situated behind the wharf. Taha notices that similar decorations to those in Taeel-Sa have been put up here too. Brown-and-maroon bunting flutter over the shoppers, and lampposts have been wrapped in green cords embroidered with white fabric flowers. Not even the defaced bronze statue of Brooma's former warlord, Al-Deeb, has escaped festooning. Set atop a tall stone pedestal overlooking the wharf, the statue would've once made for an intimidating greeting to visitors of Brooma; now Al-Deeb looks cheerfully foolish in an antlered headband, vines, and floral wreaths.

"You there, make way!"

Taha halts in the middle of the street, Sinan sharply turning his head in the direction of a sweaty Harrowlander official in a pink silk robe. The man rushes their group from the right, flapping his arms. "*Yes,* I meant you! Stand back!"

They retreat from the official's path, Atheer taking Amira's hand. Behind the man marches a line of soldiers bearing crates in the direction of a nearby warehouse. Taha traces the procession back across the wharf to an Empire barge berthed many piers over from the *Prize.*

"Long line," Reza remarks.

*Too long,* Taha thinks. None of the soldiers would recognize him—the only Harrowlanders who saw his face the night of the sinking are shark food now—but he still doesn't like the idea of standing here without his weapons, waiting for someone to take an interest in him or the unusually large falcon perched on his forearm. He peers between the soldiers at Makeen and the sailors waiting with their horses on the opposite side of the street near the entrance to the souq. After a short nod of approval from Atheer, Makeen ushers the crew into the market.

"They know where to meet us," Atheer reassures his sisters.

"*If* we ever get past," Imani mutters.

Taha glances at her, stubborn desire rousing in him again. Should he admit his feelings to her before they part ways today? He doubts there'd be any point. When Imani said in the prison that she wanted him to like her, it wasn't that she wanted *Taha* to like her specifically. She wants *everyone* to like her, as she believes she deserves. She won't ever reciprocate his feelings, not least because of what he did to her. Anyway, how could he admit his feelings to her if he can't even articulate them to himself?

Taha doesn't know, and now he's distracted by her frowning at something on their right: a redheaded Harrowlander woman in her early twenties, wearing a brown belted dress with sweeping lace-trimmed sleeves. She's surrounded by a slew of soldiers, though it takes Taha a moment to work out why she's several heads taller than them. She's standing on a large crate outside the harbormaster's office, surveying the wharf through a golden spyglass. A Harrowlander official hovers close by, quill darting across the pages of a leatherbound notebook. Watching on beside him is a burly, bearded Brooman in a green turban adorned with a symbol wrought in silver, impossible to make out under the glinting sun, though judging by the stevedores waiting around him, he's likely the harbormaster.

The woman finishes glassing the arriving Empire barges, says something to her official, and then peers at the soldiers carrying cargo past Taha and the others. By the time Taha realizes who she resembles, Imani has said, "We need to find a way around right now," and Atheer is looking at her too. The color leeches from his already washed-out face, and although Taha suspects the answer, he asks the question anyway: "Do you recognize that woman?"

"Yes," Atheer rasps, as if he has shattered glass in his throat. "Princess Blaedwyn. Glaedric's younger sister."

"Does she know you?" Reza asks.

Another pointless question. Blaedwyn knows Atheer very well. The spyglass lowers and she smiles at him, foxlike. A smile that says, *There you are, little mouse.*

"We've been discovered," Amira says, tugging her brother's hand, but Atheer has sprouted roots. He's not blinking; he's barely breathing. Taha assumed that Atheer, a Wandering Captain who faced monsters alone, was born incapable of feeling fear; he had courage stitched into his lining. But Taha just hadn't yet discovered *what* Atheer feared. It isn't ghouls or djinn, ghosts, giant sand serpents, the barren wastes, or merciless sun. It's *her.*

Blaedwyn addresses her soldiers. Some disappear behind the harbormaster's office. A moment later, a horn blows a drawn-out bellow that propels alarm across the wharf and into the souq.

Stevedores, sailors, clerks, even the drivers of wagons being loaded with cargo, abandon their tasks to find safety in alcoves and alleyways between warehouses, the door of every building in sight beginning to swing shut. The first instinct of the people here is no longer to fight but to yield. They must've learned that lesson the hard way when Glaedric attacked Brooma.

Blaedwyn points at Atheer and, in a voice that cuts through the chaos, as clear as a bell, she shouts, "Arrest that man and his companions!" Then she hops off the crate and slips into the crowd of advancing soldiers, vanished like a deadly serpent in long grass.

Taha raises his arm, making a clicking sound with his tongue. Sinan understands and launches into flight as the line of soldiers hauling crates in front of them slows, and the men begin to turn. Imani pushes her brother. "Go, Atheer, before we're captured. *Run!*"

# 5

# IMANI

ATHEER FINALLY COMES BACK TO HIMSELF AND shoves through the soldiers. We sprint after him across the street into the souq, agitated with fleeing shoppers wafting the scents of hot spices, roasted nuts, and floral perfumes. The soldiers leave the wharf shortly after us, surging through the crowd like the prow of a ship breaking water. Between them, I catch glimpses of red hair and the flutter of a brown dress. Blaedwyn.

Taha runs beside me, the gold ribbons of his mindmeld with Sinan swirling in his eyes. A moment later, the shadow of his mindbeast glides over us and continues deeper into the souq. Atheer doesn't even notice the falcon; he's anxiously looking around, as if the soldiers are about to crawl out from under the fruit stalls or peel off the hanging displays of rugs.

Ahead of us, the open-air souq transitions to a wide, yellow-walled lane. Back on the *Prize,* I studied a map of our route to the city gates. Narrower lanes branch off this one farther down, which will allow us to escape into the city's labyrinth of streets. But we don't reach it.

Soldiers burst out of a walkway formed by a cluster of stalls and cut us off. We're forced to a hard stop, Amira huddling behind me as more soldiers join the group from the lane. Around us, shoppers hide behind display shelves and traders cower in their stalls. The soldiers point their swords; one of them addresses us in Harrowtongue, though I recognize only the word *surrender* before they start their approach.

"He's lying," Taha says to Atheer.

"About what?" I ask.

"He said our lives will be spared if we surrender to Princess Blaedwyn," Reza translates.

Atheer raises his hands by his head and speaks out of the corner of his mouth. "Spared or not, our lives are over if we're captured."

"Then we fight our way past," says Taha.

"Any way we can," Atheer agrees.

"Well, we better do it now before we lose our chance," I say, glancing over my shoulder. A frenzy of soldiers has been lured from across the wharf by the relentless blowing of the horn.

A familiar shadow flits over Blaedwyn's men in front of us. Sinan has returned with Taha's recurve bow clutched in his talons. The falcon dives, talons opening; Taha catches the bow with one hand and pulls an arrow from the quiver on his back with the other. The soldiers trade baffled glances. The man at the fore waves his sword, giving his order. Atheer walks toward him with hands still raised, speaking.

"What's my brother saying?" I ask Taha.

"He says we aren't going to surrender, and if the soldiers don't step aside, they'll be hurt."

Some of them laugh. The one at the fore is insulted. He points the sword at my brother's chest. Atheer comes to a standstill, a gust of humid wind wrapping his cloak against him and divulging his frightfully lean silhouette, unarmed and unarmored. The sun dips behind the clouds; the souq hushes. The soldiers wait for us to surrender; we wait for the soldiers to step aside. But it's clear that this will end in only one way.

The soldiers charge us. Taha nocks an arrow; the ground trembles as Reza entreats the earth with his affinity. I push off my back foot, flushing magic into my hands. The metal of the head soldier's sword sings to my iron affinity. "Drop it," I order. The sword is ripped from his gloved fist, clangs on the stone, and spins under a stall. My dagger flies into my hand, glowing bright blue as it transforms into a sword.

But our combined efforts pale beside Atheer's.

My brother lunges at the advancing soldiers. Magic bursts in the air as he changes skins, launching as a man and landing on the stone as the roaring Lion of Qalia, golden-skinned and fiery-eyed, with a glorious golden mane. Taha puts an arrow in a soldier's neck before Atheer arrives, but once he does, there's little more the rest of us can do. Horror warps the soldiers' faces; still, they raise their swords. I tense as Atheer leaps into them and the blades glance off his hide, but he pays them no mind. He swipes, mauls, and throws them aside, sending shrieking shoppers clambering over each other to escape. He finishes with them quickly, leaving behind bloody, misshapen carnage I can't make sense of and don't want to linger on.

He reverts to his human form, breathing hard and wincing from some unnamed pain, and points us on. Behind us, soldiers cross the center of the souq, shouting at us to stop. I stash my dagger and run after Atheer into the lane. The people who didn't flee or take shelter inside one of the shuttered shops press themselves against the rippled stone walls or huddle between the parked wagons, as motionless as carvings. They stare at my brother as we dart around them, and I think they're seeing in him what Farida and the other rebels must have during the battle for Taeel-Sa: hope.

"Soldiers are heading directly for us," Taha announces. Golden bolts storm in his eyes; Sinan sweeps high above the souq. "Two dozen, at least."

Atheer cuts around a pushcart, glancing at the hunter running on my right. "Scout us a path away from them. We'll use the nearest intersection—"

"They might make it there first," Taha replies, vaulting several toppled boxes of fruit, his deep-blue cloak whipping behind him.

But if we're to have any hope of defeating our enemy, we must escape Brooma to find Qayn's magic. Atheer was right when he said that our lives are over if we're captured. But not just our lives. Those of our families and friends—our entire nation.

I look over my shoulder. People shrink away from the armed men flooding the lane, yet for some inexplicable reason, my eye is drawn to their shadows on the walls. Strangely, they don't look like the outlines of the soldiers sprinting at us. These shadows are dense, precise, slow. Almost as if they don't belong to anybody but themselves—

"There's the intersection!" Taha calls.

I look forward just in time to vault a fallen stool. The intersection's entrance is a few hundred feet away, crowded with shoppers trying to peer over each other's heads, and barreling down the lane from the other end are the soldiers Taha saw through Sinan's eyes. They identify us as their quarry in seconds and draw their swords.

"Faster!" Atheer urges us breathlessly.

I go as fast as my body will permit me; I leap over a stack of woven baskets and dodge a statue of a slender, winged deity bearing a large sun disk upon its crown, the plaque on its plinth reading SHAMASH. The soldiers realize we have an escape route in the intersection and speed up too. But we're closer to it than they are. At this pace, we'll round the corner first, and the lane is busy there; the shops and workplaces are still open, and people are milling about, confused but curious—there'll be snaking alleyways to take, crowds and carriages to vanish between.

I don't notice the sound of Amira losing her footing and falling. Her screams for help rise above the noise, but only once we're just thirty or forty feet from the intersection. I almost stumble from how abruptly I stop to turn around. Reza is already running back to where she's struggling on the ground all the way past the statue, while a few fleet-footed soldiers have raced ahead of the horde to reach her. She tries to push to her feet but falls back down, clutching her ankle, and resorts to dragging herself forward.

"She's injured!" I exclaim.

I break into a sprint, Atheer and Taha loping back for her too. The soldiers behind us reach the intersection, physically barring our escape. Now we're surrounded, and they're advancing on us, swords at the ready.

"Get off!" Amira shrieks. A soldier has the end of her purple cloak pinned under his boot. I pull out my dagger; she rips her cloak free and scrambles away. The soldier stumbles a few steps before righting.

"Surrender!" shouts another behind us.

With a crack, the winged statue of Shamash breaks free of its plinth and hovers. I'm confused until I notice that Reza is magically manipulating the stone. He jogs forward and spears it down the lane into the soldier making another attempt at Amira's cloak, taking out two more who arrive behind him. Shock choirs from the people clustered against the walls. Amira resumes crawling, but we have only moments before more soldiers reach her.

"You two help Amira! I'll clear the way here." Atheer runs past me in the opposite direction, and I have no time to protest my brother's facing off with thirty-odd swords by himself. Reza makes a scooping motion with his arms as he navigates the chaos of the stalls toward my sister. The ground quakes and cracks, radiating fissures from one side of the lane to the other. A soldier picks Amira up by the waist and swings her around to hand off to the others. I'm still too far away to even throw my blade. Unlike Taha, Reza, and Atheer, I'm useless.

Sinan darts over us with a piercing scream, then dives and sinks his flourished talons into the eyes of the soldier holding Amira. Blood spits onto his cheeks. He howls and drops her to the ground as it groans. A pit forms on the edge of the lane; from it, Reza drags up stone shards and hurls them at the soldiers, knocking several men back into their fellows.

"Crawl to me, Amira!" I yell, weaving between two wagons abandoned at odd angles.

She bravely pushes to her feet and hobbles up the lane toward me, tears streaming down her face. She winces every time she puts any weight on her injured ankle, but she doesn't stop, and neither do I.

"You get Amira," Taha shouts from beside me. "We'll keep them back!"

Soldiers have already clambered over each other to chase her. Sinan arcs above them for another dive. I stash my dagger and get ready. I'm going to throw her arm over my shoulder and carry her to safety while Reza and Taha hold the soldiers back just long enough for all of us to run. And then what? The intersection. *Atheer.*

I glance back. He's in his lion skin, loosely surrounded by an audience as he fights the soldiers, but only a few remain standing. More important, *he* remains standing, as victorious as dawn's first light.

Hope swells in my chest as I return my focus to Amira, but again, the shadows distract me. They're no longer where they belong. They've stepped off the walls and entered the lane, and some don't resemble people. They're wolves, gigantic spiders, winged serpents. . . .

I trip on something and fall. The stone roughly meets me, sharp pain reviving in the wound under my ribs that I sustained when I fell off my horse in the Vale. The panic in the lane crescendos. Children wail for their parents. People bang on the closed doors of the shops, begging to be let inside.

I look up, disoriented. Shadowy creatures swarm the lane, and terrified shoppers begin overturning display tables to hide behind them. Pottery shatters; brass lanterns bounce and roll across the stone. The gigantic shadow of a reed-thin person peels off the wall in front of Amira. She screams and drops to the ground, curling into a shaking ball. The soldiers carry her back into their ranks as Taha helps me to my feet. A moment later, a woman with fiery hair emerges at the front of the group. Princess Blaedwyn.

Her arrival quiets all but the young children. With a flourish of her hands, the skeleton of a shadowy horse appears and gallops at Reza, a spike sprouting from its skull. He's stationary, with a heap of stone suspended before him. Ready to strike but perhaps too dazed to do it, he stares as a batlike beast sloughs off the horse's back and elongates to immense proportion, ascending above the lane. I locate Sinan in the sky, tiny in comparison. The falcon attempts to fly out of the monster's path, but the bat isn't subject to wind or the limits of flesh. For every five feet Sinan puts between them, the bat stretches until it simply opens its giant maw and engulfs him. Below, the charging shadow horse inclines its head and drives the spike through Reza's chest as they collide, then it bursts into tendrils of darkness that slither along the ground away from him. The stones Reza had conjured drop in a pile of rubble. He keels over beside it, twitching, and Sinan lands a few feet away.

Taha's breath catches in his throat. I realize he's still holding on to me and look up in horror at the gold ribbons fading from his glassy eyes. He lets go and staggers forward, but he makes it only a few steps before he drops to his knees and his bow clatters on the stone beside him. Far behind us, Atheer unleashes a mournful roar.

Smirking, Blaedwyn sweeps her hands, and shadows reach up the walls. Shapes appear from the murk, hints at horrors that make people weep. I see gnashing fangs and swiping claws, splashes of blood; eyes blinking in the windows of burning houses, mouths screaming; impaled flesh, broken bones; rows of chained figures marching; a pile of corpses and more being thrown on—

I double over, nauseated. The shadows congeal in a pool at Blaedwyn's feet, and slowly a large beast surfaces from it, vaguely crow-shaped, its wings threaded with spikes. It lifts into the air above her and hovers there, every beat of its wings threatening to shower the spikes onto us. Blaedwyn proudly appraises her creation while drinking from a small flask that she removed from her belt. I smell it, our sacred Spice. Blaedwyn is a sorcerer with an affinity for darkness. I've only seen it manifested once before, in retired Captain Nasreen of the Asiya clan, who spoke at the barracks years ago. The affinity is even rarer than the light affinity that Auntie possesses. I asked her once if people who possessed it did so because there was something dark about their personalities. She answered, *There is nothing inherently evil about darkness. Even the light can burn if it shines too brightly.*

"Surrender to me or die," Blaedwyn declares, hooking the flask on her belt. The quality of her voice mesmerizes: light and lethally sharp, like the watered-steel knives crafted by weaponsmiths back home.

Taha closes his fist around his bow, bruised knuckles straining. "Die, then." He jumps to his feet, pulling an arrow from his quiver.

"Taha, no!" I shout.

Blaedwyn snarls; the crow beats its wings, releasing barrages of spikes made of darkness and death. But even the light can burn.

Taha nocks his arrow. The spikes rain over the lane. I reach into my pocket for a small leather pouch and slip out from it the crystal vial with the white orb coiled inside: Auntie's undying light. I pull the stopper free and thrust the vial over my head. I barely understand the enigmatic practice of animancy that created it, but the light is woven with a piece of Auntie's soul, her goodness and dedication to defending others. That has to count for something.

Taha releases the bowstring. The spikes are feet away when the light explodes from its crystal confines and rises over his head, a fierce, shielding star radiating serenity that subdues all the crying. The spikes collide with it and dissolve; the crow and other monsters fragment to nothingness, leaving only the natural shadows behind. People rejoice, praising Shamash as the light returns to its vial. I reckon that Taha's arrow has hit Blaedwyn. The soldiers are hollering at each other, and the princess is being smuggled back into their ranks.

Atheer suddenly shakes my shoulder. "Imani, we need to leave!"

"What about Amira?" I exclaim, slipping the vial into my pocket.

He starts dragging me away. "She'll be fine for now, but I can't fight anymore!"

"Then let me fight!" I escape his grip, reaching for my dagger.

"No! There're too many soldiers!" He grabs me again, his fingers pressing red smudges into my clothes. I notice then that he's holding on to me with one arm. The other is hanging awkwardly by his side, and blood is soaking through the chest of his tunic. "Imani, I'm *injured*. I need *you* to find Qayn's magic."

"Me?" My heart skips erratically, my body suffusing with sickening heat. "Wh-what about the warning?" I stammer, but I don't wait for an answer. I sprint back to Taha as he lowers his bow. "We need to retreat!"

I don't know if he hears me. He makes to go to where his cousin and falcon lie. I pounce on him with two hands, holding him in place. "Taha, my brother's injured! You're the only one left who can warn the Council that Glaedric is coming!" He tries to push me off, but I dig my nails into his bicep. "TAHA, they'll capture you! You must see your mission through!"

He jerks his head and looks back at me, slick ebony hair falling over his forehead. *"Damn the mission,"* he seethes.

I can't believe my ears. "B-but our people—"

"My cousin."

*Is dead or dying!* I want to shriek, but I can't deal the crushing blow. I can't demand that he abandon his family for our nation's safety as he demanded I abandon Atheer. I refused to do it; he has the right to refuse too, even if it's hypocritical.

Tears slip down his face as he prizes my fingers from around his arm. "I'm sorry. Be safe, Imani." Then he bolts beyond my reach, heedless or doggedly defiant of the soldiers rushing at him.

"Imani!" Atheer shouts behind me.

"Be safe, Taha," I whisper. I turn and run up the lane, my breath rasping in my chest.

# 6

# TAHA

TAHA SPRINTS ACROSS THE LANE TO REZA. HE'S FELT fear like this only a few times before—when Mama was dying; when he discovered Rashiq, his dog, mortally wounded; when Baba first turned his rage on him; the first time he killed—and he's acutely aware of how sweaty and shaky he is, how loudly his blood is drumming in his ears; how intensely desolate the world appears even in the sunlight, robbed of color, as distant and flawed as a stranger's half-finished sketch discarded in disgust for being too bleak.

He slides to his knees between Reza and Sinan, glancing at his falcon's lifeless body before grasping Reza's tunic. "Sit up and give me your hand. I'll pull you onto my shoulders."

Reza rolls his limbs barely an inch either way. Taha looks at the soldiers heading for them and swallows the spidery panic crawling up his chest. "We've got to hurry. I'll carry you." He shifts into a squat and pulls Reza up by his tunic. His cousin exhales and slumps onto his shoulder. Taha whines; he can't stop himself, only half realizes he's done it. "Hug me so I can hold on to your hands," he pleads.

"I can't. The shadow hit my heart. It was so cold." Reza slumps a little more and presses the side of his face against Taha's shoulder, tears resting on his cheeks. "I'm done for, man."

Taha can't control his breathing, ragged like a wounded animal's. This might be it: the thing he didn't know he'd been dreading all these years. "No, it's going to be fine!" he exclaims, then he drapes one of Reza's arms across his chest and takes his hand. "Lean into me while I stand—"

"Go, Taha, while you still can." Reza pulls his hand away and falls flat on the ground.

Taha tries to ignore the spiders crowding his throat. He wraps his arms under Reza's shoulders and hoists him up, but Reza collapses onto him, locking them in a macabre hug. Taha bows under the weight, too paralyzed by terror to do anything meaningful. He only knows that Reza is too heavy, and their chance of escape is almost gone.

"Please, just try to move!" he cries as Reza becomes too difficult to hold up. He eases his cousin down on the stone and grabs at his tunic again. "Think of going home and seeing your family, your father! Think of finding Fey! We can still run if we go *right now.*"

But Reza has given up. He lies flat, blinking at the powdered sky, his breathing sluggish. Not even the promise of a better tomorrow is enough to lure him back. Maybe he knows it's a lie anyway. The best tomorrows were the ones behind them.

"Don't let him win," Reza murmurs, feebly tugging Taha's sleeve. "Promise you won't."

The first of the soldiers arrive as Taha leans over him. "Who do you mean?"

"Your father . . ." He reaches up and lightly touches Taha's cheek. "Your father is a sad, angry, broken man . . . and he's trying to turn you into one too."

But Taha is already there. Damaged, his heart slipped out through a crack and shattered long ago. "My father loves me," he whispers; the words sound so hollow to his ears.

A tear rolls down Reza's face. "Let someone else love you, Taha . . . the real you, as I always have."

"But nobody else will accept me!" Taha presses his forehead to his cousin's, bawling now. "Please don't go, Reza! I'll miss you too much; I'll miss your jokes and your company and your funny drawings! Your smile! *I'll be lonely without you.*"

Reza places his hand over Taha's, a touch as light as a feather. Suddenly Taha is six again, back in the orphanage where he was left after Mama died giving birth to his little brother, Taleb, and his father couldn't take care of them. Afraid of everyone and everything. Wondering why the children he saw in the streets had mothers but the Great Spirit had seen fit to steal his away. Wondering what she'd done wrong; worrying that it might have been his fault. Wondering why, even after Uncle Omar learned of his and his brother's fates and took them in, and many months had passed, his father still barely spoke, didn't cry, and never hugged Taha or kissed baby Taleb. Wondering why they didn't deserve from him the love that Uncle Omar gladly gave Reza and his other children. Wondering why.

"Raise your hands! You are under arrest by order of His Majesty!"

The soldiers have them surrounded. Taha sits back on his haunches, gazing at his cousin. But Reza isn't breathing anymore, and his eyes are closed.

*"No,"* Taha gasps. "No, no, no."

He palms Reza's face, waiting for his warm, coffee-brown eyes to flutter open and his chest to rise on a vigorous breath. But Reza is still, so is Sinan, and Taha knows now that there was never any hope in the world. No justice.

"This is your final warning!"

Taha doesn't surrender; he just doesn't fight back when the soldiers close manacles around his wrists. They pull him to his feet, remove his quiver, and search him for weapons. His warning for the Council is taken from his pocket, and then he's presented to a ruddy man in an open-faced brimmed helm, who gawks at Sinan.

"My, what a spectacularly large falcon!" he says in Harrowtongue. "Have it stuffed and mounted, Grimbald—it'll be a gift of this hallowed season for His Majesty."

"Stuffed," Taha mumbles, not understanding.

"Yes, sir, and the body?" says Grimbald.

The soldier tugs Taha away. "Burn it."

"NO!" Taha tears free and folds himself protectively over Reza. "Don't burn him! He has to be buried!"

He's dragged to his feet again by the soldier in charge. "Why is that, boy?"

"He belongs to the earth; he must return to it," says Taha. "Please, just let him rest. Let the earth take him."

The man shoves Taha forward. "Burn the body and toss the ashes in the bay."

Taha shouts and thrashes against his captors; they silence him with a punch. Dazed, he's shuffled between them back to the souq; they slap and elbow him, they kick him in the backside and laugh; some yank his ears while debating the idea of chaining him to a wall and using him for archery practice, "bollocks first." Someone mentions transporting him to the "vanguard with the girl." Then a hood is thrown over his head and he's shoved into a carriage.

Yet even with the wheels spinning, Taha is still back in the laneway, holding Reza's face. He will always be back there, helplessly watching his cousin die. Just as he watched Mama's eyelids droop shut and never open again. It was supposed to be a joyous afternoon when his brother was born, but Taha is assured now that no blessing ever comes free. He was gifted a beautiful baby brother, and in return he had to say goodbye to his mother. Maybe Reza and Sinan were killed because Imani spared his life. Maybe the lives he's taken must now be repaid.

He tries to distract himself with the present. Although the scratchy hood obscures his vision, Taha could try to use his magic to find out where he's being taken. But the mere thought of reaching out to another falcon frightens him; it reminds him of what Sinan saw and felt before he was killed—the blue sky blotted out by a black wave he couldn't outpace. The freezing darkness enveloping him. His body erupting in tremors; his small falcon heart beating faster and faster until, suddenly, it stopped.

Taha sits up, gasping. He's desperate for comfort, some sort of relief from this pain. Something his father said comes back to him: *Ignore your heart. It feels too much, and feelings are only rust on a blade, eating its power.*

But Taha has been eaten through already, and the few strands that remain holding him together are as fragile as breath. He weeps to exhaustion and, in his stupor, listens to the soldiers marching around the carriage as it heads down the Spice Road.

# 7

# IMANI

ATHEER IS IN TROUBLE, MOVING SLOWLY. EVEN breathing is paining him.

"Careful," he says as I sling his arm over my shoulder. "I think my other arm is broken."

Numbness spreads through me. We can't leave Brooma immediately to find Qayn's magic as we planned. Atheer urgently needs a physician, but I don't know if we'll even survive long enough to find one.

The entrance to the intersection ahead is marked by mangled bodies and scattered swords. Atheer's awed audience, all of them in their teens and twenties, stands around the debris, watching our approach. Behind us, Taha kneels between his cousin and his mindbeast, both motionless. He presses his forehead to Reza's as the soldiers close around them. For a fleeting moment, I think we've been forgotten about, but then a soldier in a steel helm points at me and others start up the lane after us.

"Qayn, I need you," I call out.

Frankly, I don't know what he can do to help, but just seeing Qayn materialize beside me eases some of my panic.

"Atheer's injured and his arm might be broken," I say quickly as he evaluates the situation behind us. "What do we do?"

Qayn looks back at Atheer, then the wide-eyed people near the intersection in front of us. "The only thing you can. Ask for help." He beckons at the crowd. "Yalla ya shabab"—"Let's get on with it, young people." It's the only invitation they need. Nods are exchanged, and three people rush over to escort us, one leading, two at the rear holding dead soldiers' swords. The rest drag pushcarts away from the walls and begin piling them around stalls in the center of the lane. A brown-skinned girl in a green veil hops onto a bench.

"The gods have sent us our liberators!" she proclaims to the timid crowd. "Cower no more! Defend Nirgal's Lion and the Bearer of the Light of Shamash!"

Goosebumps dot my arms. A few months ago, I didn't even know Brooma existed; a few weeks ago, I was selfishly determined to forget Alqibah behind like a bad dream. Now my fate is tied to this land and its people, who rush out into the lane to act as shields at our backs, pushing any object they can across the path to hinder the soldiers' advance.

Around the corner in the next lane, the black-skinned young man leading us slows to speak to Atheer. "You must be seen to. I know a healer not far from here who will look after you."

"Can you get us to them safely?" I ask.

"Yes." He points ahead. "Stop at this clothing shop. The owner is my Uncle Bashir. My name is Karim."

"I'm Imani. This is my brother, Atheer, and our . . . friend, Qayn."

I sense Qayn glance at me as we shuffle into the shop. We're met by Bashir, a broad man in a white *thobe* stitched around the square neckline with silver thread. He's joined by a younger man who resembles him enough to be his son. Both gaze at Atheer as if my brother is constructed of precious jewels.

"The boy who became a lion," Bashir murmurs dreamily. "Touched by Nirgal's vengeful hand."

"He's injured, Uncle," Karim says. He gestures at Atheer's bloody tunic, and I point out my brother's possibly broken arm.

Bashir snaps out of his reverie and locks the front door. "We'll take him to Taslima. Labib, wrap the wounds."

His son layers a long veil around Atheer's torso and knots it, being careful to avoid nudging the arm. Bashir bustles past the rows of tunics, abayas, dresses, and srawel to a curved doorway obscured by a curtain of stringed beads. We hurry after him through a corridor to a door that opens onto a very narrow lane. Judging by the similar doors and crates left stacked against the walls, the lane is backed onto by shops on both sides.

Bashir points at a pushcart resting against the wall of his shop. "Lay him on it."

We ease Atheer onto the bed of the cart while Bashir and Labib do something inside the shop. Atheer's cloak falls aside as he sits, revealing the blood seeping through his tunic around to his back. I inhale sharply; Qayn turns on Karim with frightening intensity.

"Just how capable is this healer of yours?"

"E-extremely, the gods are my witnesses," Karim stammers. "She mended many fighters when the invaders attacked Brooma." He shrinks under Qayn's gaze until he can tolerate it no longer and excuses himself to go help Bashir and Labib.

"Don't worry about me, Imani, I'll be all right," Atheer says. He takes my trembling hand and pulls me closer with his good arm. "Follow the street signs to the northern gates out of Brooma. Makeen and the others will be waiting at the burial grounds with the horses. There's coin and supplies in Raad's saddlebag, and Qayn will guide you. Find us at Maysoon's teahouse when you return to the city."

"But what about Amira?" I object, voice rising. "What if they kill her?"

"They won't," he says adamantly. "I know how Glaedric thinks. He'll keep Amira safe as a high-value prisoner."

Tears sting my eyes. "A prisoner, Great Spirit help her! What if he tortures her too?" My voice breaks. "It's not fair, Atheer. She's innocent and kind; she's nobody's enemy. She shouldn't have been involved in any of this—"

"Find Qayn's magic," Atheer interrupts me. "Do whatever you must to help him. He will save us all; he'll save Amira. Can I trust you with this, Imani?"

My pounding heart is about to burst from my chest. As a child, I dreamed of becoming a Shield and protecting my people from monsters, and that's exactly what I did. But my Shield duty was never this personal, the enemy never so monstrous. Now my sister's life depends on *every* step I take, *every* decision I make, *every* thrust of my blade. What if I slip? Choose the wrong path? What if my blade misses even once?

Atheer squeezes my hand. "You can do this."

"I must," I rasp, squeezing back, "or else . . ."

We share grim nods. Bashir, Labib, and Karim emerge from the shop holding reams of fabric.

"To hide you," Bashir explains as they begin arranging it around Atheer.

My brother kisses my forehead and lies down, ashen and breathing choppily. I've never seen him so helpless. He's the bravest warrior I know, as indomitable as Qalia's walls, yet somehow both are being threatened. This is a nightmare, but I can't wake up.

"We weren't supposed to part, Atheer," I say, standing back from the cart to give the men space to work. "We were separated for so long, and now we're going to be separated again after such a short time back together."

*Perhaps separated for the last time, forever,* whispers a fearful voice inside my head.

"We were meant to stay together," I repeat, louder and more desperate now, my heart heavy with the memory of us seated on the bow of the *Lion's Prize* only days ago, reminiscing about our family and the home we thought we'd see shortly, all of us filled with the hope and promise of a new dawn. A promise now broken, a light ebbing.

"Please forgive me, my Bright Blade," he murmurs weakly. "Believe we'll meet again in better times, for good."

I want nothing more than to believe that. But after all we've lost, my faith is straining, and I sense the cold dark of forever on the wind, like the approach of an evening storm.

A moment later, Atheer is concealed from my sight. The three men leave a gap in the fabric for him to breathe through and run the cart down the lane. I follow them, trying to take comfort from how good a disguise the cart is. But the longer I look at it, the more I'm reminded of the prison cart in Taeel-Sa that transported bodies into the lighthouse to be heartlessly dumped down the cliff, where they decay to dust without dignity or remembrance, as if they aren't innocent casualties of violent occupation but detritus, useless things broken beyond repair and taking up too much valuable space. As I wait for Karim to unlock the gate, a rootless dread finds purchase in me, strangling my present and pledging itself to my future, assuring me that I will only ever be safe by the steadfastness of my own blade. Should that blade fail, I will perish, and all I love shall follow.

Karim lets Qayn and me out of the gate and gives us a nod before joining his uncle and cousin pushing the cart away in the opposite direction. I'm desperate to go with them and protect Atheer, but if I do, I won't be able to find Qayn's magic, and then who will save Amira?

Qayn takes the lead, guided by street signs directing us to the northern gates. Brooma spreads out around us in mudbrick and stone painted in a mellow palette of whites, yellows, and sandy browns, interspersed here and there by the greens of date palms and potted citruses. But it's difficult to appreciate the city's unadorned beauty. I'm consumed by my siblings' fates. Taha's too. He tried to save Amira without being asked; he put himself in harm's way to defend her, and he was captured for it. He might even have been killed moments after I fled, cut down alongside his cousin and his falcon.

I should be relieved that my worst enemy after King Glaedric has been dealt with, but the anguish that strikes me is bone-deep. What if I was wrong about Taha? The Taha I know would never have wept in front of us like he did over Reza's and Sinan's lifeless bodies. He would never have said, *Damn the mission.* The Taha I know would've urged us to leave Amira behind. He would've prioritized the fate of our nation over the fate of his cousin. He wouldn't have apologized to me back on the *Lion's Prize.* But Taha was right when he said that I still don't know anything about him. And now he's gone, and I'll never learn the truth. I'll never know whether we could have defied the perilous waters between us to find some common land to stand on. Whether the intimacy we fleetingly shared could've become something more enduring.

Qayn and I reach the gates farthest from the wharf. An alarming number of soldiers enter through them into the city, but most stop only to purchase tobacco, coffee, and small goods before leaving, and their ceaseless movement means the guards are concerned more with keeping the traffic flowing than with stopping anyone. We exit unharmed, but I'm too deadened to feel relief.

A makeshift military camp has been established in the fields outside Brooma, where arriving forces are welcomed before being sent southwest down the Spice Road again. There are even more soldiers here than those we saw leaving Taeel-Sa, and I can only assume that Glaedric has rallied his armies from across Alqibah to his cause.

We take a rocky path away from the camp and follow an old sandstone wall to the entrance of the burial grounds. The sailors are there, waiting for us with our horses.

Makeen throws up his lanky arms. "What happened back there? Where's Atheer?"

"Taken to a healer," I say with an unnerving degree of control. "Glaedric's sister was on the wharf. She saw Atheer and sent soldiers after us. We had to fight them, but Atheer was injured."

Makeen falters, looking around me. "What about your sister? The cousins?"

Again my words emerge unaffected. "Amira was captured. I believe Taha was too. Reza was killed."

"I'm sorry," Makeen chokes out, the sailors murmuring commiserations behind him. "Gods, I even feel a little bad for those two bastards."

Qayn brushes his hand over Raad, my brother's black stallion. "A young man named Karim and his uncle Bashir and cousin Labib took Atheer to a healer named Taslima near the souq. Alert Farida and find him as soon as possible. We're to go on alone."

"Understood." Makeen releases the lead rope and turns to me. "Which horse do you want to take?"

Each one evokes painful memories, fears, guilt. I wish my horse was still here and not left behind in the Vale of Bones. Badr was stolen from me so suddenly. Her death was a bad omen that I should've heeded, the first loss of many.

A sailor holds up Aesif's rope. "This boy's strong and he follows Raad's lead well."

"Take Fey's mare if you prefer," Qayn says quietly, rifling through Raad's saddlebag.

I shake my head. "Aesif will be fine." *Perhaps it's fated,* I think as I climb into the colt's saddle. *Raad and Aesif. Thunder and Storm.* Taha's horse agrees; he bobs his head and snorts happily at Raad when I bring him alongside.

The sailors bid us goodbye and good luck as we canter down the path. In minutes, Qayn and I are alone again. The Djinni Slayer and the Djinni, her last hope.

# 8

# TAHA

AT THE END OF A BUMPY CARRIAGE RIDE, TAHA IS chained to a beam inside a sweltering tent. Soldiers move around outside, wheel axles squeak, camels grunt, and heavy objects thud on the ground. He spends a few hours here, judging by how dehydrated he is when he's finally walked along a rocky path, pushed down to his knees, and released from his hood. An army encampment throbs with activity around him.

"Water," he croaks, but a canteen is already being shoved into his dusty hands.

"You're the one who sank my brother's ship." A woman's voice.

He lowers the canteen from his lips, water dribbling down his chin. Princess Blaedwyn saunters over the clumps of tough-grass toward him, her long red hair rippling in the hot wind. Her shoulder has been bandaged, her arm draped in a sling. She's very much alive, and that's not how Taha wanted to leave her this morning when he shot her.

Hundreds of soldiers gather on the scrubland behind her, burdening a spiraling line of camels with supplies. At the end of the caravan, camels are tethered to wagons with wide wheels, presumably adapted for the journey through the immense dunes of the Swallowing Sands, looming on the near horizon. This is the beginning of the invasion, and it's his fault that nobody in the Sahir has any idea it's coming.

"My brother described to me how you used your falcon to burn his ship. He'll be tremendously pleased when he learns I've captured you."

Blaedwyn stands over Taha, smirking. Though the princess is as willowy as a blade of grass, her belligerence makes up for her lack of physical menace. Rather than ponder the riddle of how Glaedric could have known that Taha sank his ship, he fixates instead on the black threads radiating from Blaedwyn's blue irises.

"It was a decent shot you took," she says, sharp-tongued, "but it could've been better. I imagine you were aiming for my heart? I was certainly aiming for your cousin's."

He throws the canteen and lunges at her, snarling in Harrowtongue, "Give me another try. I won't disappoint!"

His fingers graze the smooth skin of her neck, but despite her injury, she agilely hops out of reach, and a soldier yanks his chain, dropping him face-first on the gravel.

"Brute!" Blaedwyn exclaims, her cheeks flushing an angry red to complement her hair. "I think someone needs to be taught his place!"

She turns to the well-proportioned soldier standing a few paces behind her. He's about thirty-five, with anemic blue eyes and blond hair cropped high on his head. His appearance signals eminence amongst the soldiers. He wears a brown surcoat with maroon trimmings, the chest emblazoned with a shield depicting a stag on one half and a wolf on the other; he wears glimmering chainmail on his arms, and from his belt hangs a scabbard capped in the decorative golden pommel of a longsword. Two teenaged soldiers flank him, one bearing an Empire flag, the other what must be his steel-antlered helm.

Blaedwyn beckons him with a crook of her finger. "Educate this young man, Ser Ulric."

"Your will, Your Royal Highness." Ulric strides across the grit, and as the soldier comes closer, Taha sees that he possesses the choleric gaze of a man who has taken one too many blows to the head and is apt to lash out if someone gives him a look he doesn't like. Curiously, the whites of his eyes share the same filamentous discoloration as Blaedwyn's. They must be suffering from the same ailment. It's a symptom not unfamiliar to Taha, but before he can contemplate it, Ulric has grabbed a fistful of his hair and thrown him to the ground. A single kick splays Taha on his back and sends pain ricocheting through him. Groaning, he rolls onto his knees, but Ulric shoves him back into the dirt.

"Stay down, boy."

Taha throws his shackled arms over his head just in time to block Ulric's next kick. His head still throbs, and his arm bleeds where he took the brunt of the blow. He manages to stand, only to be struck again. His ears pop; he hears everything too loudly for a second, and then the encampment sinks beneath monotonous ringing. Ulric pulls him over with the chain and starts throttling him with it. Taha wheezes, struggling in vain to fit his fingers under the chain; it's pulled so tightly that his flesh is ridged and his jugular vein is as thick and stiff as rope. His knees buckle, and Ulric drops the chain and lets him fall. He coughs violently, a monstrous headache climbing up from the base of his skull.

"He takes punishment well," Blaedwyn remarks, excited.

"Too well. Like flogging a carcass." Ulric is slightly winded from his assault and speaks between fast breaths. "You won't get through to him that way."

Blaedwyn crouches in front of Taha and peers into his face. He glares back at her, teeth gritted. Has she forgotten his last two attempts on her life, or is she flaunting her absolute confidence in her guards?

"I could do more than get through to you if we had the time," she says softly, almost intimately. "Alas, my brother will want you delivered to him . . . intact."

She stands, signaling some soldiers. Moments later, a short, hooded figure is carried out and dropped on the scrub. Taha recognizes the girly peach dress with the sheer sleeves.

"Amira," he says hoarsely.

She freezes, her head twisting toward his voice. "Taha?" she squeaks.

Blaedwyn smiles at him. "It was careless of me not to formally introduce you to Ser Ulric, but you understand him better now than you could've with words alone." She nods at the soldiers behind her. "Ser Ulric is Marshal of the Vanguard, the first and best of our army to be crossing into the Sahir. You will be going with them as Ser Ulric's model prisoner. Do bear in mind that if it weren't for your actions in Taeel-Sa, many of his men would be sailing home for the Holy Season. Loyal as they are, I sympathize with their frustrations at having to remain in service here. You'll make amends to them by assisting the Marshal with whatever he asks of you."

Taha pushes to his feet. "I'm not going to help you invade my homeland," he croaks while massaging his tender neck.

"Oh?" Blaedwyn tilts her head. "Ser Ulric?"

He plucks the hood off Amira. She recoils, her wet eyes darting until she locates Taha. Ulric calmly lifts the chain attached to her manacles and winds it around her neck. She cries out, looking to Taha for help. He senses Blaedwyn watching him too, searching for a tender spot to press on. His father has long cautioned him against admitting weakness to anyone: *Once people know you have vulnerabilities to exploit, they will exploit them. Perhaps tomorrow, perhaps a decade from now. Vultures never forget where the wounded fall.*

Before Taha was sent after Atheer, he was convinced there was nowhere his armor was susceptible to cracking under the right pressure. But the moment Ulric tightens the chain around Amira's neck, he jumps forward.

"Don't hurt her."

Amira's face purples; she pushes onto her knees, whining and scratching at the chain.

"Stop him!" Taha demands of Blaedwyn. "Please! I'll do as you ask!"

She makes him endure a protracted leer before nodding to Ser Ulric. The man releases his chokehold. Amira collapses to her knees, spluttering, and Taha can hardly stand the sound of air howling down her throat. He's seeing in her his half sister, Nura, though he doesn't know why; Nura never wore expensive silks and makeup.

"Amira is now your ward," says Blaedwyn. "Disobey Ser Ulric and your punishment will be meted out to her without exception. Until we meet again, Taha, firstborn of the Grand Zahim." She leaves him to meet with the Marshal, who's now innocently inspecting the clear sky and daytime moon as if he weren't just strangling a defenseless girl.

"How do you know who I am?" Taha calls after Blaedwyn.

"A little bird told me," she replies without looking back.

She must mean Atheer and the secrets he gave up during his

torture. But as Taha and Amira are marched to the front of the Vanguard, Taha realizes that the only reason Atheer would tell Glaedric anything about him is because Glaedric has an interest in Taha's father as Grand Zahim—and in any of Bayek's vulnerabilities he might exploit. . . .

Taha and Amira are helped onto camels and chained to the saddles. The men preparing the caravan around them are different from the mostly teenage soldiers Taha's seen patrolling the streets of Taeel-Sa, spitting and swearing, as keen to smoke their pipes as to serve their king. The youngest of these men are in their late twenties, with quite a few older than that. Those tend to be heavily armored in steel plates and bucket helms and have poleaxes roped to their saddles. Other soldiers dress lighter, in a mix of chainmail and padded leathers, and are armed with swords. The remainder are longbowmen, protected by light helms and padded jackets. Even the camels wear leathers and plate. But no matter the configuration of their armor, every man is serious-mannered and practiced in the way he checks over his equipment; his flushed, battle-hardened face is free of fear, despite the unknowns that await him. They have been specially selected for the Vanguard. They are the lethal tip of Glaedric's spear.

Ser Ulric takes his position a few camels ahead. One of his subordinates fixes the Empire flag in a holster on his saddle; the other helps him don a mail coif, over which he slips his helm. When the Marshal is ready, both young soldiers blow curled horns. The camels grunt and stand, including the one to which Taha is chained, and Ser Ulric leads the single-file procession toward the Swallowing Sands.

The closer they come to the dunes, the more potent the ancient protective enchantment that reaches for them. Under a thin cap of confusion, Taha's mind moves slower, his sense of direction threatening to blur. It was his father who taught him the secret paths through the Sands. *Follow in my steps, Taha, and you will never go astray.* Taha could find his way back to the Sahir blindfolded, yet he's never been so adrift, robbed of a greater sense of direction, like a compass arrow endlessly spinning, unable to settle anywhere again. Without Reza and Sinan, Taha is lost. Even if he manages to get home, the ones who helped make it home are gone.

He begins fervently praying that the enchantment triumphs over Ser Ulric and that the roughly one thousand souls of the Vanguard lose the path and are doomed to wander the endless dunes until death. Taha would gladly go with them to ensure the safety of the Sahiran nation, but there's another reason too: so that he never has to confront the emptiness waiting for him on the other side.

Ser Ulric crosses the threshold into the dune sea, and a sigh of searing wind showers them in sand. Taha pulls the hood of his cloak over his head and hopes the Great Spirit hears him.

# 9

# IMANI

WE RIDE NORTH AS IF THE SOLDIERS ARE ON OUR heels. Qayn leads the way, cutting a stoic figure on Atheer's black stallion. I watch him as much as I do the flat fields of Brooma, gradually becoming knolls and woodlands around us. Qayn first appeared to me in the Forbidden Wastes as a fearsome enemy to be destroyed, no questions asked. Now he's the only one left who can help me if I get into trouble or need somebody to talk to. As our route wends, high and lonely, toward the serrated mountains of Ghazali, I begin to feel a nervousness about him that has nothing to do with fear.

For a time, I assume that our destination is the grand gray city nestled between the peaks. We could reach Ghazali by evenfall, but in the late afternoon, Qayn diverts us to the village of Tull-Barak, a pretty cluster of pale stone built in the shadow of an immense forest.

I tether Aesif to a post on the main street. "Why have we stopped here?" I ask Qayn quietly, glancing around. But

Tull-Barak is the first place I've come across in Alqibah where there isn't a single Harrowlander in sight.

Qayn has pulled one of Atheer's black cloaks from the saddlebag and slung it across his shoulders. He fastens the clasp and nods at the hills above the village, blanketed in olive trees. "I sense my magic in the Zeytoun Forest. We'll buy supplies before continuing."

Before I can remind him that we already have supplies, he's swept up the cobblestone street between gawking villagers. I follow him, contemplating the dark green hills. Why would Nahla hide his magic in a forest? Nothing about the place stands out as dangerous, save for the risk of getting lost or succumbing to nighttime temperatures if improperly dressed. And yet, the longer I gaze upon the Zeytoun Forest, the more insecure I am in my conclusion. Qayn is clever, but we wouldn't be searching for his stolen magic if Nahla weren't more so.

He stops at a building on the corner and reads the wooden sign nailed to its front wall, proclaiming it HATEM'S GROCER AND SMALL GOODS. I enter a few moments after to find him between the shelves, scooping roasted chestnuts into a bag while an elderly man who must be Hatem beams at him from behind the counter.

"Why?" I mutter to Qayn. "We already have enough food and water."

"Information isn't free," he replies.

He collects apples from a basket, dons a handsome, good-natured smile, and takes the fruit and chestnuts to the counter. "Good afternoon, sir. May we purchase these?"

Hatem bobs his head enthusiastically, though somehow his brimless felt cap doesn't move. "Good afternoon to you both! I've not seen you before. You must be travelers."

Qayn pulls our coin pouch from his pocket. "We're visiting

friends in Ghazali, but we've heard much about the beauty of Tull-Barak and thought we should stop on our way."

"Oh, how very kind of you! Visit Aya's workshop down the street if you have the time. She's a most wonderful sculptor." Hatem finishes checking the items. "One *ruban,* my boy."

Qayn places a bronze coin on the counter. "I'm fascinated by the Zeytoun Forest."

Hatem hums a gravelly appreciation. "It is an ancient place unlike any other. Here in Tull-Barak, we have called it our Taj-Al-Akhdar for hundreds of years."

*Green Crown.* Is that why Nahla hid Qayn's magic there, all for a simple play on words?

Hatem frowns suddenly. "Oh, but do be wary if you visit. The forest belongs to Asyratu, the Bright Lady of Serpents and Olive Trees. It's her home, and her priestesses protect it fiercely."

"Serpents?" Qayn echoes. The sharp corners of his lips lift in mild amusement but drop when Hatem says, "The forest *teems* with them."

"Do the priestesses forbid people from visiting?" I ask Hatem.

"Not at all. People pilgrimage from across Alqibah to seek the Lady's blessings. But"—Hatem leans in, finger held aloft—"it is said that if you pluck an olive or kill a snake at dawn, there will be a spear in your back before sundown. If you visit, be *very* careful where you tread, and make sure you have enough food and water with you. The forest is large."

"Thank you very much for your help." Qayn shoves the apples into the bag of chestnuts and stalks out of the shop.

I hurry after him onto the street. "Are you sure you sense your magic in the forest?"

"Snakes," he seethes, glaring into the sunset. "Vile thief. Sadistic *trickster.*"

We stop at our horses. "Qayn, I don't understand."

He stuffs his purchase into the saddlebag and begins untethering Raad with flicks of his wrist. "Now I'm certain my magic is in that forest. Nahla hid it there *knowing* my aversion to them."

"To snakes?" I ask.

He cuts his eyes at me. "I *hate* them."

"But you're a djinni; your kind transform into them all the time."

"Not me," he swears, indignant. "I would never."

"Why not?" I stop him from hoisting into the saddle, but realizing I'm being intrusive, I pull my hand from his wrist. "Sorry. You don't have to tell me."

But my touch, brief though it was, seems to make a convincing counterargument against Qayn's reserve. His expression opens and he sighs. "It's nothing complex, Slayer. We all have something that sets our teeth on edge. For me, it's snakes."

"That's it?" I ask.

Something flashes in his gaze that makes me doubt his next words. "That's it."

I'm curious, but I know not to pressure for more. I nudge my cloak aside and rest my hand on my dagger. "Well, whatever the cause of your aversion, you have my word: I'll keep you safe in the forest."

His brows rise and he hovers a hand over his chest. "My very own Shield, pledged to protect me from harm? I'm flattered."

"You're smug," I correct, a scowl emerging.

A devilish smile touches his lips. He comes close and, in a low voice, says, "Don't worry. You'll have your very own monster soon enough."

I don't know why my heart has started pounding. "Of course,"

I say, as dryly as possible, "No good deed goes unpunished, after all."

That coaxes a sweet laugh from him. "You know, I think of everyone I've ever met—everyone who has ever feared my shadow—I'll enjoy proving *you* wrong the most."

I pretend a frustrating heat isn't building up in my cheeks. "Is that a compliment, an insult, or a threat?"

"None," he drawls. "It's an invitation."

I've exhausted my ripostes and stand before him, tongue-tied and hating his irresistible dimples. He sees he's won, climbs into the saddle, and turns Raad around, his black cloak rippling in the breeze. I push Aesif into a canter and follow him out of Tull-Barak, my face still burning.

If we weren't so keenly searching for the fork in the path between the rocks and long grass, I'm certain we would've missed the narrow trail that inclines steeply to the Zeytoun Forest. Once we're on it, we set a faster pace, and Tull-Barak soon resembles the toy villages my cousins are fond of building, for which Atheer used to carve tiny horses and wagons. The trail fuses with another from the north, and someone has lined this one with stones to distinguish it more easily. But nothing demarcates our entrance to the forest except for the olive trees, and then, heeding Hatem's warning, we proceed carefully lest one of our horses squash a snake under hoof. They make their presence known immediately, and there are plenty to be found—brown, bark-colored, and spotty, retreating along branches and slithering out of our path. At the sight of them, Qayn flinches, curling his fists around his reins.

"How heartless you are, Nahla," he hisses to himself in a breathless rage.

I've never seen him so anxious. "It's all right. They're more afraid of you than you are of them, Qayn. Keep riding. Raad is trained not to spook."

He does, but he remains contracted in the saddle, tensely surveying the trees.

After some time, we're confronted by a junction of three widely diverging trails and a landmark between a pair of unlit lampposts. The trees cluster especially closely here, and I have to light the oil lamp attached to Aesif's saddle to decipher that the landmark is actually the granite base of destroyed stonework.

"If it was a sign with directions, it's gone now." I look at Qayn, who's lighting his lantern too. "Do you know which way to go?"

"Naturally," he answers.

I expect him to confidently press on, but he hesitates for a few moments before setting off along the middle trail. Apprehension creeps up my spine as I follow him. *Don't be foolish,* I chastise myself. *He said he knows where we're going.* But what if Qayn is lying? Or worse, what if the reason he hesitated is because he knows what's ahead of us, and he's afraid?

# 10

# TAHA

THE SWALLOWING SANDS TRY TO LURE TAHA TO HIS death. He doesn't know what the men of the Vanguard might be seeing, though a few have already succumbed, galloping off to chase figments conjured by the enchantment. Taha sees Reza, as happy as anything, waving and calling his name from only a few feet off the path. So close. Taha wishes the soldiers had put his hood back on. He concentrates on the manacles trapping his wrists. He's thankful for them now; if they weren't chaining him to the camel, he would've been lost already.

"Taha! Over here, man!"

He glances up. Reza jogs alongside the caravan, sand spraying around his calves, a great big smile on his beautiful face. "Why are you ignoring me? I thought you'd be glad to see me again!"

"Great Spirit." Taha bows his head and breathes through waves of nausea.

"Come on, let's get out of here! What are you waiting for?"

Taha squeezes his eyes shut until Reza cries out in pain. Then Taha sits up, head swiveling. He finds his cousin again, still only a few feet off the path, on the left now. Reza is clutching his chest, eyes wide with shock, his ordinarily warm brown skin grayish.

"Help me, Taha," he begs, voice sick. Dying. "Why didn't you help me?"

Taha hunches forward in the saddle, sucking air, but it's only getting harder to breathe, as if guilt is burning a hole right through his chest and all the air is just leaking back out. He can still hear his cousin's whimpers.

"Why'd you deserve to survive and I didn't? Why don't I get to go home and see my father? You can make this right. Trade places with me. Please?"

"Stop it," Taha growls, clamping his hands over his ears. "You're the enchantment. You're not Reza; he's *dead.*"

Reza is quiet. He stays quiet from then on, and when Taha finally summons the courage to sit up again, his cousin is walking away from him along the knife's edge of a sand dune in the distance. Framed black against the setting sun in one blink, gone in the next.

They reach the Sahir well after sundown, trading the seemingly endless dune sea for an open desert shedding baked heat under a crescent moon. The Vanguard—or what remains of it—exhales in relief. In the glance that Taha steals over his shoulder, he spots at least a dozen empty saddles. Ser Ulric patrols down the length of the caravan to inspect the damage, but the missing soldiers elicit little more than a grimace from him. Hundreds of his men now know a way through the Swallowing Sands. The venture was a success.

The Vanguard moves on after a short break, though the end of the caravan stays behind to unpack what Taha guesses will be the Empire's first encampment in the Sahir. Ser Ulric leads the remainder of the men across starlit plains, pausing occasionally to consult a map and the night sky. Past the middle of the night, the Vanguard stops for good, and the men grunt and groan as they leave their saddles. Taha's ankles are chained together, and he's brought to a campfire over which one of Ser Ulric's subordinates is cooking bread. The Marshal sits on a rock nearby, chewing a strip of cured meat and consulting the map draped over his knee. Behind him, another subordinate erects a tent.

Taha is shackled to a wooden post hammered into the earth near the edge of the fire's warmth. A few minutes later, Amira is shackled to it too. Her eyes are bloodshot from the strangling; her neck is covered in bruises. She sits beside him, massaging it gingerly.

"Thank you for earlier, with *him,*" she says, glancing at Ser Ulric. "I'd be dead if you hadn't intervened."

Taha only nods. After Ulric and the other senior soldiers eat, he and Amira are given handfuls of crusty bread, water, and blankets. Men are put on watch, others retire to sleep around their own campfires, and Ser Ulric disappears inside his tent. Exhausted, Taha lies down. His heavy bones sink into the hard earth of his home; he stares at the stars, thinking of Reza staring at the sky in his last moments. With the distance the Vanguard covered, it feels like it should be long ago that his cousin was taken from him, but it was barely a day. The wound is raw enough to still be bleeding.

"What happened to the others?" Amira whispers, crawling over. "My brother and sister?"

Taha pulls his hands from his face. "Escaped, I think. Imani mentioned that Atheer was injured—"

"Badly?" she interrupts.

"Just injured," he says. "They ran off while they still had time."

"Great Spirit, I hope they're safe. And Reza ran too?"

He doesn't know why she cares to ask. He mustn't answer for a long time. She inches closer. "Taha? Did Reza get away?"

"No."

Her breathing quavers. "But he's not here with us, is he?"

"No. He's gone."

"I'm sorry," she whispers after a moment.

A tear slides down his face. He's glad for the dark and their distance from the exposing firelight. "Why should you be?"

"You both tried to save me when you could've run away instead." Her voice is hoarse and limps along. "I don't know what I'm even doing out here. Imani warned me that I wasn't prepared, and I didn't listen. Things would've turned out differently if I had. Atheer wouldn't have been injured; you wouldn't have been captured; Reza wouldn't have been . . . I'm so sorry."

"Me too," Taha mutters, and puts his back to her.

He doesn't realize he's fallen into cold, dreamless sleep until he's being shaken awake.

"Arise, boy. You've got work to do."

Taha sits up, heart stamping. Ser Ulric is crouched by his side, one hand on his arm. He groggily looks past the Marshal and the ghostly shadows of soldiers on the tent. It's nearly dawn; the sky is pallid, the rocky desert tinged cool blue. Amira is curled in a ball close by, fast asleep, and the Vanguard is still resting. The Marshal is undressed down to a tunic, and there are noticeable shadows under his eyes. He must've been roused from sleep not long ago too.

"Tedgar, one of my squires, has gone missing in the desert," he says.

Taha's head is full of sand. "Squires? I don't—"

"The boys training under my charge," Ulric clarifies.

The two teenagers who personally attend to him. Ulric

summons a soldier to unchain Taha from the beam, then he pulls Taha up and shuffles him past the fire to the tent. Shifting in the dirt here is one of the squires, a nervous flaxen-haired boy of sixteen.

"Tell Taha what you told me, Whitmund," Ulric grunts.

"Me and Teddy sneaked off for a walk and found some old ruins out there." Whitmund points a skinny finger at the arid sprawl beyond the tent and the bank of rocks it's set against. "Ted wanted to explore them, but I said we should head back before our absence is noted. Then this beautiful girl came out of the ruins, waving at us." Whitmund swallows. "I warned Ted that this could be the locals waylaying us, but Ted wasn't having it. He kept going on about how unbelievably beautiful the girl was, and she *was,* truly. He said he'd meet me back at camp in a short while and went off with her into the ruins. That was a couple of hours ago now. . . ." Whitmund hangs his head. "Forgive me, Ser Ulric. I should've been more responsible."

"Absolutely right you should've, you bleeding idiot." Ulric's admonishment shows a fair amount of restraint. He turns to Taha. "You'll find Ted. Mayhap he left the girl's company and lost his way back to camp."

Taha sighs. "Save yourself the trouble, Ser Ulric. That was no girl in the ruins, only a monster wearing the guise of one. Your squire is dead."

Whitmund goes as pale as a salt flat. The shadow of fear even passes over Ulric's stern face.

"His Majesty told me of your monsters. I thought they were fables."

"They're very real, and much of the Sahir is theirs," says Taha. "Only the foolhardy travel through the wilderness without protection. I'm of no help to you."

Ulric claps his hand on the back of Taha's neck. "You bloody well are of help to me, boy. Princess Blaedwyn said you're trained to fight the damned things."

Again Taha wonders about the source of Blaedwyn's knowledge. Ulric presses his thumb into Taha's windpipe. "You listening? You do as I order, and I order you to find my squire. Gutner, grab the girl."

A black-haired soldier untethers Amira from the beam, rousing her into a squealing panic. He clamps her mouth, shushing her, as he carries her over to the Marshal.

"This is to remind you of what'll happen if you refuse my orders or try anything else while we're out there." Ulric looks Amira over coldly and says in accented but fluent Alqibahi, "You're coming with us for a walk."

"She can hardly stand," says Taha, motioning at her leaning her weight on her strong foot.

"Then she'll be carried."

She directs her confused gaze at Taha. He raises a hand. "It's all right, you're safe," he says in Sahiran before swapping back to Harrowtongue. "Ser Ulric, I'll find your squire. But I need a weapon."

"I'm your weapon and no fool. Ready my armor, Whitmund." Ulric nods at the other two soldiers. "You'll join us. Keep them separated."

He enters his tent with Whitmund, and Gutner takes Amira back across the camp. She doesn't lift her gaze from Taha for a second, as if she's afraid of losing sight of him. It doesn't seem right. Only a few days ago, she probably would've been glad to never see him again.

The Marshal exits the tent in his chainmail and padded jacket, a sword on his belt and Whitmund at his heels carrying a bucket helm and a bag. Their group sets off in the direction identified by Whitmund, Amira unceremoniously carried on Gutner's back. Taha has already noticed where the boys' steps have disturbed the grit.

Ulric hikes beside him with one hand on his sword. "Ted was meant to be on a ship home to observe the Holy Season. You may think this a vain endeavor, but I would look upon it very kindly if you were to find him."

"I'll find him," says Taha, tracing the faint tracks between patches of white wormwood, "but he may not be in the condition you hope for."

Ulric gives a disapproving grunt. "He's still only a child. The son of a friend."

"Am I to assume you'll be just as moved when you encounter a Sahiran child?" Taha asks.

Ulric grabs his arm, stopping him. "I'm not in the habit of killing children, boy. Don't make me start."

Ulric shoves him forward, though still doesn't see fit to remove Taha's ankle restraints. He presses on, maneuvering awkwardly across uneven gravel and stumbling between boulders painted orange-blue by the twilight. Fortunately, the boys' path proves easy to follow, leading Taha directly to ruins on a mound. The large walled complex of pillars and squat buildings around a taller central hall is likely the remnants of an ancient temple.

"What sort of monster lurks here?" Ulric mutters as they approach. He's put on his helm now.

"I believe the girl was a *si'la,*" Taha replies, "a powerful type of shapeshifting djinni that lures travelers to her den to devour them."

Ulric's lips pinch. "And how do we kill her?"

"All djinn are vulnerable to the same thing." Taha nods at the sword on Ulric's belt. "Steel."

Whitmund points at an archway in the complex's exterior wall. "Ted and the girl went through there."

Gutner sets Amira down. The other soldier hands Taha a lit torch, then the soldiers and the squire arm themselves with their swords. Taha would prefer to be wielding a weapon too and not be bound like a beast going to slaughter, but he settles for the torch, raising it above his head with two hands as he steps through the archway and into a narrow laneway piled with sand. Footprints are imprinted in it—rather, footprints and *hoofprints.* The "girl" would've been wearing a long dress that fell over the si'la's cloven feet—the one part of the monster's body that cannot be magically disguised.

Taha follows the prints through the shadowy complex. A few of the buildings on the outer edge appear well preserved, but closer to the center, the stone underfoot is peppered with fissures, and many buildings are tilting or crumbled entirely into chasms. The pair of tracks meander between the hazards, pausing by pillars and intact wall carvings, with the si'la's prints always in the lead. She was luring Tedgar deeper into the ruins and farther from escape. He can imagine that the boy was enthralled by her unreal beauty, made all the more mysterious because of their language barrier. She could communicate only in coy smiles, laughs, and tugs of the hand, and she was successful. The tracks end at the entrance to the temple in the center.

Taha extends the torch through the gap in what remains of the doorway, but the interior is dark, suffused with a stuffy heat.

"In there?" whispers the Marshal.

The soldiers behind him exchange an apprehensive glance, Amira chewing her lip as if she means to eat it.

"Yes," says Taha, "and if you truly want me to save your squire, you'll free me of these chains and give me a weapon."

"One or the other, boy, but not both. Give him your sword, Whitmund."

The men tense as Taha trades his torch for the squire's short-sword. Ulric palms Amira's shoulder. "Now remember—if you try anything you're not supposed to, I'll throw her down and crush her skull with my boot."

Taha's glad Amira doesn't understand Harrowtongue. He enters the temple with Whitmund lighting the way at his elbow. The torchlight reveals pillars spotted with bright blue and green paint, and rounded archways carved in the cuneiform of ancient Sahiran. It also reveals the floor, deeply fractured under the safe-looking carpet of sand. In some places, chunks have sunken into jagged pits that would break an ankle if stumbled over, but Tedgar's footprints blithely wander around them and deep into the temple. The heat Taha felt at the entrance intensifies, as if he's moving toward a blacksmith's furnace. He finds its source in the same place where Tedgar's tracks abruptly end: a vast hall, its floor fallen away to a pit from which the nearly intolerable heat rises. Taha peers down into it. He can't make out any footholds along the walls, but a faint glow emanates from the pit's depths.

"This must be the si'la's den," he whispers to Ulric. "She's taken Tedgar down into it."

Ulric nudges his squire. "Rope."

Whitmund produces a coil of it from his bag, and Ulric winds it around Taha's waist.

"We'll lower you down."

"Alone?" Taha asks.

Ulric flicks his eyes up, annoyed. "I'm not afraid of ghosts, boy. It's men I worry about." He finishes the knot. "When you get down there, free the rope and tug on it three times, that way we know to pull it back up. We'll tie it around that pillar there and be down after you. *Three* tugs, no more, no less. You tug on it twice and I'll think you're in trouble and drag you up."

The soldiers grip the rope. Taha turns his back to the chasm, kneels, and shuffles to the edge.

"Be careful," Amira whispers from the doorway.

Taha looks up at her. For the briefest of moments, he sees Imani instead, fretting over him in the shadows. That she'd care about his safety is implausible, but his pulse still skips before he realizes he's seeing things. Still, he wonders what happened to Imani, if she survived Brooma, or if . . .

He pushes the painful thought away, nods to Amira, and eases over the side.

The rope strains, digging into him, but it holds. Whitmund places the torch in Taha's other hand, and the men lower him into the si'la's den.

# 11

# IMANI

WE RIDE UNTIL OUR LANTERNS STRUGGLE WITH the darkness, then we journey through the forest on foot, tugging our horses along behind. I take point and stomp my boots with every step to alert any snakes on the path ahead. So far, it's remained clear.

"I appreciate the caution," Qayn tells me quite sincerely, but he remains anxious, flitting his gaze over the long grass on either side of the path as if anticipating an assassin.

Eventually we encounter another broken granite base by the side of the trail. The trees end, the starlight flares, and a river roars somewhere below. Qayn halts to stare across a ravine and what remains of a stone bridge clinging to its sides. Someone has etched a message into the stone: THE PATH TO THE BRIGHT LADY ENDS HERE. Offerings have been left under the message—wilted flowers, flasks of oil and honey, and pouches of incense.

I tie Aesif to a trunk and venture to the edge of the bridge. The middle has fallen to the rushing river below, leaving an impassable gap, yet the bridge's entrances on both sides are intact.

"Someone's destroyed this bridge somehow," I say.

"Nar al-aswad," Qayn replies quietly.

"Blackfire?" I glance at him, then back at the bridge, noticing the scorch marks on the stone. "You're right. It's blown a hole right through the middle. But who would do this?" I think back to Tull-Barak. "Perhaps Hatem was wrong and the priestesses of Asyratu are trying to stop people from visiting the forest after all."

"Regardless, I sense the three jewels of my crown on the other side," says Qayn.

He goes to tether Raad to a different tree, carefully assessing it first for the presence of snakes. I follow him, chewing the inside of my cheek. The light of my lantern lands on a scattering of long wooden beams cast off in the grass beside the trail. Frayed rope is still threaded between a few.

"Qayn, look! Someone must've built a makeshift crossing. Perhaps we can restore it." I jog over and try to lift one of the beams, only to realize I'm overestimating my strength. I trudge back to him. "Never mind, they're too heavy. We'll have to look for a different path in the morning. But this side of the forest surely connects with the other somewhere."

"Somewhere," he mutters. "It could take us days to find a way across, and even if we do, we may be far from where I sense my magic."

"I know, and I want to get over there as much as you do, Qayn, but what choice do we have?" I pause as an idea occurs to me. "I think I could throw my dagger to the other side and summon you from it there. You'll be able to go on alone so long as you keep the dagger with you."

Alone, in the dark . . . with snakes?" He shudders, shaking his head. "No, we need a way to cross to the other side together."

As urgent as the situation is, I'm relieved that he rejected my offer. It was too risky. What if Qayn got lost or into trouble? What if a stranger stole the dagger from him, or he accidentally dropped it somewhere out of reach, just far away enough that the magical binding triggered and trapped him inside the blade? We'd both be stranded.

"I could teach you a way across using magic," he says, sliding his gaze over to me. "I did promise to share my knowledge as part of our deal."

I look nervously across the ravine, to the olive trees growing like feathers on the backs of the hills, black beneath night's cape.

"I've no intention of hurting you, only of helping you." Qayn's voice possesses the quality of honey. "I wish you would see that there's so much more than hostility that we could share together."

There's that word again, *together,* rebounding between my warming ears. It demands interrogation. Is there an "us" emerging, or do we remain the Djinni Slayer and the Djinni, forever destined to balance on the sword's edge of enmity? I don't know, but I yearn for friendship, even with someone of his kind. The realization flusters me, as if I've levered up a garden paver and the bugs under it are skittering away from the light. That's me, fleeing my own reflection in the mirror. Perhaps I should finally confront it, as Taha said, and discover who looks back. It would be someone lonely, I think, made so by their own doing.

"Very well, Qayn," I say. "Teach me."

"Happily." He leaves the bridge, sliding his hands into his pockets, and ambles along the forest's edge. "During our last lesson, aboard the *Prize,* you told me that your dagger is an extension of yourself. Is that why you can summon it to you if you're separated from it?"

I follow him. "Yes, I call upon the dagger to come to me, in the same way someone calls upon their arm to do something."

"But you only know how to call your blade back to you, not how to join your blade where it has gone." He turns, burying his bare feet in the loose soil, and looks at me. His words are already doing something to my mind, maneuvering it like wet clay to fashion new shapes with the matter.

He raises a brow. "Is that correct?"

"You're asking if I can go to my dagger—"

He comes over. "Give me the dagger."

I oblige him. Qayn walks away with it, curiously inspecting the blade before he drops it in the dirt.

"Summon it back to you."

Using the little magic left in my veins, I hold out my hand and pull on what Auntie called "the magical tether" that sorcerers like me share with objects of our choosing. The dagger flies back to my fist. Qayn is already walking over, palm out.

"May I?" He takes it away and drops it in the dirt again. "Now, rather than the dagger going over to you, *you* go to the dagger—but not by walking here."

"*Oh,* I see! That's brilliant, Qayn. I could cross the bridge by—*oh* and think of the other applications! Being able to reposition in battle—" I falter. "But how do I do that?"

He collects the dagger. "Your affinity attunes you to iron, which is why you feel that this dagger is an extension of yourself to command. That concept can work both ways if you change the angle of your perspective even slightly. In fact, it *must.* You see, for the dagger to be part of you, you must be part of it."

"Brilliant," I echo. "But I still don't understand how—"

"It's a matter of perspective, nothing more. See this?" He points at himself walking. "I'm coming over to you. But if a man bends to buckle his sandals, would you say he is coming over to his feet?"

I scratch my head. "Well . . . no . . ."

"Why not?" Qayn stops before me.

I feel like I'm sitting a Trial at the Order of Sorcerers, except my teachers have been replaced by a djinni of intimidating beauty. "I—I don't know."

"Think about it," he says.

I try, but after an embarrassing minute of silence, I realize that I'm only repeating Qayn's riddle in my head, with no result.

"I still don't know," I confess.

"Shall I repeat the question?"

My cheeks flush. "*No.* I heard the question; you're just not speaking to me in terms that are easy to understand."

He looks off, pointed silhouette emanating regal displeasure. "I suppose you aren't wrong. I'm attempting to communicate a magical concept in nonmagical language. It's something I haven't had to do in a very long time." He sighs, handing the dagger back to me. "Meditate on it. I'll make camp."

I reluctantly sink down onto a fallen log and repeat his question in my head. The answer is on the tip of my tongue, yet infuriatingly out of reach. I wipe my mind clear and try again. Qayn starts a small fire; he unpacks food, water, and our bedrolls. I feel the minutes passing like sandstone grating across my skin. Soon, even the seconds will hurt to squander. I can't dawdle in the hills above Brooma, meditating like one of the Order's ascetic elderly sorcerers, while Amira is Glaedric's prisoner and the Harrowlanders are invading my home.

I jump to my feet. "Qayn, I've had an idea. It's not something I would suggest if time weren't so precious, but . . . might I better understand the lesson if I bound you to my soul? Like we did last time." I have to deliberately keep an even tone.

"Naturally," he says, studying me over the fire. "If we were soulbound, I could reach you directly and precisely convey my meaning in my own tongue. You proved yourself a quick study last time; I imagine the outcome would be the same this time. But"—he returns to stoking the fire—"I would rather we didn't."

It wasn't long ago that he was trying to convince me to bind him to my soul. The rejection stings, and I no longer have the comfort of being oblivious to my own behavior. Since I left Qalia, I've been confronted by it at every turn. "Is this because of what happened the last time we were soulbound?"

"Yes." He stabs the kindling, disturbing the flames. "You invaded my privacy and forcibly viewed my most painful memory."

I remember the lavish room in the First City, before the place was destroyed by Hubaal the Terrible on the Desert's Bane's orders; the sprawling bed of silk that Qayn slept in alone, wearing his crown of light; the garden he later disappeared into, overcome by rage and despair. I never found out why.

"I'm sorry, Qayn, it was wrong of me. I promise I won't do it again."

"An apology doesn't undo the hurt you inflicted."

"Nothing would," I say half-defensively, sliding my dagger into its sheath.

"There is something that could prove your promise is sincere. Let me view one of your painful memories. My choice. Do that, and I'll share my lesson with you."

I cross my arms. "I don't know if that's a fair exchange."

"It's an opportunity to foster trust between us," he says. "You may decline and return to your meditation if you wish."

"If I don't get across this ravine, you don't get your magic," I remind him sharply.

"Until we go around," he says. "I suppose I could wait; I've only been doing that for a thousand years."

Icy fear trickles down my back. Qayn doesn't have anyone to worry about but himself. Setting aside his self-professed concern for us, he floats imperviously above our troubles. He could be reunited with his magic tomorrow or years from now. What difference does it make? Little to him, everything to me.

"Treat the exercise as if you're building a bridge across a ravine," he says, standing before me again.

I glare past him at the fire, at once a mass of thorns and defenseless skin. "Qayn, to my soul I bind yours, your liberty mine to command until a time determined by me, after which you will return to your first binding in my dagger. Do you accept?"

"I accept."

I shut my eyes as our souls meet and the boundaries that define and divide us erase. Though the binding completes, I don't open my eyes. I've been transported to a shadowy corridor of closed, mismatched doors in the cold palace of Qayn's being. Doors I long to fling open on the knowledge hidden within; doors I promised I would never open again without his consent. Qayn slinks along my own corridors, but I remain still and unobjecting, wondering where he'll go. Apprehensive about confronting my own pain.

He pushes open the door he wants; I instinctively know where he's gone, and panic moves me there too. Afternoon sunlight warms my face; I hear the flowing Azurite River and the bustle of Bashtal around me. Qayn stands aside on the stone bank, watching. Present-me reluctantly joins him as Taha emerges, sopping, from the water and kisses past-me. I avert my gaze, but I can only endure the memory without protest until Taha stammers, *Forgive me, I—I didn't mean to do that,* and my own voice returns, thick with disappointment, *You didn't?*

I turn to Qayn. "Stop this."

But it's already over. I'm moved to the dark corridor outside as the door swings shut. Qayn has gone elsewhere, to a place that even I don't know, and he's whispering in his mysterious tongue the lesson I desperately need—but at what cost has it come?

"It's done," he says.

I open my eyes. We're back in the forest, standing face to face. I can't read his, but I suspect he's wrestling a smirk.

"Are you happy now?" I ask.

"Happy to see you suffer? No."

"I'm sure you aren't," I mutter to the moon peeking between the branches above us.

"I understand your pain more than I wish I did," he says. "I was manipulated by someone I loved, someone for whom it wasn't enough to rebuff me. She tended my feelings as if they were flowers to grow and then stomped on them."

"Nahla," I say, looking back down.

He bows his head. "I bared my soul to her, and she destroyed me. At times, I'm convinced she never intended to love me in return. But other times, I think that our love was more real than the sum of all else, until her heart was won over by a darker temptation. . . . A thousand years, and I still haven't decided which hurts more."

I experience a frighteningly strong urge to comfort him, to feel his touch and be the cause of his dimpled smile, and even the rational internal voice reminding me that Qayn is a djinni isn't enough to chase away the desire. But I'm too afraid to reach out to him and change the nature of our relationship, so I do nothing.

He sighs and returns to the fire. "I suppose there's no good in dwelling on the past when we have the promise of the future. Sleep on my lesson. If you're the quick-witted apprentice I suspect you are, it should make sense soon. Oh." He half turns to look at me. "When you're ready, declare our soulbinding ended, and I will return to the dagger."

Return and leave me to my sad memories, or stay, our souls entwined in this most dangerous, forbidden union between a monster and his slayer. But we're allies now, and however much that truth might upset me at any other moment, in this one, I find it agreeable. It makes it easy to voice what I really want.

"We can keep this binding for now, unless you object," I say.

His brows rise slightly. "I don't object."

"Then it's settled." I brusquely sidestep him to the camp, and he soon resumes stoking the fire. After a few minutes of silent work, we gather around it as if nothing has changed, even though very much has.

# 12

# TAHA

TAHA SETS DOWN ONTO A MUSTY PILE OF FABRIC AT the bottom of the pit. The si'la's den is larger than he expects. Only this area is exposed to mildly fresh air through the tunnel above him. The rest of the pit descends underground, where light twinkles from a fissure in its depths. Even at this distance, the fissure emits heat harsher than what one would find at noon in a hammada. But he can't tell what the source of the light or heat is, and between that opening and him, the pit is shrouded in darkness.

He places the sword and torch on a narrow rock shelf and undoes the rope from around his waist. He tugs on it three times and arms himself again, though he can only raise the torch or strike with the sword but not do both at once. With the rope retreating up the tunnel, he studies the fabric bunched under his boots. It's clothing: the cloaks, tunics, and srawel of lonely travelers lured here before Tedgar.

Ulric drops onto the pile beside Taha with a soft grunt. He draws his sword, but he's removed the glove from his other hand.

Without warning, he summons a ball of fire in his palm. Taha stares at the steady flame, understanding dawning on him. Both Ser Ulric and Princess Blaedwyn are sorcerers, and the black filaments in their eyes are a manifestation of the improper use of misra. Magical obsession.

"Have you heard anything?" Ulric whispers.

Taha tears his gaze from the flame, shaking his head. Ulric's lips press into a bloodless line. He doesn't gesture Taha forward until Whitmund and Gutner have climbed down too.

Taha enters the pit first. After he descends roughly 150 feet, the light of his torch uncovers hills of abandoned possessions and bones picked clean, and his every breath taints with death. On his next step, he accidentally kicks a goat's skull. He tenses, listening to it clatter loudly down the decline until it hits something and stops. He adjusts his sweaty grip on the shortsword and presses on, torch raised. The obstacle is a bloody bed of skeletal remains and a set of torn clothes.

"Staggnir's scepter, it's Ted," Ulric exclaims. He extinguishes his magical flame and pushes past Taha to kneel by the bones. Whitmund shuffles over too, wide eyes glistening in the light of the torch he's holding. Ulric begins unfastening his cloak. "Will the beast be about, boy? I need to say a prayer and wrap Ted up to send back to his family. His mother's going to be beside herself."

Taha rakes his gaze over the darkness and stops again on that far-off light glimmering from the fissure in the stone. Something obscures it momentarily—something sneaking into the fissure.

"The si'la is still here," he says. "But if you remove my restraints, I can deal with it."

The sight of Tedgar's remains must convince Ulric that the Sahir's monsters aren't fables after all. He reluctantly nods at

Whitmund, who frees Taha's wrists and ankles. Then Ulric settles into whispered prayer, and Whitmund and Gutner stand guard. Taha stalks to the passageway; the pit narrows, the ground descending at a steep angle. Sweat sticks his tunic to his chest, and the heat soon becomes so intense that even breathing is difficult. When he reaches the passageway's entrance, he has to stop to gulp air, and then he steps through it onto a stone balcony protruding over the dizzying drop of a vast cavern perforated with gigantic hollows.

"What is this?" he murmurs, staring over the balcony's edge at what he can only comprehend as an immense gash in the earth far below. Searing light weeps from it, and a sense of something similar to what emanates from the Sanctuary in Qalia: the presence of magic, but this of a kind distorted and frightening.

Suddenly a voice: "It is a Door between your realm and ours. Few, if any, of your kind have looked upon one before."

He twists to see the si'la pressed against the wall at the end of the balcony. She's in her true, grotesque form, not wearing a familiar face or one that might seduce him. Her features are plucked from an amalgam of beasts, at once recognizable and foreign, like her tail, capped in a scorpion's stinger. Her jaundiced, protuberant eyes keep wary watch on his sword; her excessively large mouth sags in a frown, saliva dribbling over her purple lips onto her bristly chin with every rasp; her mottled, jagged wings curve protectively over her distended belly, the skin of which glistens with a transparent excretion. The Shields' Almanac describes her condition: *When gorged, the si'la is greatly weakened and unable to disguise her natural appearance.*

Taha tosses the torch down and grips the sword with two hands. He readies to strike, but the cavern suddenly vibrates, raining dust on his shoulders. The gash in the earth vents light that scorches his eyes, and from the abyss rises the tapered head of a giant sand serpent. The black monster slides its gleaming, scaled heft out of the gash and along naturally formed ridges to a hollow in the cavern's far wall. It disappears inside; the cavern shakes with the serpent's glide, the rumble competing with the *shhhhhh* of its mass slithering against the stone.

"Where is it going?" Taha demands between hard breaths.

"The surface," answers the si'la.

He marvels at the cavern. "This is it, then, the source of the monsters. Shields have been searching for this place for centuries."

"There are many open Doors in the Sahir. Some very high, some very low."

"Doors can be closed."

"Not these," she snarls, indignant. "Only the one who opened these Doors can close them, and they gave their word that they will not."

Taha looks back at the si'la. "Who?"

She shrinks against the wall, hissing softly. "The Invulnerable. You call them by another name."

His brows lift. "You mean the Desert's Bane."

"Indeed. It is thanks to them and their Doors that we found refuge in your realm, and what a plentiful, peaceful realm it is. We no longer need to eat our own to survive. Here we have plenty of flesh for feasting." She leers at his chest, despite her belly freshly bloated on Tedgar's corpse.

"What sort of monster was the Desert's Bane?" he asks, dragging her bulging gaze up again.

"One with no kin. . . . I could show you." The offer is uttered in a different voice—a woman's, silky and tempting.

"How?" he asks, intrigued.

"A portrait . . . if you give a blood oath to spare me."

He glares at her. "And leave you to continue luring victims to your den."

She smiles, saliva oozing between her sharp, bloodied teeth. "We all must eat. This is my price for knowledge."

A blood oath isn't a trivial agreement; it's a magical promise made at the risk of his life. Should Taha break his oath, he'll pay in blood. Bargaining with monsters is conduct he loathes, but he'd be a fool to deny her when he's stumbled upon something that rewrites Sahiran history and could change the course of its future. The threat of the Harrowlander army is a mortal, pressing one, but this Door is the answer to a question that has haunted his nation for a thousand years: Where are the monsters coming from? If he could understand its mechanism, he could find a way to close the Doors permanently.

"A blood oath," he agrees.

Her dewy torso shivers on a giggle, and then she peels her back off the wall. "Man of flesh, in return for showing you a portrait of the Invulnerable, you will leave this place having done no harm to me, and me, no harm to you."

Taha presses his finger to his blade, drawing blood, and lets the scarlet droplets fall onto the stone between them. "I swear this oath."

"And I." She bites her hand and lets her purple blood drip on top of his. A moment later, the pool turns to dust. Satisfied, the si'la faces the wall on his left and beats air over it with her wings, whispering in her guttural tongue.

Taha faces the blank stone, his heart pounding. A figure slowly appears in black scrawls, with horns of fire, a fanged snarl, clawed hands, and a vaguely human body cloaked in smoke.

Taha can hardly fathom that he is the only Sahiran alive who has looked upon the Bane's form.

"See what is written." The si'la traces a claw across glyphs scratched alongside the portrait. She reads: " 'For Their gift of shelter, bear witness and give thanks to Their Names—The Invulnerable, Maker of Fair Covenants, Opener of Doors, Provider, and Gracious Host of All.' "

"They almost appear as a man here," says Taha.

"Almost. But they are no man."

He frowns at her. "You speak of the Bane as if they still exist. Our people destroyed them."

Her lips twist into a devious smile. "How? You cannot kill what doesn't die."

Ulric's shout from the pit interrupts them. "Oi, boy! Do you hear me?"

The si'la points a claw at the passageway. "Our bargain is done."

Taha wants to probe her lies. Instead, he steals a last glance at the eerie portrait, grabs his torch, and slips through the passageway to the pit. Ulric's summoned flame waves in the gloom at the tunnel's entrance.

"Speak now or I'm leaving without you!"

"On my way!" Taha calls back, jogging up the slope.

The rope is dropping back down when Taha reaches the tunnel, the others having already gone up. As he's hoisted to safety, he stares at the glow shimmering from the passageway, entranced, and he doesn't blink until it's gone from his sight.

# 13

# IMANI

MORNING FOG IS CLINGING TO THE OLIVE TREES when I rouse. I have the pressing sense that I'm close to unlocking a vital piece of knowledge and the key is magic, so while Qayn feeds the horses, I perform a tea ceremony. I'm draining my cup when I finally solve his riddle.

"Of course," I groan, setting it down. "The man doesn't go to his feet; he *is* his feet. He's already there."

Qayn laughs, patting Raad's nose. "Your magical aptitude is quite remarkable. Let's put your newfound understanding to the test, shall we?"

We pack up camp, leave water for the horses, and return to the destroyed bridge. The gap in it looks to be roughly thirty feet. I find a clearing about double that length and throw my dagger across it while running. I inhale and, on the exhale, imagine sending away the world with my breath, leaving just me and the spinning blade that is also me. And in my body and soul, I grasp that I am here, where I land from my stride, and I am here, where my blade flies.

I go from sprinting to spinning as my body joins the dagger, and I become this perfect slice of brilliant blue steel parting the mist. It's the strangest sensation, and yet oddly comfortable. I cross forty feet in a blink before slamming my boots back down like lightning striking the ground, the dagger in my hand, now rapidly stashed on my thigh, my other fist rising in triumph.

"That was incredible!" I crow, startling the pigeons cooing in the trees. Intoxicating, powerful—a skill I must refine and build upon. With Qayn's help, I'll never again have to be as helpless as I was back in Brooma.

I jog over to him. He's applauding, dimples flashing around his smile. "Well done! You've yet to disappoint."

"Tell that to yourself!" I sling my arms over his shoulders, but before I can cringe at myself, he hugs me back.

"I would, but I'm not terribly fond of lying to myself." He chuckles as we part. "We make quite the alliance, wouldn't you agree?"

"Enthusiastically." I narrow my eyes, probing like a hound. "What other clever lessons do you have hidden away, hmm?"

His black eyes gleam; his smile widens. "The likes of which you can only dream of. Then again, anything that you dream of having, I could give you. And anything that you dream of becoming, I could make you."

All at once, I'm mesmerized by the unabashed splendor of his features, the long, fine sweep of his lips, so accustomed to graceful speech. "For what in return?" I ask. "Surely this kindness doesn't come free."

"I said that I *could,* not that I would," he snaps abruptly.

I recoil. His curled lashes flutter, confused lines sweeping across his forehead. He closes the new space between us with a step. "Forgive me. It's a terrible fear of mine, being exploited again. I'd like nothing more than to have a companion to whom I could bare my soul. Someone I could trust. For them, I'd grant any wish they asked."

Could that companion really be me? Qayn and I are both discarded fragments seeking to become whole again. What if we could find completeness in each other?

I blink, remembering that Qayn and I are soulbound. He could be feeling this, and if he's just toying with me, I'm making a fool of myself right now. Hurriedly I turn my focus inward and intuitively locate the boundary between our souls. I only need to concentrate on raising a defensive wall there for one to materialize, and now I feel a little more alone again in my own head—though, truthfully, I don't know if I prefer it or not.

"I hope you find that companion," I say stiltedly, looking anywhere but at him.

"As do I." He clears his throat. "Would you like to practice again?"

Practice never hurts, but time is scant, and I'd prefer to leave this awkward moment behind sooner rather than later. I shake my head. "No, I have it. Let's cross while the day is new."

I replenish my magic with more tea from my flask. Using this skill sapped my stores to near exhaustion, and as with every ability I've learned, it'll be some time before I'm experienced enough to temper how much it drains. With my magic full again, I stand at the edge of the broken bridge and concentrate on where I want to land, then I move several paces back.

"You'll join me when I reach the other side," I say to Qayn.

He smiles weakly. "Check the area for snakes first?"

"You got it." I sprint to the last of the shattered stone and jump. My heart hoists into my throat as I sail across the chasm, legs kicking. I lob the dagger across the rest of the gap before

I plunge through it toward the river below. But Qayn's lesson proves too powerful for my fear. *I'm here, falling,* I tell myself, teeth gritted, *and I'm here, soaring!*

I cross the gap fused with my blade and land, boots down, on the other side of the bridge, dagger in hand. "Incredible," I gasp, pawing the sweat off my forehead. Quickly I scan the dirt and grass for any scaly offenders, but there are none. "It's clear!"

Qayn materializes beside me, lightly touching my arm. "Excellent work. This way."

We return to the trail we were following last night. The chilly mist clears as the day matures. Qayn begins to move with more conviction. Courage too. Eventually he takes the lead, and his walk becomes a jog, light-footed and breathless. We climb the winding trail for hours, though the time feels much shorter, and suddenly Qayn stops and stares up at where the trail crests a hill.

"My magic is here." He turns and gathers my hands, holding them against his chest. "At last, Imani. A thousand years I have searched and longed for the jewels of my crown. A thousand years I have suffered defeat. And today it ends, thanks to your help."

He grins and scrambles up the hill, setting off small avalanches in his wake. I run after him, excited, relieved, yet nervous over what we may find—and what may happen when I help restore Qayn to his power. I don't know if Atheer discussed with him how he'll uphold his end of the bargain, but as we summit the hill, where the sunlight dims and the wind picks up, I realize that it's much too late to do anything about it.

The trail transitions to a pretty stone-edged path weaving between ancient olive trees. Farther ahead, a granite stump juts from the earth. It's the plinth of a statue since removed—hacked away, judging by the toothed marks in the stone. Shattered granite crunches under my boots as I approach it; the culprit, a metal chisel, sticks out of the dirt beside the plinth.

"Imani, look."

I follow Qayn's gaze beyond the plinth. A skeleton lies face down in the grass, wearing a purple robe with gilt-thread embroidery in the pattern of serpents and boughs, an etched spear discarded a few feet from its hand.

"A priestess of Asyratu," I say, looking back at the ruins of the statue. "Who would do this?"

We pursue the path between the trees in search of answers. Here and there in the long grass we glimpse crumpled purple fabric, heads of dark hair as stiff as hay, skeletal fingers, bloodied spear tips, and then the brown-and-maroon padded jacket of a skeletal soldier, slumped at the base of a tree.

I stop at his boots. "The Harrowlanders were here."

Qayn abandons my side, head bent into the driving wind. I run after him past empty crates, chisels, rakes, hammers, and ruts in the soil left by wagons that have cut across the path and carelessly scattered the border stones. We ascend the bloodstained steps of a magnificent granite temple with long arched windows and a domed roof, past another dead priestess and the soldier she defeated. The temple doorway has been left exposed, the doors themselves having been removed, and the engraving over the entrance reads THE TEMPLE OF QUEEN MOTHER ASYRATU.

The light through the windows illuminates a vestibule stripped bare, except for the remains of a shattered vase, a soiled rug roughly rolled and pushed aside, and one statue of Asyratu, depicted with flowing hair crowned in boughs, her nude form embraced by serpents. The stone under her feet is marred by jagged indentations; in some spots, whole chunks of stone have been chiseled away. In the wall above the door exiting the vestibule, there's a depression in the stone where something large and rectangular previously lay flat; the few colorful tiles still embedded around the edges indicate that it was a mosaic, which has been lifted and removed like the stonework.

"The Harrowlanders sacked this temple," I realize aloud. "The priestesses must have tried to stop them by destroying the bridge, but they forced their way over with the makeshift crossing and plundered everything of value." I meet Qayn's eyes. *"The jewels."*

He dashes out of the vestibule and across a circular anteroom into the temple's central space. Here, bathed in light pouring through a round ceiling window, is a mighty statue of Asyratu nursing a babe. Though the same jagged indentations mar her base, the Lady defied the Harrowlanders to remain in her home, and whoever tried and failed to evict her vented their frustration by desecrating the statue. Half the Lady's face is missing; one of her breasts has been gouged off, her forearm smashed apart, her body tormented by stab marks. I haltingly read out the statue's Alqibahi inscription: " 'Long ago, the Lady appeared to Her devoted with a Gift: three stones forged of Her gods-essence and brought forth into the mortal realm to be guarded with the blood of Her ardent—a Light to sustain those who seek Her Mercies, burning bright where Her Crown remains upon Her Brow.' "

"Here." Qayn glides his fingertips over Asyratu's crown of boughs. The three central prongs each have an indentation to support a jewel. Each prong is empty. "They were supposed to be HERE!" he shouts, the muscles in his slender neck straining. Tenderly he traces a tear down Asyratu's crumbled cheek. "The jewels were supposed to be *here,*" he whispers, and then he tilts his forehead to hers and weeps.

"We'll find your magic, Qayn," I assure him as a buzzing fills my head, and the vast room suddenly feels suffocatingly small. What if we don't? Without Qayn's magic, we have no answer for the Harrowlanders. I have nothing with which to save my family and my people.

"Can you sense where the jewels have gone?" I ask him hopefully.

Qayn slips off the statue like silk draping. "It was happenstance that I sensed them here when Atheer passed through Brooma. Since the jewels have been in this one place for a millennium, Asyratu's statue bears the trace of my magic." He tilts his head to the inscription. "This describes the Lady appearing to her devoted. That was Nahla, bringing the jewels in disguise. She may have used the magic of the misra to amaze and sway the priestesses into defending the crown with their lives."

"To their very last breaths," I murmur, looking across the bloody tiles.

"An honorable defense of a dishonorable thief," he says bitterly. "I understand now why I thought I sensed my magic a few times on the trail. The jewels were carried away by the Harrowlanders. They could be anywhere now, and it'll take me time to follow such a faint trace. It could be a *long* time."

"Great Spirit help us," I whisper, looking around desperately. A wooden crate near a plinth catches my eye. A note has been discarded on its lid. I hurry over and lift it to the light. Something in Harrowtongue is inked neatly down its length.

"Qayn, look at this." I take it to him. "Did you ever learn to read Harrowtongue while you were bound to my brother?"

He accepts the note and skims it. When he finishes, he shuts his eyes, crushing it.

"What is it?" I ask, wringing my hands. "What does it say?"

"It says that the crates contain precious cargo from the

temple, due to be carried on a ship under royal contract departing Brooma for the port of Darkcliff in Harrowland." He drops the note and slumps on a hunk of stone with his head in his hands. "The jewels are listed among the cargo."

"The jewels are in Harrowland," I mutter, staggering over to Asyratu and her despoiled crown. The statement hardly makes sense to my ears.

Qayn raises his head to stare at nothing. "Are you amused, Nahla?" he calls out, his black gaze chillingly empty, inhuman almost. "You're at peace with your family in the great beyond. You robbed me, vilified me, tried to kill me. . . . You must think you got away with it too. . . ." His voice drops. "But it's not over until it's over."

"Until our very last breaths," I say, looking again at the bloodied tiles. I go and kneel before Qayn. "Everyone everywhere depends on our stopping Glaedric before he reaches the misra tree. We can't do that without your magic. This won't be easy, but we have a way to Harrowland in the *Lion's Prize.* And if not, Farida will surely know someone else who can sail us there."

Qayn considers me from between the wavy strands of hair dangling over his brow. "And then?" he asks.

Complications leap off the question like embers, so many they spark a wall of fire that I almost can't negotiate. Almost. But if there's anything positive to take away from the time that I spent with Taha, it was his attitude of never giving up.

"We find a way or make our own," I say. "But we can't do anything until we return to Brooma and let Atheer and Farida know what's happened." *That's if my brother is still alive,* I think, but I don't voice the fear. We have enough burdens to shoulder for now. I pull Qayn to his feet. "Our best bet is to look for

Farida at a place called Maysoon's Teahouse. It's operated by a friend of the rebellion."

I collect the note and head for the entrance. Qayn lingers by the door to the central room a few moments longer, gazing at wounded Asyratu. In the afternoon light outside, I notice something troublesome swimming in his eyes.

"What were you thinking about back there?" I ask.

He reaches up to a low bough hanging over our path. His fingers brush an olive, but he moves on empty-handed.

"I was thinking about who will look after the forest now."

# 14

# TAHA

THE WISE TRAVELER NEGOTIATES THE DESERT IN THE early morning and night. The Vanguard rides the length of the scorching day. Quickly the sunburned men learn why Sahirans wrap their heads and faces in fabric, and they do the same. They stop regularly to drain their waterskins, paying no mind to conserving their stores. But it's time, not security, that occupies the Vanguard, and at the pace it's moving, Taha estimates that their first destination is imminent: the wealthy town of Ebla, situated at a junction of routes by the lifesaving waters of the Ayn al-Sama spring, one of the largest tributaries of the Al-Ayn River. Home to roughly three thousand unsuspecting souls.

Ser Ulric stops the Vanguard at sunset and sends scouts on foot to a low plateau. The rest of the men stretch their legs, quench their thirst, and smoke, keeping noticeably quiet in conversation. Taha is permitted to pace a patch of sand between several soldiers, who part a minute later for Amira. She hobbles in and slides down against a boulder to massage her ankle. Taha glances at Ser Ulric, farther up. The Marshal is deep in discussion with his senior soldiers and probably forgot to order Whitmund to keep the prisoners separate.

Taha sinks against the boulder beside Amira. "How's your ankle?"

"Sore," she sighs, "but not worse."

"Then it's healing."

She nods, still massaging it. "I saw the bundle that the Marshal brought up from the pit."

"Ulric's 'squire.'" He says the word in Harrowtongue before returning to Sahiran. "His attendant, Tedgar. A si'la had picked his bones clean."

"Spirits. Was the si'la there? I didn't hear any commotion."

Taha has been waiting for Amira to ask. "Something strange happened down there," he says, watching the soldiers check their armor. "I saw something that you need to know, in case something happens to me."

She listens closely to the account, her shock and intrigue growing. That she's grasped the gravity of the situation makes Taha feel better.

"I know we have other things to worry about right now—" he starts, but she shakes her head.

"This is a groundbreaking discovery. If only my siblings could know; Atheer was searching for the source of the monsters for years. The Council must be informed of the Door's location—" She stops, her face creasing. "*If* the Council remains."

"Great Spirit willing."

After a moment, Amira shifts in the sand to face him. "As we're speaking of the Desert's Bane—I agree with the position you took about Qayn during our meeting."

Taha nods, studying her. "I remember you didn't seem convinced by him . . . not the way your sister is."

She grimaces. "It's hard to understand, even more if you know that I was the one who encouraged Imani to bind Qayn in the first place."

"Imani was opposed to the binding?" he asks curiously. "She told me as much, but I didn't believe it."

"Opposed?" Amira snorts. "She wanted to slaughter Qayn the moment she laid eyes on him. But you've seen Qayn's beauty and heard his clever speeches. . . . It's a challenge to resist his charm."

"And now Imani is devoted to him," says Taha, resentment churning his insides.

Amira glances at him with a peculiar look. "Imani's devoted to Atheer. Don't misunderstand me, I love our brother too, but Atheer isn't impervious to Qayn's manipulation. Now Farida and the whole Taeel-Sani rebellion are effectively doing Qayn's bidding through my brother." She sighs. "To be frank, when we landed in Brooma, I was going to ask to go home with you and Reza, if you'd have let me."

"Why?" Taha asks.

She looks up to the plateau. "I thought if we could reach Qalia, I could research what Qayn told us about himself and the First City. His accounts are all so . . . *substantial.* There must be some record of him in the Archives somewhere."

"Not if everything he's told us is a lie."

"You don't think his magic was stolen?" she asks.

"I believe it was, but even if his crown is somehow an implement and not just a talisman, I know he can't do with it any of what he's promised. No djinni can."

"Not even a djinni that's over a thousand years old?"

"So he says." Taha shrugs. "Anyway, the lifespans of djinn

vary widely. Well-fed si'la can live for four hundred years, and that's just what we've documented. What about Hubaal? Giants are technically a class of djinn, and he's also over a thousand years old."

"I suppose . . ." Amira chews the inside of her cheek before leaning in. "I have a different concern. What if Qayn *can* do what he says?"

Taha shakes his head. "No. He'd have to be an ifrit, and ifrit don't exist."

"But say they do," she insists, "and Qayn *can* summon a magical army. What if, once he's done with the Harrowlanders, he turns that army on us?"

Taha shrugs again. "I really doubt that, but if it's true . . . then your brother has doomed us, no matter what we do—Hold on."

The scouts have returned to Ser Ulric. Taha climbs to his feet as Ulric looks over the heads of his men and locates him. A few seconds later, Whitmund is sent sprinting over.

"The Marshal's summoned you!"

Taha's ankle restraints are removed, and he's walked alongside Ser Ulric and some of the senior soldiers to the plateau. Below the crest, he's given a spyglass and made to lie flat on his chest.

"Tell me what you see," says Ulric quietly, lying next to him.

Taha looks through the glass at the Sahir's first major patrolled road. It runs against the other side of the plateau toward Ebla, an elegant brushstroke of eggshell-yellow limestone buildings and the fanning green heads of date palms that make up its wealth-generating plantations, all set at the base of the mountain from which gushes the Ayn al-Sama spring. He follows the road down from the town's arched entranceway, guarded by two

Sentries in emerald cloaks, to a drove of bleating goats and their herder; a pair of young men steering a wagon stacked with trays of pomegranates; a few lone travelers and, riding slowly toward town from the right, a group of eight. Taha's fingers tighten around the spyglass. Nine, if he counts the sun jackal trotting tamely alongside the squad. A large, imposing mindbeast, the domesticated jackal is golden like its smaller canine cousin, but the tips of its fur are a bright orange-red that glows like fire when touched by the daylight.

"They're warriors." Ulric's hot breath hits his cheek. "Sorcerers, like you, eh?"

Dressed in the same armor that Taha left in his saddlebags back in Brooma. "Shields, yes," he answers, and immediately regrets saying anything.

But Ulric is a hound; he already knows. "What kind of sorcerers? One has your affinity with the wolf-dog."

"Jackal," he says through his teeth. "I don't know about the others."

"What are they doing here?"

"Routine patrol." Should Taha have lied and made it seem less like the squad has their guard down? He doesn't know, but every word he utters might be the one that gets these Shields killed.

Ulric cranes toward the officers lower on the rise and tells them, "Start the push." Taha grasps his grave error then. It doesn't matter what he says; the Vanguard has come here to do one thing.

"Permit them to surrender," Taha says quickly as Whitmund waves a red flag below. "They're more valuable to you alive."

"They're less dangerous to me dead," Ulric mutters, peering at them through the spyglass.

Taha chills to the bone, despite the afternoon heat. Senior soldiers disperse through the Vanguard, giving quiet orders. The men climb into their saddles and line up in formation, but the longbowmen scramble up the plateau on either side of him. Now Taha is in the grip of a fever.

*"Please,"* he whispers, turning back to the Marshal. "Let me talk to the Shields. I'll convince them to surrender."

"You try anything of the sort and I'll flog you." Ulric slings his arm and leg across Taha's back, pinning him to the rock. "You're going to lie here in silence and learn that resisting His Majesty is a fool's game."

"You're no more than a murderous thief, Marshal," Taha grunts.

Ulric appears genuinely hurt. "I'm protecting the Empire. Your people can't be left alone with magic."

"Why not?" Taha demands. "We never did anything to you."

"Not *yet.*" Ulric looks over the edge of the plateau again. The squad has stopped in front of it on the road below, but the beastseer has left her horse and wandered into the brush toward the rock, led on by her sun jackal, who must've sniffed out the sweaty soldiers on the crest. The jackal assesses the plateau with fiery eyes, its long, pointed ears strained. The beastseer is concerned, but some of her squadmates start riding on again.

"Probably a hare," calls one. "Come on. The inn is waiting."

Taha tries to shift his shoulders, but Ulric is heavy in his chainmail and leathers. Taha could still shout and alert the Shields to gallop away, at least.

"Bear this in mind, boy," Ulric whispers in his ear. "You so much as squeak and I don't spare a soul in Ebla. Everyone gets put to the sword and flame, and you'll be right there, up to your ankles in their blood. Ask yourself if eight lives are worth it."

Tears prick Taha's eyes; his heart pounds between his ribs and spine as they're crushed together, but Ulric suddenly pulls away. The Marshal isn't worried about Taha disobeying him, and why should he be? Defeat is unavoidable. There are eight Shields with magic; the Vanguard numbers in the nine hundreds, with roughly fifty of its longbowmen alone stationed on the plateau. They wouldn't be here if Taha hadn't prioritized his feelings over his duty to warn the Council. He demanded that Imani sacrifice Atheer to protect their people's future, didn't he? That was easy enough, so why was leaving Reza behind so impossible? Because Taha is a hypocrite. He is everything his father despises, and every Sahiran death in this invasion is his fault.

Ulric gives a signal. The longbowmen rise and let arrows fly. Horses whinny and grunt. Taha hears them thudding on the road, then Ulric yanks his head back and forces him to look over the crest at the Shields sprawled beside their downed horses. Only the beastseer still stands between her dying horse and the dead jackal. Her mouth is agape, wide eyes staring at the arrow run through her chest leathers into her heart. She gasps and collapses onto her back in the grass.

The shepherd, a man in a blue thobe and a white turban, wandered a little too close with his herd and saw the attack. He turns to stagger up the road to the Sentries at Ebla's gates. Two arrows throw him to the grit. Another hits the driver of a wagon farther up, knocking the man off his perch, and the longbowmen don't spare the mule pulling the wagon. Even the Sentries at the gates are accounted for. The pair have barely grasped that they're under attack before longbowmen in the grass riddle them with arrows. The road falls quiet and still. The assault was so swift, not a single person cried out.

"Now you'll have your chance to negotiate surrender." Ulric drags Taha down the plateau behind the retreating longbowmen. He's chained to the saddle of a camel alongside the Marshal's and transported past the plateau to where the land lies even with the road. The Vanguard continues to Ebla, but Ulric waits for soldiers to search the dead Shields. One man jogs up the road carrying stolen items. Taha recognizes the pouches of misra in his arms.

"Spice?" Ulric opens a saddlebag. "Drop them in."

Another soldier drapes the beastseer's body over the back of Ulric's camel. Her unseeing eyes watch Taha during the ride to Ebla; a stream of crimson flows from her wound and down her fingers onto the road. Taha recognizes her as the Shield he once saw in Beit al-Sahiran, the headquarters for the Order of Sorcerers. She was walking through the expansive central gardens, smiling at her sun jackal yelping playfully at her side.

The Vanguard assembles around Ebla's gates; a smaller force flanks the town's low mudbrick walls toward the mountain. Last night, Taha spied Ulric's map of the Sahir. It depicted the mountain path to the town of Tir, Ebla's only escape apart from these gates. That's where the men are going—to cut off anyone who flees.

The ordinarily empty fringes of Ebla rapidly speckle with the Vanguard's newly lit lanterns; the ghostly men of steel, linen, and leather stare, hard-faced, under the small circles of light. Incredibly, nobody in Ebla has noticed their arrival yet; they have no idea how drastically their lives are about to change.

Ulric stops outside the open gates and slides his antlered helm over his coif. "The horn, Whitmund."

The squire blows the curved tusk, producing a flat, deep bellow. Confused voices rise from within Ebla, then screams from the other side of town and a corresponding horn. The smaller force is signaling that they've secured the mountain pass. Now there is no escape for anyone.

Whitmund blows the horn in shorter intervals for perhaps a minute, then unfurls an Empire banner and accompanies the Marshal through the gates. Taha rides on Ulric's other side; the rest of the Vanguard filters through in orderly rows of three. He expects panic to engulf Ebla. Some townspeople flee, but most retreat into doorways or huddle under sconce light outside shops in shocked silence.

"Greetings, people of the Sahir, from the Great Harrowland Empire across the Swallowing Sands," Ulric announces in Alqibahi. "I seek audience with the person in charge."

Nobody moves. Ulric looks across the townspeople, his menacing antlers rotating.

"I did as you ordered earlier," Taha speaks up. "If Ebla surrenders, will you spare its people?"

"If Ebla surrenders," the Marshal agrees.

Taha clears his throat and says loudly in Sahiran, "Someone alert Ra-is Suleiman immediately!"

"What is the meaning of this?"

A group hurries down the street, consisting of seven Sentries and a short, balding man in gold spectacles. Ra-is Suleiman speaks with the same pomposity as his late merchant cousin, Farhat of the Azhar clan, whom Taha sent plummeting to his death from the balcony of his villa one rainy night a couple of years ago. Only a ruby-encrusted goblet of wine and a pair of silk slippers were left behind, arranged to imply a drunken accident. Suleiman traveled to Qalia for the burial, claiming that his cousin had been the target of harassment over his vocal opposition to Bayek's election, and that the stress, if not something more nefarious, led to Farhat's death.

Ulric removes his helm and balances it on his saddle. Suleiman stops as if turned to stone.

"W-who are you?" he stammers.

The Marshal smiles. "Ser Ulric. And you are?"

It's a moment before Suleiman responds. "Ra-is S-Suleiman. I am the head of Ebla."

"Well met, Ra-is Suleiman." Ulric descends from his camel, armor clinking, and nods at Gutner, riding in front of Taha. The soldier brings Taha down and unchains him from the saddle, then Ulric takes him by the elbow and shuffles him forward.

Suleiman's eyes bug out before vanishing behind his fogged spectacles. "Is that *you,* Taha ibn Bayek of the Al-Baz clan?" he splutters, polishing his spectacles with his jacket sleeve.

He shoves them back on his face. "What is going on? Who are these men?"

"Answer him, boy," Ulric directs.

"They're part of a very large and powerful army from a distant land," says Taha, "and they're marching across the Swallowing Sands as we speak. Their final destination is Qalia, and they come with the intention of subjugating us for our magic."

Suleiman stares at him. "An army . . . from across the Sands . . ."

"Yes. It's not a wasteland—"

"But the Council—"

"The Council concealed the truth from us," Taha admits. "It was to protect us, because there are cities like our own across the Sands—"

"But the Sands are protected by an impassable enchantment,"

interrupts Suleiman, as if he can simply reason his way out of this problem.

"The enemy has clearly learned ways through it, Ra-is Suleiman!" Taha steps forward, pressing his palms together. "Please, listen to me. Whatever this man asks of you, *do it.* Don't attempt to fight back. Agree to peacefully surrender Ebla."

Suleiman looks as if a frog has just landed on his face. "*Surrender?* You mean, let this man take control of my town?"

"*Yes,* Ra-is, don't you understand?"

"Take it for what purpose?" he asks.

"To own it!" Taha shouts desperately. "To use it! To strip it of its wealth!"

Suleiman shakes his head, jowls jiggling. "No, no, this man can't just come here and demand I hand over Ebla. It's not his to control! The Council will never allow it!"

Taha despises Suleiman and his ilk, but now he feels only deep sadness for the man. Suleiman's naïveté is the naïveté of every Sahiran, comfortably isolated from the world.

"Ra-is," Taha enunciates, "if you do not give Ser Ulric control of Ebla, he will take it from you by force."

"My proposition is straightforward," says Ulric. "Either you surrender Ebla, its people, and its resources to us, and every civilian goes unharmed, or"—Ulric removes his glove and summons a tall flame in his palm, startling the townspeople—"you refuse, and every person in Ebla, young and old, becomes our enemy whom we will fight and destroy without mercy. The choice is yours."

Ulric extinguishes the flame and replaces his glove. It takes a moment for everyone to understand what he's said, and then they break out in cries for the Great Spirit's mercy, others demanding action from Suleiman.

The *ra-is* shrinks in his stiff jacket, sweating so much, it's a miracle he has any fluid left in his body. "Gold," he bleats at Ulric, "however much you want! I'll give it to you if you leave us in peace."

Ulric grins. "Thank you for the kindly offer. I do value a cooperative leader. But I'm taking your gold regardless."

Suleiman starts mumbling to himself. "I—I don't understand, I don't—"

"Ra-is, please!" Amira struggles down from the camel in the second row. Ulric nods at Whitmund, who releases her chain from the saddle. As she hobbles forward, Suleiman's jaw drops.

"You're Muamer's youngest! Amira?"

"Yes. My father has spoken of you before."

Suleiman suddenly relaxes. "I purchased a beautiful gelding from him, oh, perhaps four years ago now, for my middle son, Ayad—"

"Ra-is." Amira cuts him off. "You must heed what Taha is telling you. Look what they've already done!" She points at the dead beastseer draped over the back of Ulric's camel.

The Marshal obligingly drops the body at Suleiman's feet. He stares at it, his chin twitching. "Marwa? But I spoke to her just yesterday morning, before her squad went out on patrol—"

*"Please!"* Amira shrieks. "Save your people and *surrender*!"

Suddenly Ulric has drawn his longsword. "Time's up, Ra-is Suleiman. Will you live in peace or suffer in death?"

In a rising tide of noise, the townspeople plead with Suleiman to surrender. But the reality of the situation has finally dawned on him, and he needs no more convincing. He raises his hands at Ulric.

"Ebla is yours."

His Sentries place their swords on the road, and the townspeople hush in anticipation of what horror comes next. Taha braces for Ulric to renege on his promise, but the Marshal bows slightly.

"A very wise choice. Your people will be spared, provided you and they continue to follow my orders."

Suleiman dabs a silk tissue across his upper lip, saying, "You will find me most accommodating."

"Very good. In a moment, we'll go for a walk through Ebla and you'll tell your people what's expected of them." Ulric returns to Taha and Amira. "Your contributions are noted. You'll continue as my messengers." He looks down the line of the Vanguard. "Close the gates! Man the patrols!"

Taha meets Amira's teary eyes as Ebla's gates slam shut. Again he glimpses the ghost of Imani floating over her features. Suddenly he feels as if the very marrow in his bones has been eaten away by regret and he's liable to fracture in a dozen places at once. Why didn't he just tell Imani how he felt when he had the chance? She would have spurned him, but at least she would've known. Neither of them would go to their fates under any impression but the truth.

"I'm sorry," Amira sobs to him. "If it wasn't for me, you and Reza would've escaped with the warning!"

Maybe. But Amira isn't a Shield or a Scout. She didn't pledge herself to protect her nation, as Taha did. The guilt is all his.

# 15

# IMANI

UPON OUR RETURN TO BROOMA, QAYN AND I waste no time finding the pier listed on the note from Asyratu's temple. We take cover behind a fence opposite a heavily guarded warehouse. "I sense a faint trace of my magic there and on the docks," he says. "The jewels were shipped out from this location with the rest of the plunder."

We watch as two coaches arrive and a Harrowlander official emerges from the warehouse to supervise the soldiers unloading cedar furniture adorned with pearl inlay. They carry the pieces into the warehouse's open door, through which other items are visible to us: a stone animal bust; an opulent cloak—a camel-fur *bisht* encrusted with precious jewels—hanging on a stand; and a painting of an esteemed Brooman family, seated in the grand courtyard of a home they were probably forced out of by the Harrowlanders.

Once we've had enough of the sickening display, we set off to find Maysoon's Teahouse. Brooma's dusty streets greet us with the scents of spices, fresh meat, incense, and horse manure, a pungent aroma enlivened by the wet heat that's so stark in contrast to the temperate Zeytoun Forest. To describe Brooma as busy would be an understatement. Wagons clog the thoroughfares; quiet street sweepers do their duty beside loud vendors bruising shins with their handcarts; teenagers shouldering crates and ceramic jars dodge obstacles; and crowds in colorful thobes and shawls gracefully flow into every gap with the intuition of water.

It should come as no surprise that the teahouse is located in a bustling laneway, but perhaps I was expecting something slightly more clandestine. A river of customers streams through the entrance of the trilevel building, its frontage marked by the ornate latticework of protruding *mashrabiyas.* A smoking waiter in a black-and-white-striped thobe and matching vest leans against the wall outside, studying our approach over his pipe.

"Salaam." His greeting is accompanied by a puff of fragrant smoke.

I clear my throat. "Salaam. We wish to have our tea leaves read by Yara."

After a tense moment of reflection, the waiter crosses the stoop into a dim space purring with chatter, clinking glasses, bubbling shisha pipes, and the strum of an oud. We follow him between potted ferns and carved wooden partitions; I catch glimpses of people seated on bright cushions around short tables, sipping herbal teas from clear glasses. Between them weaves a brown-skinned woman with long black hair set in a loose braid, shrewdly watching over the teahouse. The waiter catches her eye as we pass and signals her with a small nod; the woman returns an approving one, pointing her gaze at the ceiling.

"That was Yara," he says when he notices my confusion. "She runs the place."

The waiter leads us upstairs to a door in a private corridor. He knocks, silencing the heated conversation happening on the other side, then he unlocks the door and pushes it open. Fresh air flows over me from a mashrabiya in the opposite wall; through the tight hexagonal gaps in its latticework, the undressed façade of another building and the tops of some palm trees are vaguely visible.

At the waiter's encouragement, I inch my way in. The furnishings are few and simple, almost an afterthought to the room's purpose as a rebel's refuge. A desk on my right is nearly hidden under piles of scrolls; letters spill from open crates onto the carpet about its feet, and still more correspondence is heaped upon side tables and lounges. The walls show the same treatment: every spare space is plastered with annotated maps; sketches of the port and surrounding warehouses; portraits of Harrowlander officers, labeled with their names and positions; paintings of warships and men in steel armor; diagrams of street checkpoints, comments scrawled in the margins; Empire posters announcing new laws or warning against the breaking of others.

"Imani?"

I spin around to see Atheer gingerly pushing out of a chair by a long, cluttered table. Farida rises from her seat at the other end, and Makeen straightens off the wall he's leaning against.

"Welcome back, you two!" my brother exclaims.

I rush over with tears in my eyes and stop him from standing. "Don't get up! Please, sit, rest. I can't tell you how happy I am to see you alive, Atheer." I ease him down again, noting the thick bunching of bandages under his tunic and the splint on his arm.

He pulls me into a seated hug and kisses my temple. "Not as happy as I am to see you, Bright Blade."

"Maysoon helped us find Taslima," says Farida as she rounds

the table to greet me. "We brought Atheer here as soon as it was safe to move him."

I surprise myself by hugging the captain. I think I surprise her too. Her brows lift, but she hugs me back, warmer than ever.

"Thank you for looking out for him, Farida. I take it Taslima was a capable healer." I part from her and nod at Makeen, who returns the gesture.

"Gifted," says Atheer, pulling Qayn into a hug too. "Steadiest stitching hand I ever saw, before I blacked out." He notices my alarm. "I'm all right now, Imani. Wounds closed, bone set."

I blow out a breath. "And Amira? The warning to the Council?"

Farida shakes her head. "No good news there, unfortunately. I sent some of my crew to scout southwest, but the soldiers turned them off the Spice Road. They had to go through the wilds to get near enough to see the Swallowing Sands. Glaedric's men have set up camps all along the perimeter, and they're watching the skies as keenly as the ground."

"He's guarding the entrance to every path," says Atheer. "We can't get a warning through, and we don't know where Amira was taken, but the crew didn't see her."

My heart sinks so low it lands somewhere in my heels. "I wish we had better news on our end."

"You didn't find the jewels," says Atheer.

"We found where they *were,*" Qayn answers bitterly. "A temple in the Zeytoun Forest that had been ransacked by soldiers. Imani found paperwork that said the jewels were among the cargo shipped back to Harrowland for the king."

Atheer, Farida, and Makeen exchange glances but no more. I frown at them.

"What's going on? None of you are surprised."

Atheer clears his throat. "We already suspected that the jewels are in Harrowland. Now we know how. Farida, show her."

Mystified, I follow the captain to a painting hanging in the opposite corner of the room. Elegant script in Harrowtongue frames a young, robed man seated on a royal throne; in the stained-glass window behind him, two stags are depicted locked in battle against a rising sun. The young man has been rendered in exquisite detail, but the painter has heaped the most attention upon the dainty tiara resting across his forehead. Each of the tiara's three prongs supports a distinctly shaped stone effusing radiant beams of light.

"The *jewels,*" I breathe.

Qayn brings his face so close to the painting that his nose almost brushes it. "Where did you find this?"

"Here," says Farida. "Maysoon collects Empire propaganda. This piece had been hanging in their enclave in the city's center under guard. She wasn't exactly transparent about how she came to possess it."

"What does the painting say?" I ask.

Farida translates the words: " 'In the stead of His Majesty King Glaedric, Prince Kendric the Bright hails you home for the Holy Season.' As soon as Atheer saw it . . ."

"The jewels are unmistakable," he says. "I'm sorry, Qayn. It seems Glaedric's younger brother has had them set into a headpiece."

"Younger brother?" I huddle beside Qayn for another look at the painting. But Prince Kendric barely resembles Glaedric. Though he shares the blue eyes of his siblings, theirs are round and forceful. Kendric's are long and tapered, and his gaze is withdrawn, as if his looking out at the world is a clever illusion. Unlike their pointy, close-set features, Kendric's are soft and generously spread out, his thin mouth a pouting line, his pale skin as dimensionless as parchment. And with his long, vividly yellow hair, I can see why he's been titled Prince Kendric the Bright. All the more so with those magnificent jewels glowing on his brow.

Atheer breaks the tense quiet. "We can still get them back. Farida and her crew are more than willing to sail us to Darkcliff, but . . ."

"But?" I echo uneasily, turning back to Farida.

She's already gone to inspect a map on the table. "We'll need to cross the Serpent Sea to get there. I've made the journey only once, as a teenager at my father's side, and it was . . . unpleasant."

"That's a nice way of putting it." Makeen scoffs, his brown skin shading a sickly olive hue. "I thought we were dead the night that storm rolled in. To this day, whenever the water gets rough, I imagine the howling wind and Captain Fadel shouting orders at us in the near pitch-black." Makeen shivers. "I don't know how we made it through."

"Yet you're willing to do it again?" Qayn asks, joining us at the table.

Makeen's eyes take on something of a mad glint. "Qayn, after everything we've endured and all the people we've lost—I'd cross the Serpent Sea in one of Muhab's empty wine casks if it means you'll throw the Empire out of our lands."

Qayn grins at that, Farida and Atheer chuckling. I'm still nervous.

"Is there no safer route to Darkcliff?"

"Several," says Farida, "but they'd take so much time that they're not worth considering."

I sigh, looking down at the map and the waters depicted around the coast of Alqibah. "Very well. We brave the Serpent Sea, whatever it has in store for us."

"Which brings us to our next problem," says Qayn. "None of you have been to Harrowland. You need a guide."

"A sympathetic Harrowlander," Atheer agrees.

"Ugh." Farida pulls a face. "Do they even exist?"

An uncomfortable heat rises inside me. Without warning, my heart starts to race; I hear an ocean wind whistling in my ears, I feel things soft like overripe fruits pressing against me; I smell death, and before I know it, words are spilling from me. "There was a soldier in the prison in Taeel-Sa . . . a boy, my age. He came upon me in the lighthouse when I was trying to escape. Told me he'd been threatened with execution if he didn't agree to join the army and come here. He let me go. . . . He saved my life."

The room is silent. I force my heavy gaze up to find Atheer watching me, his expression pained.

"I'm sorry I put you through that, Imani," he says, but I wave my hand, eager to move the conversation on.

"Qayn is right," I say in a steadier voice. "I don't like the idea, but we don't understand Harrowlander customs or what we should or shouldn't do to avoid attracting attention. We need a guide. If we're really lucky, someone who can help us get to the prince."

Farida throws her hands up. "Fine, fine. I'll speak to Maysoon. If *anyone* could find us a trustworthy guide among the Harrowlanders, it'll be her. But the help won't come free. She'll want valuable information in exchange. There's nothing she likes more than knowing what others don't."

Atheer grins. "Perfect. Then tell her about our magic and what Glaedric is up to."

"Omit mention of my crown," Qayn interjects. "It's best if that part remains a secret."

Farida bobs her head dutifully. "I'll keep the details of our purpose in Harrowland to a minimum. In the meantime, we'll need a few days to ready the ship and do some repairs."

After a short discussion of preparations, Farida and Makeen leave, and I help Atheer to the washroom. As I wait for him in the hall, I realize I still have a view of the main room, and Qayn, though he doesn't notice me watching. He's returned to the painting again, staring longingly at his stolen jewels as if hypnotized.

# 16

# TAHA

THE VANGUARD REMAINS IN EBLA UNTIL ANOTHER force arrives in the afternoon to take over. By then, the correspondence tower has been barricaded, men of fighting age have been separated out and marched off to the date plantations, and the soldiers are inspecting properties for weapons, gold, and anything else of use, all of which is piled into wagons lining the streets. Taha doesn't see more than that. The Vanguard thunders out of Ebla via the mountain path. A few hours later, Ser Ulric orders the slaughter of a fleeing merchant's caravan outside Tir and seizes the town as he did Ebla. It's clear then that he intends to take the Sahir by surprise, one settlement at a time.

And the settlements fall. Again and again, Taha and Amira are forced to convince their fellow Sahirans to surrender. But some refuse. In a vineyard in Beit Sena, a pair of agriculturalists seconded from the Order of Sorcerers command the grapevines to strangle and kill several soldiers, their short but deadly revolt aided by workers armed with hook knives. Ser Ulric sets the group alight and hangs their charred bodies from the town gates as a warning to anyone else thinking of resisting. Then he turns his fury on Taha and Amira, sobbing into her hands.

"I thought the only sorcerers we had to worry about were Shields like you, boy."

Taha looks away from the smoking remains swinging in the night air, but he can't ignore the smell. He battles nausea to explain to Ser Ulric that the Order assigns sorcerers from civilian occupations, such as agriculture and engineering, to settlements across the Sahir.

Ulric listens while sipping from his flask of misra tea, black-threaded eyes nitid with possibility. "Sorcerers need Spice," he says between greedy swigs, "so where's it kept?"

That's how the Marshal learns about the Maktab, the Order's offices located in each major town center, where misra is securely stored. After that, the Maktab becomes the first place Ulric searches when the Vanguard seizes a settlement.

In the grasslands of Arsus, the owner of the gristmill refuses to surrender his flour and strikes a soldier with a shovel. For that act of disobedience, and in full view of his pleading family, Ser Ulric ropes the miller to the back of his own wagon.

"I hope the flour was worth it, old boy," he says, and waves off the soldiers on the driver's perch. They take the wagon down the village's main street, dragging the screaming miller across the cobblestones until he's dead. Then, when the supplemental force arrives, the Vanguard packs up and moves on.

They're always followed by this surge of soldiers who take over administration of the settlements, allowing the Vanguard's consuming tide to roll on. Steadily, the men trade their camels for powerful Sahiran horses, making their advance even more efficient. If a settlement has a correspondence tower, it's immediately barricaded to prevent warnings from being sent. No one is ever prepared for the Vanguard's arrival; one settlement has no idea that its neighbor down the road was taken only a few hours earlier.

Only the monsters succeed in thinning the Vanguard's ranks. Late one night, Whitmund alerts Ser Ulric that almost a dozen men have been lured away by strange lights floating through the wilderness on the edge of camp. "A clan of djinn," Taha explains when he's brought to look at the mesmerizing orbs. Soon after, agonized screams and cries for help reach the camp. Ulric orders a patrol of the perimeter in full plate armor, and, perhaps remembering how he found Tedgar, he doesn't send after the missing men.

The Vanguard attacks through most of the nights and sleeps only a handful of hours before moving on, sustained by tobacco and strong Sahiran coffee. Taha searches the men for the same cracks of fatigue that he feels forming in himself, but the Vanguard forges on as if it's cursed with a hunger that cannot be satiated until this task is done. For Taha, the days are blurring. When the Vanguard makes camp along the river after seizing Karkesh, he can't recall whether Ebla's surrender was five days ago or seven.

As he and Amira are shackled to a beam by the campfire, Ser Ulric emerges from his tent carrying bowls of ground misra. He prepares enough pots of tea for roughly fifty excited men, and within fifteen minutes the magic takes hold and a crowd gathers to spectate. Misra tea has a euphoric effect the first few times it's drunk, and that has never been more manifest.

The newborn sorcerers scatter, laughing raucously. Several

discover their affinity for fire and run across the fields setting trees alight and hurling blazing spheres into the sky. They even try to set each other on fire; one soldier succeeds, and his fellow is saved only because another man learns that he can unleash a gale that extinguishes the flames and knocks the soldier on his roasted backside. The men with earth and water affinities join the mock war; rocks and clumps of dirt go flying alongside filthy curses; one man is pitched over by a stray boulder; another drops down a pit that opens suddenly at his feet. A chortling soldier lopes across the field with water from the river suspended over his head. His magic exhausts before he reaches the battle, and the water soaks him, a fish bouncing off his shocked face. Even Ser Ulric admits a boisterous laugh at that.

"How any of them can smile after what they've done is beyond me," mutters Amira before turning her back on the spectacle to rest.

The soldiers churn through their stores of magic and return for second, third, and fourth mugs. Their consumption of so much Spice in one session should alarm Ser Ulric, but he's constantly sipping from his own flask of tea, so it doesn't. Finally, the men wear themselves out and retire to rest, leaving behind damaged fields.

Ser Ulric catches Taha's eye on his way back to his tent. "Not bad for whelps, were they?"

"Easy enough if you don't care how much misra you're using," he retorts. "But if you don't temper them, your men will develop a magical obsession. I assume you know what that is."

Ulric chuckles. "It's not an affliction if you never run out of misra, boy." With a wink, he vanishes into the comfort of his tent.

Taha is woken at dawn by a nightmare about Reza running from skeletal shadow horses. A falcon hovers high in the pale sky above him, much too large to be a messenger.

"Sinan?" he murmurs, sitting up.

"What's that?" Amira stirs beside him. "Taha, are you all right?"

"Good, you're awake." Whitmund abruptly appears and begins undoing their chains. "Do you want to bathe in the river before the men go down? You won't get any privacy otherwise."

Taha looks back up at the sky, but the falcon has gone. Or it was never there in the first place.

"What did Whitmund say?" Amira asks, nudging him.

He frowns, massaging his stiff neck. "He asked if we wanted to bathe in the river before the men do."

Her eyes light up. "Oh, *finally*." She nods at Whitmund and says yes in Harrowtongue.

Whitmund takes them down to the water alone, some blankets slung over his arm. Taha helps him hang them from a tree growing over the water to create makeshift curtains. Whitmund removes Amira's manacles and gestures at the curtains, and Taha translates his warning: "He says you have a few minutes to bathe, and that this is just because we've been helping the Marshal, so don't think of running off."

She restrains an eye roll, rubbing her raw wrists. "Like there's anywhere left to run to."

They wait for her to step between the curtains before Whitmund takes Taha farther downstream. There he removes Taha's wrist manacles and replaces them when Taha has pulled his cloak and tunic off.

"Ankle restraints go back on when you're finished." Whitmund removes them and draws his shortsword. "Go on, then. Unless you're embarrassed."

Taha peels the rest of his clothes off, tosses them on the bank, and stands boldly. "Do I look like I have anything to be embarrassed about?"

Whitmund looks away, red-faced. "Don't waste the few minutes you have gloating."

Taha wades into the cool water with a relieved sigh and begins scrubbing the dirt off his arms.

"Anyway, you have a lot of scars," Whitmund adds.

"So? I've never met anyone who didn't like them or couldn't look past them."

"How'd you get that many?" Whitmund asks.

"Fighting monsters," Taha replies, running water through his hair.

It's not the whole truth. Some scars he got fighting people. Some he earned at his father's hands. He wears them equally without shame, precisely because of something his father told him when he was small and still learning his bloody way around skinning knives. *I'll be covered in scars by the time I'm half as skillful as you,* Taha lamented while his father bandaged the deep wound in his hand. *I pray it's so,* said Bayek. *Scars teach the flesh not to fear. Scars are armor.* Taha is almost wearing a suit of them at this point.

"Do you come from a family of warriors?" Whitmund asks after a minute.

Taha doesn't know why the squire is bothering with conversation, but he tolerates it because Whitmund granted them the small comfort of bathing.

"Hunters," he says. "But my father was a Shield too before he became Grand Zahim."

"Curious. Is hunting lowly work here?"

"To some," Taha says stiffly.

"Shame. Our gods are fond of hunters, especially in the Holy Season. Even so, it's still astonishing for your father to go from a hunter to a king!"

That annoys Taha. "The position of Grand Zahim isn't inherited, like a king's throne," he corrects. "You have to be chosen by the Elders of our society. It's a merit-based position." *One that's also usually reserved for the already powerful,* he thinks with some resentment, but he leaves his answer there.

"It's really all so curious," says Whitmund. "What about your mother? Is she a hunter too?"

"She was." Taha clears his throat. "She was also very gifted at making clothes and items out of pelts."

"But no longer?"

"No." He wades out of the river and begins drying off with his cloak. "She died giving birth to my younger brother years ago."

"Oh . . . I'm sorry. You must miss her."

Taha doesn't answer and finishes drying off.

"Do you only have the one brother?" Whitmund asks.

"By my mother. I have step-siblings."

The squire makes a face. "I have six brothers, five of whom are knights. They're expecting I'll become one too."

"A knight?" Taha pulls his sirwal on. "You mean a warrior like Ser Ulric?"

Whitmund nods. "If I do my duties, Ser Ulric will knight me too, otherwise I'll have to become a priest and go around singing hymns and blessing babies and reading dusty tomes all day." He makes that face again.

Taha dons his tunic. "You mean if you help the soldiers slaughter my people and steal from us."

Whitmund turns the vibrant pink of a saltwort flower. "We're here to civilize you and give you peace, for your good and that of the Empire."

Taha can't help his derisive laugh. "Oh? And if we don't want your assistance?"

"You'll get it anyway because you don't know what's good for you." Whitmund points his sword at the manacles, his goodwill depleted. "Put those back on, hurry up."

Taha fits the manacles around his ankles. "Well, I won't wish you luck becoming a knight, Whitmund. Frankly, I hope you take an arrow to the heart and never see home again." He stands up holding his damp cloak. "Ready when you are."

The Vanguard takes the walled town of Sur-Marra that afternoon. As in other towns, Ser Ulric marches Taha and Amira through the streets with the *ra-is'a,* a woman named Mahar, to explain the situation to the townspeople before the next force arrives.

"The gates are locked!" Mahar declares to the scared people watching her from behind windows and ajar doors. "Do not fight back or attempt escape! You are safe so long as you do what you are told!"

At the end of the main street, shawled women and small children huddle outside a dressmaker's shop. Ser Ulric gestures at them.

"Send these people home, ra-is'a."

Mahar translates his order to the group. The women bow their heads and shepherd their children on. Ser Ulric watches them go, but then suddenly seizes the wrist of a woman clutching her young son's hand.

"Not this one." He leads the pair back over. "Taha, how old were you when your mother passed?"

Taha tenses, confused. "How did you know—" He falters as Whitmund jogs past to assist the Marshal, and recalls their conversation by the river. *"Snake,"* he spits. The squire sends him a blank stare.

The anxious woman is stood in front of him, her son's trembling hand prized from hers. "No, please!" she cries, reaching for the boy again.

Ulric points his sword at her neck. "Stop," he orders in Sahiran.

She utters a high-pitched whine and clamps her hands over her mouth. Tears spill over them as Ulric hands the boy off to Whitmund.

"Well?" he asks Taha in Harrowtongue. "About this boy's age, would you say?"

The boy looks frantically from his mother to Ulric and then Taha, whom he seizes upon intensely. "Please don't let him hurt my mama!" he begs.

"Almost seven," Taha rasps, his body wracked by tremors.

The Marshal frowns as if that upsets him. "Must've been hard, growing up without her. I bet you feel the pain of her loss every day."

An angry tear drips down Taha's face. He swipes it away. "What do you want, Marshal?"

"Tell me about Fort Hannirami. I noticed it on a map I found in Suleiman's office."

Amira gives a panicked peep, even though she's probably only recognized the words *Hannirami* and *Suleiman* from Ulric's statement. Taha stays quiet, nauseated from how hard his heart is pounding.

"Fort Hannirami," Ulric repeats. "That's a garrison, isn't it?"

"Maybe, don't know. Never been there."

Ulric studies him. "Forts are usually called so because of their function."

"Could also just be a name," says Taha.

"But you don't know for sure."

He shakes his head.

"That's funny. You see, Amira"—Ser Ulric gestures at her—"confirmed it's a garrison for Shields when I asked her to translate the name for me yesterday. If she knows it, you certainly should."

"I'm so sorry, Taha," she whispers behind him. "I didn't realize why he was asking me about Fort Hannirami."

An internal fire burns up Taha's spine. He palms the sweat off his forehead as Ulric addresses him in a low, threatening voice.

"You've been obliging since we entered the Sahir. For that, I'll let you correct your lie before I see to it that this boy grows up without his mother too. Do you know what Fort Hannirami is?"

"Yes, it's a garrison," he confesses. "I've been posted there twice before."

"Wise choice. How much Spice is kept inside?"

"Enough to supply the squads who pass through it for six months at a time."

"Staggnir's beard, *six months.*" Ulric licks his lips. "And how many squads might I expect to find if I went there now?"

Taha's shoulders sag. "You intend to attack it."

"Oh, what gave me away?" Ulric summons flames along his sword; they leap at the tip and almost catch the woman's shawls. She recoils from the fire, its light dancing in her green eyes. Green like his mother's.

"Tell me about the fort," Ulric demands.

"I will if you let them go."

Ulric extinguishes the flames and nods at Whitmund, who pushes the boy back to his mother and tells them to leave. As they hurry away, a horn blows at Sur-Marra's gates, signaling the arrival of the supplementing force.

Ulric saunters over. "Speak fast. If you lie again, I'll put the next village to the torch."

*Some lives for many others.* Warriors for civilians, his father might reason, and slim as it is, it's the only comfort Taha can find.

"Fort Hannirami is the largest fort on the doorstep to Qalia," he says. "It's situated near at least a dozen settlements, so on any given day of the year, it might host three or four squads—between twenty-four and thirty-two Shields. They'll spend a night there before setting out for their assigned patrol in the area. Five senior Shields are permanently posted there."

"And the misra?"

"Kept at the back of the fort, in the administrative area facing the river." Taha steps forward. "Marshal, please give them the opportunity to surrender."

"Wolves don't know how to surrender, boy." Ulric sighs, sheathing his sword. He sounds tired. "It's not in your nature. As soon as you see your opportunity for flesh, you bite. I don't care to live looking over my shoulder."

The following night, Ser Ulric unleashes the Vanguard upon Fort Hannirami. Taha and Amira are gathered on a hill nearby, guarded by Whitmund, Gutner, and four others.

Whitmund hands Taha a spyglass. "The Marshal left you this."

He reluctantly uses it to watch the hundreds of horses galloping across the floodplain below. Ser Ulric rides a white stallion at the front, the large shield on his arm painted with a stag to match his gleaming antlered helm, his long maroon cape fluttering behind him. He'd be resplendent if he weren't so contemptible. Taha has never seen the Vanguard move this fast, but with Fort Hannirami, they can rely on the element of surprise for only so long. The garrison has been constructed on a mound to lift it off the floodplain, and it's protected by wooden palisades and a watchtower. The warning bell should begin tolling at any moment, but it doesn't.

Amira shifts restlessly beside Taha. "How could the Shield-on-watch not have noticed them yet? Or is the watchtower for show only?"

"No, it's always manned in case of bandits," he says. So why hasn't anyone detected the advancing army? The sound of the horses is thunderous. The Shield-on-watch doesn't even need to see the Vanguard to realize there's a serious problem.

"The torches in the watchtower are unlit," Taha notes, looking again.

"Does that mean there's nobody in the fort?" Amira asks.

He lowers the spyglass and, with his naked eyes, follows a messenger falcon fleeing the garrison's correspondence tower south. "No, there's somebody."

The Vanguard surrounds the fort on three sides, horns blowing. While two soldiers use their wood affinities to rip the gates open, Ser Ulric evaluates the correspondence tower, from which another falcon has just escaped. That incites him. He dismounts, draws his sword, and enters the fort, flanked by heavy cavalrymen and trailed by dozens more. Taha braces for the Shields to ambush the soldiers, but nothing happens. After a few minutes, flames climb the tower, spewing smoke into the sky. Three more falcons depart in close succession as it's engulfed, but one bird is killed by an arrow. The men begin emerging from the fort carrying large bags that they sling over their horses. That's when Whitmund brings Taha and Amira down.

Ser Ulric is waiting for them in the field outside the fort, the air around him stippled in flying embers. He stops his horse beside the one that Taha is chained to.

"You lied to me."

"I didn't. There should've been Shields here," says Taha defensively.

"Oh, there were, up there." Ulric points at the burning tower. "Don't know how many. They had the doors barricaded while they sent falcons." He holds out a scroll that he must've taken off the slain messenger bird. "Read this out for me."

Taha accepts the paper with a mixture of curiosity and dread. " 'Crisis Order Invoked Under Authority of Shield Captain Rashida of the Jarrat clan at Fort Hannirami—Foreign armed force advancing south on horseback. Sur-Marra, Karkesh, and others under their control. Retreat to Qalia immediately. Warning has been sent to the Council. Shields are en route to you to aid evacuation.' "

Taha's hand shakes. The falcon he saw yesterday was real; it was a mindbeast from a nearby squad that must've alerted the senior Shields at Fort Hannirami.

"Brave individual, this Captain Rashida," Ulric remarks. "Sending warnings right up until the fire claimed them."

Taha imagines the captain's last moments as she heard the soldiers advancing on the fort, knowing this was her last stand. Then came the roar of the flames, the intensifying heat as the fire closed around her and the smoke thickened. But still she inked her messages and attached them to the falcons, compelled by the oaths she swore to serve her nation. If only Taha had been as brave in Brooma; he could have saved Captain Rashida's life.

He holds out the scroll. "The Council knows you're coming now, Marshal."

Ser Ulric is hardly upset. He takes it, smiling at the men carrying crates away from the burning fort. "About time. I'm itching for a fight."

# 17

# IMANI

MY DAGGER FLIES ACROSS THE ROOF OF THE teahouse and lands in my fist. I jog toward the far end of the roof and throw it. "I'm here," I whisper, shifting my focus from my boots to the blade spinning ahead of me. "And I'm *here.*" My body vanishes; my essence joins with the steel. A moment later, I materialize on the other side of the roof with the dagger glowing in my hand.

"Impressive." Qayn emerges from the shadows of the doorway. "And you've already made my lesson more magic-efficient."

How long has he been watching me? *Perhaps this was payback for me watching him in front of the painting.* I sheathe my dagger, sighing. "The *Prize* is being readied to depart. Not much else for me to do but train, is there?"

"And practice your Harrowtongue."

"I've been doing that too," I retort dryly in the invaders' language. A few days ago, Qayn offered to start sharing his knowledge of Harrowtongue through our soulbinding. Ever since, bits and pieces of the language have been spontaneously coming to me.

He smiles, though it's unclear whether he's pleased with himself or me. "Then we're just about set," he says, running his hand through the potted citruses lining the roof's border wall. "Farida did say Maysoon might've found us a guide."

"Over a *week* ago. We haven't heard anything since." I collect my cloak from the outdoor lounge and sling it over my shoulders. "I feel sick with worry about Amira. Atheer promises that she'll be protected, but I just can't stop thinking the worst." I shake my head. "Don't mind me."

Qayn runs out of potted plants and presents me with a pale flower. "I understand, Imani. There's nothing more torturous than not knowing whether your family members are safe or not."

My fingers slow on the clasp. I've pondered the matter of Qayn's kin before, imagining what they must be like, but I never expected that he'd raise the subject with me even indirectly.

I accept the flower, conscious of our hands brushing. "From what I've gathered, djinnis can have families too."

"And mothers who love them." He watches me from under the dark curve of his lashes as I tuck the flower into the clasp of my cloak. "Yes, I had a family."

"Had?" I echo. My earlier curiosity feels deeply inappropriate now.

"They were killed by a rival tribe," he says. "They all perished in the attack but me, and—"

A door slams downstairs, interrupting him. Several voices clash and someone thuds up the short stairwell to the roof.

"Imani, you there?" It's Farida.

I have to pry myself away from Qayn to go to the door. "Is something the matter?"

She stops on the middle step. "Our guide is here."

My relief over her announcement is quickly surpassed by caution; our guide, after all, is a Harrowlander.

I follow Farida down to the main room, where a broad, brown-skinned woman with a mess of salt-and-pepper curls is waiting. Beside her in a black hooded cloak is a small, pale Harrowlander man of nineteen or twenty, delicate-featured under his messy tousle of blond hair.

Atheer leans against the table nearby for support, his chair pushed back. "Maysoon, this is my sister, Imani," he says, gesturing at me as I enter.

Maysoon swivels to face me, her beaded necklace swinging and bushy brows rising. "Ah, greetings at last, young lady! And this handsome fellow must be Qayn!"

I wince, glancing at Qayn as he comes to stand beside me. "The Whisperer" must be an ironic nickname. Maysoon hasn't said much, and my ears are already ringing.

"Now that we're all present: you asked me for a guide—" Maysoon claps her hands together and turns to the Harrowlander, who gazes back at her with the calm aloofness of a cat. "And here he is: Skerric Gray, the son of a nobleman. *Lord* Skerric if he's to be addressed properly, though he has never insisted on it. As one of my most reliable sources of information, Skerric has proven extremely helpful to the rebel movements in Brooma and Ghazali. He's traded me confidential army documents, sensitive information about officials—"

"Is he a soldier himself?" Qayn interjects, scrutinizing Skerric.

"No, but very good at making them fall under his spell. Too good. The only reason it took me so long to get ahold of him was because he'd changed lodgings to evade one of the lovesick officers he was using for information." Maysoon stops to huff, considering a smiling Skerric the way a mother might consider her naughty but otherwise sweet son. "Anyway, he was sent here to spy on his house's competitors and any business ventures they might be making in Glaedric's new territories, but he fell into the business of selling secrets rather than smuggling them out. This young man is like us: no love for the king. Calls Glaedric's talk of peacekeeping and civilizing 'insulting nonsense.' "

"Really?" Farida folds her well-built arms, treating Skerric to a surly look. "I have a hard time believing that."

"Have as hard a time as you like. His actions speak for themselves," Maysoon retorts.

I glance at Atheer. "He does sound helpful indeed."

Maysoon inflates slightly, as if that compliment was for her just as much as Skerric. "And he's very clever. Well aware of what's going on in your homeland."

"Is that true?" I ask Skerric in Harrowtongue. "You know about our homeland?"

"The secret country across the desert, yes," he replies in a collected, posh voice. "Glaedric has gone to invade it for its magic Spice. A knight of the Vanguard told me—one of the warriors of Glaedric's elite forward force," Skerric clarifies. "His tongue had been loosened by drink, you see, and he was searching for something impressive to say. He even told me there are sorcerers there who can manipulate fire, water—"

"Steel." I free my dagger and transform it to a longsword and back again.

Skerric breathlessly tracks the glow rolling along the blade. "So it's true. And the rumors of Princess Blaedwyn commanding the shadows?"

I think of Reza being impaled by the shadow horse; Sinan

swallowed up by the darkness. Taha, weeping over their bodies. I shouldn't want to, but I wish I had protected him. Saved him. Stopped him from stubbornly going to whatever fate it was he chose, even if he fought tooth and nail against me and never found it in his flinty heart to forgive me. I would endure his resentment, because whatever happened to Taha after we left him there in Brooma . . . it can only have been worse.

"They're not rumors," I say, sheathing my dagger. "Blaedwyn has some of our magic."

"That is alarming." Skerric goes and places his hat and travel bag on the table. Then he crosses his arms and, in competent Alqibahi, says: "Maysoon tells me you have a scheme you wish to involve me in."

Maysoon flicks her eyes at me. They're glittering with a greedy hunger for the specifics of our plan that Farida denied her. As she's not one accustomed to being kept in the dark, I'm sure the many possibilities have been gnawing at her ever since.

"Come with me, Skerric," I say.

Unlike Maysoon, whose confusion fastens her brows to her hairline, Skerric maintains a cool poise as he follows me to the painting of Prince Kendric. It's only when Qayn stands on his other side does his composure crack and his cheeks begin to redden.

Qayn introduces himself before gesturing at the painting. "This tiara Prince Kendric is wearing has been made using jewels that belong to us. We want to steal them back."

Skerric stares at him blankly. Maysoon reacts for both of them.

"You want to rob the prince of the tiara on his head? *In* Harrowland?" She waves her arms wildly. "What could be so important about these jewels that you'd risk a venture this dangerous?"

"They have sentimental value," Qayn answers coldly. "Can it be done?"

His uninviting tone is enough to silence Maysoon, for now. Skerric returns his gaze to the painting and exhales an astonished chuckle, as if he can't fathom having to even answer such a question. "No, it can't be done."

"Why not?" I ask.

He puts his fingers to the chest of his black doublet. "Why *not*? Prince Kendric is a recluse. You want to rob him of something he's wearing, but he never leaves Darkcliff's royal citadel."

"We'll break into it, then," I say.

He laughs again, louder. "I don't think you quite understand what you're suggesting. You can't *break* into the citadel; nobody ever has. It's impregnable."

I battle my rising anxiety that this plan is dead before it's even been hatched. "By your estimation. Let us worry about it when we get to Darkcliff."

"And how will you get *into* Darkcliff?" He feigns pitying surprise. "Oh, you don't know? Our country isn't as welcoming to the open movement of foreigners as Alqibah is. There are few exceptions under which you'll be permitted into the city, especially during the Holy S—" He stops himself, withdrawing slightly, gaze clouding with thought—and possibility.

"You know of a way, don't you?" I say, inching closer.

He considers me carefully. "You transformed your dagger into a sword. Are you a warrior of some kind?"

"Yes, a Shield. I fight monsters back home."

*"Monsters?"* he murmurs with a bewildered frown. "Well . . . are you good at it?"

"So I'm told . . ."

Cunning comes alive in his gray eyes. "Then yes, I've thought of the only way that gets you into Darkcliff and the citadel."

Everyone crowds closer to Skerric, including Maysoon, who makes no secret of her curiosity and occupies the chair right in front of us. Only Qayn remains perfectly still but for his eyes—they slide from the painting to settle on Skerric.

"De Wilde Hunten," says the pale man. "The tournament is being held between the Empire's finest warriors in six weeks. People believe that after it's won, everything will be well in Harrowland for the next seven years."

"It's a ritual to guarantee future prosperity," says Qayn.

Skerric nods approvingly. "People travel from across the Empire in the hopes of participating. Of course, many Harrowlanders believe it's a bad omen if anyone other than a Harrowlander enters, let alone wins the Hunten, but since a foreigner has never won yet, it's not been forbidden."

"You mean to exploit a loophole," I say.

Skerric reveals a thin, wily smile. "To great effect, I hope. This painting confirms that Prince Kendric will be leading this Season instead of his brother, and he's evidently had this new regalia made for the occasion, so I've little doubt that he'll be wearing it at the tournament. If you win, you'll be permitted to meet him inside the citadel. But you'll need a sponsor to enter the Hunten. Once you have a sponsor, you go from being a challenger to what we call a *fyghtor.* This very minute, there will be sponsors in Darkcliff looking for their challenger, and they pay fees to people who find challengers for them. *Those* people are called *myddilmen.* During the Holy Season, interfering with myddilmen and their challengers—even those of foreign origin—is strictly prohibited. Still following? I could act as your myddilman and find you a sponsor. In the meantime, you'll be permitted to enter and freely move about Darkcliff as a challenger, and no one can stop you regardless of how dreadfully it bothers them."

"That's clever," I murmur, my skin tickled by exhilarated goosebumps.

Maysoon beams. "Told you he was."

"And you're sure that if we win the tournament, we meet the prince?" I ask.

"Once the Victors are announced, the Empire revels for three days," he says. "It's tradition for the leader of the Hunten to participate—you'll celebrate *with* Kendric in the citadel's banquet hall if you win. It is the absolute closest you could ever get to him, and it's the only way into the citadel."

"Being close isn't enough," says Atheer. Wincing, he limps over to Skerric, who considers my brother's broken arm with inexplicable disappointment. "Prince Kendric needs to be vulnerable too."

"Hmm." Skerric begins inspecting his nails, though from what I can see, they're perfectly manicured. "I've heard that Kendric has quite the habit for wine. If someone exploited that, they could create for themselves an ideal opportunity to pluck the tiara right off the prince's head." Skerric cuts his eyes at us, alight with a malicious sparkle. "Pay me by winning. The prize for Victors is gold, land, and knighthood, which confers the status of minor nobility. Take your jewels and your knighthood, and leave the gold and land to me, less any coin you need for your troubles." He preemptively raises his hand to silence any objection. "It might seem that I'm asking too much, but bear this in mind: I must still find someone in the city willing to risk bad luck and the curses of the superstitious to sponsor a young, foreign woman-warrior. That is not going to be easy, if it's even possible."

"A foreign woman-warrior." My fingers graze my chest. "You mean me."

He looks across our group. "Yes, and another warrior if there is one amongst you. Most fyghtors enter the Hunten in pairs to maximize their chance of winning."

"It'd just be me," I say, pulling his inquisitive gaze back from Qayn. "Does that matter? What sort of tournament is the Hunten? You mentioned that it's between warriors."

"I did." Skerric is suddenly cautious. "Have you ever wondered why Harrowlanders took so quickly to the Valor Grounds here? The Hunten is similar in format."

My heart plummets. "It's a battle to the death."

"It's a hunt in a sacred forest. Your prey just happen to be other fyghtors," Skerric unhelpfully adds.

"You're not doing this," Atheer says while Farida curses and Maysoon tuts.

"But you can win!" Skerric quickly assures me. "You have an advantage no other fyghtor does. *Magic.*"

"It's not about an advantage. I don't want to participate in the butchery," I exclaim.

The pace of Skerric's speech triples. He was detached before; now his personal investment in this plan is manifest. "Give me a chance to explain. There's no trickery involved in the Hunten as there is in the Valor Grounds. Every fyghtor enters because they *want* to participate. They're under no illusion as to what happens, and they're sponsored by the wealthiest nobility. They have excellent armor, weapons, and training. They're the very best of

Harrowland, willingly fighting to earn the Empire seven more prosperous years. They're happy to sacrifice their lives to honor Staggnir and the other gods."

Atheer touches my shoulder. "You *don't* need to do this, Imani. We can find another way—"

"Into the citadel? You can't." Skerric is vehement now. "You can't sneak your way in, you can't deceive your way in, and you definitely can't slaughter your way in—your blades would snap before you exhausted the guard force protecting the prince. This is the *only* way to reach Prince Kendric, and short of getting yourself indentured as some noble's servants or being personally invited into the city on business, it is also the *only* way for you to be in Darkcliff at all."

Skerric sighs. "I won't lie and tell you that the tournament will be easy, but you have magic, a magic that allows you to manipulate *weapons*. You may as well bring a sword to a duel where your opponent is armed with a broomstick! And as for your reservation about the 'butchery' of the tournament—take heart. The other fyghtors will want to kill you, not out of the gallant spirit of the season but out of a petty hatred for who they think you are: an impertinent girl from a land of savages, who foolishly thinks she can flout her lowly place in the Empire's natural order."

I smart at his remark, crossing my arms. "Well, now I actually *want* to fight in the Hunten. Imagine how much my victory would chafe King Glaedric."

"Chafe?" Skerric titters. "It'd send him mad with rage. The Hunten is chiefly a fight for the king to defend his right to rule. If his fyghtors lose, he is, in effect, giving away some of that right to the Victors and their sponsor. I can think of no greater insult to him than your winning."

"There's just one glaring problem," I say. "How do you think the audience will react when they see me using magic against the other fyghtors? Not well, I suspect."

Skerric is unperturbed. "As I said, the Hunten takes place in a forest, not an arena. It isn't a spectacle like the Valor Grounds are; it's a holy ritual and a test of power for the king. Your audience of nobles in the nearby tower aren't there to be entertained, even if they try to catch glimpses of the hunt between the trees. They're there to bear witness to the Victors who emerge at the end. *You,* because you'll be able to freely use your magic."

"And I'll come out of it with the jewels too," I say, catching Qayn's eye. He gives me a small nod. "Very well. If there's no other way, I'll do it."

"Not alone you won't." Atheer forces himself to stand without leaning on any furniture for support, but it's clear that doing so is draining him.

It's a disheartening sight. "You're too injured, Atheer," I say. "Your arm won't even be out of splints by the tournament, let alone fully healed."

He's dejected, but where his body may be broken, his Beya clan stubbornness remains intact. "Take someone else, then," he says, looking to Farida for help. "Someone in the crew, perhaps? Do any of them have training with a sword?"

Farida gives an apologetic shake of the head. "I'm sorry, my love."

"Atheer," I say, gently but firmly, "I'm not asking anyone in Farida's crew to risk their life in the tournament in addition to risking it just getting us to Darkcliff. In any case, I'll have an easier time if I don't have to worry about looking after someone else."

Atheer looks as if he wants to argue, but he perhaps realizes it's futile and sinks mutely into his chair again, gaze downcast.

"What about a sponsor, Skerric?" Qayn speaks up. "You didn't seem confident about Imani's prospects earlier."

Skerric gazes at the painting, eyes squarely on the tiara on Prince Kendric's brow.

"You focus on winning. Leave the politics to me."

# 18

# TAHA

THERE'S NO FIGHT TO BE HAD.

The Vanguard passes through empty settlement after empty settlement. As it draws closer to Qalia, avian mind-beasts interrupt the stillness and flood the sky. Ser Ulric orders his soldiers with weather affinities to conjure mist and clouds to shield them from view.

In Halaf, only one person has defied the Crisis Order and remains behind: the elderly Abu Hamza, relying on a cane to stay upright. He watches the Vanguard's approach from the balcony of his stone farmstead on the hill above town, and when he refuses to answer Ser Ulric's questions, Taha is sent over to speak to him.

"Did you receive the order to evacuate?" Taha calls up to the balcony.

Abu Hamza grips the railing, nodding. "First the Sentries knocked on my door and told me to pack up and leave for Qalia because an army was on the way. 'An army,' I said. 'An army of bandits?' They couldn't answer me. In Halaf, the carriages and wagons were gathered to carry people away, but I told them I wouldn't leave. As the last were going, two Shields knocked on my door and asked me to join them. 'We can't stay behind to protect you,' they said. If I refused, they would have to move on."

Taha is aghast. "So why didn't you go with them? It's an offense to disobey a Crisis Order, regardless of your personal opinion of it."

Hand shaking, Abu Hamza parts his jacket on an old leather baldric and the curved pommel of a sword hanging from it. "Whoever these men are, they can take Halaf. They can take the Sahir and do whatever they wish with it. But I will not give up my home." He rests his knobby hand on the pommel and stares down at Ser Ulric. "I am eighty-eight years old. This home is my birthplace. My late wife and I spent sixty happy years here. We raised our children; we celebrated their weddings and the births of their children; we buried my parents. I buried her just down the hill there. This is where I will die too. No, I will not give up my home, not to one thief or ten thousand. I will defend my land with my ancestors' sword, and you will have to kill me first to claim it."

The soldiers whistle and chuckle. Taha dreads learning what torment is in store for Abu Hamza and has to force himself to confront Ser Ulric. The Marshal is grinning. Panic crawls up Taha's chest. He suddenly feels unhinged, something torn loose and flailing violently in a relentless storm. But then Ser Ulric says to the Vanguard, "Have a look at the guts on this chap! Reminds me of my own grand-*atta,* Staggnir guard him."

The men actually applaud Abu Hamza. He stares back at them, tremoring but with his hand staunchly on his sword. Ser Ulric nods up at him. "Well met, Abu Hamza. You have defended your home with valor. We will not encroach upon it."

He has Whitmund tie a maroon sash to the farmstead's sign and scrawl upon it SER ULRIC HAS SPARED THIS MAN AND HIS HOME.

He isn't as kind to the men in the coach so overburdened with valuables that their horses are struggling to pull them up the road out of Bis-Amna. Ser Ulric orders soldiers to surround the coach. The occupants beg him for their lives, offering pouches stuffed with gold and jewels, and everything in the coach if he'll permit them to run into the countryside and never be seen again. They beg, each and every one. He doesn't care for any of them.

"It's your greed that killed you!" he shouts, hurling a ball of fire that engulfs the coach and its occupants whole, fire so hot it robs the moisture from Taha's eyes and sears his cheeks. A few horses over, Amira screams and folds, covering her ears. Some soldiers laugh, but Whitmund flinches and takes to studying the small thorn tree by the road instead of Ser Ulric, still throwing fire at the coach. In seconds, the stench of charred flesh fills the air, and Amira becomes so hysterical that Gutner turns their horse around and rides back into Bis-Amna. Judging by the look on the soldier's face, he was glad of the excuse.

Taha is too numb to even gasp. The bodies vanish beneath the smoke; the coach cracks and disintegrates to ash. He wonders at Ser Ulric's erratic behavior. From merciful to merciless, with no stop for rest somewhere in between. Only when the deed is done and the Marshal drinks from his flask of tea does Taha begin to understand. Aggression and uncontrollable outbursts of magic are signs of magical obsession, and Ser Ulric, a man already accustomed to violence, is suffering from it severely. Maybe he knows it too. Of all the men he could look at when he turns from the remains, it's Taha at whom he directs his tense gaze. Taha senses a question amidst the black threads. Fear too. But

Ulric may still be capable of feeling guilt. In Bis-Amna, a teary woman emerges into the main street and begs for mercy for herself and her sick mother, with whom she stayed behind. Ulric excuses them both, ties the maroon sash to her door, and orders soldiers to fetch supplies for the women.

The Vanguard doesn't press on for Qalia once it's ascertained that Bis-Amna is otherwise empty, as they did with the other settlements they passed through today. Whitmund seats Taha and Amira on the street in the shade while the men pick through the town's remains.

"He burned those men," Amira mumbles, staring at the soldiers raiding the abandoned bakery across the street. "He could've spared them as he did the old man in Halaf, but for no reason at all, he decided he wanted to use his magic and burn them." Her chin quivers. "What did my brother do, Taha? He didn't mean this to happen to our people . . . he was trying to help. He was doing the right thing, wasn't he?" She looks at him imploringly, eyes wet. "Great Spirit, I *hated* you for what you tried to do to him, but now I'm scared that you might've been right, only too late. And I don't want that to be!" Her tears escape, hard and fast.

Taha doesn't know why he sees himself in her grief or why he too doesn't want that to be, whatever *that* is. But pity slips his chained arms over her shoulders and pulls her against him.

"I think I understand Atheer now," he says in her ear. "The Harrowlanders committed this same violence in Alqibah. I didn't see it when I went there, but Atheer did, and he couldn't forget it once he came back home. How could he? I don't agree with how he went about things, but I understand—he was just trying to help."

She quiets after that, leans her head against his chest, and falls asleep. Taha is exhausted, but he doesn't think he'll be able to sleep ever again. Around him, the soldiers gorge on food and emerge from people's homes washed and refreshed and intent on trading the small belongings they've pilfered: smoking pipes, combs, razors, bottles of perfume, and a set of intriguing palm-sized paintings of horses.

"Wasn't right, what Ser Ulric did," Whitmund abruptly confesses when none of the soldiers are in earshot. Taha wonders if the squire is manipulating him again, but Whitmund turns away without seeking a response.

At sunset, Ser Ulric takes Taha up the street, Whitmund bringing Amira along behind them.

"You mentioned magical obsession to me a little while ago, boy. I've had some questions from my men." The Marshal keeps his gaze strictly forward-facing. "Is it normal to begin seeing and hearing things if you don't drink the tea every few hours?"

The hairs rise on Taha's arms. "What sorts of things?"

"Vines growing everywhere, reaching for you. Behaving like snakes with purple flowers blooming on their backs and bursting into dust." Ulric pauses, face reddening. "Hard to explain. Sounds mad. The whispers are as if someone's speaking in one ear and occasionally another person responds in the other." He puts on a ghostly hiss. " 'There are rules. Consequences. A balance to be kept. No bounty is without burden. This is your gift.' " And then in a deeper, angrier voice, " 'This is my curse.' " He clears his throat, signaling the end of the disturbing theater. "What does it mean? Is that part of this magical obsession stuff?"

"Yes. You've ingested too much misra—"

"Not *me,*" he snarls, hand landing on his sword. "I said my men."

He's lying, but Taha doesn't fight it. "Sorry. Your men have ingested too much misra too quickly and too often, and now they'll need ever-increasing amounts to stave off the consequences. I've heard anecdotes of the hallucinations that come with withdrawal. As for what they mean . . . nobody knows."

Ulric listens breathlessly, brow furrowed. The whites of his eyes are so riddled with black filaments, they look like shattered glass. "All right, but this magical obsession, is there a tonic to cure it?" he asks, wiping the sweat off his upper lip.

Taha should enjoy Ulric's suffering, but he almost feels a disgusted pity for the man. "Anyone afflicted with magical obsession has to be seen by specialists in the Order of Sorcerers. I don't know the treatment; it's kept secret."

"The Order of Sorcerers," Ulric repeats. "They're headquartered in Qalia, are they?"

"Yes."

He pulls Taha up the step into a grocer. "And if my men keep drinking the tea instead? Will they be right if they don't go without?"

"I don't know. I've heard that some sufferers eventually find the bottom of their appetites and sustain it until they're discovered. But most are either driven mad and not heard from again or their hearts stop from the excess of magic."

Ulric doesn't say anything more. He leads Taha down into the cellar, smelling of soil and vegetables but receiving some fresh air through a tiny opening in the stone by the ceiling. Whitmund, following behind them, takes Amira to one shadowy end; Ulric takes Taha to the other.

"We part here, boy. Don't get soppy about it." He gestures a length of chain at a stone pillar.

"Why? Where are you going?" Taha tries to step back, but Ulric holds him in place.

"Time for you to rest. The Vanguard still has work ahead of

it." Ulric chains him to the pillar, Whitmund chaining Amira to one at the other end, and then they go together to the cellar stairs.

Taha scrambles to his feet. "But why are you leaving us behind? Does anybody know that we're here? . . . Ser Ulric?"

Ulric retreats up the stairs. A moment later, the cellar door is bolted shut, and footsteps recede through the shop. Taha blinks, stunned, and then yanks so desperately at the beam that the manacles cut into his wrists.

"Don't leave us here, Marshal!" he shouts at the top of his lungs. "DON'T LEAVE US TO DIE!"

But Ser Ulric does, and the Vanguard rides on. In its wake, Bis-Amna is as silent as a burial ground.

# 19

# TAHA

BIS-AMNA DOESN'T KEEP ITS SILENCE. HOURS LATER, the cellar door opens, and a soldier Taha hasn't seen before comes down with food and water.

"Where's Ser Ulric?" Taha demands hoarsely. When he wasn't shouting for attention, he was promising Amira that they weren't going to die of thirst down here as she feared.

The young man places a tray by the beam and hands him a waterskin. "Ser Ulric moved on with the Vanguard. We're responsible for you now."

Taha doesn't know how much longer they spend captive in the cellar before they're finally escorted to Bis-Amna's southern gates. Parked on the road outside is a coach with wood nailed over its windows—the transport has been repurposed to carry prisoners.

"Where are you taking us?" Taha asks, struggling against the soldiers surrounding them. They force him over the coach's threshold into the dark after Amira. He turns back to the door just as it slams shut, and begins banging his fists on it. "Where are we going? Answer me!"

"Home," comes the muffled reply.

A soldier raps his knuckles on the side wall, and the carriage jolts into movement.

"I wonder if we'll get to see our families again," says Amira from the bench.

Coldness snakes around Taha as he counts every mistake he's made since leaving Qalia. Every moment of weakness and act of hypocrisy, every failure and order disobeyed.

He slumps on the bench beside her. "Home," he murmurs, but rather than Qalia's grand walls and the brothers and sisters housed within, he thinks only about the man he'll have to confront when he gets there.

The coach stops suddenly. Taha's head rocks against the wall, ending his shallow nap.

"What's going on?" he asks, sitting up.

"Don't know, but it's storming," Amira says from the corner, her voice barely audible over the rain buffeting the roof. What isn't audible is the coach door swinging open. Cold, wet air billows over him, accompanied by faint light and a soldier who throws something at them.

"Put these hoods on and come out."

Taha obeys, shuffling first into the drenching storm. It soaks him from head to toe, though he doesn't mind; it's been some time since he last bathed. He is walked along cobblestones up a steep incline. Vague shapes appear through the fabric of his hood. He senses men walking around him, hears their ghostly voices and the *clip-clop* of horses' hooves through the deluge.

At the top of a hill, he crosses a threshold, and the rain pours onto a roof instead. He's led up some stairs, without Amira by the sound of it. Soldiers mutter around him, papers shuffle, chair feet scrape tiles. Someone is saying ". . . been another attack of those bloody monsters . . ." but Taha doesn't hear any more. He enters a quieter space, where his boots sink into a rug and the warmth of a hearth plumes on the backs of his knees. His hood is plucked off, and he finds himself in a long, opulent room with several soldiers, Ser Ulric, and King Glaedric.

Taha has seen the king before but only through Sinan, at a distance. Up close, the late-twenties man is so much blonder, paler, taller, and the whites of his cold blue eyes are cracked porcelain, like Blaedwyn's and Ser Ulric's. Glaedric wears heavy steel-plate armor, browned and gilded in elaborate vine-and-rose patterns, the shoulders molded into stag heads; attached to them, a heavy cloak trimmed in animal pelt. His helm is on a nearby table, antlered like others Taha has seen but imposingly tall where they were wide, the face cast to resemble a stag's pointed silhouette.

"Welcome home, Taha, firstborn of the Grand Zahim," the king says in lackadaisical Harrowtongue. He turns sideways and looks out a large window at well-maintained gardens enclosed by a stone fence. Beyond it, fields and farms sprawl in the shadow of Qalia's defensive walls, overgrown with climbing jasmine and rosebushes.

Taha searches the room for something to orient him. Although many furnishings have been removed, the marble-inlay flooring and stucco ceiling carvings belong in the home of someone obscenely wealthy. He must be in a villa in Jawhara, the leisure town exclusive to the richest Qalians. The fields past the villa's fence line are marred almost beyond recognition. Trees have been felled, long lines of trenches dug, fences removed and new ones erected. Clustered behind tall palisades across this desolate expanse are tents, wagons, horses and hounds, stacks of hay bales, wood, stones—and soldiers. Thousands upon thousands of soldiers, so many more than he's ever seen in one place. They're either huddled around firepits under canopies or busy at work, many of them using magic to unload wagons, stack stone, cut wood, and, farther afield, assemble siege engines.

"Look upon the child of the marriage between Harrowlander industry and Sahiran misra," drawls Glaedric.

Taha focuses on the siege engines. Some are in the process of being constructed, but some have already been completed and are facing Qalia on the encampment's outskirts. The most numerous are catapults. The taller engines with slings are trebuchets. He's seen one of these towering weapons of war before, near Taeel-Sa, where it was used to breach the walls and browbeat the Alqibahi king into submission; but he also recognizes the design from a similar machine on display in the Qalian Museum, constructed by the ancient engineer Al-Jazari. The smallest siege engines in the field are bolt throwers that look like oversized foot-drawn bows.

Taha's knowledge of these machines is purely theoretical, but he's seen Taeel-Sa's mutilated walls and its buildings reduced to rubble. Not counting any response from the Council, a sustained assault with this many engines would eventually punch a hole through Qalia's defenses. Yet the engines aren't being used. They sit idly, appearing to him through the rain like the abandoned relics of a battle fought long ago. Just as curious is their distance from Qalia—he doubts any of the engines could reach the city from here. They're useless.

It must be the rain. The mud would be constantly shifting under the engines' wheels, making operation impossible. The soldiers must be waiting for the rain to pass to begin their assault. He lifts his gaze to search for the storm's limit, but the skies above Qalia are sunny. Spitefully so. This violent welt of a storm is localized exclusively above the army encampment. It's of magical origin, a storm that can't be expected to pass according to natural laws—and only one sorcerer alive can sustain a storm of this size for any length of time: Yasmeen Zahim.

Hope warms Taha's body. There's an active defense of the city; that means archers on the ramparts and other sorcerers, including Imani's auntie and his own father. He hasn't deciphered how yet, but they must be what's keeping the Harrowlanders from setting up any closer.

He goads Glaedric in the man's own tongue. "Even with your stolen misra, you still cower before Qalia, sodden and shivering."

"Do you think this storm is the trouble?" The king raises a gloved hand at it and laughs. "I hail from the Far Northern mountains of Weildūn. There, storms with no beginning or end scream in your ears all hours of the day and night. I am very accustomed to the rain, Taha." He stands beside the younger man, manifesting the mildest frown. His frosty eyes crawl over the clouds. "No, there is only one obstacle that I have yet to surmount."

A flash paints the room white as an immense bolt of lightning smashes into the earth about six or seven hundred feet from the siege engines. Branches of electricity splinter off the central bolt and strike nearby trees; they explode, fire leaps off their tops and burns in defiance of the rain; a deadly blue current ripples across the water pooled in the area. This all happens in the time it takes Taha to flinch, and on the heels of the destruction comes a boom so loud it rattles his racing heart against his ribs. Even the stags on Glaedric's shoulders jerk up; the king shuts his eyes until the light withdraws from the room.

"Baba," Taha murmurs. He forgets his fear of his father,

overtaken instead by a mean-spirited joy. He sneers at Glaedric, gesturing at the encampment. "Your child is powerless. Your supply of misra is finite; ours isn't. Your sorcerers are inexperienced and suffering magical obsession; ours draw on centuries of knowledge. You will never win against us."

"I've already won." Glaedric nods at Ulric, who leaves the room. "My forces have recovered substantial misra from your towns, your garrisons, and the bodies of your Shields. Your father controls Qalia, but I control the Sahir. Everything I need, I have right here in your land."

The si'la said something similar about the Sahir. *Here, we have plenty of flesh for feasting.* Taha's ancient homeland is a mighty lion, and these Harrowlanders are vultures, waiting for it to die. They're flies come to lay their maggot eggs and sustain their progeny on its carcass.

Glaedric speaks with a concentrated fury. "You say Qalia has infinite misra. It will need every grain to fend me off. Even once my supply is exhausted, I will keep the fruits of my labor. As we speak, I build more powerful engines to outrange your father's remarkable affinity, and I will build as many engines as I must to discover the limits of your sorcerers waiting on the ramparts to stop my missiles. I will destroy the walls one day, but long before then, I will launch fire, poison, and pestilence onto your city's streets. Your sorcerers will be run into the ground trying to repel me while sustaining their increasingly demoralized population. Your father is capable of this magic now; but will he be in two weeks, two months, two years from now, when my men once again forge forward in the depths of night and he is roused from his meager slumber to drive us back? A burden like that erodes a man's heart."

Glaedric stoops closer to Taha. "Someone told me you come

from a clan of hunters. You understand, then, when I say that Qalia is a boar, and like a boar scurrying through the forest from a relentless hunter, it will ultimately tire and fail, not because death is a mercy but because it can evade it no more. And when it cannot, I will enter, and none shall be pardoned my wrath." He straightens again. "Magic can protect your city from me for only so long."

The bloody phantoms of Qalia's fate rise before Taha's eyes, shadowed by the souls of the innocents slaughtered already. Glaedric's war is a war of attrition, a bet that Qalia's sorcerers will succumb to his ceaseless barrage before he exhausts his capacity to fuel it. A bet he might win, as Atheer warned. Qalia's misra is limitless, but so is Glaedric's appetite for war.

Riding along the villa's fence line to the encampment is a bannerman, small in stature, with a tumble of blond curls escaping the bottom of his helm. Both soldier and horse are armored in chainmail, but the banner remains tightly pinned against its pole.

"If you're so confident in your victory, why have you brought me here?" Taha asks, watching the bannerman.

"I'm pleased you asked. The answer is *time,* a resource even more precious than misra, though you wouldn't think so, considering how people squander it. Not me. I value my time." Glaedric gazes at Qalia. "Your city is an extraordinary fortress, and your people possess knowledge that has blossomed in secret for a thousand years. I have no desire to destroy what I wish to make my own. I want to end this siege before it begins."

Taha is barely breathing as he watches the bannerman ride past the war engines and out onto the fields. As the rider nears Qalia, he unfurls a white banner of truce. It seems to be effective; he hasn't been struck by an arrow or a lightning bolt. Yet.

"That messenger carries a letter of my terms to your Council," says Glaedric. "Do you want to know what they are?"

Ser Ulric returns to the room. Taha glances at him, remembering his promise to slaughter everyone in Ebla if Ra-is Suleiman refused him.

"Don't trouble yourself threatening the Council," Taha mutters. "They won't surrender. They'll fight you, and they'll outlast you."

"You've not even heard my offer."

"Don't need to; I can guess. Fight and fail or surrender and survive."

Glaedric smiles at someone over Taha's shoulder. "Close."

Soldiers grab Taha. He thrashes as he's dragged back out of the villa and pushed into a spacious carriage waiting just outside the gilded front gates. Glaedric, Ser Ulric, and a long-faced soldier whom Ulric refers to as Ser Alfred clamber in with him, Glaedric sitting on the cushioned bench to his right.

"There's a proverb in Harrowland that goes, 'A wolf must have her prey, a wounded man must have his revenge, and a war must have its dead,'" he says. "I've offered your Council an opportunity to surrender and join the Great Harrowland Empire. But if they're determined to fight this war against me, they'll face the consequences of their choice first."

He opens the curtains, filling the cabin with light. They're traveling through the encampment, soldiers eagerly flanking the path to watch the procession. Another procession is happening elsewhere. Sahiran prisoners are being marched from tents in the center, among them children, manacled and chained to the persons before and behind them. Taha's hands grow restless with the urge to dive on Glaedric and strangle the life from him, as much as he can steal before Ser Ulric wrenches him off.

Their carriage maneuvers between palisades and over trenches and stops near the siege engines. The door opens and cold air gusts in.

"With me, Taha," Glaedric calls over his shoulder as he exits.

Taha steps out of the carriage into the rain. Glaedric, now in his helm, accepts a broadsword from Ser Ulric and strides with it across the grass to a flooded hollow. Another soldier pushes Taha down to his knees in the murky water, mud spitting onto his beige sirwal. Glaedric stands on the hollow's edge and tilts his face up at the city. As Taha stares at the tall man and his gleaming broadsword, he realizes that the first casualty of Glaedric's siege of Qalia will be *him*.

But Taha refuses to give Glaedric the fear he wants. "I'm glad to die for my nation," he declares through the rain filling his mouth. "Do you hear me? I am glad to die for my nation!"

Glaedric looks down at him. "I doubt your father would be glad to watch me torture and decapitate his firstborn. A spyglass pointed from those ramparts will disclose every one of your pained snivels and pleas for death."

Taha's face gathers. "You want to try to trade my life for the city?"

"I'm not *trying* anything." Glaedric sneers. "Few men would choose the lives of strangers over their own son's."

Taha almost weeps. Glaedric doesn't know his father, and Taha fears he himself doesn't actually know Bayek either. He used to be convinced that the only reason Bayek bothered being hard on him was because he cared. But so many people lately have said that Bayek is a bad man who doesn't love Taha. Or he does, but his love isn't good enough, and Taha can't help but feel that that's a reflection on *him* and what he deserves: nothing.

"And what about the Council, your people?" Glaedric goes

on. "How will they feel once I start in on my prisoners? Will they be glad for their shut gates and encircling walls when the severed heads of children rain upon their city? I doubt it."

*"Children?"* Taha is certain now that Glaedric was conjured in a djinni's nightmare. "How could you ever describe what you're doing here as civilizing us?"

Glaedric is confused before his grin flashes behind the helm. He crouches beside Taha and speaks in the hushed tones of one divulging a secret. "You've heard my father's rhetoric. He believed it was his divine mission to civilize primitives. A great number of my men still subscribe to the notion. Gives them honorable purpose, I suppose; helps them overlook the violence inherent in the expansion of empire. Me? I don't care to civilize you. Why should I need to? Look at the wonder before us. I understand the truth perfectly well, Taha, make no mistake. I'm here to own you and your civilization."

"But *why?*" Taha asks.

"Why not?" Glaedric wistfully appraises Qalia. "There is no greater pursuit in mortal life than to assert ourselves. Once I possess the misra tree, I will ascend to godhood and stand shoulder to shoulder with Staggnir himself. I'll be greater than your Great Spirit. Won't that be something?"

Taha bows his head to the muddy water. His own reflection stares back at him, warped by disbelief and terror.

# 20

# IMANI

THE SEA TRAFFIC AROUND BROOMA IS SO HEAVY that it's four days before the *Lion's Prize* is cleared to depart for Darkcliff. By then, Skerric has briefed me about the Hunten, and I'm desperate to reach open ocean so I can start training for the tournament. But we have to survive the Bay of Mist first.

I keep silent watch with Qayn and the sailors at the railing as the *Prize* inches along the Bay's choppy waters through thick, humid fog. Atheer helps us vigilantly scour the white for other vessels from his seat on the gangway, and a sailor by the bow regularly sounds a horn to make our presence known. At the helm, a pipe-smoking Makeen steers the ship alongside Farida, who guides him using a set of notes, a compass, a spyglass, and a speaking trumpet.

"Whoa, watch out!" she suddenly hollers into it.

I jump back from the railing as a merchant vessel glides out of the fog alongside us, sailing in the opposite direction. It's so close that I can see the moles and scars on the faces of its alarmed crew. I could almost board it with one foot still on the *Prize*!

Farida limps to the railing above, yelling, "You're too close!"

"But this is our lane!" the bewildered captain yells back in Alqibahi as his helmsman adjusts their heading and their crew hurries to slow the ship.

"The lanes have been changed to give more space to the warships!" She points at a brightly painted cask anchored in the water as a buoy. "Keep left of that!"

The captain puts a hand over his heart in thanks. I blow out a long breath and rejoin Qayn at the railing.

"A near head-on collision. Not the most auspicious start to our journey," he remarks dryly.

I watch the gap grow between us and the merchant vessel, saying nothing. But instinct warns me that an impending fight to the death might be the least of my worries.

After hours of restrained sailing, compliments are exchanged at the helm, the crew cheers, and the fog releases the ship. A deep-blue sea extends before us, the horizon speckled with vessels. I lean over the railing and peer back. Brooma lies at our stern, the yellow coast showing in patches through the mist before vanishing again.

We sail on in this direction for a while. Atheer goes belowdecks to lie down, and Qayn follows him, intent on finding the plums I packed for the trip. Farida limps down the gangway, tying her hair back from her sweaty face with a red scarf. She joins me at the railing, massaging her thigh. I nod at it.

"Forgive me if this is a rude question, Farida, but how did you injure your leg?" I ask.

"I'm proud to say I broke it fighting for Taeel-Sa," she

answers. "When the Harrowlanders attacked, our king called on every able sailor to defend the Bay of Glass. My father and his crew volunteered on one of the ramming vessels. We were good, but after Atheer gave us misra, we were *very* good."

I recall something else she once said to me. "Your affinity is for water, isn't it?"

She winks. "The ramming vessels were already fast, but I made ours glide as if we were sliding on oil. We sent quite a few warships to the bottom of the Bay before we were boarded. We defended the ship, but I twisted my leg in the fight and took an errant blade to the face." She pats a hand over her black eye patch.

"That must've been terrifying."

"Was at first, realizing I couldn't see out of this eye anymore," she agrees. "Thought I'd lost the other too, there was so much blood. But my father wrapped me up and gave me the courage to get back on the oar. We made it to shore with only a few casualties."

"Your father was a brave man," I say.

"Had the heart of a lion, he did, which is probably why he took to Atheer so quickly." She grins at me before continuing her story. "After we lost the city gates, the Harrowlanders started using catapults within the walls to force our surrender. A boulder came flying at the position some fighters and I were holding. I jumped out of the way, but when I landed—" She makes a blunt cracking noise. "Broke my leg. Couldn't believe it either, the jump wasn't serious. But my leg must've been weak since the fight on the Bay. And with the battle still raging, I suppose I didn't give it a chance to heal right. Been a trouble ever since."

It's a wonder how calmly she relates the tale. "I'm sorry you had to endure something so harrowing."

"I could endure it and much more," Farida says. "It was my

father's death that almost ruined me. He dreamed of seeing us defeat the invaders. When the arrow hit him, the only thing that kept me going was Atheer's promise to him that we'd make that dream come true. Here we are, still fighting for it. Hey." She points over the railing at where it looks like a giant has taken a bite out of the land. "You've never seen the Gulf of Fire, have you? It's full of shipwrecks. Even fishermen don't venture too far out, though the waters are rich."

"Why not?" I ask curiously.

*"Ghostfire,"* she intones. "Tales speak of it appearing on the water, sometimes hovering above it; it can hunt a ship and send it adrift, as if the flames are alive. Even when you pass the Gulf, you aren't safe." She points farther up the land. "The Sahiran coast is notorious for playing visual tricks on sailors, appearing farther away than it really is. That's why the waters are marked with skulls on seafarers' maps and ships always give it a wide berth. It always sounded like magic to me, even before I knew magic was real."

"That's because it *is* magic," says Qayn, who leans on the rail beside us, holding a purple plum. "Part of the same enchantment that protects the Swallowing Sands. It extends through the Gulf of Fire and around the Sahiran coastline."

I marvel at the Gulf's vast, tranquil waters. "The Unknown Sorcerer was truly prolific. Scholars are still debating the means of the enchantment and how one person could be responsible for it all."

"I suspect they were strongly motivated," Qayn replies. He sinks his teeth into the plum's soft flesh, drawing a surge of juice around his sharp canines.

"You mean by the Great Spirit's commandment." I ripple my fingers along the damp rail. "I don't know. . . . It seems contradictory that the Great Spirit ordered us to keep the lifesaving misra to ourselves but also wanted us to be merciful and kind to others."

"It's almost as if history is inked by the victors in the blood of the vanquished." Qayn finishes the plum and tosses the exhausted pip overboard. "Tell me, who benefits from your being merciful and kind to others?"

"Everyone," I answer.

"And who benefits from the misra being kept to the Sahiran people alone?"

"We do."

"No. The people who control the misra tree do. Consider it." He pushes off the railing. "There's another plum belowdecks with my name on it."

"Captain," Makeen calls from the helm.

Farida pats the railing as Qayn saunters off. "I think that's enough philosophizing for me." She returns to the helm; a minute later, she and Makeen resume a lighter conversation about last night's card game.

Alone and with nothing to do, I move farther up the deck and begin running through some dagger drills. Skerric said that the majority of fyghtors in the Hunten enter as pairs, and they are all men. I'll be outnumbered in almost every battle and most assuredly the smaller combatant. There'll be time later to practice my swordwork, but I intend to exploit the disparity in size and strength by getting close and using speed to outmaneuver my opponent's defenses. That means focusing on my footwork and on recovery and defensive positions. The benefits of magic aside, being steady on my feet is paramount. Even the slightest misstep could spell my doom.

Though I'm moving through each drill slowly and precisely,

I work up a sweat and eventually have to lean on the railing to catch my breath. That's when Muhab, the black-bearded bosun, appears, wielding a bucket and mop.

"I have it on good authority that swabbing the decks makes one better with a blade."

I decide against interrogating that statement. I want to be a productive crew member, and I doubt that I'd be any use on the complicated rigging.

"What's the point of swabbing the decks anyway?" I ask, taking the mop and bucket from him. "You'd think we'd want to keep the ship as dry as possible."

"Salt water protects the wood from decay and keeps the planks swollen, which stops that stuff out there"—he points at the sea—"from seeping in here."

Before long Atheer returns to the deck for some fresh air and notices me.

"Let me take over, Sis," he says, reaching with his good hand for the mop. "I'm feeling better already."

I pull it out of reach. "Let's wait until you're feeling even better, hmm?"

Grudgingly he resigns himself to sitting on a stool nearby to keep me company. Muhab joins us soon after, though the bosun keeps a close eye at all times on his sailors clambering high in the rigging.

"Do either of you know where our foreign passenger is?" he asks. "I haven't seen Skerric since we set sail. Hope we didn't forget him on the dock in Brooma."

"He's resting in the captain's cabin," says Atheer.

"Oh, good," says Muhab. "I'm glad he's catching his breath after the hard nothing he did all week."

I dunk my mop in the bucket, snorting. "To be fair to Skerric, he answered my questions about the tournament, and I had a lot."

"That was the least he could do," says Muhab. "I heard he's getting paid quite handsomely for his 'help.' "

"No, just a little more gold and land to add to his reserves," I say, straight-faced.

A nearby sailor chuckles. Atheer remains unamused.

"I asked Farida to let him lodge in her cabin for the duration of the journey. To be honest, I was worried about his safety in the crew quarters."

"You were wise to be," says Muhab. "We're furious that Glaedric's thieving little brother got his hands on Qayn's magic and now Imani has to win a fight to the death for even a chance to get it back." He sniffs, crossing his burly arms. "It's salt in the wound, having to ferry a Harrowlander back to his castle as well."

I notice Atheer watching me with a familiar sadness. But I don't want to give him or anyone else the impression that I'm nervous or worried about the Hunten, so I ignore the first part of Muhab's comment entirely.

"Does Skerric really own a castle?" I ask, slapping the wet mop on the planks. "I suppose it must be true. Maysoon did describe his house as prominent."

"Ooh, *prominent.*" Muhab twirls his hand grandly. "Is that why he's been spared the rigors of work? It's too unseemly for a lord to be seen doing anything other than lounging around?"

"Shopping and stuffing your face are also acceptable activities," calls a sailor above us, referring to Skerric's several leisurely visits to the souq over the last few days, which always seemed to culminate in him returning to the ship eating a sweet dessert. Every sailor within earshot bursts into laughter.

Atheer shakes his head at them. "Come now, you lot. Yes, he's a nobleman, not a sailor, and he's on our side."

"Oh. I didn't realize it took a sailor to do this." I mop a single plank, inciting another wave of derisive laughter.

"A monkey could do it!" Muhab exclaims. "Want to know how I know?" He leans in, squinting. "I once saw a ship in Taeel-Sa that had not one but *two* monkeys in vests swabbing the decks."

"The monkeys were in *vests*?" I round my lips. "How mannerly of them."

Atheer groans. "You did not see that, Muhab."

"I swear on the gods, I did! Where's Khaled? He saw it too."

"And was this sighting before or after you drank a cask of wine?" Atheer asks.

"That's enough chatter," says Farida from the railing above us, interrupting Muhab's rebuttal and the snickering sailors. "We're coming up on the Serpent Sea. I want everyone attentive."

Muhab regains his gruffness. "Understood, Captain. Back to work, all of you."

And just like that, the playful mood on deck evaporates. Atheer slowly goes up the gangway after Farida, and Muhab returns to the rigging. I look off the side of the ship for what's changed, but the sea is the same as before: vast, blue, and secretive.

# 21

# TAHA

THE PRISONERS ARE MARCHED OUT OF THE ENCAMPment and lined up. Taha kneels under Glaedric's broadsword, while Amira is left to shiver in the hollow beside him. Stewards erect a small canopy, and Glaedric removes his helm and retreats to a chair under it to be spoken to by officials bearing maps; he listens, sipping hot misra tea, while a young man polishes the king's helm and sword in the corner.

The bannerman returns in the late afternoon, his flag of truce saturated by the rain and slapping limply against the pole. Yet despite the hours spent waiting for death in this forsaken field, it seems to take the bannerman even longer to finally reach them, his horse's hooves throwing up clumps of mud. He dismounts and marches over clutching a leather pouch in his gloved fist.

"Your Majesty." He greets the king in oddly accented Harrowtongue. "The Council has given their answer."

Taha's eyes widen. The bannerman's voice is familiar—

"And?" Glaedric snatches the pouch. The bannerman stands

back and removes their helm. Blond, curly hair bounces away from the steel bucket and falls to frame a bronze Sahiran face.

Taha straightens. *"Feyrouz?"*

She glances at him and Amira and quickly returns her attention to Glaedric. Taha can't understand it. She isn't a prisoner in Bashtal; she wasn't executed there either. She's here, very much alive, cutting a slim figure in the enemy's mail, surcoat, and cloak.

"Ah yes, your companion," says Glaedric. "You'll have time to talk once Qalia is mine. Sooner rather than later, I hope."

Fey clears her throat. "The Council has agreed to surrender, Your Majesty. All soldiers within the city will hand themselves over imminently. The Shields will exit first."

Her announcement distorts in Taha's ears. Amira wails frenziedly. Officials and stewards applaud and cheer. Glaedric laughs.

"Staggnir's sons, excellent news! You see, *never* underestimate the comfort of a familiar face delivering hard news!"

Fey bows. "Yes, Your Majesty."

The rain turns to a drizzle, and a gigantic swirl of light forms above Qalia. Glaedric skips into the hollow, sloshing water around as he points his sword at the light. "Look at that! Has there ever been a more glorious flag of surrender? Tell me!"

His subordinates hurry to agree that there never has been and never will be again. Taha is so desensitized that he feels only the most caustic edge of his rage. He lunges at Glaedric and crashes them both into the water, roaring "YOU DIE HERE!" as he clambers onto the king's chest.

The muddy water recedes from Glaedric's startled, ashen face. Taha drives his fists down on it, but he's launched onto the bank before he can connect. He grunts and rolls onto his back, pain bolting through his ribs. He feels as if he's been hit by a carriage, but it was actually Ser Ulric, pointing a sword at him as Taha gets to his feet.

"Move an inch and I'll gut you, boy. Don't force me."

Taha splays his hands, gasping, "Easy, Marshal. Easy."

Soldiers crowd Glaedric, and the stewards pull him out of the water. He pushes them out of the way and marches at Taha, seething: *"You dare lay a finger on me?"*

A chill finds Taha, too cold to belong to the late storm. He starts shivering; his rain-spiked lashes crystallize, and the hairs dangling over his forehead glisten with beads of ice. The chill constricts, emptying his lungs of white steam. He gazes in horror at the frost creeping across his tunic. Even his blood is freezing, the thud of his heart slowing. *Magic,* he realizes sleepily. Glaedric's affinity is for the cold.

The king closes an icy fist around his neck. "Your pathetic life was promised in exchange for the city, but if you make an attempt on me again, I will freeze your heart and smash it to pieces with a hammer." He shoves Taha away and turns on his subordinates. "Secure the brute and the girl and fetch my horse. And wipe this mud off me!"

The chill melts away, but the burns on Taha's neck remain. While soldiers carry Amira to Glaedric's carriage, Fey crosses the grass to her horse.

*"Traitor,"* Taha barks at her back. "The only mercy for Reza is that he isn't here to see what became of you!"

Her head jerks up. She looks over her shoulder, eyes shining, body turning as if she's preparing to come back and demand answers. But Ulric marches Taha off toward Glaedric's carriage before she can.

The other prisoners return to the encampment; the Vanguard

rides from the other side, trailed by foot soldiers marching to Qalia. A loud groaning emanates from the city as the golden gates are drawn open.

Ulric shoves Taha into the carriage. Amira is already inside, pressed against the rain-spotted window. The Marshal doesn't follow, instead staying out to speak with the soldiers on the perch. Once the Vanguard reaches the city, a short horn is blown and unarmored Shields begin to exit the gates with their hands over their heads. They're surrounded, chained, and marched away, and the same is done to the Sentries and Swords who exit next. Meanwhile, a black stallion is brought to the king in barding enameled dark brown to match the color of his armor. His stewards assist him into his gilded helm and fasten a dry cloak to his shoulders, then he climbs into the saddle and sweeps the cloak's length over the stallion's hind. He's soon joined by six others on horseback. A large Empire flag unfurls, borne by the man at the very back, and they begin their ride toward the city, blowing curved horns.

"It's really over," Amira says, watching them go. "We lost our home to the Harrowlanders."

Taha hears her but doesn't comprehend any of it. The journey across the Sahir was long and punishing, yet on reflection, it was a grain of sand in an hourglass. His homeland, secure for a millennium, stolen in a heartbeat.

Ser Ulric climbs inside the carriage holding two pairs of wrist manacles. As they roll on to join the king's procession, he fits the end of one pair around Amira's wrist and the other around his own. He turns to Taha with the second pair, saying, "Missed me in my absence?"

"I think you broke one of my ribs," Taha mutters as Ulric chains them together.

"Just one? You're lucky." He yanks his hand back, tugging Taha's forward.

Taha pulls it back, teeth gritted. "Why?"

Ulric offers up his hotheaded grin. "If your father tries to strike me down, he won't strike me alone. We'll go to Staggnir together, never to part again."

Taha would rather go to Alard, the Land of No Return, alone.

Flanked by the Vanguard's heavy cavalry, the carriage enters the shadow of the archway housing Qalia's gold gates, which prompt an appreciative whistle from Ulric. They stop there behind Glaedric and his convoy, and several figures exit the open gates to meet the king.

Amira clambers onto the seat beside Ulric and looks out the window behind his head. "It's the Council!" she exclaims. Her fingernails dig into the cushion. In a lower voice, she says, "Come on, Auntie, you must have a plan."

Ulric laughs at that, and then he twists to look out the window too. "Say, which one is the Grand Zahim, boy?"

Taha looks at his father, towering over the other Councilmembers. Bayek emanates proud power in a black thobe and sweeping bisht, his short ebony hair hidden under a black keffiyeh held in place by an *agal* of corded goat's hair, daylight slanting across the angles of his stern, sculpted face. In some respects, it's like looking in a mirror. Both tall and broad of shoulder, they share the same square hairline and jaw, but Bayek's eyes lie dark in the shadow of his strong brow, made darker by the black kohl he uses to line them. At Taha's initiation into the Shields, the mother of another initiate remarked to Bayek that, apart from their eyes, Taha resembled him very much. Taha feared his father would scoff at the comment, but Bayek gazed at him with some fondness and said, *Yes, every day, my son reminds me more of myself when I was a young man.* It is the greatest compliment Taha has ever received.

He has to clear his throat to speak now. "The man in the middle."

Ulric whistles again. "Big man. Mighty impressive what your father can do with his magic. Lightning bolts worthy of Thunor." The muscles around Ulric's eyes twitch. Frowning, he reaches for the flask of misra tea on his belt, as if the mere mention of Bayek's magic has stirred his thirst. "You don't look too glad to see him, though," he adds between mouthfuls.

Taha may as well have been carved from deadwood. He's petrified in his seat, seeing the contempt on his father's face; *feeling* the rage that must boil Bayek's blood when soldiers approach the Councilmembers to restrain them. Did Bayek really surrender Qalia to save Taha's life? It's unbelievable.

Wrists chained, the Council is marched back through the gates. The carriage creaks in after Glaedric's convoy and the Vanguard, leading the greater army into the city. Taha never thought he'd see it, but the street opening onto Main Square is entirely empty; all the fearful faces are peeping out at them from the windows of surrounding buildings. Just as well. The Vanguard disperses down the laneways, accompanied by Qalian officials using speaking trumpets to instruct people not to leave their residences.

Glaedric stops the convoy to marvel at the ancient marble monolith in Main Square. Erected by the Council of Old, the monolith is crowned by a claw supporting a glass funnel that houses a swirling light, magically sustained by Aziza Zahim and the team of sorcerers who work under her. The light cascades through fissures in the monolith's length, illuminating the carved branches of a tree symbolizing the misra tree in the

Sanctuary. Though the convoy eventually leaves it behind, soldiers break away from the column to remain. Wagons crowd the square, and spiked palisades are pulled from their beds and set up at the entrances. The same is done at intersections. Street by street, neighborhood by neighborhood, soldiers separate from the pack to establish permanent control. Yet when the Sanctuary's glittering golden domes come into view, it doesn't seem as if the column has thinned at all.

The procession ends in the gardens outside the Sanctuary, a cluster of domes and minarets now emptied of officials who've lined up under the cypress trees. While the convoy dismounts and Glaedric removes his helm, Ulric pulls Taha and Amira from the carriage and takes them to the Zahim, waiting at the foot of the steps.

"Auntie!" Amira shouts, frantically waving her free hand.

Aziza tears up, nodding and smiling at her niece. Taha forces himself to meet his father's gaze, but he's unable to read Bayek's expression, if he even has one.

Amira is barely within reach when her auntie gathers her in her chained arms. "We thought we'd lost you!"

"I'm so sorry for running away and hurting you all," Amira blubbers.

"What matters is that you're back." Aziza lowers her voice. "What about Imani?"

"Free with Atheer in Alqibah," Amira whispers back.

Aziza's eyes shine. "He's—"

"Yes, Auntie." Amira smiles. "Atheer is alive."

But if Bayek had ever been worried about Taha since the Scouts left Qalia—or is relieved now—he doesn't show it. Taha reaches for him anyway. "Baba," he says, then kisses his father's hand and taps it to his forehead in a traditional sign of respect. Maybe it's his father's touch that does it. The tears escape him, despite every attempt he makes to stop them. "Forgive me," he says, his face hot.

Bayek pulls his hand away. "No more, Taha," he orders gruffly. "Show the invaders no weakness."

"Yes, sir." Taha dries his face and hardens his expression, but his eyes are raw, his breathing hare-quick. For some reason, Ser Ulric is watching him.

"This is Atheer's doing, isn't it?" Bayek asks, eliciting uncomfortable glances from Aziza and the other Zahim.

Taha gives a restrained nod. "He was the king's captive; told him everything. We freed Atheer, but it was too late for us to . . . do anything . . . by then."

Amira glances at him, evidently grasping the meaning of his double-speak.

"Atheer," Bayek mutters. "Entitled fool doomed his nation while his betters bent over backward to defend him." He turns on the Council, targeting the small Treasurer, Aqil, who earlier dismissed Atheer's involvement with the Alqibahi rebels as nothing of consequence. "Perhaps you understand now how the brush fire that consumed Ayadin began with a single, insignificant spark."

Aqil looks as if he's swallowed his own tongue.

Glaedric finishes removing his helm and coif, freeing his sweep of silken hair. He points at the Sanctuary doors. "Take me to the Garden of the Misra."

Bayek has to wrench his glare from Glaedric to follow the other Zahim into the Sanctuary. They make their way across the marble-floored foyer and into the Sanctuary's fragrant depths. Glaedric can't contain his giddy excitement; he points and gasps and gazes adoringly with round eyes at the vaulted honeycomb ceilings, the constellations of stained-glass lanterns, the geometric and scroll mosaics lining the long walls of arcades, the columns of stucco relief wrapped in gold and inlaid with jewels.

"Breathtaking craftsmanship," he gushes as they walk, his steel boots thudding obnoxiously on the tiles.

A few minutes later, Aziza pauses at a pair of engraved wooden doors and announces, "The Garden of the Misra," before pushing them open.

Glaedric eagerly shadows the Zahim through the doorway. Ser Ulric moves too, tugging Taha and Amira along, but Taha drags his feet. He's never looked upon the misra tree before. Only Zahim are permitted to do that, and his father never extended the permission to him. Ser Ulric wouldn't care about tradition even if he knew it. He wrenches Taha through the doorway and, like Glaedric and the other men, gasps as he lays his sickly eyes on the tree. Though the garden around it is beautified with elaborate flower beds and statues, they're invisible beside the tree's magnificence.

Glaedric stops on the path and raises his hands. "It's perfect!" he proclaims.

Even that doesn't adequately describe the Great Spirit's gift. The air is alive with the tree's magic, the late light twinkling as if gold dust floats in its beams. Glaedric removes his gloves, drops them on the paver at his feet, and ambles under the tree's generous canopy. There he lays his hands on its pristine trunk and presses his cheek to the bark.

"It's perfect," he repeats, inhaling deeply, "and it's *mine.*" He smiles, exuding more self-satisfaction than Taha thought possible from one man.

But it's the despair on Bayek's face that Taha will never forget.

He'll see it in his nightmares for years to come, if he survives that long, and now he feels paper-thin, strained around the understanding of what Amira said in the carriage: It's over. They've lost their homeland to the Harrowlanders.

Glaedric has to peel himself off the tree, and even when he addresses his soldiers, he's a man separated from his lover. "Keep the Councilmembers under watch until the magic has left them," he murmurs, glancing back at the tree.

As Aziza is led away, she gives Amira a heartening nod. Taha receives only the tail end of his father's glare, which reluctantly shifts from Glaedric to him.

# 22

# IMANI

I'M SWABBING THE DECKS THE FOLLOWING AFTER-noon when Farida orders us to batten down.

Sailors curse; others lose their color. I'm not so bewildered that I don't know to be worried. The crew were just at ease, trading jokes between the rigging. Now they're silent, serious, and working fast.

I trail after Muhab with my dripping mop, waiting for the bosun to finish shouting orders. "What's happening?" I ask the second I get my chance.

"Farida senses a storm." He notices me looking at the clear sky. "Don't be fooled, Imani. They start fast in the Serpent Sea. I advise you to steel your nerves." He calls a sailor over and says to me, "Help Mina secure things below. We don't want anything flying around if we get caught up in it."

I tip my bucket out overboard and hurry after Mina through the hatch. "How likely are we to be 'caught up' in this storm?" I ask her.

She replaces my mop and bucket with rope. "It's not a matter of *if* but *when.* Let's get to work."

I'm glad to be engaged by the mess of loose items strewn through the crew quarters. Even with the escalating howl of wind over the ship, I don't get a moment to worry about whether my nerves actually have the spongy consistency of cake. Any door that might swing open is lashed shut, and anything Mina and I can't stow away, we tie down. That includes Qayn, whom I discover lounging on a bunk, head buried in a sailor's book of bawdy tales.

"Qayn, didn't you hear? A storm's coming." He peers at me over the pages as I fling rope across his stomach. "I've been ordered to secure everything belowdecks. If you don't move, I'll interpret that as your wish to be tied to this bunk for the foreseeable future."

Sighing, he pushes the rope aside and stands. "This is drivel anyway." He tosses the well-thumbed book into a trunk and goes off to help the sailors closing the porthole shutters.

Steadily the deck gets dimmer and stuffier. I reunite with Mina to help her tie barrels against a beam.

"Why is it called the Serpent Sea?" I ask as we work.

"During a storm, a ship rides the waves as if they're the spine of a giant serpent so sailors used to spread rumors that it was home to sea monsters. I hope you have a strong stomach." She secures the knot and looks around. "That's everything. Take a break while you can."

It's an offer I'm happy to accept. She returns abovedeck and I ease onto a barrel, mopping my brow.

"They aren't rumors, you know," Qayn says, strolling over and sitting on the barrel beside mine. "The Serpent Sea owes its name to Tiamat, the greatest sea serpent to ever exist. In this realm, at least. She was very fond of these waters once. I imagine she's broadened her horizons now."

I stiffen. "I didn't know any monsters existed beyond the Sahir."

"Some. The Unknown Sorcerer wouldn't have been aware of Tiamat's existence, or else they would've factored her majesty in when creating the enchantment."

I look for the closest porthole, half expecting an enormous yellow eye to be staring back at us. The shutters are all down now. Perhaps for the better.

"Will Tiamat try to hurt us?" I ask.

"Not with me aboard. We're old friends. Good ones. She owes me a favor, in fact."

The ship bobs, sliding me off the barrel. I hop back onto it. "A favor for what?"

"Saving her life." He raises a hand. "It's a long story, and I'm not much in the mood to tell it."

A disbelieving smile creeps onto my face. "How does one befriend a monstrous sea serpent? Was there much to talk about between you? I mean, besides sinking ships and destroying cities and the like."

Qayn returns the smile. "Was there much to talk about between you and Taha? I mean, when you weren't berating or trying to kill each other, and kissing occasionally."

He may as well have poked me in the chest, so sore do I feel. "Why would you say that?"

Qayn shrugs, laughing now. "Perhaps next time you'll think twice about casting aspersions."

I fold my arms, grumbling an apology.

Qayn is still smiling. "And I am a *little* curious. What was it about Taha that you liked so much? He's handsome, certainly, but he could be rather dull."

"What's it to you?" I say sharply. "And I didn't like him *so much.* I didn't like him at all!"

Qayn tuts. "What if Tiamat has a change of her many hearts and devours us? Do you really wish to spend your last moments telling lies?"

"Surely I'm needed elsewhere," I mutter, looking toward the hatch. The ship's rocking has worsened, and I'm having to hold on to the barrel to keep from falling. But then, as if I'm skirting a whirlpool, I'm sucked right back into the conversation. "Regardless, you sound awfully jealous of him."

As soon as I say it, I search for any sign that Qayn is, indeed, jealous, even though I shouldn't. He's a monster and we're only allies, *maybe* friends. Yet he's begun appearing in my dreams. Quietly walking by my side, eating a plum under a tree, brushing Raad; simply smiling in the sunlight, as beautiful as one can possibly be. I can't stop it from happening, and what's worse is that I wake from the dreams craving his company. I can't decide if it's genuine desire or a side effect of our binding and his influence. Either way, I dread how he'd taunt me if he ever found out.

"Jealous of Taha?" Qayn reflects on that for a moment, but I know it's just for show. "Perhaps a little. You can have your charms."

I roll my eyes. "Oh, thanks."

"I'm more perplexed," he goes on, brow furrowed. "Taha had an ox's strength, but he wasn't clever or creative, hardly curious. He couldn't write you poems or dance with you. Paint you. He has no understanding of . . ." Qayn mulls his words and settles on "true pleasure."

"Oh, but you do," I scoff, my heart beginning to skip.

"I write exceptional poems," Qayn says seriously. "Nahla and I exchanged them often. And I have a very good eye for portraiture. You've seen the beauty of the First City. I designed and built it all—I even crafted the purple flowers after a dream I had. Nahla's favorite color was that particular shade of lavender." He half smiles, one cheek dimpled. "Don't even get me started on my dancing."

I have to rely on every ounce of self-control to resist asking for a demonstration, and every scrap of theatrical ability to disguise my nerves. "Very well, you've convinced me," I say, throwing my hands up. "I should pine after no one else but you if I have any sense in my head."

"None of my admirers have ever regretted it," he assures me before sighing dramatically. "And who knows—I *suppose* you could win my heart if you put in some effort."

*Oh no.* He *has* sensed that I've been dreaming of him. He's not flirting with me—he's mocking me! I set my jaw.

"Let's speak candidly, Qayn. We both know I don't have what it takes to win your heart." I free my dagger and twirl it between my fingers. "This blade, on the other hand. What do you say? It feels right. Me, the Djinni Slayer; you—"

"The object of your hunt." He smirks and leans closer as if the dagger between us doesn't exist. "Has something of a romantic ring to it, don't you think?"

There's no triumphing over him. He always finds a way to have the last laugh, to maneuver into the position of power before the battle is done. I replace my dagger on my thigh, hoping I can think of one last pointed reply, but I'm interrupted by a sudden barrage of rain over the ship. We rise off the barrels, listening. A bell tolls. Farida shouts, but the wind quickly surpasses her, and even the tolling becomes inhibited in comparison.

We hurry abovedeck into pouring rain. The afternoon's clear sky is now a solid bank of dark blue; at our stern, a whirl of black. The sea is angry, its sharp-toothed waves gnashing behind us in wide undulations. I'm horrified to see that Atheer is working with the sailors to strip the masts of canvas, pulling at the ropes using just his good arm. He notices us and points at the hatch. "Shut it!"

We drag the wooden shutter over the hatch. I bolt it and jog over to him. "You should be belowdecks!" I shout, taking a length of rope and helping to pull.

"We need every hand to reef the sails!" he shouts back. "The storm could damage the masts if we don't!"

After yelling something at the sailors near the foremast, Muhab gestures angrily over my head at the closed door of the captain's cabin. Everyone must be out here battling the storm except Skerric. There's no chance that he hasn't realized he may be needed on deck.

"Find out what he's doing!" Muhab shouts to me.

Atheer frowns, shaking his head, but I don't dare disobey the bosun. I navigate the slippery deck up to the cabin door and bang my fist on it.

"Skerric? Are you in there?" I call in Harrowtongue.

No response.

I open the door. The window is shuttered, making it hard to see anything. I push inside just as the ship skates down a wave and slams the door shut behind me. Farida's bed creaks.

"Who's that?" Skerric asks in a small voice.

"Imani." My eyes adjust and I notice Skerric hiding under

the blanket. "We need help out there. The storm's about to get very bad."

The blanket drags away. Skerric stares back at me, messy-haired and as pale as a wisp of smoke. "I *want* to help, but I've seen how the crew look at me whenever I leave this cabin—even you sometimes—and I've heard their jokes." He sinks into himself. "They wouldn't want me out there. I'd only make things worse."

I feel guilty for having joined Muhab in mocking him yesterday. "I'm sorry, Skerric, it was wrong of me to make you feel that way. As for the crew, I'm afraid they just don't trust you."

"I don't blame them," he says, slightly defensive.

"Then why not try to earn their trust? If there was ever an opportunity for that, it's now. We need to all work together to keep this ship afloat, or we're sunk."

His throat moves thickly. The silence between us fills with the desperate shouts of the sailors, the storm's rising menace.

"Thunor forgive us this day," Skerric whispers. He pushes the blanket aside and frees himself of the rope he was using to lash himself to the bed.

Muhab is glaring murderously at the cabin door when it opens. But at the sight of Skerric descending the gangway after me, he swaps his glare for a milder frown. Some of the sailors even spare curious glances as Skerric joins me at the ropes beside Atheer and Qayn. More surprising is how he takes to the rigging, with such strength and natural skill that he can hardly be distinguished from the junior sailors. Muhab has no choice but to treat him as one and returns to barking orders.

The rain quickly gets worse, as if the storm were taking a breath and now it's exhaling. Freezing water pours down on us. The ropes become hard to grip, the deck gets even harder to stand on, and over the stern shrieks a malevolent gale. But only a small square of canvas remains on the masts, and Muhab said that as soon as the job is done, almost everyone is to go belowdecks to wait out the storm.

Suddenly the ship surges on a monster wave. I hug the railing as we're thrown back at the sea, the gray-green water rushing up to meet us. We crash into it hard; sailors shout, the ship shudders and swings. A young man lies limp on the deck by the mainmast. Above him, ropes whip free, and a section of previously reefed canvas drops open and is grabbed by the wind. Now we're no longer fleeing with the storm at our stern. The wind is buffeting over our starboard, where another, even more monstrous wave is lifting off the sea.

"HOLD ON!" Muhab bellows.

The wave collapses over us. The ship keels. Everything slants before I'm hit by the frigid water. I fold around the railing, Atheer holding on to me, and for some accursed reason, I think of the silver beach under the prison in Taeel-Sa. The cold water I fled into with the tower of bodies at my back. . . .

The ship swings out of the trench and bobs upright, still fighting. I gasp for air. Hissing water chutes off the deck through the scuppers, but the hatch to the crew quarters has wrenched open and water is flooding belowdecks. The unconscious sailor who was lying near the mainmast is gone.

"Man the pump!" Farida shouts from the helm.

I blink, dazed, and search for the missing sailor. Farida yells at Makeen; Muhab shouts at the sailors. The ship twists. Another wave, as big as the last, stands over us and falls.

I brace for death, yet the wave doesn't crash. I stare up at it, an ant before a giant, struggling to comprehend why the world has halted. Then I see Farida by the rail above us, body contorted as if she's pushing an invisible wall, face rigid with concentration, the muscles of her arms straining through the sodden sleeves of her tunic. Of course. Her affinity is for water.

She roars and shoves the wave back with stunning force; it folds in the center and collapses on itself, turned inside out before it's accepted by the befuddled sea. Makeen wrenches the helm to put our stern to the wind again, and the sailors shake off the shock and return to the rigging.

"Man—the—pump!" Farida repeats breathlessly.

"Hurry," Atheer says, ushering me, Qayn, and Skerric to a bronze machine in the center of the deck with two handles, one on either side. "Push," he rasps, working the handle one-armed. I join his side, Qayn and Skerric taking up the other.

"You can't exert yourself like this," I say as I throw my weight behind the handle. It rotates with great effort; piping in the machine's center emits a glugging noise, and stinking water spews out and rolls across the deck to drain through the scuppers.

"I'm fine!" Atheer replies. "And it's not as if I'd ever leave you up here on your own! What kind of big brother would that make me?"

Not mine. My big brother got himself arrested in Taeel-Sa defending a stranger from a group of soldiers. My big brother would walk through death's door to help others if nobody stopped him. Worryingly, I don't even know if *I* could stop him.

We persist under the battering storm, clinging to the levers when water comes seeking over the bow. The ship bounces violently on the churn, groaning in my ears; it flies and falls, and the furious sea demands blood. The sailors work in near silence around us, all hearts and minds concentrated on this final task: surviving.

Through the curtaining rain, I see Atheer's expression change. He pulls away from the pump handle and staggers for a nearby rope, exhausted. I'm about to beg him to seek shelter below when the ship plunges. He loses his footing and slips, his head and body aligned with the mainmast. The unconscious sailor flashes in my mind. My brother is next.

I lunge, one fist still gripping the lever, and catch the back of his tunic. My shoulders spasm; the muscles of my chest wall burn as I stop his fall. I scream regardless; my relief is a sluggish thing, but my panic is agile.

Qayn appears at my side and grabs Atheer before my brother's weight can tear him from my already tenuous grip. Together we get Atheer back on his feet, but he struggles to stand fully upright and keeps clutching at his bandages. Yet he still says, "I'm all right," over and over again, and returns to the pump handle.

I look around, desperate for somebody to intervene. Thankfully, Muhab's already noticed and is coming over.

"Belowdecks now, Atheer! That's an order," he adds when my brother opens his mouth to argue. And then for good measure, "I'll carry you down myself if I must."

Atheer gazes at me forlornly as I take hold of his good arm. "Come on," I say, "we must be quick."

He acquiesces in despondent silence and limps with me down into the sopping darkness of the crew quarters. I lay him on a bunk nearest to the faint light filtering through the still-open hatch. More sailors arrive to take shelter now that the canvas has been reefed, and one lashes my brother to the bunk despite his protests. But it's obvious to all of us that Atheer is too weak to hold on by himself.

"Rest," I urge him.

A tear escapes down his cheek. "I should be the one looking after you, Imani."

Perhaps it's a blessing that there's no time to talk. I swallow my distress, squeeze his hand, and race abovedeck, the hatch shuttering behind me. Immediately the ship slides off a wave and slaps the surface of the water. I grab the railing, staring in muted horror at the icy sea rolling across the planks past my boots. Despite all this physical sensation anchoring me in the present—the biting cold of the rain, the roar of the storm and strained groans of the ship, the taste of salt—our predicament feels unreal. A nightmare. Even time has slowed, and in the yawning gaps between the seconds, I see with unblemished clarity the beautiful faces of my family. The home we left behind and may never return to.

Then time regains control of itself, and so do I.

I return to the pump, being worked on one side by Skerric and Qayn, on the other, by Muhab. As burly as the bosun is, he's relieved when I join him.

# 23

# IMANI

THE STORM ABATES AT DUSK, BORED CLOUDS DISbanding to terrorize elsewhere. It happens so quickly that when the warmth of sunset touches my skin, I don't recognize it right away. The hatch opens, and sailors ascend from the dark. They look haunted, as if they'd been trapped down there with ghosts. We continue to pump water out of the ship's hull until Farida finally instructs us to stop. By then, I'm so accustomed to the rotating motion of the handle that letting my arms hang by my sides feels wrong.

The crew gather before their sodden captain, her commanding figure framed against the red sunset and the water, gray-black but for its apricot crests.

"The *Lion's Prize* survived," she says hoarsely, looking across them. "But not all of us will sail another day. Bassem paid our toll for passage over Yamm's seas. Let his sacrifice never be forgotten."

I drop my head as the sailors shed quiet tears. I didn't even know the young man's name until now. Bassem died fighting as hard for his family as for mine, but he'll never see his family again. He won't even go home to rest.

A few minutes of sorrowful silence pass. Farida thanks her crew for their courage and sends them to various tasks. But before their ranks can thin, she turns to the small figure hiding in the shadow of the mainmast behind me.

"Skerric."

He nervously approaches her, glancing at hard-eyed Muhab standing to her right. "Captain," he says.

She stares down at him. "You were safely hidden in my cabin when the storm caught us."

He shrinks in his boots, cheeks flushing. "Yes."

"Yet you later changed your mind and joined my sailors on the ropes. Why?"

He glances at me. "Imani was quite clear that our collective survival depended on the actions of every individual aboard without exception."

Farida nods slowly, contemplating that. Then, "If someone told me that one day a Harrowlander lord would help save my life and the lives of my crew, I would've cut the filthy liar from navel to neck. But that's what you did today, though you were under no obligation." She holds out her hand. "You have my thanks."

Skerric's face shades a bright strawberry red. He gladly shakes her hand, and it's not lost on me that Farida made sure the gesture was witnessed by as many sailors as possible. To my relief, none of them seem to have taken offense at it.

The rest of the crew disperses to its tasks. I leave Qayn resting on the gangway and descend into the crew quarters to find Atheer. He's sitting on the edge of the bunk, and his tunic and soaked bandages have been peeled away. I have to cover my mouth to stifle my gasp. His ribs are purple and his torso is covered in injuries, including the freshly stitched stab wounds he sustained in Brooma.

Yet the bald, bearded ship's physician kneeling beside him is heartened by the sight. "Not a single case of separation of stitches," he says when he notices me. "Your brother is extremely lucky."

"I think we have very different definitions of luck, Hashem," says Atheer dryly, watching the physician uncork a jar of ointment.

Hashem merely smiles. "The ship is still floating. I'd say we're the luckiest people alive right now."

I quietly wait for him to finish cleaning and bandaging Atheer, but then Farida arrives and alternates between fussing over my brother and making him laugh, the resulting movement of his torso frustrating Hashem's attempts at precisely applying ointment. Finally, the physician has enough and politely sends the captain away.

"I'm sorry about earlier," I say to Atheer once Hashem is gone too. "I know how much you wanted to help."

Atheer's gaze drops. "I should've done more."

"Atheer, you're *injured.* You're allowed to rest. Stopping to look after yourself doesn't suddenly undo all the good things you've done for others." I crouch before him. "Listen to me. You are allowed to let someone else do the fighting once in a while. It doesn't make you any less of a warrior to ask for help."

"Someone else," he murmurs. "You."

"I'll try my best to hold down the fort on my own until you recover," I say.

That upsets him for some reason. "And you'll succeed, Imani," he says, agitated. "When I saw you go back out into that storm,

I realized why I'd been refusing to step aside. I was . . . *scared.* Scared of failing you and not keeping you safe. But *you* saved *me* out there. You've become the warrior I always said you would be. I guess I just didn't expect the day to creep up on me so soon." He sheepishly palms his nape and then shakes his head, frustrated again. "I spent all of last week telling myself I'd be recovered in time to enter the Hunten with you when I should've been helping you prepare. Can you forgive me?"

"There's nothing *to* forgive, Atheer. Even if you aren't with me in the Hunten, your lessons will be." I stand up as a group of sailors arrive to clean the crew quarters.

"Then we'll start tomorrow," says my brother, gingerly rising too. "And when we're done, those fyghtors aren't going to know what hit them."

Any training regime requires, as a matter of course, a rested body and mind, but I'm too worried about another storm to fall asleep. Every time wind gusts over the deck, I startle, and when the ship encounters a steeper wave than usual, I imagine Atheer falling and bolt upright on my bunk, almost whacking my head against the low ceiling. After that, I decide some fresh air might be in order.

Qayn is on deck, watching the water. All the starlight in the sky must be concentrated on him; he's almost glowing under it, as cold and perfect as polished obsidian. Suddenly I'm unusually nervous and considering another attempt at sleep. But he notices me before I can sneak away.

"Trouble sleeping?" he calls over his shoulder.

"As usual." I join him at the railing, feigning nonchalance. "I didn't get to thank you earlier for being there when Atheer fell. Another second and he would've slipped from my grasp."

"You're welcome. I'll always be there for you if I can," he says.

I watch him out of the corner of my eye. "That's very generous of you."

"You sound disappointed," he says, a smirk flickering on his lips.

I frown. "Huh. I was going for skeptical."

He can't restrain the smirk. I knew he wouldn't. He swaps his stance, putting his back to the rail. "You know, Imani, sometimes I think you'd prefer me if I played into your wicked monster fantasy."

I can't help but snort. "Perhaps you're onto something. After all, a monster I'm not allowed to destroy is like—"

"A piece of *baklawa* you're not allowed to eat," he finishes for me.

I stare at him. "Did you just compare yourself to a dessert?"

He treats me to a mischievous grin. "Be honest. What would you give to get your hands on a piece of forbidden baklawa?"

"Depends on the baklawa," I say.

"The sweetest, freshest, stickiest piece of baklawa ever made," he replies in the kind of low, smooth voice that should be outlawed.

"What if I prefer *maamoul*?" I ask innocently.

His eye twitches. "But this piece of baklawa is better. No, it's the *best*. Nothing compares."

"Are we still talking about you here?"

"Depends. Do you want to get your hands on me?"

My heart flutters in my chest. I fight to suppress a grin and lose, so I'm laughing when I say, "To throttle you, certainly."

He smiles. "You really are at your most charming when you're being hostile."

"I am? Then you must be just about in love with me by now."

He's silent, gazing at me. The moment is brief, but when he breaks it by chuckling, I feel like an age has begun and ended between us. "Just about. You must be the same."

I clam up, even though we're only jesting. "Where would you get such an idiotic idea?"

"From you, naturally." His grin returns as he leans closer, his arm brushing mine. "Being soulbound is an interesting experience."

"What are you talking about?"

"I see your dreams sometimes," he reveals in a silky voice.

My jaw drops. I hurry to shut it and compose myself. "How could you? I mean, I don't see yours."

"Suppose I'm a little more adept at keeping that wall up when I'm asleep."

He may as well have just told me that there's been a giant hole in the ship's hull ever since we departed Brooma! "Well, I don't know what you *think* you've been seeing, Qayn, but it wouldn't be my dreams—" I gabble, darting my eyes around to make sure the few sailors on night watch aren't looking this way.

"I saw the one where we held hands."

"They don't mean anything," I blurt out, tugging the neck of my tunic. I know it's freezing out here, but I can't feel it. I'm insufferably warm.

"The heart speaks through dreams. You asked me if we could dance in this one." His grin widens until his dimples show. He takes my hands and, when I don't object, he rests one on his shoulder, then he wraps his arm around my waist and pulls me close. "I didn't know you cared for dancing."

"I don't know if I do," I choke out. "I've never really danced before."

He looks offended. "No life is lived until you dance under the stars."

"But there's no music, Qayn."

"*We* are the music makers."

He begins humming a soft, happy song and slowly leads me in a circle across the deck, moving with relaxed grace. I've about forgotten how to coordinate my feet, but I can't concentrate on where I'm stepping or how. All I can think about is just how close we are. Kissing distance.

"I have no idea how to dance," I lament in a nervous attempt to appear casual.

Qayn stops humming for a moment. "You don't need to know. You only need to *feel.* It's as good a guiding sense as any other."

That's precisely what I dread: letting my feelings take the lead, only for them to strand me somewhere I can't escape from.

Qayn picks his song up again, grinning as he guides me in a twirl. When he tips me backward and I yelp, digging my nails into him to hold on, he laughs out loud, transformed into a joyful boy for whom the sun still shines. But at other times, he looks up at the stars or across the sea in pensive wonder, and that's when I gaze at him openly, my heart tumbling over itself.

He eventually catches me doing it. "Don't send me away after you return my magic," he murmurs. "When all's said and done, let's go on an adventure. We can explore far-flung lands together, go dancing in places you won't believe exist. What do you say?"

"I think bringing me to dance anywhere is criminal."

He flashes a cheeky grin. "I'm going to take that as a yes."

"Perhaps."

"No, I will most certainly take it as a yes."

I burst into laughter. His breathing hitches, his pupils dilate. He gazes at me with such intense, vulnerable longing that I become a moth flown too close to a tantalizing flame, and I have to part from him before I'm consumed.

"I'm sorry," I mumble awkwardly, massaging my neck. "That was fun, but I should try to get some sleep before training starts. Thank you for the dance lesson, Qayn."

"It was my pleasure. And the offer will remain, Imani." He nods, smiling on his return to the railing.

With his back to me, I feel as if I've been kicked out of a dream. I rush belowdecks and locate several objects with my shins before I collapse onto my bunk. Sleep is far away, but I make no attempt to hunt it down. I stare at the ceiling, and when a big wave rocks the ship, I forget to flinch.

# 24

# TAHA

IF NOT FOR THE COMPANY OF BIRDS, TAHA WOULD'VE gone mad. He's never been so close to home yet felt so far away; he's never been this restless or lonely. The songbirds on the balcony outside are freer than he is. He's going to spend the rest of his life in a cage.

The apartment's front door opens behind him. He half turns to see Ser Ulric standing in the frame.

"His Majesty has summoned you, boy."

Taha glances at his reflection in the hanging mirror on the way out. Shadowed eyes glance back at him; his jaw is coated in fine stubble, and the shorn sides of his hair are growing out, the top getting so long that it keeps falling over his brows at inconvenient moments. He looks spent and feels bankrupt, but at least something's happening. Anything is better than the nothingness of indefinite imprisonment.

Ser Ulric escorts him through the Sanctuary's myrrh-scented halls, accompanied by Whitmund, Gutner, and four other soldiers.

It's an excessive force, given that Taha has nowhere to escape to, but so is Glaedric's occupation of the Sanctuary. Soldiers patrol every corridor, office, and hall. The Qalian officials have been permitted to return, but they work in the company of Harrowlander counterparts, who watch the Sanctuary in motion as if attempting to understand a complex mechanism before assuming control over it.

"Why have I been summoned?" Taha asks.

"His Majesty has a special task for you." Ulric tosses a frown at him. "What happened to your hand?"

Taha glances down at his swollen, purple-black knuckles. Last night, after hours of pacing and thinking about how he's never going to see Bayek or Taleb gain, he punched a hole in the bedroom door and almost broke his hand. He can barely close his fist now.

"What do you care?" he says, tucking it behind him. "Where's Amira?"

"She was sent home."

Taha feels as much relief for her as envy. "Why can't I go home too?"

"Because wolves need to be kept busy or they turn to trouble, don't they?" Ulric looks pointedly at Taha's fist again.

They step out into the sunny Garden of the Misra. Like the rest of the Sanctuary, it's undergone a transformation. Stacks of crates are arranged on the path near a long table piled with rolls of linen and a miscellany of tools, including shearing knives and hammers. Behind it sit two soldiers armed with quills and parchment.

King Glaedric stands under the misra tree, sipping from a white porcelain cup. Despite Qalia's dry heat, he's wearing a thigh-skimming mahogany doublet over iron-gray breeches, with a black cape trimmed in animal pelt slung over his shoulders, the two sides of its gold clasp molded into stag heads that lock antlers when the clasp is closed. His outfit is wholly inappropriate for the climate, yet the king's face remains as matte as bone, his irises floating in a black sea. Magical obsession. He's probably been drinking misra tea continuously since taking Qalia and is keeping cool by using his affinity on himself.

Bayek and Aziza Zahim are standing beside the table when Taha arrives, and Glaedric is busy delivering some speech to them in confident, if not fully fluid, Sahiran: "Of utmost importance is the proper storage of the Spice for transportation over sea. You should find the materials you need here, but if you require anything more, alert one of my men and it will be arranged."

"Your Majesty." Ser Ulric announces himself.

Glaedric drains his tea and glances at Taha. "Your son will assist you in the task," he says to Bayek. "Consider it an act of goodwill from me to you, Grand Zahim, that you may peacefully spend time with your firstborn."

Bayek is less moved than the stone busts in the garden. "Your so-called goodwill doesn't disguise your insult of ordering me around like one of your donkeys." He directs the remark at Ser Ulric and the soldiers, then he gestures at the tree. "Qalia is yours, invader. Take it, and don't rely on me to assist you with anything more."

Aziza glances at Bayek with some anxiety. Taha doesn't know how to feel. Disappointed that his father refused the opportunity for them to work together after so much time apart? Or should he agree with Bayek's refusal to help Glaedric rob the Sahir of its most precious gift?

Not at all amused, Glaedric smiles. He strides over to Bayek, the animal pelt of his heavy cloak whispering along the pavers at his heels. "I am a reasonable man by choice, not nature. Choose carefully which face of mine you wish to confront."

"Neither frightens me," Bayek replies.

"Let's see if your son feels the same." Glaedric places his teacup on the table and turns to Ser Ulric with a sweep of his cloak, throttled fury in his gaze. Unspoken communication passes between them. The Marshal hesitates for a fraction of a second, then releases Taha's chain and backhands him across the face. Taha drops to the pavers, shocked thoughtless. His eyes water, his nose runs, but he's quickly back on his feet. It's the product of training, when his own father would knock him down and call him weak until he stood back up. Now Bayek gazes at him dispassionately.

"Again," says Glaedric.

Ser Ulric strikes Taha, who tumbles to one knee, ears ringing. Pushes to his feet.

*"Again."*

Still no response written in Bayek's brow; even his hands hang relaxed. Ulric's fist connects with Taha's jaw, but the Marshal catches him by his blood-dotted tunic before he can fall.

"Stay down after this one, boy," he mutters, and throws him to the ground.

Taha's head spins even though he's lying flat. Groaning, he rolls onto his knees, his shaking fingers scraping for purchase between the pavers. Glaedric gives Bayek an expectant look.

Bayek shrugs. "Do you think my son hasn't endured worse?"

Taha pushes upright and spits blood in the long grass. *Great*

*Spirit forgive me for desecrating the Garden.* He has enough sense left to think of that, at least.

Glaedric nods at Ser Ulric. The Marshal heaves a sigh, tight lines crowding his mouth. He punches Taha in the eye. Taha totters back, fireworks flickering in his vision; his socket feels as if it's been dislodged and pushed back into his brain. Over the ringing, he thinks he hears Glaedric say, "Again!" but he can't be sure. He doesn't count the blows he sustains after that, only notes that Ulric's frown deepens and his face becomes so red that he looks like he's about to pop. It takes him longer every time, but Taha keeps getting up. He has to prove to his father that he isn't weak. He may have failed his mission in Alqibah and doomed their people, but he isn't weak.

"You see, invader?" Bayek proudly nods at Taha. "My son exemplifies the indomitable spirit of the Sahiran warrior. Each time you knock him down, he stands up again."

Glaedric draws his sword. "He won't after I kill him."

Ulric is lightning-quick to intercept his king marching furiously down the path. "The boye's mara weorth for thee am lif, me rihtwis cyning," he mutters urgently in a poetic Harrowtongue Taha has never heard before.

Glaedric inspects his marshal, briefly curious, before stepping past and pointing the sword at Taha's chest. "Bend your knee, Grand Zahim, or your firstborn's heart wets my blade to the hilt."

"Bayek, please," Aziza urges quietly.

Taha's father distorts in his blurry gaze. *Please, Baba,* he thinks, *please yield and end this suffering.* He only thinks it; he could never bring himself to plead for his life before his father, who has told him more than once that strong men strive in silence.

Bayek tips his head back to confidently expose his squared jaw and the strong column of his neck. "If you had intended to kill my son after you seized Qalia, he would already be dead. You have nothing to use against me."

Surprisingly, Glaedric sheathes his sword. "My men are scouring the city as we speak. They will find your children, and your brother, Omar, and his family. Then I will have a dozen *things* to use against you, Grand Zahim. Take him away."

Bayek gives Taha a short nod before being escorted from the garden. Taha clings to that tiniest of approvals for dear life. Relief knocks around somewhere in his addled brain too. Taleb, his other siblings, and his cousins are safe. Perhaps they're all with Uncle Omar, an accomplished hunter and tracker, who has hopefully hidden them beyond Qalia somewhere the king can't find them—yet.

"Loathsome mule," Glaedric mutters when Bayek is gone.

Aziza bows her head, her hands interlinking under the billowy sleeves of her dress. "I am the Master of the Misra, King Glaedric. I can strip the tree on my own for now, if you would permit Taha time to recover."

Glaedric nods curtly. "Very well, Aziza Zahim. Begin."

Whitmund returns Taha to the apartment. He lurches in over shattered ceramics and overturned furniture—the product of last night's rage—and when he spies his bloody face in the mirror, he hurls a coffee table at it and shatters his reflection. *Better,* he thinks, and collapses on the glass-strewn lounge. It hurts to even sob. Taha has no choice but to swallow his suffering and quietly lie back. He finds himself thinking of Bayek's nod. "You made Baba proud," he tells himself. "You honored him, and he loves you for it."

A little while later, Whitmund enters bearing a box of bandages and tinctures. "I'm to patch you up."

Taha lifts his throbbing head. "Touch me and I'll kill you, Whitmund."

The squire puts the box on the floor and leaves, shutting the door behind him.

# 25

# IMANI

WE CLEAR THE SERPENT SEA THE FOLLOWING day. Atheer tells me that by Farida's estimate, we have nine days of sailing left to reach Darkcliff.

"That's nine days of training for the Hunten," he says excitedly as we're waiting for water to boil on the stove. "Hope you're ready. I'm not going to go easy on you."

I'm a bit more subdued than he is after the nightmare I had this morning. In it, I found Amira, but for some reason she was trapped aboard Glaedric's burning, sinking ship, and unlike with Atheer, I couldn't free her.

"I hope you don't," I say. "Maybe if I'm exhausted enough, I won't have the energy to constantly worry about what's happening to Amira."

He watches me pull the silver teapot off the fire and place it on a tray of ceremonial tools. "You're going to save her, Imani. You're going to save everyone."

"Yes, or I'll die trying."

*"No,"* he says, putting his hand on my wrist. "Don't think like that. You're not going to die in the Hunten."

"But if I do, I won't be afraid," I say, staring him straight in the eyes. "I want you to understand that, Atheer. When I fight for our family and our people, I am never afraid."

Something about my statement fortifies him. He squeezes my fist and leaves me to my tea ceremony. It should be unsurprising that the scent of the misra reminds me of Qayn. Fire and destruction, but something enticing in the wisps of steam too—aniseed, honey, and immeasurable potential. I savor the tea from first drop to last, and once the magic is coursing through my blood, I emerge in the sunshine to begin my training.

Qayn is seated on the gangway next to my brother when I arrive. Though he greets me with only a nod, the warmth in his eyes is enough to set my heart racing. His presence should distract me from wanting to train, but it does the opposite. I want to show him what I can do.

We start with dagger drills, continuing my earlier custom of slow, deliberate action. I practice my attack, recovery, and defensive positions while Atheer calls out adjustments in my stances and Qayn looks on in thoughtful silence. For hours, I practice stabs, cuts, thrusts, lunges, and parries. An ever-shifting audience of sailors stops to watch, clap, and call out encouragement.

Even Skerric descends from the comfort of the captain's cabin to offer his counsel: "Fyghtors in the Hunten are well protected. Mail and padding are standard, but some fyghtors opt for full plate. Now, I'm no expert in"—he waves his hands at my dagger—"but factoring your opponents' armor into your training might be sensible."

"But our warriors don't wear full-plate armor," I say. "I don't know its weaknesses."

Skerric claps his hand to his forehead. "Yes, of course. Well, I've seen plenty of suits. The ones used in battle have gaps in the joints between the plates, for the wearer's ease of movement." He points at various places on his body: groin and inner thighs, underarms, backs of the knees and elbows.

"You'll need an edgeless blade," Atheer says to me.

"A thrusting sword," I agree.

"I've also heard that axes and maces have the advantage over plate armor," adds Skerric.

But Atheer shakes his head. "They're too heavy. Imani could never generate enough force to deal a crushing blow."

Did I imagine the way Qayn just looked at my brother? As if he'd taken issue with Atheer's statement. I haven't. I'm under no illusions about my strength relative to a heavily armored man.

"I'll have better luck fighting close and fast," I say, transforming my dagger into a thin, two-handed thrusting sword. Though my arms are exhausted from working the bilge pump yesterday, I'm not ready to rest. The reminder that I'll be facing off warriors in plate armor has gifted me a second wind. I begin shuffling across the deck, practicing my lunges, jabs, and half-sword thrusts, aiming high and low.

I don't stop until Hashem collects Atheer to have his bandages changed and Atheer tells me we'll pick up again tomorrow. Skerric excuses himself too, leaving me and Qayn.

"And you told me you didn't know how to dance," he says, sauntering over. "Your footwork disagrees."

"I see I've impressed you," I say, not bothering to hide my self-satisfaction.

"You've left me wanting more." His gaze darkens, his slender face becoming serious. "I don't mean to diminish the value of today's training, but you're forgetting the most powerful weapon in your arsenal. Magic is the only reason you have any hope of winning the Hunten alone. You must use it to level the battlefield. Why settle for one blade when you can attack with many?"

I narrow my eyes. "Because I only have two hands to wield them?"

"Let your *magic* wield them, Imani. You'll overcome the disadvantage of fighting alone. Do you grasp my meaning?"

"Yes, actually," I murmur, feeling a tickle of excitement. "The blade is me; I am the blade."

I turn and lob my dagger at the foremast, picturing the weapon as my hand reaching across the deck. Before it can stick into the wood, I pull my arm back. The dagger halts midair, quivering until my concentration breaks and it flies back to my fist. I look back at Qayn. He's nodding, pleased.

"Learn to direct your blade with your magic and your hands will be free to wield another weapon," he says. "You will be one person, but you'll fight like you are several."

I sheathe my dagger. "There's something else, isn't there? I noticed how you looked at Atheer when he dismissed the idea of my wielding an axe."

Surprise flashes in Qayn's gaze. "I believe your brother was only partially correct. You can't generate enough force to deliver a crushing blow using your body. But—"

"I could with my magic."

*"Yes,"* he hisses. "Take it from me. I am not physically strong, but when I had my magic, I could reduce a man to dust with a snap of my fingers."

The idea should terrify; it *does* terrify. But it inspires me too. "How do I do it?" I ask.

Qayn has taken on a jackal's visage again, dangerous and sly. "Remember what I said last night? You don't need to know how. You only need to *feel.*" He gestures at the dagger. "Learn to control your weapon with your magic—and then strike with your heart. Who knows? Perhaps one day you won't even need a weapon for you to deal a crushing blow."

Every day after that, I get through my dagger drills and sword-work as efficiently as possible so that I can focus on my magic. Over and over, I throw my dagger and halt it midair. The time it stays suspended increases until I'm able to hold it still for as long as I want.

"Now move as if you still wield it," Qayn calls to me from where he sits on the gangway with Atheer and Skerric.

I go with his instruction even though it feels odd to swing my arms as if I'm holding an invisible weapon. But it works. The dagger slashes when I slash, it jabs when I jab. And with more practice, I learn to stab without moving my arms at all.

"How about swabbing the decks at the same time?" Muhab suggests when he finds me leaning against the railing while my dagger carves a smiling face in the side of a barrel.

Next to me, Qayn's eyes light up. "*Brilliant* idea, Muhab. But let's make it a little more interesting."

Somehow I let myself be talked into swabbing the decks while trying to magically wield a sword in a duel against Muhab and his scimitar. It's nearly impossible, even with Atheer regularly reminding me to "concentrate!" I'm either mopping or fighting, but if I try to do both at the same time, I'm knocking the bucket over and my sword is floating in circles around the deck as if it's lost. This is all to the boisterous amusement of the gathered sailors, who take to betting on the outcome of each duel. After more than a dozen of them, my sword parries Muhab's scimitar with a vibrant *shing!* and comes to rest against his throat, while I'm coolly mopping the planks. The bosun drops his scimitar, exclaiming, "I think you've got it!"

In the wake of my victory, I feel powerful. But like the magic that inevitably fades from my veins by day's end, so does my confidence. When I fall asleep in my bunk that night, the dread I first met in Brooma slithers up from the shadows to suffocate me.

I sit with Qayn on the bow at dawn the next day.

"You had another nightmare," he says, reaching into the pouch of dates between us.

Amira was captured in it, taken away screaming for help I couldn't give. Atheer trundled off, bleeding under that shroud, needing aid I couldn't offer.

"You felt powerless in Brooma."

"I feel powerless now." I focus on the date under my thumb, pressing its ridges and scraping its lustrous skin. "I'm learning more about my magic than ever before, but I'm still afraid it won't be enough to save anyone."

Qayn doesn't say anything, not even to comfort me, and I appreciate that more. He understands the senselessness of making promises against a future still discovering itself. But after a moment, he does look at me. "You grieve for Taha."

My nail punctures the date's flesh. Taha was in the nightmare too, weeping over Reza's body as the soldiers closed around him in an endless loop. There and gone again.

"Seeing him so distressed was like witnessing something unconquerable shatter into pieces," I admit. "I worry about him, even after all he did to me. He watched his cousin die and he was mindmelded with Sinan when the falcon was killed too. I can't fathom what it must be like inside his head now. And this isn't because of feelings I held for him—"

"Even if it were," Qayn interrupts gently, "that doesn't change the truth. What happened to him was unjust."

Again, Qayn doesn't come to my aid with uplifting wisdom. He interlocks his fingers with mine, and that's enough.

We sail into the black waters of the Harrowen Channel on the eighth day. The air is cold and thin, sketched with four-masted warships. Watching them glide along, I realize that my identity was almost dismantled when I went to Alqibah. What will happen to me when I confront Darkcliff's gilded streets and grand dwellings, its inhabitants relishing the wealth of pillaged lands, including mine? The thought plagues me every hour after.

That night, I dream I'm in Qayn's palace.

"This way, Imani," he whispers out of sight.

I follow his shadow down winding staircases and across grand halls to a long room with plain stone walls and an unadorned floor. Empty but for him, standing in its center, and me, crossing the space toward him.

"What is this place?" I ask.

"Whatever I want it to be."

With a sweep of his hand, he fills the room with soil, grass, and roses that bud and bloom in a cluster of heartbeats. I turn on the spot as the ceiling vaults wide and blue and a sweet breeze rolls over me. I keep turning; the roses shrink, the land folds back like a rug being put away, and in its place rise mountains, shuddering the earth as they strive for a night sky pinpricked by twinkling lights. I stare, agape, at the waterfall cascading over cliffs on my left; at the cool water rushing around my ankles in a shallow stream surrounded by date palms. I glance over my shoulder at a pride of lions ambling along the pink sash of sunset. I squint against a bright light that fades to a soft glow, and when I open my eyes, I'm back in the plain room with Qayn.

"Is this your imagination?" I ask.

"I suppose you could call it that. This is where I come to practice my magic so that I don't forget how to use it."

I exhale. "I doubt you're at any risk of that. They were magnificent illusions."

Qayn raises a brow. I respond with a frown. "You were practicing illusion magic, weren't you? Even if you were powerful enough to raise mountains and fashion rivers, djinn aren't exempt from the Law of Adjustment. You can't raise mountains and fashion rivers unless you're flattening an existing mountain and draining an existing river."

Qayn's steady gaze doesn't waver. He's waiting for me to comprehend something I can't. I have to laugh out of incredulity.

"Qayn, I *know* that you built the First City, but there's a significant difference between building a city and creating a mountain from nothing."

"Is there?" he asks, cocking his head.

I squint at him. "Are you taunting me right now?"

"No."

"But the First City was something you made out of blocks of stone that already existed. A mountain is the stone itself. How can you create stone from nothing?"

"By understanding that there is no such thing as 'nothing' and by knowing what stone is made of. You can too." He steps back and gestures at the space between us. A suspended sheet of glass appears. "What is glass made of?"

I study it for a trick, but it's unblemished, like him. "Sand," I answer slowly.

He snaps his fingers. The sheet drops to the floor and lands as a golden pile of sand. "Sand sorcerers can manipulate glass, can't they?"

I gawk at the faintly sparkling mound. "A few. . . . It's a rare talent."

"Because of the Law of Essences." He notices my astonishment and tuts. "I've been trapped in the Sahir for a millennium. I learned a thing or two about your people's magic in that time."

"Yes, but the Law of Essences is complex magical philosophy." I recall what I learned from Auntie Aziza before the subject was briefly touched upon again with the Order. "Using your example: glass is made of sand, sand is made of quartz, quartz is composed of smaller crystals. Those smaller crystals may appear elsewhere in other objects, but for the purpose of magical affinities, their composition doesn't make the objects the same. One sorcerer can manipulate sand; another can manipulate precious stones. Both materials have quartz and crystals in them, but they're different."

Qayn circles me. "Why are they different?"

"I thought you knew the Law," I say, watching him.

"Humor me."

"Their essences aren't the same. A horse and a falcon are both creatures of flesh and bone, but you would hardly consider them similar. They embody different essences. That's how affinities work." I paraphrase a passage from a tome that Auntie lent me to study: "What we now call the Law of Essences is codified experiential knowledge to help new sorcerers understand the limits of their magic."

Qayn stops shoulder to shoulder beside me, though we face opposite directions. "What a very boring, long-winded way of saying that because nobody has done it before, it must be impossible. Or so you've been told."

"No, it *is* impossible. Cautionary tales are passed around the Order all the time about once-brilliant sorcerers who are now rambling shadows of themselves because they tried to violate the Law. It's a dangerous path to venture down. Sorcerers begin seeing connections where there are none."

"But everything *is* connected. Everything is one and the same." He pulls the dagger off my thigh and holds it up. "This blade is made of iron. So are you."

I go cross-eyed looking at it. "I am?"

"Yes, and I'm not talking about your cold heart." He smirks. "I mean there is iron in your flesh and blood. But what is iron made of? What is the mountain made of? *Matter.*" He returns my dagger to its sheath. "Matter is the essence of everything, salvaged from one form and gifted to another in an eternal cycle, never to be destroyed. And misra is—"

"A key?" I suggest.

He nods. "So far, your people have used that key to access the magic that you call affinities. Speaking of the misra tree, consider this example." He floats his hand up, palm facing the ceiling. A flawless rendition of the magical tree sprouts from a patch of soil in front of us. Qayn points at the shadows of its branches on the stone. "The shadows are affinities. The tree is the magic that I speak of. Do you know the story of the sightless men and the elephant?"

"Vaguely. I think it was in a collection of parables that my mother bound and gifted to Amira a few years ago."

Qayn waves his hand; the misra tree scatters to twigs. Shadows in the shapes of people assemble where it was and begin miming his narration.

"A group of men encounter an elephant in the night. As none of them are familiar with an elephant's form, each man feels a different part of the elephant's body and proceeds to describe the animal based on his partial knowledge. The man who feels the trunk believes the elephant is a waterspout. The man who feels a leg disagrees; he's adamant that the elephant is a pillar. The man who feels the elephant's ear claims it is a fan; another who feels the tip of the tail declares the elephant is a brush. Each man believes the others are lying, and they come to blows."

I watch the shadows of the slain men fall. "Each of them proclaims their limited, individual experience to be absolute truth, and they refuse to accept that the experiences of others can also be true."

He half smiles. "Sound familiar to an institution we know?"

"Unfortunately," I mumble as the shadows go away too. "But that's not why you've told me this story. You're comparing the sightless men to my people and our approach to magic. We've experienced affinities, so we proclaim them as the sum of magic."

He gives a shallow bow. "You argue that it's impossible, yet what I speak of is the same magic that governs the practice of animancy, which permits an affinity to behave in a manner far outside the scope of your Order's understanding. They even admit that such behavior is possible, albeit exceptional, due to the 'intrusion of the soul.'"

"There's no better explanation," I say, shrugging. "The soul is one of the Great Spirit's Mysteries."

"It's not a mystery, Imani. The soul knows that, like all magical laws, the Law of Essences is a mortal contrivance."

I glide my eyes across his face. "How does it know?"

"By design. How does a raindrop know the sea? Animancy is a type of practice that even your auntie attempts to master, and as far as I'm aware, she hasn't become a rambling shadow of herself."

I consider him intently. "You discuss magical philosophy with the same degree of experience and understanding as she does, and she's Master of the Misra. How do you have this knowledge?"

He slides his hands in his pockets, looking off at something. "I've been around for some time and had many interesting encounters."

I huff. "An insightful answer, as ever, but not to the question that started this: How can I raise a mountain without flattening an existing one first?"

His black eyes return to me, glittering. "By making your affinity for matter itself."

"*What?* No." I shake my head. "Qayn, that's impossible. You've fundamentally misunderstood something—"

"I haven't—"

"If my affinity were for matter, I'd practically be as powerful as the Great Spirit itself!" I exclaim.

He grins, triumphant. "Yes, Imani. You would be."

Something immense and incredible is born between us right then. He's about to speak again when a low bellow quavers down the palace halls.

"Something's happened," I whisper.

I sit up in my bunk on the *Prize.* It's daytime, and Qayn is already peering out of a porthole. I scramble over to him. "What is it?"

He stands back for me to look. "We've arrived."

# 26

# IMANI

WE EMERGE ABOVEDECK TO FIND THE SHIP WITH bare masts, bobbing at the busy mouth of a river between towering, rugged cliffs. Imposing black stone watchtowers dot their peaks, and a blocky settlement protrudes like a sickly gray growth at the foot of the precipice on our left. Vessels sail in and out of the river mouth, but others are queued as we are, waiting for something. And stationed nearby are several long, low, lithe ships with curving prows fashioned into serpents' heads. From their strategic positioning around the river's entrance, even the menacing scarlet of their sails, I sense they're guard ships.

We join Atheer and Farida at the helm, the captain glassing the water. I point at the settlement.

"Is *that* the capital of Harrowland?"

"Oh, Imani, you must be joking," says Skerric, coming up the gangway in dark hose, black breeches, and a black doublet embroidered with silver and slashed in the bodice to reveal a maroon silk undershirt; he's slung a similarly embroidered black cape over the outfit and topped it off with a black wide-brimmed hat sporting a single white feather. Clearly, he's dressed for a homecoming.

"Darkcliff is down the River Waden," he informs us. "We require permission and a pilot to reach it." He nods at the single-masted boat sailing toward us from the settlement. "The pilot will arrive with a reeve—an officer of the king. He decides whether or not we pass. Let me deal with him."

"He's all yours. Lower the ladder!" Farida calls, shutting the spyglass.

She descends the gangway with Skerric, Makeen, and Muhab. The sailboat slows its approach, and its sail is reefed. I inch to the taffrail to peer at the Harrowlander men inside. The sour reeve is easy to identify among the soldiers, marked by the gold-clasped leather pouch clutched in his arms, and his austere yet obviously expensive clothing. His reedy frame is cloaked in a rigid, ankle-length brown coat trimmed with gilt thread, and he wears a maroon hood over his stringy silver hair, similarly trimmed, with a long tail that falls between his shoulders. He stands at the bow, impatiently staring up at the *Prize.*

"Who is your captain?" he shouts.

"I am!" The crew parts for Farida, her muscular arms folded across her chest. "Greetings."

The reeve wrinkles his long nose. "You? But you're a woman."

"And I am the captain here," she reiterates.

The reeve mutters to his men out of the corner of his mouth. The boat pulls alongside us under oars, and the reeve climbs the rope ladder, followed by two soldiers and a rougher man about Baba's age. Unlike the reeve's rich garments, the pilot's outfit is a dull-russet wool version of Skerric's that looks years away from being new.

"I am Reeve Ottiwell. This is one of my pilots, Rikald," says the reeve.

"Welcome aboard," says Farida. She nods to the pair, but only the pilot returns the gesture.

Skerric makes his way over to them, and upon seeing the nobleman, Ottiwell exhales in overstated relief. They huddle away from the crew and quietly converse. After a minute, the reeve scowls. The soldiers are displeased too, but Skerric calmly continues his end of the discussion, and whatever it is, Ottiwell reluctantly relents. After a brief inspection of the hold, Farida hands him a pouch in exchange for a scroll. He curtly nods at Rikald and leaves without so much as glancing at Skerric. Farida guides Rikald up the gangway past us to the helm. The stoic man speaks slowly, gesturing at the masts, and Farida relays his instructions to the crew below. Ropes sing, canvas rustles, and the ship starts for the mouth of the River Waden. Skerric turns and smiles up at us. We've secured our permission.

With Rikald skillfully directing us down the sinuous river, I perch at the bow to observe our passage into Harrowland. There are only cliffs at first: gray and serrated, crests dusted deep green, clefts haunted by clouds of ravens and bulbous white seabirds. The longer I study the cliffs, the more I decipher shapes carved into their grim stone. Unfeeling eyes; wolves and lightning bolts; symbols composed of straight lines and hard angles. The face of a bearded man—I wonder if I'm imagining it until our ship curls around a bend and a statue materializes through the thin mist on the cliffs above: the same bearded man but seated atop a stag with antlers as sturdy as boughs. Statues and carvings of the man appear elsewhere along the river. Sometimes he rides the stag and bears a scepter; in other depictions, he's a combination of man and beast. He's always accompanied by hounds, wolves, and ravens; in one portrayal, he rears on his hind legs, scepter held high as he directs his flock to attack a vaguely manlike monster wreathed in smoke. But regardless of what fantastic pursuit this man is engaged in, it always feels as if he's coldly staring down at the ships floating along the Waden.

"Who is he?" I ask Qayn, beside me.

"Staggnir. Father and Ever-King of the Harrowlander people."

"He's terrifying."

"That he is," Qayn agrees.

Between the ubiquitous depictions of Staggnir are watchtowers and steepled buildings from which tumble the echoes of bells. The farther along the Waden we go, the more structures that crop up. Lone buildings become settlements comprised of small square windows, gabled roofs, and clustered chimneys exhaling woolly smoke, the structures fabricated from dark wood, black stone, and unadorned iron, their stark appearance softened slightly by the presence of brown-and-maroon banners. Some settlements roost precariously on the clifftops, to be buffeted by merciless winds; but most huddle at the water's edge in the steadfast shelter of the crags. Down here, weather-beaten piers connect towns to the river scattered with slender, leaf-shaped fishing boats that twist and turn over the surface, trailing nets and the hoarse bellows of men in their rippling wakes. Occasionally the settlements above and below are united by paths zigzagging up cliff faces and rock landings to which squat buildings daringly cling.

The settlements eventually join, one to the other, like linked hands, and traffic intensifies on the Waden. Fishing boats compete fiercely with tall merchant ships and barges ferrying produce and livestock—people too, mostly women, children, and old men, all pale and weary, heads shielded under flat caps and blue bonnets; they bunch in shivering knots under the mast or balance amidst the cargo. Now and again, a ship stands above the rest, generously crewed, its stern elaborately wrought and its prow boasting an ornate figurehead of a serpent or a swan. The voyagers on board are dressed in richly colored outfits that are heavy, brocaded, and overly worked with lace, buttons, slashes, and trimmings, their heads supporting wide-brimmed feathered hats, often over masses of curls too thick and lifeless to be real hair.

By afternoon, the river widens and the distant banks are connected by a stone bridge. We enter a shallow harbor where something curious has happened to the cliffs. It's as if an enormous boulder once fell upon them from the skies and in tumbling down, carved out a recess, such that the land appears stacked in two uneven steps. A waterfall chutes from the top step, and around it, the people have erected the capital of Harrowland, Darkcliff.

The dense, smoggy city sprouts as a tight cluster of piers at the water's edge and climbs the mild slope around a winding canal in a tangle of bridges and pointy-roofed rows that crowd to the cliff walls on all three sides. Set against the distant back wall are towers that somehow connect the lower half of the city with the plateau high above; there, majestic buildings stand free of the pollution, their architecture typified by dramatic spires, pointed arches, and massive cylindrical pillars, the sunlight mirroring in the stained glass of their many lancet windows. Most imposing of all is the walled, black stone castle that hangs over the lower city from a rocky outcrop where it's been built at the base of a mountain.

But the city below it doesn't look anything like the land of gilded streets and grand dwellings that I imagined, and it is so crowded that I can scarcely make out where one structure ends and another begins. Everything appears without dimension, as if someone has painted the city onto the stone and not bothered with perspective, and even the squawking seagulls must have paper wings and be suspended by string.

The crew take in the canvas, and the *Prize* glides into port. We pass a fish market teeming with customers, harried fishermen banging their boats against the dock in a rush to offload their fresh catch, and tough, dagger-wielding old men cutting up fish in open stalls, the guts and refuse tossed onto stinking piles being swept into the sea by scruffy boys contending with greedy-eyed gulls. Gallows prominently line the docks not far from the market, and their hanging corpses are a grim warning of how crime is punished in Darkcliff.

Our ship moors in a crowded nook on the city's edge; Rikald bids us farewell and disappears in a foul-smelling haze of soot, fish guts, decay and sewage. Atheer and I collect our bags and meet Skerric by the bridge to the pier.

"The reeve didn't seem happy about whatever you told him," I say.

"That I'm a myddilman and you're my challengers." Skerric smirks. "No, he wasn't happy, and yet here we are: Darkcliff, in all its glory." He gestures at the pier. "Shall we?"

I sling my bag onto my shoulders. "Lead on."

# 27

# TAHA

SER ULRIC FETCHES TAHA FROM HIS APARTMENT days later.

"I've thought of something that'll cheer you up, boy," he says as they're walking through the Sanctuary's halls. Alone this time; even Whitmund has been tucked out of sight somewhere.

"Why would I need cheering up?"

"Because you look like tenderized steak." Ulric nods at the green silk ribbons wrapping the pillars at the head of the hall. "Have you been told about the Holy Season yet? You must wonder with the decorations. They mark De Wilde Hunten. Only happens once every seven years. His Majesty hosts a tournament between the Empire's best warriors and throws a feast for everyone afterward. People celebrate in the streets and village squares, peasants and nobles alike: drunk, fat, and happy. You'd enjoy it."

"You could if you weren't here, occupying my home."

Ulric flicks Taha's ear. "You're too sour, boy. I could leave you out overnight coated in honey and even pests would refuse you."

They pass the open door of a large office. Officials are clustered around a table inside, and at least three possess the specialized magical affinity for ink. They're jotting notes on parchment without even picking up quills. In fact, most of the Harrowlanders that Taha sees during their walk are using magic. On the way out of the Sanctuary, several soldiers use wood affinities to hover boxes inside. On the path through the eastern gardens, soldiers play dice in the shadow of a scholar's statue; the soldier with the fire affinity lights the others' smoking pipes, and the soldier with the silver affinity levitates the gambled coins in amusing patterns. They're all swilling from cups and flasks of misra tea, every single one. Taha wonders whether Ser Ulric sought help from the Order for his obsession, but he doesn't care enough to ask.

It's the Marshal who insists on conversation. "I'll tell you what's a shame. It's blasphemy to sponsor warriors from other lands for the Hunten. If it weren't, and I were rich, I'd have sponsored you. I'd wager you could wrestle a bear and win, you've that tenacity about you." He pauses to laugh, crow's feet creasing the skin around his eyes. "Don't go telling His Majesty I said that, eh? His fyghtors have won two Hunten in a row, and he's assured an easy third victory."

"What do you want from me, Marshal?" Taha asks bluntly.

Ulric nods at the soldiers guarding the gates to the barracks. They draw them open on a covered passageway leading into the training quadrangle, starkly empty where it used to be busy with Shields at all hours of the day. There is one Shield being escorted to Abishemu Hall by two soldiers.

"Captain Ramiz," Taha murmurs.

Ulric glances at the man disappearing inside the building. "Aye, His Majesty wants the veteran to start training some of ours like your Shields. The monster attacks are becoming a problem."

Taha wants to know more, but it's paramount he check his surroundings first for what new torment is about to be inflicted upon him. As soon as he realizes that Ulric is leading him to the archery range, he digs his heels into the grit.

"What's the bloody matter with you?" Ulric grunts, forcing him on.

"Why are we here?" Taha demands. The range is one of the happiest places in his memories. Often he felt more at home here than in his actual home. He can't have it transformed into a place of pain. It'd be too much taken from him.

Ulric stops at the range's edge and unshackles him. "Told you, I thought of something to cheer you up." He places the manacles on a nearby bench and returns holding Taha's recurve bow and quiver. He holds them out, but Taha just stares at them as if the Marshal is offering a snake and a scorpion.

Ulric waves the bow. "Take it; it's yours. Have a go at the range, like old times."

"Why?" Taha sheds enough fear to snatch the bow and quiver and step away. "What if I put an arrow through your temple, huh?"

Ulric sighs. It's a moment before he finds a quiet voice. "I had a father like yours. Never saw the worth in anything I did. Beat me worse than the servant boys over the smallest mistakes. 'Was making you a man,' he'd say later. I became a knight at seventeen, younger than any other man in my house. Wasn't enough for Atta. 'That was my doing,' he said after the ceremony. 'You'd have become a priest like your cousin if I hadn't made you strong.' " Ulric pauses to ponder something in the distance. Nothing, really; he's looking but not seeing. "Later, in my travels with His Majesty along the Spice Road, I came across a master weaponsmith who had crafted a sword as thin as one of your eyelashes. This thing was so deadly it could slice through steel like it was butter. But if the sword struck at the wrong angle, just once, the blade would shatter." Ulric moves a hand from his chest to Taha's. "Men like us, raised by men like our fathers, we're strong like that sword." He nods at the targets. "Have a go. Or put an arrow in me if you'd rather that. I probably deserve it after the beating I gave you, and Staggnir knows I'm due a good rest." He goes and sits on the bench.

Taha clenches his teeth so hard his temples smart, but he uses the pain to distract himself from the heavy ache of tears pressing against his eyes. He slips the quiver onto his back and takes his bow to the range. Nocks, breathes evenly, and shoots. And he never misses. Ser Ulric whistles after some arrows, curses affectionately after the unbelievable ones. "You're one of the best damned archers I've seen," he calls out at one point.

Eventually he jumps off the bench, shouting, "Think fast, boy!" and summons rings of fire around the range. Grinning, Taha fires an arrow through the ring behind him, then sprints and hops onto one of the divider posts and shoots an arrow through the ring hovering high in the air over the range. Ulric rumbles laughter, trying to best him; he fashions rings that race to close, others that float along prompting Taha to chase them. He behaves like a man with some kindness left, not like the man who burned the coach outside Bis-Amna.

He tires first, sweaty and wheezing. "Don't like stopping you," he says, confiscating the bow, "but some days I feel as old as gnawed dog bones."

Taha struggles against his disappointment. He wants to keep going until sunset, as he used to do with his father. *Years ago,* he thinks sadly, when Bayek had some kindness left in him too.

Ulric replaces the manacles and walks him back to the Sanctuary, drinking from a flask of misra tea on the way.

"Did you see someone from the Order?" Taha asks.

Ulric grunts in the negative, thumbing the flask closed. "Not had the time, have I?"

Taha doesn't think time has anything to do with it. Closer to the apartment, Ulric returns to better spirits. "Don't lie now. Did that cheer you up or didn't it?"

Taha reluctantly nods. "Thank you, Marshal."

That pleases him. "Good," he says quietly with a small smile. "Good to hear." He tasks the soldiers standing guard with Taha and goes off down the hallway, whistling.

A soldier removes his manacles and opens the apartment door, and as Taha is walking through, another says, "You have a visitor."

He slows down, bracing for an attack, but he's already inside, standing face to face with Fey.

"Hello again, Taha."

The door shuts behind him. He clenches his fists, not to deny himself an assault but to stop them from trembling. What's wrong with him? He's become too soft.

"Aren't you ashamed of yourself?" he says quietly.

He expects a scathing reply served up with a smirk, but Fey is restrained. "I had no choice but to help Glaedric."

Taha was never fond of Fey, despite her being a highly capable sorcerer and Shield. He'd tell himself it was because her shrill laughter and relentless sarcasm were annoying. Deep down, he knows he was just afraid that she was taking Reza away. Still, he never perceived her as someone who'd betray their people.

"You had a choice to die instead," he says.

Sighing, she finds a path through the wreckage of toppled

furniture and sits on the lounge. "After I was captured, I was taken to a prison cell in Bashtal. The soldiers wanted to hang me the very next day. I tried to use my affinity to escape; an officer at the station saw me. He'd been warned to keep a lookout for magic, so he sent me straight to the king in Taeel-Sa. I arrived the morning after you sank Glaedric's ship." She turns a shard of mirror between her fingers. "What a state that man was in, as furious as a viper. He already knew so much about the Sahir that he said he would kill me where I stood if I didn't offer him any valuable information. I learned then that he'd held Atheer captive for months and tortured answers out of him before you broke him out. Call me a hypocrite, a coward, a traitor—I suppose I'm all of them. . . . I must've felt a fraction of the fear and pain that Atheer endured, but it was enough to make me crumble. I told Glaedric whatever he wanted to know. I told him about our group, who we are, how we were sent to retrieve Atheer. He fixated on you—he hadn't seen you the night before, but he had seen Sinan setting the ships on fire and suspected that a sorcerer was responsible. You almost got his pregnant wife killed. Great Spirit, Taha," she whispers, as if she fears that Glaedric is in the next room. "If you'd heard how he spoke about you, you'd never sleep without a blade again. He was planning to capture you and torture you for as long as you could withstand it. But I told him who your father is and convinced him you're more valuable alive. It seems he still agrees."

Taha goes to the balcony door, his guts twisting. After a very long moment, he says, "I stopped Reza from going after you in Bashtal. I felt we had no time to spare because of the risk Atheer posed to our people."

"It was the right decision, though I know it wouldn't have been easy to make," she says.

Taha watches the songbirds on the balustrade. "It meant nothing in the end. The Sahir was set to fall months before we arrived. If I'd have stopped to save you instead, things might've turned out differently. Better somehow."

She joins him at the door. "We have magic, but nobody can divine the future, Taha. You did the best that you could with the circumstances handed to you. I wish I could say that I did the same."

He thinks of the settlements he helped the Vanguard occupy, the people he might've saved if he had gotten his warning out. He searches for bitterness at himself and her, but he finds only sadness.

"I shouldn't have called you a traitor, Fey," he says. "None of us know the decisions we'll make in a situation until we're there and it's happening to us. You're not a hypocrite, or a coward. You're a survivor, and there's a good chance that if you hadn't convinced Glaedric of my value, I'd be dead."

Her face folds; tears well in her eyes in the time it takes him to inhale. "But Reza didn't survive, did he?"

Taha's throat heaves. Habit tells him to find distraction in the songbirds again, but he can't do it. His cousin's death is something he should never look away from. If he does, he might forget things. The little details. That Reza turned back first for Amira. That he was manipulating stones to throw, hoping to create a diversion to allow Imani to save her sister, before Blaedwyn killed him. That he had enough strength in his last moments not to lament his misfortune but to urge Taha to a happiness he'd never get the chance to find for himself. Reza's ashes were scattered in the Bay—there is no burial wall with his story of valor engraved by their clan. His story is engraved on Taha's memory, in his heart and soul. He can't let it be forgotten.

He tells it to Fey and spares no details. With every word he utters, her grief expands. She sobs and wails, and at the end, slumps on the rug.

"I wish I'd told him that I loved him one last time," she whispers. "Wish I'd heard just one more joke."

Taha doesn't know how to alleviate her pain. "I'm sorry" is all he can say, kneeling beside her.

After a moment's thought, she hugs him. "Me too, Taha."

They part but stay kneeling by the balcony door, watching the songbirds. Soon a soldier enters and tells Fey to leave, and then Taha is alone again with the ghosts of his past.

# 28

# IMANI

ATHEER, FARIDA, QAYN, AND I FOLLOW SKERRIC to the docks. Only a few Harrowlanders greet us, all with stiff nods. The rest are either suspicious of us as foreigners in their city, or displeased with our presence, glaring at us as we pass. Some openly scowl, and one man even spits at our feet. I can only think that if the Harrowlanders were treated as poorly in Alqibah, the perpetrators would be promptly flogged.

The chaotic docks consist of rows of warehouses worked by wiry old men, gnarled as if hewn from the cliffs, and skinny, greasy-haired boys hardly touching thirteen, swimming in the slouchy, elbow-patched coats of absent fathers and missing older brothers. The smoking pipes they keep dangling from their grimacing mouths likely belong to older relatives too. Spiced tobaccos similar to those in Alqibah seem popular here, and I assume it's to mask the water's putrid scent.

"Doesn't that bother anyone, Skerric?" I ask, pointing at the sludgy effluent gushing from a drain directly into the harbor.

He gives me a funny look. "Anyone with a sense of smell,

Imani. But this is an improvement. Before Bertric, Glaedric's father, ordered the construction of sidewalks and a new sewer system, there were no closed drains at all. Whenever the Cliff's runoff was heavy, the drains would overflow. You can imagine what that was like."

I wish I couldn't. "What do you mean, 'the Cliff'?"

He nods at the city's top step and its splendid halls. "The Cliff." He drops his gaze to the cramped sprawl before us. "The Dark."

"Ah." I nod at the Cliff too. "How do you reach it?"

"Only nobles are freely permitted up there. We travel to and from it by lift." He mimics a pulling motion, one hand over the other, but doesn't elaborate.

Closer to the center of the docks, the piers are wide and well maintained, and the city guards make their first appearance. Armed with swords, the patrolling men wear long gray coats with dark leather fastenings, thick leather gloves and boots, and steel-pot helms that disguise their faces, which are almost always turned to the water. Grand ships are moored out on the harbor, their wealthy passengers and piles of luggage ferried to shore by knobby-wristed boys operating oar-powered barges. Merchant ships are also lightened of their loads here under the guards' watch. Much of the cargo seems to have come from the occupied lands along the Spice Road: richly dyed textiles and rugs; spices, tea, tobacco, and grains; even animals, including horses, colorful birds, and small, strange bears howling in cages. In return, the merchant ships are loaded with the products of Harrowland: soap, woven goods, leather- and ironware, just from what I see. But some of the crates are loaded into wagons and trundled off to the bridge that connects this bank of the Waden to the other.

"Where does the bridge lead?" I ask Skerric.

"The headquarters and ship yards of His Majesty's Armed Forces."

Meaning those wagons are probably carrying critical supplies destined for the soldiers in Alqibah and the Sahir, among other places. Darkcliff really is the beating heart of Glaedric's aggression.

We leave the docks and enter what Skerric calls "Lift Street," a spacious cobblestone thoroughfare running alongside the canal. The handsome frontages of its many shops bear similar decorations to those in Alqibah, but a few have also been painted with imagery promoting De Wilde Hunten: in one mural, a powerful stag with golden antlers stands on the peak of a hill against a shining sun while, silhouetted below, four fighters are locked in battle.

The street is dominated by luxurious carriages, some traveling to the docks, others to the cliff wall. The towers fixed against the wall are lined with windows, revealing platforms rising and descending the shafts within. *Lifts.* I want to look longer to find the mechanism that propels them, but Skerric leads us through a gate onto a bridge suspended over the canal. Scupper-like drainage holes pepper the stone of the canal on either side, permitting waste to seep in.

"Do watch your step from here on," he mysteriously counsels at the end of the bridge.

I shadow him onto the shoulder of a narrow street, busy with plain carriages and Harrowlanders navigating its rutted cobblestones, many of them clinking along in curious sandals with tall, wedged soles made from wood, worn *over* another pair of leather or fabric shoes.

"They're called pattens," Skerric says, noticing my interest in them. He gestures us across the street through a gap in the traffic.

I make to follow him and query the purpose of the outer shoe when Qayn says, "Careful," stopping me an inch from ankle-deep sludge trickling through a runnel carved into the cobblestone. I believe I have my answer: the purpose of pattens is hygiene, not fashion.

I exhale in relief, giving Qayn a nod. "Thank you."

"I did tell you to watch your step," Skerric says over his shoulder.

We hop over the waste and continue up the opposite side of the street. In glaring contrast to Qalia, which is perfumed by incense trees magically maintained by horticulturalists from the Order, Darkcliff *stinks.* One street of candle and soap shops all but vanishes in a nauseating miasma of animal fat that paints the walls with a glistening sheen. Past the stinking leather tanneries a few streets over, it's as if we've stepped into an open carcass. The shops here are butcheries, evidenced by the meat hanging from hooks and draped on shelves in the shade of the eaves. The street is so narrow in places that I can open my arms and touch both sides at once, the constriction made worse by the butcheries with their wood-framed upper floors jettying over us by several feet. The clustered architecture does an excellent job of trapping the scent of blood and offal rising like steam off the gory surplus of gizzards being dumped into the runnels by red-handed boys who, as soon as their ghastly duty is done, scurry back inside to collect more. Crowds of customers haggle with the butchers over their chosen cuts; others collect bagged orders and clamber back into carriages waiting at the top and bottom of the street, as it's too tight to accommodate them. Everyone is seemingly accustomed to the conditions surrounding them.

And what filthy conditions they are. Though Skerric mentioned a new sewer system, construction on it seems to have been halted midway. Some streets do indeed have sidewalks, but often only one side has been completed. Most of the drains remain open, if not partially covered, while the runnels are generally too shallow to accommodate the volume of waste, forcing it to leach across streets already polluted with horse dung and settle in silty piles and opalescent puddles, only to be disturbed by carriage wheels, street sweepers and, to my total horror, barefoot children. Compounding Darkcliff's sanitation problem is the uneven slope upon which the lower city has been built—in one spot where the slope is steep, and gravity helps move the tide of sewage toward the canal, we must ascend a damp, unlit stairwell burrowed tightly between buildings in order to reach the next street farther up, dodging the vile-smelling water dribbling down the stairs and pooling in the cracks of the cobblestones below. It quickly becomes apparent that if you want a favorable place to settle in Darkcliff, you must go up.

Skerric notices me staring in disgust at an open drain. He slows beside me and Qayn and speaks in a low voice.

"As you can probably tell, Glaedric isn't as enthusiastic about the new sewer system as his father was. His Majesty's passion lies *elsewhere.*" Skerric directs our attention to a slogan painted on an opposite wall: " 'The Empire's advance abroad will ensure glory and plenty at home!' You'll appreciate the illustration for the people who can't read."

It depicts a soldier in silhouette bearing the Empire's flag and staring out at a sandy expanse; behind him is a slice of Darkcliff with clean streets and smiling, well-dressed, well-fed people. Skerric's mockery of the propaganda intrigues me, since little about the Dark impacts him as a nobleman. Yet much like his skill on the rigging, the ease with which he navigates the city's labyrinth of pin-thin streets belies his station in society.

"I assume you reside on the Cliff," I say, eyeing him.

He pulls his hood lower. "I keep a residence there, yes. But we won't be staying in it."

"Why not?"

We slow on a long, crowded street with views of the harbor. On the sidewalk outside the three- and four-story terraced housing, women scrub clothes in tubs of gray water and hang the dripping fabric over fences while simultaneously keeping watch over their infants cooing in baskets nearby and the group of children rolling an old carriage wheel down the cobblestones past some drunken old men smoking and spitting in the runnels. There are no guards among them, and they don't seem to mind that we're here.

"It would be sensible to avoid attracting the attention of my nosy neighbors," says Skerric. "Nobody can legally interfere with us, but they can certainly try."

"What about an inn on the Cliff, then?" I ask, still hopeful.

He shakes his head. "One look at you and the innkeepers will suddenly find themselves booked up, if you know what I mean."

I return a disappointed nod. I was secretly looking forward to seeing how a Harrowlander lord lives, but I suppose I'll be seeing inside the royal citadel soon enough.

Skerric stops us outside a building with cracked white walls, thatched roofs, and a few small, shuttered windows. Despite its ragged appearance, the building bears an elegant name: THE SWAN OF SHOREHILL—and if I blur my eyes, I can make out its namesake in the patches of paint still clinging to the sign.

Skerric nods at it. "I've heard that the lodgings are cheap and the innkeeper is very hospitable. You won't have to worry about guards snooping around either—this street is technically outside the city's administrative jurisdiction."

He goes first into a warm, dark room tinged orange by a crackling hearth. Careworn men nurse mugs at a long table, gazing blearily at our entrance. The oldest stands, pointing a crooked finger at us.

"The Swan isn't open to *fremde.*"

"It's open to challengers for the Hunten," Skerric counters smartly.

The old man concedes a phlegmy, disapproving "Suppose so." But he does sit back down, and the others at the table resume their conversations.

"What does *fremde* mean?" I whisper to Skerric on our way to the desk.

"It's an unfriendly word for foreigners in Old Harrowtongue," he answers. "Prepare to hear it a lot, but don't worry. We have a saying in this city: 'Even the mite is mighty in the season of the Hunten.'"

# 29

# IMANI

TO MY SURPRISED RELIEF, MY SMALL RENTED ROOM smells agreeably of hay, linen, and wine, and for an extra fee, the innkeeper supplies us with clean water that's been collected from a conduit on the Cliff. Given that dusk is near, Skerric advises us to rest for the night and departs. After a dinner of fish-and-vegetable soup, we retire to our rooms, and I'm so exhausted from training and relieved to rest on solid, dry ground that I fall asleep immediately.

Skerric collects us in the morning after my tea ceremony. He has a band of blue paint around his eyes, and his fingertips are stained gray—"the traditional sign of the myddilman, made using the stone of the cliffs," he explains as we're climbing into the coach he's hailed for us. Once we're seated and moving, he says to me, "Good, you wore your armor as I asked."

I adjust the scabbard holding my dagger-turned-sword. "Why did you? Have you found potential sponsors already?"

"Not yet. But that's where your armor and sword come in. I hope you're ready to put on a show for the Cliffsiders."

Our arrival at the lifts is heralded by the incessant squeak and grind of gears. We disembark in the cool shadow of the Cliff on a street lined with carriages. While Skerric pays the driver, I stare up at the towers striping the face of the dauntingly tall stone precipice. Windows reveal the lifts' complicated pulley system and the boys and young men whose backbreaking labor makes it run. Dressed in brown doublets and breeches with white hose, pairs of them work to raise passengers while four are needed to operate each cargo lift. The towers are barred from street access by fences capped in lethal arrow finials. Guards are stationed along the fence line and amassed around the wide entrance. Though the gates are open, those entering must first pass the inspection of the guardhouse, and there is no way to slip through unseen.

We join the line behind two girls in black dresses and matching bonnets. One carries a sweet-smelling cake covered by a white silk tissue; the other is laden with bags of coffee.

"A noble's servants," Skerric says in my ear.

There are many of them waiting in line with items they've presumably collected from the Dark for delivery to a noble above, and there are a few boys dressed like those down at the docks, dragging carts stacked with casks.

As we inch forward, I notice a thick tower that's separate from the rest. It's blocked off by its own fence and entered via a single door in a windowless stone façade; the number of guards protecting it outnumbers the sum of the guards watching over the rest.

"What's that?" I ask Skerric, nodding at it.

"*That* is the only way in and out of the Royal Citadel," he whispers. "Now you understand why I said you couldn't break into it."

I tilt my head back and look up at the walled castle, perched high above the city, that I noticed earlier from the *Prize.* From this angle, it's possible to see that the outcrop on which it's built is actually a peninsula unconnected to the cliff on three sides. If the lift is the only way to reach the Citadel, the snowcapped mountain behind it must be impassable. Skerric was right. It's a fortress.

At the front of the line, Skerric introduces himself to the guards as our myddilman. They look us over disdainfully but motion us through. As we gather outside a tower to wait for our lift, a white four-horse carriage arrives on the street; a baby-faced nobleman steps out in a wide-brimmed, feathered hat and a rose brocade doublet, surrounded by guards in matching ankle-length dark-rose jackets. The servants whisper excitedly, twisting in line to look at the noble.

"What is taking those *liftenboys* so bloody long," Skerric grumbles, peering up the tower shaft at the descending platform.

The nobleman leisurely taps up to the gates in heeled boots. One of his guards, a knight in plate armor, marches ahead to the guardhouse and cuts in front of the waiting line. The nobleman, meanwhile, smiles amiably at the servants curtseying and bowing to him.

"He seems famous. Who is he?" I ask Skerric.

"Doesn't matter; the lift is here."

It lowers into view, and a liftenboy with dark circles under his eyes waves us over, his workmate waiting on the wooden platform inside. We clamber onto the lift, but before the second liftenboy can reach for the crank to start it up, someone outside shouts.

"Crush me under hoof," Skerric mutters, palming his forehead, sweaty despite the chill inside the tower.

A liftenboy jogs out and returns with the guards and nobleman.

"What's going on?" Atheer whispers to Skerric, who's begun tipping his hat forward to shield his face.

"Apologies," the liftenboy waiting by the crank says to us, gesturing at the step. "You'll have to take the next lift."

We're being shooed off the platform so the famous nobleman can take our place, even though Skerric is also a nobleman, but perhaps there's some social hierarchy involved that I'm not aware of. I try to peek at the young man without making it obvious, but he's already inspecting our group. Suddenly his eyes light up, and he struts past the guards and liftenboy.

"*Riccy?* Is that really you?"

Skerric tenses. The nobleman reaches the step to the platform and gasps. "It *is* you! One day you're working these lifts; the next, you've disappeared! You've not been hiding from me, have you? You stood me up at the theater, although I can't blame you. Graubard's always been a bore; I don't know why I keep asking my father to fund his plays."

I sense Qayn dropping the wall shielding his soul from mine. I do the same and immediately hear his voice in my head: *"Working" the lifts isn't something a nobleman would do.*

I cut my eyes at Skerric. *Perhaps our nobleman isn't noble at all. It would explain why he was strong on the rigging.* He pulls ropes for a living, and we've been duped.

Skerric resembles a pomegranate wearing blue makeup and a feathered hat. He keeps his head bowed, stammering, "G-greetings, Lord Clarus. It's lovely to see you again."

"Likewise. You look well." Clarus sees us bunched around Skerric and cocks his shaped brows. "What's your business with foreigners?"

Skerric finally raises his head so that Clarus can see his face. He's hardly begun his explanation that he's a myddilman when the knight in plate armor barges into the tower and jogs up the steps.

"Is there a problem, m'lord?" He pauses beside Clarus on the scaffold. The second his eyes land on Skerric, they bug out. "Well, well," he crows. "If it isn't the former Lord Ashton Hargrave!"

*"Lord Ashton?"* Clarus floats a gloved hand to his stiff lace collar, tittering softly. "I believe you're mistaken, Ser Brunwald. This is Skerric, a commoner. He's been my regular liftenboy for years."

"He's a commoner now, certainly, but he *was* the son of the disgraced House of Hargrave before his father was hung for treason, m'lord." Brunwald juts his head forward. "Didn't I have you arrested for thieving, Ashton?"

Atheer and Farida exchange wild glances. I feel Qayn's unease marching in step with mine.

"I really must insist you're mistaken, Ser Brunwald." Clarus points at us. "Riccy is a myddilman for these challengers. Quite bold of you, Riccy, liaising with foreigners! I'd ask my father to sponsor them if he weren't such a superstitious fellow. Oh, but that means you've been traveling? On whose coin and pleasure, may I be so nosy as to ask? I might have a word with them for stealing you away from me."

Skerric makes a noise as if something is dying in his throat. Brunwald speaks through grayed teeth. "*Riccy* was supposed to have been sent for judgment. What crooked game are you playing at, Ashton? You don't really think you can escape arrest and resume befouling this city, do you?"

I hear Qayn's voice in my head again: *We can't let Skerric be taken away by Ser Brunwald. Do something before the situation gets out of our control.*

Do *what*? Setting aside Brunwald's armor, I can't just attack him. Doing that will guarantee that every guard in the city is sent after us.

My eyes dart over the lift's ropes, the steel wheels and crank. My magic surges, my iron sense homes in. As Brunwald reaches for Skerric, and Clarus shrilly rebukes the knight's flagrant violation of the Holy Season, the crank swings back and the wheels above us spin. The lift grinds to life and screams up the tower shaft, leaving both Clarus and Brunwald behind. Cursing, Skerric grabs the rail; Atheer and Farida hold hands, and the liftenboy gapes at the ropes moving over the wheels without his laying a finger on them.

We judder to a halt at the top, and the crank wrenches back to its starting position and locks the platform.

"By Staggnir's beard!" the liftenboy marvels, hands raised as if he fears disturbing anything.

We hurriedly depart the tower without another word. Unlike the lift grounds below, which were a field of black scree, these are gardens of trimmed hedges and blooming flower beds. We take a paved path into the thick cover of trees, and I instantly draw my sword on Skerric.

"You've been lying to us since we met. Who are you really? Lord Ashton, the son of disgraced nobles, or Skerric, the liftenboy?"

He stands as straight as a beam, his face tight with rage. "*Both.* People used to call me Lord Ashton Hargrave, Earl of Somerford, before King Glaedric Brand ruined us."

My anger gives way to caution. "How is Glaedric involved in this?"

"He implicated my father in a treasonous plot and had him executed." Skerric turns his glare on a finch singing in a tree.

"The rest of my house was spared, but we were stripped of our noble titles, our army, and our lands."

"Army?" Atheer shuffles closer, good hand pressed to his bandages. "Your house was that powerful?"

"My parents were the Duke and Duchess of Attencraw. Yes, the House of Hargrave was powerful, and very wealthy." Skerric's lip curls. "But the smaller House of Brand managed to unify the warring Far North under their banner and marched south. Once they began earning the support of the priesthood, my parents understood that the House of Brand couldn't be ignored. So we became their closest allies. During the War of Elders, Hargrave men, including my father, fought alongside Bertric. We helped put Glaedric's father on the throne. Never mind that he rewarded our loyalty by declaring himself the sole owner of Harrowland, which suddenly meant our ancestral lands were 'royal grants' from him instead." Skerric heaves a sigh. "It's a long and complicated affair, all right? You only need to know that a few years after Glaedric became king, he framed my father—the same man who rode alongside *his* father into battle—and then, in a self-proclaimed act of mercy, he seized our wealth rather than sending us to the gallows. A house from the Far North was installed in our place, likely as a means for Glaedric to buy their loyalty. The House of Hargrave was left destitute, and rather than starve, I decided to come to Darkcliff seeking work as a commoner."

Pity dowses the last embers of my anger. "That's why you care about the state of the Dark."

"I lived in that filth for years," Skerric seethes, "two streets over from Butchers' Row. Yes, I care, and I care that Glaedric is now inflicting his greed and treachery on blameless people across the seas."

"The work you found—it was as a liftenboy?" Qayn asks.

"At the age of fifteen." Skerric dabs the sweat off his forehead with a worn silk tissue. "The pay was chickenfeed, and the labor can only be described as immoral in its demand. But I was given ample opportunity to pickpocket the nobles I brought down from the Cliff." He glances warily up the path. "Brunwald eventually caught wind and had me arrested. I escaped, but I couldn't stay in the city. I wound up disguised as a soldier aboard a warship to Alqibah. Once we arrived, I fled duty."

"And began selling your army's secrets to Maysoon," says Farida.

He primly adjusts his hat. "The House of Hargrave must be rebuilt somehow."

"Gold and land would help quite nicely," I say. "Is that why you want me to win the Hunten?"

Indignance paints a blush across the bridge of Skerric's pointy nose. "I would want you to win even if there wasn't a single gold coin in it for me. The insult to Glaedric would be reward enough."

"And if Ser Brunwald makes a reappearance?" I ask, sliding my sword back into its scabbard.

Skerric takes on the look of a cat about to slip into a hen-house. "That oaf can try his luck interfering with a myddilman, but no judge in this city will permit it. Shall we continue?"

Qayn motions at the path. "Onward, Lord Ashton."

"Skerric," he corrects, striding off. "Ashton hasn't returned from the Halls of the Dead yet, and when he does, it won't be as a lord."

With their wrought-iron lampposts, ornamental trees, and not a single open drain in sight, the spacious, clean streets of the Cliff are the opposite of those in the Dark. Overlooking them are majestic stone buildings with pictorial stained-glass windows and marble steps out front, upon which serious men in heavy robes gather to converse and stare at us as we pass. Paintings of King Glaedric hang wherever they fit; he considers us from inside entrance halls, behind the windows of private residences, and from within specially carved recesses on the streets. Many of the buildings are separated by gardens featuring gold statues of haughty men, though nobody considers these displays with any interest or envy. In the slate Temple of Staggnir, the Ever-King is cast against the blue-black in solid gold; he appears mounted atop a glittering spire, and elsewhere behind curving glass windows wielding a gold scepter tipped with a diamond as big as my fist.

"Such astonishing wealth," I say as we round the temple's pebbled grounds.

"Ah, the Great Star diamond, Glaedric's *humble* contribution to the faith," says Skerric. "Yes, the priesthood has grown rather corpulent off of the House of Brand's exploits."

But excessive opulence isn't exclusive to the Cliff's buildings. Single-oar boats float along the pristine waters of the canal, leisurely conveying passengers who read, doze, and embrace in bored passion. Inside a teahouse scented with the spices of home and furnished in the style of Taeel-Sa, people smoke shisha on beaded cushions, the lamplights dancing off gems in the foreign-origin jewelry piled upon their wigs and around their necks and fingers, as if there's an ongoing competition to see who can step out of their home the most ornamented. None of the nobles appear engaged in any labor, trade, or profession; even water is delivered directly to the doors of their dwellings and waste taken away by humbly dressed laborers from the Dark.

Skerric soon stops us at the entrance to a garden dotted with dozens of tall bronze statues. Nobles stroll under dainty parasols between them, admiring the statues as much as the armored men posturing, training, and dueling in their shade.

"What is this place?" I nervously ask Skerric as we walk toward the two tallest statues in the garden's center. One of the portrayed men is muscular and bearded, wearing a mixture of pelt, mail, and leather; he grips a poleaxe and glares fiercely out at us. The second statue depicts a severe man so bearlike in proportion that he almost makes the first man look slight. They're neither alone nor unique: the other statues are also of intimidating, weapon-wielding men in armor.

"This is the Garden of the Huntsmen; its statues are all tributes to Victors of previous Hunten," says Skerric. "These two men before you are Glaedric's fyghtors: Lord Wulfsyg Grim, Baron of Stanfeld, and the Ent. They've already won two Hunten, and they're tipped to win this season too, though there's been much talk of a new pair, Pat and Tenney, having very good odds too."

We stop behind a small audience of nobles watching a pair of young men duel with wooden swords. They're naked but for short trousers, a seemingly deliberate fashion choice to show off their impressive physiques.

"The garden has become a common place for challengers to display themselves to potential sponsors who might pass by," Skerric quietly explains. "We'll start here while I try to arrange meetings for you."

My heart sinks as I follow him to a pair of statues with an empty space in front of them. "Do you really think my standing here is going to convince anyone to sponsor me?"

Skerric gestures at the grassy patch. "You won't get sponsored if nobody knows who you are. The more attention on you, the better."

It's not the kind of attention I want. Nobles are already

dropping their interest in the other challengers to gawk, sneer, and point at me.

"See," Skerric whispers, "you're getting an audience. Try to impress them. Do what you were doing on the *Prize,* minus the magic."

He scurries off to watch from a nearby bench. I glare after him, sorely tempted to use him as my training dummy. He was supposed to find me a sponsor, not drop me in this garden and hope one takes a sufficient degree of pity on me.

Atheer interrupts my fuming with a nudge. "Just focus on your training, Imani. Ignore everything else." He retreats with Farida and Qayn to join Skerric on the bench.

With no choice left, I grit my teeth and draw my sword.

# 30

# TAHA

TAHA IS HELPING AZIZA ZAHIM STRIP THE MISRA TREE when Ser Ulric collects him for a meeting with Glaedric.

"Extraordinary tree," Ulric says as they walk through the Sanctuary. "You've been husking it from dawn until dusk, and it still looks untouched." The Marshal is conversational, as if they're friends. Even his hand resting on his sword is more for the comfort of the stance than for protection. It was a kind thing he did, taking Taha to the archery range, but Taha refuses to trust him, nor can he look at Ulric without seeing the faces of the people he ruthlessly murdered across the Sahir. But if Ulric is easy in manner, he might be willing to speak honestly.

"How is my father?" Taha ventures.

"Healthy and quarrelsome as ever. Why should you care, boy? He hasn't asked about you once."

The statement hurts right in the breastbone. But Taha knows that the reason Bayek hasn't asked about him is so Glaedric doesn't get the idea that Bayek's love for Taha is something to exploit.

Yet Taha still finds himself blurting out, "My father loves me. Don't compare him to yours. You and I aren't alike either."

"No? Then how come I know how much your guts are squirming right now?"

Taha answers Ulric with an angry silence. They take a wide staircase to the next floor. In one of the corridors here, the Marshal notices a painted scene of Shields battling ghouls and stops Taha to inspect it.

"The monster attacks are getting worse," he says, bringing his nose up to the paint. "I was under the impression that monsters prefer isolated places where there aren't too many people who can fight back."

"That is typical for most types of monsters," says Taha.

"Is it?" Ulric considers him keenly, leading Taha to suspect that this is neither a painting nor a conversation that Ulric happened upon spontaneously. "These monsters are going up to towns with no concern for how many soldiers are around. A pack of hyena-men killed ten outside Sur-Marra in broad daylight two days ago. The men beat them back but killed only a few. The rest scampered off into the farmlands."

Taha should want to laugh about the soldiers' suffering, but there are Sahiran civilians in Sur-Marra who might be in danger.

"What was done with the soldiers' bodies?" he asks. "They mustn't be buried before a steel stake has been driven into each man's heart."

A rut forms between Ulric's brows. "Why? What happens if they are?"

"The dead soldiers return to life as werehyenas and seek out others for their clan."

Ulric narrows his eyes. "But they'd be buried deep—"

"They will claw their way out of the graves, Ser Ulric. What about ghouls, the monsters in this painting—have there been any incidents involving them?"

The Marshal turns his cracked-glass eyes to the painting. "Aye. Some have taken the graveyard near Halaf. . . . They're eating the dead."

"Curse you to Alard," Taha hisses. "This is why we need Shields patrolling the Sahir, but you stupidly slaughtered them all!"

Ulric shoves him back a step. "It's done, boy. What happens when the ghouls finish with the dead?"

"What do you think?" he says, returning. "They'll turn their appetites on your men stationed at Halaf."

"Shit," Ulric mutters. "Then the beasts need to be cleared out of the graveyard as soon as possible."

"The soldiers don't understand what they're doing, and they're going to make the situation worse," Taha says harshly. "To kill a ghoul, it must be struck with one forceful blow to the head or chest. The weapon doesn't matter, but something made of steel is always preferred, to be safe."

"Why not two blows—make sure the thing's really dead?" asks Ulric.

"Striking a ghoul more than once makes it stronger. Your soldiers will only succeed in creating an enemy they can't defeat."

Ulric stares at him, deep in troubled thought, sweat plastering short blond strands to his forehead. As if urged on by an unexpected breeze, he starts Taha moving again. "I sat in on a meeting this morning between His Majesty and your Shield veteran, Captain Ramiz. He swore that the locations and increased incidence of attacks are concerning and unusual, and he couldn't tell His Majesty why it's happening. Was he hiding the truth?"

"The truth that'll save you?" Taha scoffs. "No. I can't tell you why it's happening either, but I can corroborate that what you've described is concerning and unusual."

Ulric is the dominant participant in any conversation except where King Glaedric is involved. He has nothing to say now, and that leaves an unsettling emptiness between them.

They reach a door guarded by several soldiers, more ambling on patrol in the corridor. Ulric brings Taha through it into a well-appointed office of dark cedar furniture brightened by the light shining through open balcony doors. Glaedric sits on the edge of a desk, one thigh draped at an angle, as he sips misra tea. Ulric leaves Taha standing there and goes to shut the door.

"Hello, Taha. Feyrouz told me you led the party that freed Atheer from my captivity," says Glaedric, swirling the tea in his cup. "She accounted the members as you, your cousin Reza, and Atheer's two sisters. Is that correct?"

"Yes," Taha answers, watching Ulric take a position at the other end of the desk.

"I recalled something earlier today about the night you sank my ship that I had previously overlooked." Glaedric drains the cup and places it on the desk. "Imani made her way onboard accompanied by a young man whom Atheer identified at the time as his relative. Black hair, black eyes, slender build."

Taha frowns at first, then: "Oh. That would've been Qayn."

"The djinni Imani has bound to her." Glaedric leers. "I asked Feyrouz about him first. She said he'd slipped her mind. Did he slip yours too?"

Taha half shrugs. "Qayn is nobody of importance, so I didn't think of him when you asked."

"Was Qayn still bound to Imani at the time of your arrest in Brooma?"

Taha nods. The king extends a bone-white hand. "Why? Qayn's sole purpose was to guide your party to Atheer's last whereabouts. Does he continue to provide Imani magical service?"

Taha restrains a mocking laugh. "No, Qayn has no magic of his own."

"He couldn't, say, encourage other monsters to attack my men?" Glaedric asks.

Taha's brows jump. "You think *Qayn* is behind the increased monster attacks?" Now he has to laugh. "No. As I said, Qayn has no magic of his own. He's the most pathetic and useless of his kind."

"And yet Imani hasn't ended her magical contract with him."

Taha falters. This conversation has hidden thorns.

Glaedric starts rocking his booted foot. "What *are* the three of them doing now, do you think? They haven't attempted a return to the Sahir, but I can't fathom Atheer and his sister simply going into hiding." Glaedric collects a scroll off the desk. "This warning for the Council was in your pocket when you were arrested. It's evident what your plan was. So why did you travel to Brooma rather than to Bashtal for a more direct route back to the Swallowing Sands? You wouldn't have been caught. You would've sent your warning, and your cousin would still be alive."

Taha clenches his fists, a resentful heat rising in him. "We thought Brooma wouldn't be as busy as Bashtal."

"It's not because Atheer had other business in Brooma?"

Glaedric stalks his answers like a starving hunter pursues quarry. If Taha isn't careful here, he'll seal his fate by stumbling into a trap.

He takes too long to answer. Glaedric slides off the desk. "Come with me, Taha."

The king leads him onto the balcony. They aren't alone; a longbowman stands in the corner between the potted citruses. Glaedric acknowledges the masked man with a nod before leaning on the banister. Taha stands a few paces behind him, watching the longbowman inspect the gleaming head of the arrow he just pulled from his quiver.

Glaedric presses a finger to his lips and motions Taha to look over the balustrade. In the courtyard below, Bayek sits at a stone table with Captain Ramiz and two other senior Shields whose names escape Taha now. They're deep in discussion over a marked map of the Sahir and don't notice that they're being watched.

Glaedric nods at the longbowman again. The man nocks the arrow and points it down at the courtyard. Taha looks from the arrowhead to its target: Baba, seated with his back to them. At this angle, the arrow would land in his heart, killing him instantly.

"What do you want?" Taha rasps.

"Answers, quickly and quietly," says Glaedric. "What are Atheer and Imani plotting? And before you think to lie, know that I can confirm your story with Amira."

"They have a plan with Qayn to stop you."

The king's face goes as taut as a burial mask. "How? You said the djinni has no magic."

"He doesn't. He says it was stolen and hidden from him. They're trying to find it to restore his power. He's promised to summon them a magical army to defeat you."

Glaedric raises a hand over his shoulder. The longbowman relaxes the bow and pulls away from the balustrade. "Can a djinni really do such a thing?"

"No," Taha says emphatically. "There's rumored to be one type of djinn, called an ifrit, that *might* be capable, but they're an ancient myth."

"Monsters were a myth to me before I came here," says Glaedric. "What do you know about ifrit?"

"Very little, because they're not real," Taha replies bluntly.

Glaedric shakes his head. "Atheer is exceptionally astute. He must have good reason to believe that Qayn is capable, or he wouldn't have agreed to help. How do they intend to find the djinni's magic?"

Taha narrows his eyes. "What does it matter? Qayn's promise is a lie. I tried to convince them to return to the Sahir instead, but Qayn has them fooled."

"I asked you a question, Taha. Answer it or I will kill your father and do worse when I find your siblings," Glaedric warns.

Taha hastily glances at the longbowman waiting on Glaedric's signal. "Qayn said his magic takes the form of three jewels that were once part of a crown. When he gets the jewels back, he can reforge them into a new crown and access his magic again."

As cunning as Glaedric is ordinarily, he proves predictable now. "Could the crown be used by someone other than the djinni? A person?"

A person named Glaedric. Taha stifles a sigh.

"Theoretically, yes, but practically, no. Anyone who has ever used a monster's talisman or implement has died because of it. Qayn said as much, that a person could use his crown but doing so would result in severe, unpleasant physical effects and death. He counseled against it."

"Of course he did," Glaedric snaps. "He's already been stolen from once. He was lying to ward you off."

Did Glaedric not understand what Taha just said? He tries again. "Qayn wasn't lying about that. "We have a thousand years of documented history proving it's impossible for a person to survive the use of a monster's implement—"

"Qayn isn't just *any* monster," Glaedric interrupts crossly. "You said so yourself, he's an ifrit, and you know very little about them. Who's to say these same rules apply to his kind and their magical implements?"

"You want the crown," Taha says, monotone. "Despite having the misra tree under your control. All the magic you could need, right here."

"But it's not *all* the magic available to me, is it?" Glaedric retorts. "I'm already dealing with these monsters. I don't want to be fighting a magical army as well—I want to be commanding it. Where are the jewels now? Brooma?"

Taha would sooner get the bookshelf to listen to reason. Glaedric is only hearing what benefits him, and disregarding or misrepresenting what doesn't. But why should Taha care? He's been approaching this conversation the wrong way. Even if Glaedric will never get the crown, Taha should encourage him to go after it. The fool's errand might prove enough of a distraction from his occupation of Qalia—and if Glaedric is distracted, his hold on the city is weakened.

"Qayn sensed their presence north of Brooma, yes," says Taha. "He didn't specify, but he gestured at the region below Ghazali on a map. Atheer and Imani were planning to go there when we were captured."

"North of Brooma. Below Ghazali." Glaedric sweeps his stiff cloak and walks a short line across the balcony with his head bent. Suddenly he stops and points at Taha. "You're going to steal the crown for me."

Taha's eyes widen. "What? How? I told you, I don't know where the jewels are."

Glaedric grabs him by the tunic. "I *do*." He cuts a look at the longbowman, then shoves Taha into the office. Ulric follows and closes the balcony doors after them.

"You said north of Brooma, below Ghazali, didn't you?" Glaedric pours more tea into his cup. "Some time ago, my men discovered a magnificent temple in an olive forest there and shipped its artifacts to Darkcliff for academic study and display. I remember the manifest because of the sheer number of items on it. A set of three precious jewels of unknown constitution were listed amongst the cargo, though I thought nothing of them at the time."

Glaedric fills a clean cup and hands it to Ser Ulric, sweeps his cape aside, and perches on the desk again.

"Later I received correspondence from my brother about those same jewels, in which he went on about their entrancing, magical qualities. Like most of Kendric's letters, I dismissed it as drunken rambling, but he said he was having the jewels mounted in a new headpiece. I don't believe in coincidences. We must confirm that those jewels are the same ones Atheer and Imani are searching for. You'll follow their steps from Brooma. If they departed for Darkcliff, we'll know these are the right jewels and pursue them."

To Harrowland—Taha hasn't even been home yet, and now this devil wants to send him across the seas. Leaving Qalia again is the last thing he wants to do, but if it means Glaedric leaves too, it's a sacrifice he's willing to make. Glaedric's absence here could open up a much-needed opportunity for Bayek and the other

Councilmembers to strike back against the invaders. But Taha has to confirm Glaedric's intentions before he agrees to anything.

"Do you mean that you'll come with me?" he asks. "What about Qalia? The misra tree?"

"They'll still be here when I return, under the capable care of my sister. You've met Blaedwyn, I believe." Glaedric smiles coldly. "Bring me the djinni's crown and your attempt on her life will be forgiven. I may even be moved to spare the lives of your siblings when I find them. Refuse, and they'll be slaughtered alongside your father."

"Your Majesty." Ulric speaks up. "If you're confident that the jewels are the same, could you not ask Prince Kendric to send them—" The Marshal stops.

Glaedric finishes gulping tea, nodding. "You see the quandary. The djinni's magic is inaccessible to me if he doesn't forge the jewels into his own crown first. Is that correct, Taha?"

"That's my understanding," he says, "but Qayn won't forge the crown under duress."

Glaedric hops off the desk with a liveliness that's intimidating in a man of his height. "I can torture anyone into doing anything." His sincerity grates on Taha.

"Qayn is a being older than a thousand years—"

"If he feels pain, he can be conquered," says Glaedric.

"You'll have to catch him first." Taha edges the frustration out of his voice. "Qayn is magically bound to Imani. She has the power to release him from the contract at any moment, and if she does, he'll be returned to the Sahir by the enchantment over the Swallowing Sands and you'll never find him. He's lived for a thousand years already, waiting to get his magic back, and he could very well live for another thousand."

"Time," Glaedric mutters, looking at Ulric. "He has the time; I don't."

Ulric places his empty cup on the desk. "I believe there's a ready solution, Your Majesty. Permit Atheer, Imani, and the djinni to go about their plot without fear that they're being watched. Reveal your hand only once the crown has been forged."

Glaedric nods, turning to Taha. "Can you find them?"

Taha ignores the small, anxious rise of his pulse. Even if Glaedric does get his hands on the crown, and captures Atheer and Imani in the process, he'll use it only to discover that its power isn't greater than that of the misra tree—and then he'll die. Taha should've known that the only person who could succeed in killing Glaedric is himself. Any possible risk posed to Atheer and Imani is worth that outcome.

"They spoke of lodging with a woman in Brooma," Taha says. "I can ask her for their whereabouts."

"The boy's arrival alone might arouse their suspicions," says Ulric. "He should take the younger sister with him."

Taha turns his head sharply, and a lock of hair lands in his eye. He shoves it back, blinking. "Amira? No, she'll never agree to deceive her siblings."

"She will if her mother's life depends on it. Useful thing, filial loyalty," says Glaedric with a grin. "In any case, Atheer and Imani are more beneficial to me alive. They'll be captured along with the djinni once he has forged his crown."

"Provided it hasn't already been forged," says Taha.

"I'm still here, aren't I?" Glaedric peers at the sky out the balcony doors. "Ser Ulric, have your squire arrange a wash and shave for Taha and collect clothes for him for a monthlong journey. Send someone else to fetch the girl, tell her to pack a bag as well. We'll depart this afternoon."

"Yes, Your Majesty."

Taha digs his heels into the rug as Ulric tries to usher him to the door. "I want to see my father before we leave."

"No, but you can see him as much as you like after you bring me the crown." Glaedric smiles. "Off you go, Taha."

# 31

# TAHA

AT NOON, TAHA IS TAKEN DOWN TO AN EMPTY meeting room where his belongings and armor have been heaped on a table. A little while later, Amira is escorted in by soldiers and told to wait. He calls her from the back of the room, where he's using a glass vase as a mirror to put on his cloak.

"Taha!" She scurries over, studying his clean-shaven face through a frown. "Ser Ulric came to my house and said I have to help King Glaedric with something or my mother's going to be killed!" She slides a bulging bag off her shoulders, fumbling with its weight, and drops it on the rug. "They ordered me to pack for a monthlong journey!"

"So you packed some books?" Taha fastens his cloak and turns to inspect the mouth of her bag, which is struggling to stay closed around a book jammed in at the top.

"Important reading, yes." She folds her arms. "Glaedric interrogated me about Atheer and Imani's plan to find Qayn's magic. Just what is happening?"

He glances at the door. It's still shut, but soldiers are standing on the other side. They have to be quiet.

"Glaedric thinks the jewels are in Harrowland with his brother," he says softly. "He wants to take us to Brooma to find out whether Atheer and Imani went to Harrowland after them. If they did, that's where we're headed too."

*"What!"*

*"Hush."* He glances at the door again. "Glaedric wants me to take the crown once Qayn has forged it. He's threatened to kill my father and my siblings if I don't."

Her jaw drops. "Is he mad? What am I saying, of course he is! Did you also warn him about the consequences of using the crown?"

"Yes. He doesn't believe it. He wants the crown, and he intends to arrest your brother and sister."

Her lower lip wobbles. "Not to—"

"No. He said they're more beneficial to him alive."

She stares at him. "Are you lying, Taha?"

"*No.* Look, I understand that you have no reason to trust me. But do you really think that if Glaedric executed Atheer and Imani, your auntie would keep helping him with the misra? Everyone has their limit, Amira. He needs Aziza Zahim's help, even more now that his men are being attacked by monsters out in the Sahir."

"They *are*?" Amira starts biting her nails. "But what does he need me for?"

"To make me appear less suspicious to your siblings, given our . . . history."

"Fine, I understand that. But should we really—"

Something thuds outside, silencing them. Taha checks to see that the door hasn't been cracked ajar before gesturing for her to continue.

"Should we really give Glaedric Qayn's crown?" she whispers.

"Of course we should," Taha whispers back. "Using it won't make Glaedric any more powerful than he is now, but it *will* kill him."

"How quickly?" she asks.

"In most cases, death is immediate."

"And in the cases where it isn't? We don't know the crown's power. If Qayn *isn't* lying about his magic and Glaedric manages to use it for even a few hours, the consequences could be devastating."

"Yes, but if Qayn isn't lying, there's no telling whether it's safer to trust him with it," Taha argues. "Which monster is better?"

"The one we know more about," says Amira, going to her bag. "I found this—"

The door opens and Ser Ulric enters, ending their conversation.

They don't pick it up again that day. Glaedric arranges a convoy of carriages and heavy cavalry, and they set off a couple of hours past noon. To Taha's dismay, Bayek and Zahra, Amira's mother, are brought along in a prison coach at the front of the convoy. Taha and Amira are loaded into their own carriage, traveling between two carriages carrying Ser Ulric and more than a dozen soldiers. Between the prison coach and one belonging to the soldiers is Glaedric's, a giant of a coach pulled by six grotesquely muscular horses in dark barding.

The excursion is the first time Taha has seen Qalia since its fall. The city is overrun with Harrowlanders. Soldiers patrol every street, and officials supervise the exchange of goods and coin inside every business; other officials are joined by soldiers in inspections of homes, presumably looking for items of value. Their collective use of magic is excessive and at times reckless. At a checkpoint, a soldier takes offense at a man's manner and blasts his wagon into pieces with a summoned gale-force wind, wounding several others in the line. On a street near the gates, a pair of soldiers arrest a woman and make her shed the gold jewelry concealed under her shawls, leading Taha to suspect that the shrewd-eyed official who accompanies the soldiers has an affinity for gold and, like a hunting dog, has been tasked with identifying any civilian trying to smuggle out the precious metal.

People attempt to go about their lives as usual, but the pervasive presence of the invaders is an undeniable reminder that Qalia has been shifted off its axis. The most painful proof is the gallows in Main Square. A banner hangs above the long row of executed that reads FOLLOW THE LAW, OBEY YOUR KING, LIVE IN PEACE.

For hours after they leave Qalia, Amira pores over a leather-bound tome of fragile pages, stopping often to make notes in a separate journal. Taha attempts to continue their conversation from earlier, even asking her about the story she's reading, but she silences him with a raised hand.

They stop in the evening for a break. Taha doesn't see his father; the prison coach is parked in such a way as to obscure Bayek and Zahra's being taken in and out. Shortly after they're given dinner, lanterns are lit and the convoy goes rattling through the night, their path frequently illuminated by a soldier who pulls together tangles of light and throws them high into the air, where they hang for a few minutes before burning out. Though the convoy strictly sticks to the main travel routes, Taha has heard too much about errant monsters to be able to rest.

The following afternoon, Amira makes an abrupt announcement while he's attempting to nap through a particularly rough stretch of road.

"It's not a story. It's a collection of ancient poetry and illustrations."

"Huh? Oh." Taha rubs his eyes, yawning. "How interesting."

She tuts, carefully shutting the book, though she marks the page she was reading with her thumb. "I myself prefer tales of adventure and intrigue, but I'm reading this for a reason. I searched the documents in my mother's home office for references to anything related to what Qayn told us about himself."

Taha sits up straighter, immediately curious about what might've been found in the office of the Qalian Archives' Arch-Scholar. "Right, I remember your saying you wanted to do that. Did you find anything?"

"I think so. This book was inside a special glass case at the very back of a locked cabinet that took me two whole days to pick open." She pouts, as if that's someone else's fault. "With the book was a long note in my mother's handwriting. She describes meeting with a man who had inherited the book among other items from his late mother. He had made inquiries of a dozen other scholars about its possible historical value, but not a single one had met with him before my mother did." Amira smiles proudly. "You see, this man had come across one of my mother's hobby projects on display in the Library of Qalia, in which she'd found and collated a series of anonymous poems that other scholars had overlooked. Have you heard of it?"

"Uh, I don't think so," says Taha, as if he actually knows of any scholarly displays in the Library of Qalia. He's never so much as set foot in the old building; the few books he's ever read were from his father's shelves, about hunting, weapons, and monsters, with the occasional political treatise thrown in.

"Oh, well, my mother proved, through an analysis of the penmanship, materials, and contents, that the author of the poems was actually Al-Leyl, the famous polymath—" Amira stops, smiles. "It's not relevant. What *is* relevant is that the display led this man to believe that my mother might also see the value in his book, particularly as it's not attributed to any author. The book was found by the man's great-great-great something or other, a caravan driver, on a bandit's body near the edge of—get this—*the Vale of Bones.* What else was on the bandit's body? A map with notations indicating that he and three of his companions had been exploring the Vale for treasure. The map was lost, so I couldn't confirm that the bandit had been in the First City, but the most important item survived." She holds up the book. "I began reading about an hour before Ser Ulric arrived. I've not gotten through much, but listen to this." She flips to a page, steadies against the carriage's swaying, and reads out a passage framed by a sketch of flowering vines: " 'His gift was a pearl in a green sea; a bed of purple for he and me; a stem of bounty for family; prosperity guarded by immensity; a secret bought naked in the shade: divinity.' "

Taha knits his brows, pretending to understand. Amira traces the words with her finger. "Qayn said he built the First City for Nahla as a gift. It was made of white stone. 'His gift was a pearl in a green sea.' "

"The green sea is the Vale," he says. "The cedar trees, before Hubaal destroyed them."

"Yes, and this next part—'a bed of purple for he and me'—refers to the purple flowers that were all over the city. The symbolism of a bed speaks to the nature of Qayn's relationship with Nahla."

"As lovers," Taha mutters.

"Scandalous, isn't it?"

"It's disgusting and unnatural." He hates how defensive he sounds; hates more that he's now thinking about Imani and Qayn together. He waves a hand at the page. "What about this next part? 'A stem of bounty for family.' "

"I don't know enough about Qayn to explain that, but the part after that: 'prosperity guarded by immensity'—"

"Hubaal the Terrible."

"*Yes,* the giant Hubaal." She shuts the book and lays a hand over its cover. "I'm certain that this journal belonged to none other than Nahla. From what I've decoded so far, Qayn *was* telling the truth about his history with her, which means his magic was *at least* powerful enough that he could build the First City with it."

Taha sits back, tapping his thumb against his thigh. "But if this book is to be believed, Qayn might actually be an ifrit and could summon a magical army."

They gaze at one another as they realize the dreadful implication of his statement.

"What do we do?" Amira asks. "Who do we trust?"

"I don't know." Taha sighs. "We can never trust Glaedric, but we can confidently guess what he'll try to do with the magic, before it kills him."

"Conquer more lands and oppress more people," she says. "We don't know what Qayn would do."

"Save us, supposedly."

She chews her lip. "And if he's telling the truth about that too, then by helping Glaedric, we're taking away our people's only hope of defeating the Harrowlanders. . . ."

Taha points at the book. "You need to figure out as much as you can before we reach Brooma. There might be an answer in there—"

Before he can finish his sentence, their carriage comes to a sudden halt.

# 32

# TAHA

AMIRA SLIDES OFF HER SEAT WITH A YELP, THOUGH she has the presence of mind to raise the book over her head before she lands, saving it from damage. Taha helps her back onto her bench and peers out the window. The convoy has stopped, and Glaedric is stepping out of his carriage, pointing at the front wheels.

"What's happened?" Amira crowds in at the window beside him.

"There might be a problem with Glaedric's carriage." Taha opens the door and jumps down to the grassy road they've been following between some hills. It's stiflingly hot in the sun, but a cool southern wind is blowing, and the blue stain of a storm is visible in the distance. He glances at the soldiers' carriage behind him; a few of the men are already jogging over to Glaedric's. He goes after them, Amira at his side, though she's more intent on looking at the prison coach at the front.

Ser Ulric is addressing the drivers when they arrive. "What's causing the noise?"

"It's insufferable," Glaedric complains.

One man mops his forehead, nodding. "Forgive me, Your Majesty, I imagine it is. The dry heat's the trouble. We'll check the wheels again and give them a soaking for good measure—"

Taha takes advantage of his relative freedom in the moment and climbs a nearby hill for a better view of their surrounds. His eyes wander across the mountains on the horizon, the storm clouds hanging over them, then he drops his gaze closer to a hamlet and its farms. There's not a person in sight, and one of the homesteads has been reduced to a pile of rubble. He might attribute that to the Vanguard if something else hadn't made its mark in the fields and left behind long, winding trenches and huge circular pits alongside mounds of soil.

He lopes back down the hill to the convoy. The drivers, Ulric, and Glaedric are still in conversation; the other soldiers are gathered around the third carriage, lighting smoking pipes and talking loudly.

"King Glaedric, we need to leave," says Taha.

The king flashes an irritable glance over his shoulder. "How dare you interrupt me while I'm speaking."

"You've no time for wheel maintenance, and those men over there need to stop making noise." Taha gestures at the smoking soldiers, who quiet the instant their king looks at them.

Glaedric turns, curious now. "Why?"

He points at the hill. "There's a giant sand serpent nearby. We need to move as soon as possible."

Ser Ulric turns to the drivers. "Give the wheels a quick once-over and prepare to depart."

The men move off, presumably to fetch tools.

"What did you say?" Amira asks Taha in Sahiran.

He replies out of the corner of his mouth: "There are signs that a giant sand serpent—"

"Show me." Glaedric appears by his side. "While they're dealing with the wheels, show me the giant sand serpent."

"You can't see it, only the signs of its presence," says Taha.

Glaedric extends a floating hand. "I would like to see."

The men setting tools on the ground exchange glances. Taha has no choice but to return to the hill. Glaedric shadows him, trailed by Ser Ulric, a dozen uneasy soldiers, and Amira, who creeps after them unnoticed.

Taha stops Glaedric at the top of the hill. "Do you see the pits? That's where it would've come out of the ground, and the trenches would've been left behind by its body. It's very unusual for it to be here."

Glaedric cups a hand over his squinting eyes. "Oh, yes, I see. *Fascinating.* It must be an enormous creature. Would it still be close?"

Taha instinctively glances at the prison coach. "It could be. Giant sand serpents tend to frequent areas more than once, which is why we—"

Glaedric starts down the other side of the hill toward the pits. Taha freezes; Ser Ulric jogs to the crest.

"Your Majesty?" he calls out.

"Stay where you are, Ulric! I just want to get a little closer!"

Ulric stares after Glaedric, confused.

"Magical obsession," says Taha, drawing the Marshal's worried gaze. "It's making him careless and overconfident." It's the same reason why Glaedric didn't care about or believe the consequences of using Qayn's crown.

Ulric blinks a droplet of sweat out of his eye. "How dangerous is it for His Majesty to go down there?"

"The closer he gets to those pits, the more likely he's about to get himself killed." Taha shrugs. "He did order you to wait here."

"Don't be smart, boy," Ulric says gruffly. "Anything happens to His Majesty, the girl here pays for it. Come."

He drags Taha back down the hill. "Ready yourselves," he orders the soldiers as they pass. He stops at the third carriage and opens the trunk. Taha's bow and quiver are inside.

"Take them, quickly."

Taha works through a string of curses by the time he's slung the quiver onto his back and run back up the hill, where the cavalrymen are sweating in their armor and Amira is biting her nails. Glaedric is already halfway to the pits and still pressing ahead in lordly strides, long arms swinging. Their group crosses a decent distance after him before Taha realizes that Amira's followed them with a sharp stick. For someone so clever, she's frustratingly foolhardy.

Taha stops to meet her. "It's too dangerous for you to come with us."

"But I can help you," she says, raising the stick.

"What do you bloody think you're going to do with that, girl?" Ulric demands, stopping a few paces behind him.

"It's better than nothing!" she exclaims, cheeks flushing peach. "I just want to help."

Her sincerity is sad. Pathetic, really. When she snuck after them to the First City, blithely surviving in the way lucky people do, Taha attributed her actions to Beya stubbornness and the arrogant belief that they must be involved in everything. But now he thinks Amira is just anxious for someone to confirm that her efforts are worthy; *she* is worthy of having around. Taha always assumed she was popular in her circles the way Atheer was. He was friends with everyone, he knew everyone's names and they knew his. But maybe that wasn't real either, not meaningfully, and that's why Atheer had time in his busy schedule to associate with somebody like Taha.

None of that erases the present danger. "Just don't come any closer," he implores in a quieter voice. "You're smarter than anyone else I've ever met. You need to decode that book, but you can't do it if you're dead."

She sighs but nods. "I'll stay here."

"Thank you."

Taha sprints after Glaedric with Ser Ulric and the soldiers. The king has reached the edge of a sunken pit and bends over to peer into it.

*"Hell-l-l-o-o,"* he calls, flinging a rock down.

"Stop!" Taha grabs his elbow before he can throw another one. "You'll get yourself killed!"

Glaedric springs to his feet, yanking free of Taha. "Touch me again and I'll cut off your hand like they do to thieves in Alqibah." He tosses the rock into the pit and heads for a trench, faster now.

Taha is tempted to let the mad fool wander to his death, but Bayek and Zahra's fates are tied to Glaedric's until he gets Qayn's crown. Taha runs after him, sliding his bow over his shoulder. "Stop!" he repeats.

Glaedric only stops so that he can hop into the trench left behind by a massive serpentine body, then he walks quickly along it, marveling. Taha jumps down after him, Ser Ulric on his heels, the soldiers waiting outside the trench.

"You must return to the carriage!" Taha calls.

"Once I'm done," Glaedric replies. "Do you think I'm afraid of the pests you call monsters?"

"I think the opposite! But would you rather be eaten by a giant sand serpent for curiosity's sake or survive to wear Qayn's crown?"

Glaedric halts. "Quite right, the crown," he says in an abruptly different tone.

He doesn't resist Ser Ulric helping him out of the trench. He pauses there to dust his breeches while Taha climbs out and the soldiers jog over. The ground starts to shake just as they arrive.

Glaedric frowns. "What's that?"

The tremoring intensifies; Taha remembers the serpent back in the cavern with the si'la, coiling and sliding along the walls, the *shhhhh* that he still hears when he's too drowsy to hold his nerve. The ground judders and there's a sound he can only understand as the earth taking a deep breath. Glaedric stares over his shoulder, as pale as milk. Taha physically feels the serpent's presence as it rises from the soil, and the shadow it casts . . .

He turns and confronts it, reared against the thunderous sky. As thick and tall as a tower, armored in gleaming reddish-black scales each the size of a door, it has a tapered head with tiny gold eyes intersected vertically by slitted pupils that ravenously assess their surroundings for a meal. And they've found one in Amira.

The serpent's jaw opens on long, lethal fangs, prompting Ser Ulric to exclaim a curse too offensive to repeat. Taha pulls the bow off his shoulder. Glaedric kicks him in the calf.

"Don't attract its attention, halfwit! You'll get us killed!"

"Run," Taha barks at him. *"Now!"*

But Glaedric grabs his arm, fist like a pincer. "You're running with me. I need you alive to get me my crown." He looks at Ser Ulric. "You and your men deal with it."

"They've never fought one before!" says Taha. "They'll die!"

Glaedric tugs him forward. "Yes, Taha, that's what soldiers *do,* they *die.* Now move!"

*To Alard with this devil.* Taha roughly jerks out of Glaedric's grip as the serpent hisses at Amira. She screams, holding up the stick like it's a spear. Taha shoots an arrow at the serpent's head, but it begins its descent toward Amira in the same instant. He misses; the arrow bounces off a scale near the serpent's eye. A second later, Glaedric's sprinted off for the hill, seething. But Taha was never under the impression that his arrows could pierce a giant sand serpent's armor. What matters is the proximity of the arrow to the beast's vulnerable spot: its eyes. The serpent flinches, its hefty body wobbling, and looks up at him nocking another arrow. The Almanac says these monsters are clever. Taha's certain it's realizing that one of his arrows—if not this one, then the next—is going to land in its eye. Enough of them and he might just kill it.

The serpent hisses again and launches onto the dirt, causing the earth under Taha's boots to throb. Amira drops the stick and collapses to her knees, covering her head with her arms. But the serpent is heading for him now.

"Come on!" he goads in a shout.

He shoots again; the serpent dodges and the arrow bounces off its cheek. But Amira has realized that the serpent has forgotten about her—for now—and thankfully, she doesn't squander the opportunity he's created for her. She sprints for the hill and clears the serpent's reach, leaving it slithering across the field toward Taha.

Ser Ulric draws his sword, prompting the men behind him to do the same. "How do we defeat this thing, boy?" he shouts, summoning flames along the steel.

"Go for its eyes!" Taha shouts back.

Ulric raises his flaming sword; the men spread out. Taha nocks an arrow and aims for the beast's golden eye but doesn't shoot. He must be sure before he releases the bowstring; he must know his aim is true. He holds the arrow; the serpent raises its head, mouth open, and dives at them. He shoots; the arrow hits the pupil. The serpent roars, buffeting them in stinking, hot mist. He shoots another arrow and rolls out of the monster's path. He misses, but Ulric tumbles to the opposite side and manages to slash the serpent's other eye. The enraged, wounded beast slams to the earth, knocking the Marshal and several soldiers aside. It cuts past and coils back up behind them, weeping black tears. Taha is already on his feet, shooting. He needs just one or two more direct hits to kill it. But his arrow narrowly reflects off the spines of the serpent's brow as it dives on them. And in a heartbeat, Taha understands that he's forfeited their lives with that one failure.

Lightning opens the sky. A deafening screech quakes his insides; a gust of fresh wind beats over them. Past the serpent's head, Taha spies the familiar silhouette of a bird of prey, but one much, much larger than what he knows. The serpent's jaw opens around him, Ser Ulric, and the soldiers, then closes; its fangs are seconds from impaling them through guts and spines—then the serpent is ripped away from them, and the violence of its withdrawal knocks Taha to the ground.

Shaking, he stares up at the monster with the serpent between its talons: Anzu, a gigantic bird of prey, emanating an aura of crackling lightning around its white plumage. Depicted in the Almanac as the king of the *rukh,* a noble race of rarely seen bird monsters, Anzu is said to descend on the Sahir only during thunderstorms and gales. He lifts into the sky, raining soil and grass over Taha, and soars for the mountains with the hissing serpent wriggling in his talons, bolts of lightning crackling under every beat of his wings and striking the earth. Taha doesn't get up; he doesn't think he can. He watches Anzu and the serpent as if in a dream, becoming smaller until they vanish over the jagged peaks on the horizon, where the storm finally breaks.

"You saved me!" Amira drops to her knees beside him and clutches his hand. "That was so selfless. I don't speak for anyone else, but I forgive you for what you did back in Taeel-Sa, Taha."

He's surprisingly touched. "Thanks, Amira. It was really brave of you to come to help."

He's never seen her smile so broadly. He helps her stand and collects his bow from the dirt.

Ulric comes over, holding out a stray, undamaged arrow. "You're the luckiest son of a bastard I've ever seen. Attacked by one monster and saved by another."

He waits for Taha to collect the remaining intact arrows from the dirt and replace them in his quiver; then they start back to the hill, where Glaedric is standing. Ulric seems to deliberately walk slower so that a space forms between his soldiers and him and Taha. "You had guts, not running from that thing," he says, voice quiet and earnest.

Taha glances at him, taken aback slightly by the compliment. "You didn't run either. Not like Glaedric did."

Ulric's nostrils flare. "Watch your mouth, boy. His Majesty's life is worth ours put together. It's my duty to protect it. Yours too now."

Taha knows he's risking a beating from Ulric for what he's about to say, but he says it anyway; someone has to. "Lucky man, Glaedric. He commands the absolute loyalty of experienced soldiers like you without having to give any in return."

Ulric flashes wild eyes at Taha, yet incredibly, the man remains silent and considers Glaedric for the rest of the walk back.

The king is strangely sullen upon their return. "Surrender your weapon and return to your carriage," he orders Taha curtly.

Taha hands his bow and quiver to Ser Ulric. Glaedric watches him and Amira walk back to the carriage and climb inside.

# 33

# IMANI

"TWO WHOLE WEEKS." I SLIDE ACROSS THE GRASS. "Two weeks of being laughed at." Jab. "Insulted and told to go home." Pivot. "Rejected." Stab. "Two weeks of Skerric achieving *nothing*."

I don't have a dueling partner—Muhab stood in for a few days, until we realized it didn't make me look any better to be sparring with someone at half my skill level—but there are plenty of nobles in the audience whom I'd gladly invite into my arena. Unfortunately, they have enough sense to watch me practice improvised cuts from a safe distance.

They've shown up every day since Skerric first brought me to this garden and instructed me to make a spectacle of myself. After a week, the constant stream of new faces became dotted with faces I'd seen before: the sallow nobleman who smokes as if he's a chimney in the shade of the oak tree; the pair of plump noblewomen twirling never-ending supplies of silk parasols in various hues of pink; Lord Clarus, once, and only to arrange a date with Skerric at the bowling greens, after which I learned from Skerric that it was considered progressive and fashionable amongst young nobles to have dalliances with commoners. Clarus was even so generous as to inform Skerric that Ser Brunwald had been reprimanded and wouldn't be a trouble anymore. That's how it's gone. Largely the same people coming past every few days, not to decide whether to sponsor me, not to take up Skerric's offer and invite me to duel one of their retinue to prove my skill. No, they come just to observe me, as if I were an exotic animal caged in a menagerie.

"It's not fair," says Qayn. "You're valiant in your armor and plainly very skilled with a sword."

I pause, sword held aloft, and slide my eyes over to him. He's seated behind me on the plinth between two statues of Victors, shivering despite being cozily cocooned in a black woolen cloak he insisted on purchasing a couple of days after we arrived in Darkcliff. He even found the cold intolerable enough to don a pair of black leather boots. Judging by the way he keeps fiddling with them, tying and untying the laces, he's not very comfortable with this new arrangement after a millennium of going barefoot in warm sand.

"Are you being sarcastic?" I ask, recovering from my lunge. Unlike Qayn, I have to remain on my feet, either training or posturing. *Don't drop the act for even a minute,* Skerric advised me two weeks ago. *You never know when a potential sponsor is watching.* I'm a fool for having thought securing one was even possible.

"I believe the word is *supportive,*" Qayn says. "For your future reference, being supportive is something friends do for each other to show that they care."

I purse my lips. "*Now* you're being sarcastic."

"Am I?"

"You should be. I happen to think we're making great strides in our friendship. When was the last time I threatened to kill you?"

"Hmm . . . I can't remember. Perhaps that means *I'm* winning *your* heart." He resumes the knot he was tying in his laces.

Perhaps it does. I doubt I would've gotten through the humiliation of the last two weeks without his nightly words of encouragement. And if it weren't for his and Atheer's defense of Skerric's efforts, I probably would've murdered our guide by now. The golden-haired Harrowlander gestures at me as he speaks animatedly with a nobleman in a too-tall hat. He's flanked by Atheer, smiling and nodding politely. Last week, my brother theorized that if he could speak to the nobles too, they might overcome some of their antipathy toward the idea of sponsoring a foreign warrior.

I feel a twinge of guilt. They've been trying so hard. Skerric has been tirelessly championing me from dawn to dusk, waving nobles over to watch me and vivaciously engaging them in conversation with his best, brightest smile, only to be resoundingly rejected, sometimes very angrily. He's trying—he's just not succeeding, and that's not his fault. He can't change the sentiment of an entire city, certainly not in such a short time. But the Hunten is next week, tomorrow noon is the cutoff to enter, and not a single noble is even mildly interested in sponsoring me.

Sighing, I slump on the edge of the plinth beside Qayn. He finishes the knot on his boot and looks up at me, concerned. I raise a hand.

"Don't. My future sponsor isn't watching and doesn't care that I've admitted defeat by sitting down. Because that's what this is. Defeat." I tilt my head back to the cloudy sky, touched red in places by the setting sun, and watch a black raven cross it alone. "We traveled all the way to Darkcliff, we almost sank getting here, Bassem lost his life. It was all for nothing. I left Amira and my family when they needed me most. Perhaps Taha was right: I would've better served my people if I'd gone home to defend them."

Qayn flinches ever so slightly. In some corner of the garden, someone laughs. I blink and drop my gaze.

"I owe you an apology too, Qayn. I wasn't good enough to get your magic back. Not good enough to do anything."

He places his hand over mine, still gripping the hilt of my sword. Nobles abandon the garden as dusk arrives, unrelentingly cold, but not before sparing me their last victorious sneers. They won. I didn't secure a sponsor; I couldn't defy their discrimination.

Skerric trudges over, feathered hat in his hand, trailed by Atheer. Both of them are glum—Skerric particularly morose in his blue eye paint.

"Well?" I prompt halfheartedly.

"Same as the others. You're a girl, you're small and weak, you're fremde, you're not trained in proper Harrowlander swordsmanship." Skerric sniffles. "Lord Winthorpe *also* said he hopes the law is changed and people like me are hanged for scheming to ruin the Empire, which was a nice addition to the usual rotation of insults."

I clench my fist around my sword. "They won't even give me a chance to prove them wrong."

"I doubt there's anything they loathe more than being proven wrong," Skerric says sadly. "I'm sorry, Imani."

I'm still for a moment, glaring into the falling dark as the cold nips at my eyes. Then I transform my sword back into a dagger and head for the garden gates. As the others trail after me through the streets of the Cliff, I think about what to do next.

What I *can* do next. But in the lift down to the Dark, I have to confront the shadow of the Royal Citadel hanging over the retiring, frostbitten city, and with it, the reality that I can't find any other way inside but the Hunten. The only other time Prince Kendric will leave the fortress is to give a speech at the foot of the lift right before the tournament. To get to him, I'd have to navigate crowds, guards, and those deadly fences. And even if I somehow found a way past those obstacles, what then? I could throw my dagger and fuse with it to cross the distance to Kendric on his hypothetical podium, but then all I'd have is a dead prince and his tiara in my hands, with hundreds of guards and a furious city surrounding me and no way of getting the jewels to Qayn. Futile, all of it.

Skerric hails us a coach to take us back to the Swan. Then, as we're waiting for it to reach us, he says, "There is *one* last opportunity to find a sponsor. The Proving Round. It's happening tonight, a way for little-known challengers to seek last-minute backing to enter the Hunten. Nobles come down to watch the duels, and if they like what they see, they offer sponsorship." He flicks his eyes from the oncoming coach to me, cautiously hopeful. "If you can tolerate being laughed at one last time, I encourage you to participate. This will be your chance to finally show what you can do against an evenly matched opponent. With wooden swords, of course," he adds, glancing at my concerned brother.

I open my arms. "Why didn't you mention this earlier? Obviously I'll participate! What are we waiting for?"

Skerric exhales, relieved, as the coach rolls to a stop beside us. "Take us to the Filthy Bilge," he tells the driver. We clamber into the coach after him.

"As I said, if nobles like what they see, they offer sponsorship," he says. "I must warn you that it *is* uncommon—the Proving Round is more of a show than a serious avenue of entrance—but the possibility of its happening is part of the excitement."

I sit on the bench opposite him. "And if there is someone there who wants to sponsor me, what happens then?"

Skerric grips the bench as the coach rounds a corner. "The paperwork is easy to prepare. If a noble is serious about being a sponsor, they'll carry it with them when they attend. You can have your name down and ready to be entered by this evening."

Twinkling with warm lantern lights and festooned with vines and wreaths, the Filthy Bilge is situated on the docks facing the black harbor. In contrast to the tavern's humble appearance, the road outside is lined with lavish carriages watched over by a group of smoking drivers sharing tobacco and matchboxes.

I pull my hood low as we approach the tavern. The waiting crowd allows Skerric to pass through to the pair of men guarding the doors. He says something to them that I don't catch, and we're let in. A stage has been erected in the center of the large, stuffy room, and drinks flow freely from a counter in the corner. Haughty nobles peer down from the mezzanine at the duel that's just finished; the loser slinks off into the crowd while the victor remains posturing onstage with his wooden sword. The spectators applaud noisily; many exchange coins, presumably to pay out bets. A few of the nobles are muttering to each other, but none are leaping at the opportunity to sponsor the winner.

The spectators notice that Skerric is wearing the blue eyepaint of a myddilman and make way for us, less from respect and more from a keen eye for profit which they quickly turn on me in my armor. With my hood partially concealing my face, nobody's realized yet that I'm not a Harrowlander man. The crowd closes in around us as we reach the counter and Skerric speaks with the barman. Their conversation is mostly drowned out by the rowdy audience, but I swear I hear the barman say, "You're late," as if he were expecting Skerric's arrival, even though that wouldn't make any sense. A minute later, Skerric tells me to remove my hood. I would prefer not to—I can predict the response already—but I can't hide forever. At the sight of my exposed face, the crowd erupts in laughter and hateful insults.

"Is this a joke?" the barman shouts to Skerric over the noise. He gestures a thumbs-down.

"What's the matter?" I ask, tugging Skerric's arm.

He leans closer to me. "The barman's refusing to let you join the Proving because you're not Harrowlander and you're a woman."

The barman returns to stubbornly watching the stage, but I raise my voice to a volume he can't ignore. "Tell this fool that I demand to put on the greatest duel he's ever seen!"

The people around us blow raspberries and jeer. A muscle feathers in the barman's jaw. He shoots me a glare before he hops onto the tavern counter.

"Oi!" he shouts at the crowd. *"Quiet!"*

The tavern hushes, save for whispers and giggles, and almost everyone turns to the barman. "This little fremde girl here demands to put on the greatest duel we've ever seen."

The tavern shakes with laughter; nobles titter from the comfort of the mezzanine.

"What do you say?" the grinning barman hollers. "Is there anyone here interested in seeing the little girl fight for an even littler chance at sponsorship?"

Silence. I can even hear bubbles pop in the foam of a drink nearby. The barman continues calmly: "How about anyone interested in seeing her taught a lesson?"

The crowd's response is thunderous; even the nobles applaud. The barman soothes the riot with a flap of his hands and turns back to Skerric.

"Answer enough for you? I'd rather not waste the other challengers' time or the time of our generous patrons. Leave, before I have my boys throw you out."

"That's not fair," I exclaim. "I'll happily teach whoever you send me a more valuable lesson!"

Grumbles move through the crowd. The barman groans. "Come on, girlie, does it look like any of the nobles are interested?"

"The entire purpose of letting me participate is to *get* them interested!" I retort in frustration. "You won't even give me a chance! Who are you to stop me from demonstrating my skill? No, I'm not a Harrowlander, but I'm a part of the bloody Empire!"

Atheer touches my shoulder. "Let it go, Imani."

I glance at the crowd. Their glee is transparent enough that I can see the hostility underneath it now. We're surrounded by people who hate us.

Suddenly, a confident voice dominates the opposite corner of the tavern: "The young lady makes a good case."

The man who spoke is standing on a chair to look over the crowd at us. He's in his mid-forties, with a wavy mop of chin-length dark hair flecked in silver, and a heavy brow set over smart gray eyes. His doublet and breeches are simple in design, muted in color.

"Who is that?" I whisper to Skerric.

"*That* is Mister Hardy," he answers through a gratified grin.

"I would like to see her fight for the potential of my sponsorship," Mister Hardy declares.

The crowd murmurs; the barman's face colors. I gawk at Mister Hardy. "He does? But why isn't he sitting with the other nobles?"

"Because he *isn't* noble," Skerric replies. "He made his wealth through industry. He even invented the modern lift system and sold the design to Glaedric's father."

"Let us have our evening in peace, Hardy," complains a nobleman. "The spectacle is supposed to be the challengers, not you and your spiteful jousts against the Empire."

Hardy laughs and turns to the crowd. "Contrary to popular delusion, a foreign woman winning the Hunten would be a *good* omen for people like us. After all, we share more in common with this young lady of the Empire than we do with—" He points at the mezzanine.

"You should be flogged!" squawks a noblewoman craning over the banister with a slice of cake in one hand and a goblet in the other. "There would be chaos without the natural order. We all have a duty to respect and uphold it for the good of Harrowland."

Hardy frowns, dusting his shoulder. "Do take care, Lady Weiss. You're dropping crumbs on us."

The crowd quiets, palpably uneasy.

"Bring her onto the stage, my good man," Hardy tells the barman.

"You'll do no such thing," directs another nobleman from the mezzanine.

"Uh-uh." Hardy shakes his head. "To forbid the young lady when I have expressed interest constitutes interference with a challenger and their myddilman. I hardly think either of us wishes to spend the remainder of our evening before a judge, do we, Lord Elmer?"

The nobleman strangles the banister. "Very well, Hardy, have your duel. Wynstan," he calls, leaning over to peer down into the crowd, "teach her a lesson."

"Yes, my lord," someone calls back.

The barman runs a finger between his collar and his neck before nodding at me. "You're on." And the crowd is boisterous again, except now there's a curious undercurrent of anxiety to their excitement.

I shuffle after Skerric, my heart starting to pound. My opponent, Wynstan, has already climbed onto the stage, armed with a wooden longsword. The tall, wiry blond is about twenty-two years old and impressively long limbed. I should be afraid to challenge him, slightly nervous at least. I'm only impatient. This duel has been due for two weeks, and I've accrued much resentment during the wait.

"Imani, once you're onstage, we're barred from helping you," says Skerric. "The duel continues until one of you concedes or a winner is declared."

And it's clear the barman has no intention of permitting otherwise—men have formed a human barricade around the stage.

"No problem," I say. With a smile, I hand my cloak and dagger to Atheer, accept my wooden longsword from Skerric, and make for the stage. The barricade parts for me to climb up. The stage is taller than it looks, and I tower over the crowd packed wall-to-wall in the tavern. The front doors have been thrown open too, permitting everyone who was waiting outside to cram in ahead of the show.

"Shall we engage in a friendly bet, Lord Elmer?" Hardy calls up to the sour-faced nobleman.

There's a sudden surge of people frantically exchanging slips of paper and coin with men wearing flat caps with black feathers tucked into them. Wynstan paces opposite me, waving his arm to incite the crowd's fervor. But a few people are betting on me to win—I know as much because they pause to study me before they nod and hand over their coins to the bookmakers.

The barman drains his mug and hops onto the stage, raking back his greasy brown hair with his fingers. "Get your bets in now and get them in big!"

Wynstan cracks his neck, leering at me. Atheer's tense face hovers into view behind the barricade. I nod reassuringly at him and, on the way, notice Mister Hardy now leaning with his back against his table, arms folded. Giving me that shrewd stare that demands I don't waste this opportunity.

The barman orders the end of betting and raises his arms, about to signal the start of the duel. I catch Qayn's eye in the crowd. He drops his soul wall, so I do the same.

*Remember to strike with your heart.*

The barman drops his arms and hops out of the way.

# 34

# IMANI

I STEP FORWARD, SWORD POINTED. WYNSTAN THROWS his sword down and lunges.

I react out of instinct and stab. The wooden point strikes him in the chest—it would kill him if this were a real battle, but it's not, and this is only a practice weapon. He endures the blow and shoves the sword away with such aggression that I relinquish my grasp on it, intuiting that this is no duel with rules and points to score. This is a barefisted battle, and the winner is the last one standing.

I step right, narrowly dodging his lunge, and push off my back foot with arms extended. I shove my weight against his torso and drive him across the stage, to the roar of the audience. For a moment, I think I have him, but it's a short moment. He twists in my pincer grip and elbows me in the side of the head, forcing me to stumble. A second later, he's tackled me. I crash to the stage, the back of my head thudding against it; spots dance over my eyes as the crowd bays for blood. Wynstan sits on my chest and immediately begins crushing my throat.

"Yield, fremde!" he demands, spittle flying.

I buck to try to pull a knee up to wedge between us, but he pins his to the stage, locking me in place, and I can't argue with his weight. I start to wheeze and tug at his wrists. Distantly I hear Atheer yelling at the barman to stop the fight, his voice strained with fear.

I throw a fist at Wynstan's head. In the time it takes to fly across the gap between us, my iron sense alerts me to Wynstan himself. I don't understand how, but Qayn told me that there's iron in our flesh. This is proof. I seize upon it with the pitiless frenzy of someone lashing out from the corner they've been backed into. Magic burns in my blood; my fist meets his jaw, and my magic spasms as if I'm pulling all my muscles at once. The punch is nowhere near forceful enough to throw Wynstan off me, yet he barks in pain and jumps as if I'm made of fangs.

*That's it,* Qayn whispers to me across our souls. *Strike with your heart. Bend him to your will as you do your dagger.*

I scramble to my feet. Wynstan, now on his hands and knees, glares at me over his shoulder. "What'd you do?"

"I know what you did. You ignored the rules of this duel."

"No," he seethes, pushing to his feet, "you *did* something to me just then!"

The crowd is already so sensitive to my presence that Wynstan's implication of underhandedness changes their excitement to anger in an instant. They begin hurling allegations of cheating, looking to the barman for rectification, even though Wynstan plainly cheated first. But they don't care, because they're not here to see a fair fight—they're here to see me beaten to a pulp. And that enrages me like nothing else.

"Yes, it's called being better!" I raise my fists and roll my shoulders. "Now are you going to stand there whining, Wynstan, or are you going to yield?"

The noise surges again. Teeth bared, Wynstan marches at me, fists brought up too. He throws a punch as soon as he's in range, which is sooner than I expect, owing to his long limbs. I dodge but don't clear it fully. His knuckles clip my jaw; I stagger, faintly dizzy. He strikes at my temple. I throw my arms up, remembering that Atheer once told me a blow to the temple can kill. My magic surges; everything in me seizes again. Wynstan's fist meets my raised forearm and a bit of jaw, but there's noticeably less power in his punch than there should be, and suddenly his expression has distorted as my iron sense reaches into his body and starts pulling at whatever it can find. He yowls in agony, retreating from me like a wounded spider yanking its limbs in.

*Careful,* Qayn warns, *you're making it obvious.*

I stop whatever I'm doing, but the crowd has noticed that something's amiss. Some chant, "Cheater!" Others demand I be checked for a hidden weapon. The rest are too enraged for words and push and shove for the stage. The barricade gives way to a younger man who bears a striking resemblance to Wynstan. It must be his brother. He throws something across the stage. Wynstan catches the sheath.

"You're not allowed to use a real weapon!" I protest.

Wynstan pulls the dagger free, short blade gleaming hot under the lanterns. I look to Atheer and Skerric for help. Atheer's still yelling at the barman, but the barman is ignoring him, and the men around the stage have closed ranks.

I look back just as Wynstan pounces. I grab his wrist, stopping the blade inches from my face. He grits his teeth and pushes down. My arms tremble; my boots slide back on the stage. Panic flares in me, and magic rushes to my hands.

"Drop it," I growl in Sahiran.

But instead of his dropping the dagger, my magic plucks it from his hands and throws it across the stage. The crowd's mystified outrage crescendos; the barricade parts. Someone grabs my arms and pins them behind me. Wynstan's brother.

"If a lesson's what you're looking for," says Wynstan, and then he lunges at me. He doesn't demand that I yield. That opportunity has passed. He's not going to wait for the Hunten either; he doesn't have to—he's going to kill me here, and nobody is going to intervene.

He swings at my head; I brace for pain, a broken jaw, and darkness. But someone else hurtles across the stage, dressed in a manner I recognize, and tackles Wynstan to the ground before climbing onto his chest. One fist cages Wynstan's throat; the other begins pummeling him.

The noise in the tavern suddenly becomes too loud to comprehend, and I feel as if I'm floating in suffocating silence. The barricade disperses, several men climb onto the stage, Wynstan's brother releases me, and they all turn their attention to the mystery attacker. But he's no mystery to me, with his burnished-ebony hair, hard-cut jaw, and bright-green eyes. It's Taha.

It takes four men to drag him off Wynstan. By then, blood is glistening on Taha's bruised knuckles and Wynstan's face, and it's smudged across the stage.

"I said *the fight's over*!" screams the flushed barman.

I stumble back as Taha throws the men off him and straightens to his full, formidable height. The lantern lights blur and bleed around him in a feverish haze. Am I dreaming? He's not the person I left in Brooma—and even the person I left in Brooma was beginning to show cracks in his façade. This Taha is covered in cuts and bruises just healing over, and when he finally looks up at me, I sense that he's survived terrible things.

An exhausted quiet intrudes upon the tavern. Mister Hardy interrupts it with enthusiastic clapping, startling almost everyone. He grins at us as he climbs onto the stage, accompanied by a girl in a plain black dress and bonnet who resembles him enough to be his daughter.

"Watching your fight has been *the* most fun I've had in a tavern all year!" he declares, shaking my hand. "Everyone, give them a round of applause for the fantastic show. Go on!"

The crowd obeys; the tavern fills with applause and whistles. It's almost magical how masterfully Mister Hardy soothes their inflamed passions. He shakes Taha's hand next.

"You have proven yourself most worthy, young man, young lady. I will gladly sponsor you both for the Hunten."

The applause quickens. My foggy brain fumbles over his offer, and I look at Taha in shock. He's even more perplexed. Of course he is; he probably arrived at the tavern about a minute before he was leaping onto the stage to save me. I understand that last part least of all. And then he lightly brushes my arm, asking me in Sahiran if I'm hurt, and my comprehension of the world just about vanishes.

"I should ask the same of you," I reply weakly, though I'm swiftly drowned out by Skerric materializing between us.

"Oh, thank the gods, you two know each other. I have utterly no idea what's going on here, but Mister Hardy is waiting for an answer. He's keen to sponsor you as a pair."

Atheer extends a hand to Taha, speaking in Sahiran. "Did you come here to help us?"

Taha shakes his hand, nodding, and that confirms it. This is a dream. There's no other explanation.

Atheer pulls him closer. "You can start right now. Imani needs a sponsor to enter a tournament, the winner of which gets to meet the prince, who will be wearing a tiara with three lovely *jewels* in it. Understand?"

"I'll participate," he says, glancing at me.

Atheer claps his arm. "Glad to hear. It's a battle to the death."

Taha reacts so little to the revelation that I begin wondering whether he even heard it. He seems distracted; his gaze lingers on me with an emotion I can't decipher—or can't bring myself to—before he turns his attention back to Skerric, who has just eagerly communicated our assent to Mister Hardy. Our new backer directs his jubilation at the mezzanine of fuming nobles.

"Then let it be known to all that I, Everett Hardy, and my daughter, Audrey Hardy, do sponsor this young man and woman of the Empire as fyghtors in De Wilde Hunten! For the glory of the Empire, in which all people are *common* before the Ever-King's court!"

The crowd claps and boos with the double mind of someone possessed. The nobles are so offended by Mister Hardy's speech they toss wine and food over the balconies.

Skerric nods at us as I'm picking grapes out of my hair. "Mister Hardy wants to forge the oath now in one of the private rooms."

Dazed, I follow him through the crowd. Qayn appears at my side, squeezing my hand and glancing guardedly over my shoulder at Taha as he joins us too, now carrying a bag. Suddenly Amira appears from between the spectators, wearing an enormous smile, and hugs me. Again I'm certain that I'm imagining things. I have to step back to examine her and be sure I'm not embracing a stranger.

"How are you here?" I ask, holding her arms. Perhaps I should be asking if she really *is* here.

A shadow passes over her face. "We'll speak later."

I can only drift on at the mercy of the world around me,

leaving the loud, hot main room of the tavern for a quiet, comfortable back room.

Everett and Audrey sit at one side of a table in the center, Everett gesturing us to sit opposite them. Skerric urges me to the chair in the middle, Taha to the one beside me. After a long hug, Atheer sits on my left, and Amira sits on Taha's right. Qayn slinks off to a shadowy corner where the hearth light doesn't reach, and Skerric stays standing at the head of the table, rubbing his hands together, more out of excitement, I bet, than to keep warm.

Everett unfolds a bundle of papers and hands them to Audrey, who has placed her boxy carry bag on the table. She looks to be my age, but she balances a pair of slim spectacles on her gently sloping nose and skims the papers with an intelligence beyond her years.

Everett beams at me and Taha. "I'm so appreciative that you agreed to handle this matter this way, messy though it was. I only wish you'd told me, Skerric, that there would be another challenger, but perhaps the delightful surprise was worth it."

"Agreed to handle . . . ?" I pitch forward. "I'm sorry, I don't know what you're talking about."

Everett's lips round under his precisely shaped mustache.

Skerric begins talking very rapidly: "Imani, I didn't tell you because I thought a genuine reaction would be much more convincing, and I also highly doubted you'd willingly endure the mockery of the nobles in the Cliff—" He pauses to take a steadying breath and continues in a more measured manner. "Sensing that our interests would be aligned, I met with Mister Hardy the night we arrived in Darkcliff. He agreed then that he would sponsor you—"

My jaw drops. "You *knew* this entire time that I had a sponsor?"

"Yes, but I wanted to announce the sponsorship in a more

*public* manner," Everett supplies. "It was important to me that you were seen by the nobles in the Cliff these last two weeks. Seen and rejected, I should say. They don't know what I know about you—that you possess a very special quality."

I sit back, stumped. I don't know what to say to this silver-tongued man; it's hard enough just concentrating on what he's telling me. I'm desperate to learn how Taha and Amira escaped capture and found passage here, and I have a strong urge to forgive Skerric his deception—though he doesn't deserve it—and ask Everett to just hand over the paperwork already so I can pick up that conversation instead. But I don't want to offend the man who has extended us a courtesy nobody else in this city would. I silently wait for him to continue. He smiles, though it doesn't touch his eyes.

"Of course, the special quality that you possess—and I dare-say, that the rest of your party possesses—is something nobody in Harrowland could. Not yet at least." He pauses, his smile widening slightly before slipping away.

Frowning, Audrey stops rifling through her carry bag and gently elbows her father. He reaches into his breast pocket and draws out a small jar of black ink, which she uncaps and uses to wet a short quill. Everett watches her scratch words in the gaps left on the paperwork.

"I don't know if you would know this," he says. "Even Harrow-landers don't. There is a suspension on correspondence traveling in and out of Alqibah at the moment. Every letter is secretly checked by officers of the king before it's permitted through the net, and if it contains information that it shouldn't, it is conveniently lost on the journey to its addressee."

I reluctantly abandon my impatience with this conversation.

Everett just said something very peculiar, though Audrey calmly continues scratching away at the paperwork.

"King Glaedric is behind the enforced silence," he continues. "He wishes to prevent news of certain . . . *discoveries* from becoming known to the nobility too soon. I am already abreast of the latest developments thanks to my own ingenuity, so I can appreciate why the suspension is in place." Everett looks up at us now, one eye wider than the other, lending him an air of wry conspiracy. "It may appear to you from the outside that our noble class is a cohesive one, but the contrary is very much true. Even the most loyal to the king worry about their survival under the dominant House of Brand. Separately, each searches for their own upper hand. Reputation and religious duty aside, the wealthiest houses sponsor fyghtors for the Hunten in their attempts to siphon land and gold from the king. Imagine, then, what they would do if they possessed *magic*."

There's no tenser silence than the one that now fills the room. "Once again, I don't know what you're talking about," I say after a moment, as wooden as the table we're seated at.

Audrey peers at me over her spectacles. Everett chuckles. "Skerric has already confirmed it with me. Now, I don't know *how* you did what you did onstage—I am not at all well versed in the matter—but I recognized that magic was involved. You hail from the hidden land across the mystifying desert in southern Alqibah."

I don't say anything. None of us do. We sit like a row of captives waiting to hear whether we're to be imprisoned for life or executed.

"Don't be afraid," Everett says in his airy, crafty way. "Your secret is safe with us. I merely wanted to make you feel comfortable as we work together to plot your victory in the Hunten. And we must scheme, there is no doubt." He leans in so the edge of the table digs into the buttons of his navy doublet. "I will speak plainly. I want you to win the Hunten. The nobles will say the same to their fyghtors, but I mean it more than any of them. I want you to win."

"Why?" I ask.

His gray eyes glimmer. "For gold—as much as I can make. I intend to position you in the public eye as tragic losers fated to die."

"Just as you've been doing to me these last two weeks," I realize aloud.

Taha frowns at me. "That doesn't sound like a winning strategy."

"It's not supposed to," Everett agrees. "By the day of the Hunten, I'll be one of the few people in the city who have bet on you to win. And I know you will win, because I know you possess magic, and you will use it to win if you must." He smiles.

I feel a bitter sting, knowing now that my humiliation in the garden was deliberate, that the hours spent sparring and posturing in the cold while nobles laughed at me were nothing more than a waste. But perhaps I'm looking at it the wrong way. I'm certain Everett would make the argument.

"It's not just about the gold, though," says Audrey in a surprisingly commanding voice given her unassuming appearance. "Like your victory, it's about delivering a message to the nobility and the House of Brand."

Taha leans back in his chair, arms folding across his broad chest. "What message is that?"

Everett leans even farther forward to compensate. "That the winds are changing in the Great Harrowland Empire, hmm?"

I feel them as a chill whispering over me. I offer Everett a steady nod. "Rest assured. We will win the Hunten, with magic if we must."

He has a long smile, foxlike in its cunning. Audrey rests her quill in its inkpot and hands the paperwork to Everett before ringing a bell from the center of the table. The barman enters, face furrowed as if he's smelled something offensive. Everett slides the paperwork across the table and points at the end. "Under our fine innkeeper's watch, press a drop of your blood here to make the oath."

Atheer hands me my dagger. I use it to goad a crimson dome and press my thumb to the parchment. Taha does the same with his dagger. The barman watches, and when it's done, he signs the parchment and leaves.

Audrey packs up her carry bag; Everett blows on the ink until it's dry. He tucks the folded paperwork under his doublet and pushes his chair back. "I shall have this form lodged this evening. Well met, Imani, Taha. I look forward to tournament day, my noble fyghtors."

# 35

# TAHA

TAHA THOUGHT HE'D BE MORE IN CONTROL OF HIS emotions. He used to act as if Imani didn't exist; now he can't focus on anyone or anything else. Something has changed. What's he thinking? Everything has changed.

He doesn't even notice he's followed her out of the tavern until he's freezing on the step of a waiting coach. They pile into the threadbare cabin, lit slightly by a hanging lantern. It's a relief that he doesn't wind up sitting beside Qayn—he doubts he could without breaking a sweat—but he breaks one anyway when Imani sits opposite him and her knees touch his. She opens her mouth to speak, but Amira cuts her off.

"Don't ask yet. It's not safe."

Imani sits back, chewing the inside of her cheek. She stares at her sister at first, then Taha, as if she thinks with enough willpower she'll see through his shell into his mind and get her answers that way. Taha looks back at her, expecting her to break the gaze, but she doesn't. She holds it as it becomes more loaded and he feels his racing heart drowning in a muddled sea of longing and despair. He caves first and shifts his attention to the city. Darkcliff isn't what he expected, this foul, overcrowded mess of solemn black stone and wood, but the longer Taha thinks about it, the more it makes sense that this should be the city that Glaedric left behind for so many of his people.

Their journey ends at a modest inn with an ambitious name, the Swan of Shorehill. Atheer, Amira, and Qayn go in first, but Imani stops Taha with a light tug on his elbow. "Can I speak with you?"

Despite the chaos of the tavern fight, she's beautiful in her proud composure. He nervously joins her at the inn's front wall. "We shouldn't discuss anything out here," he says.

She speaks anyway: "I'm sorry for what happened to Reza and Sinan. I just wanted you to know that before anything else. They didn't deserve to die."

Taha's breathing catches. Suddenly his grief is new again, the slow-healing wound cut open and the pain he barely survived flooding out. "The Harrowlanders burned Reza's body and scattered his ashes in the bay," he says. "They were going to have Sinan stuffed and mounted for Glaedric."

He doesn't know why he tells her such an awful thing, only that he feels a little better afterward.

Her own breathing becomes tremulous then, eyes shining like silver moons. "I'm so sorry," she whispers, placing a hand on his arm.

He looks down at it; she seems surprised by herself too and pulls away. He wants to pull her back, but it's almost instinct how he finds a way to divert the conversation. "Your brother is injured."

She nods, swiping quickly at her eyes. "Atheer nearly died fighting the soldiers in Brooma."

"I'm sorry, but I'm glad that he survived."

"Are you?" She searches his face. "Or would you be happier if Atheer had perished?"

"No," Taha says strongly. "Maybe I wouldn't have gone about things the same way as your brother, I don't know, but I understand now why he couldn't ignore what was going on in Alqibah. I just regret that I had to see it happen to *our* people before I could admit that it was wrong not to intervene." Taha shakes his head. "I thought I was doing the right thing, focusing my energy on the plight of Sahirans first, but I'm starting to think that helping others helps us too. . . ." He drifts off as an elderly man with a cane shambles alongside them. At first glance, Taha thinks it's Abu Hamza from Halaf, and he's struck by the fretful need to tell him to go back inside and hide from the soldiers before they change their minds about sparing him, and hide from the ghouls before they finish with the dead in the graveyard. Then the man turns his head, and the figment fades before his white beard and pale blue eyes.

Taha swallows, looking back at Imani. Her chin is quivering, lashes batting in an attempt to ward off tears. He gestures at the door uncomfortably. "Maybe we should go inside."

She goes first, past shaggy drunkards and a polite innkeeper to a private room upstairs where the others are waiting. As soon as Taha shuts the door behind him, she demands answers.

"We were taken through the Sahir with the Vanguard," Amira explains, "the leading part of Glaedric's army, tasked with seizing settlements all the way to Qalia. The Council was eventually alerted to their approach and shut the gates, but it was too late. Glaedric used us and other captives to force the Council's surrender. He controls the misra tree now. The Sahir is his."

*"No,"* Imani whispers. She drops to a crouch and holds her

head. Her shoulders shift as if she's crying, but she doesn't make a sound. Atheer remains fixated on something on the opposite wall, standing as rigidly as a load-bearing beam. Maybe the consequences of his actions are finally beginning to feel real. It's a guilt Taha wouldn't wish on his worst enemy.

Imani collects herself and stands again. "How bad is it?"

Amira glances at Taha before busying herself with her bag. He takes over the explanation.

"People who fight back are slaughtered. Most who surrendered were allowed to live, but they've had everything of value taken from them."

Imani's breathing shallows. "Most?"

He suddenly flinches from the searing fire engulfing the men in the coach outside Bis-Amna. *The heat is coming from the hearth behind you,* he realizes, yet he still hastily steps away from the flames. That's when he notices Qayn, lurking in the shadows in the far corner of the room. Staring at him with those black, depthless eyes. Judging him . . .

"Shields," he mumbles, looking back at Imani. "The ones who weren't in Qalia at the time were killed. So were people caught on the roads between settlements." He has to force every word out; it hurts as badly as pulling thorns from his skin. The things he saw in the Sahir have simultaneously been preserved in his memory and eroded by the ten days of sea air aboard the warship that brought them here. He feels as if the events are happening in the next room and a world away at the same time.

"And our family?" Imani asks, turning to her sister.

"They're not hurt," Amira quickly assures her. "They're safe for now."

"How did you escape?" Atheer asks, pressing a hand against his ribs; his other arm is immobilized in a splint.

Amira glances at Taha again. *This is it,* he thinks, his heart beginning to pound. Even with the terrors he's withstood until now, he's uneasy. What if Imani and Atheer don't believe him? He's already been their prisoner once; he doesn't want to be again.

"We didn't escape," he confesses. "Glaedric sent us to find you. He took us to Brooma so we could speak to Maysoon and find out that you'd come here. . . . He wants Qayn's crown."

He feels Qayn's gaze on his skin. The touch of a blade would chill him less.

"Glaedric— But— How does he—" Imani stumbles over her words.

"He's holding Mama and the Grand Zahim captive until he gets the crown," says Amira. "He knows the jewels are in his brother's headpiece. Right now, he's waiting on a ship in the harbor for Taha to secretly return with information on your activities. Once he knows what you're up to, he intends to spring a trap on you and seize Qayn's crown after it's been forged. As for how we found you, it was Spirits' luck that we spotted you walking into the tavern on the wharf. We'd just arrived in Darkcliff about half an hour earlier to search for you."

Imani stares at her sister, mouth open. Amira tries to comfort her: "It's all right. Mama hasn't been hurt."

"But she'll be killed if Glaedric doesn't get Qayn's crown! If he knows about Prince Kendric's tiara, he'll find out just as easily that we're entering the Hunten to steal the jewels."

"I intend to tell him," says Taha, "and you must continue with your plan as if you never learned about any of this from us. We were supposed to lie to you and say that we arrived here stowed aboard a merchant's ship."

Atheer eases down on a chair by the hearth. "We're volunteering our necks to a noose by doing nothing. Glaedric is cunning; he'll already have factored in the possibility of this betrayal."

"Which is why we need to stay a step ahead of him," says Taha. "You have to tell us everything about how and where the crown is going to be forged."

Imani throws her hands up. "*Why?* So that *he* can know everything?"

"He *must,*" says Amira. "Once Glaedric knows what you've planned, he'll make his own plans to thwart you, and tell *us* so that we're prepared."

"And we, in turn, will find that out and be able to prepare a counterattack," says Atheer.

"Precisely." Amira looks between them. "Nothing can come down to chance or be improvised in the moment. If Glaedric senses that he's being double-crossed, he'll kill Mama and the Grand Zahim, and we'll be next."

Taha braces himself and turns to Qayn, still cloaked in the shadows. "This comes down to you, Qayn. We came here to help you, but you must be confident that if we get you your magic back, you can stop Glaedric in what will be a very narrow window to act."

A menacing laugh rises from the shadows. "My, my, is this really the same boy who was advocating to have me killed not long ago?"

Taha stiffens. "The situation has changed," he says.

"I can see that." A tone like a razor's edge. "You've sailed across the seas with the king's leash around your neck to beg me to save your father. And what else can you do?" Qayn divests himself of the shadows, though the dark jealously clings to him. "You can't give my crown to Glaedric. Let's ignore for a moment the cataclysmic havoc he'd unleash on the world before his brains began dribbling out of his ears—*your* life, and the lives of your loved ones, would no longer be of any worth to him. That's why you've come around. You understand, now that the Sahir has fallen so violently, that *you need me.* Don't you?"

Taha's fingers curl; his nails dig into his palms. "Yes," he says through his teeth, "I need you."

A long slit of a smirk cuts from ear to ear. "I have seen many extraordinary things in my time, but this change of heart . . . *this,* I place somewhere near the top." The smirk vanishes. "If you're asking whether I can stop Glaedric once he realizes you've double-crossed him but before he has your father killed in retaliation, the answer is yes, Taha, I can. As to whether I *will,* well . . ."

A frisson of fear runs through Taha. He begins rubbing the sore spot on his chest that he sustained slamming into the railing of the warship during the vicious storm on the Serpent Sea. It feels more like he's trying to massage a tangle of nerves trapped inside.

"That's not fair," Amira objects. She's brave to be challenging Qayn when they both know he isn't lying about his power. "You need Taha's help in the tournament to get your magic back. It's only fair that you give your word to save his father in return."

Qayn drops a sneer in her direction. "In the same way Taha gave his word that he'd bring Atheer back to the Sahir?"

"I acted out of ignorance," Taha says, stepping forward. "I believed I was doing the right thing at the time. But I saw what you saw, Atheer, the worst of the invaders' aggression, and now I can't unsee it. It'll follow me every day, everywhere I go, as I imagine it does you and every person in Alqibah—"

"It's all right, Taha," says Atheer, already shuffling over to meet him. "The past is forgiven."

They shake hands like old friends. Taha thought they would

never see eye to eye again, though a part of him always hoped for it. So much about the world has gone wrong lately, but this small thing feels like it's just where it's supposed to be.

Qayn turns his head to Imani. "Well, is the past forgiven? You have a say, given you were also the subject of an attempted murder."

Taha watches Imani with a resigned sadness, waiting for the inevitable resumption of conflict between them. Atheer may have forgiven him, but Taha knows that for Imani, nothing he does in the present will ever erase the things he did in the past.

"We were fighting on the opposite sides of a war," she says quietly. "We're fighting on the same side now. We must behave accordingly if we hope to win."

Did Taha hear her right? That was a measured response, absent the biting passion of resentment. Not even a sneer. But Imani *is* different somehow, wiser, more forgiving—or maybe the shortcoming is his. He never believed in her capacity to be better.

"Well, I suppose it's settled, then," says Qayn. "Who am I to stand in the way of peace? Yes, you have my word that I will save your father if you return my magic to me, Taha." He smirks. "I believe that makes us allies now. You must be thrilled."

"We still need to know how you'll forge your crown and where," says Amira.

Qayn shrugs. "It's very simple. No tools are required beyond the jewels themselves. I only need somewhere calm where I won't be rushed. We've decided it will be on the ship while we're sailing back to Alqibah."

Amira glances at Taha for help.

"I'm sorry, Qayn, but that's not enough," he ventures. "Where on the ship will you forge your crown? The captain's cabin? The crew quarters? Will you need to be alone, or can we be present? *When* will you do it? As soon as you're on the ship? Once you've exited the River Waden?" He steps closer. "Please. Glaedric is meticulous in his planning, and he won't tolerate ambiguity from me. If I can't give him specific information, he'll suspect that you don't trust me, and then Amira and I won't be of any use to him anymore."

"And neither will our parents," Imani says solemnly, Amira nodding.

Qayn considers Taha through narrowed eyes. Taha's guts churn, but he forces himself to gaze back at Qayn as steadily as possible.

"There's something else to bear in mind," Taha says. "If Glaedric feels it'll be too complicated or difficult to steal the crown from you on the ship, he'll engineer a reason that forces you to forge it somewhere more favorable to him."

Qayn laughs coldly. "So what you're telling me is that I should make it as easy as possible for Glaedric to rob me."

Taha grimaces. "Unfortunately, yes. That way, Glaedric's plan will be a simple one, which will make counteracting him simple too."

Qayn heaves a sigh. "As you wish. I will forge my crown on the deck of the *Prize* as soon as we've departed the River Waden. Tell Glaedric I need the aid of the fresh air," he adds with a smirk.

A fast knock sounds at the door, startling them.

"It's Skerric," comes a Harrowlander's voice from the other side. "Just returned from the Filthy Bilge!"

Imani opens the door, and the fine-featured blond who was assisting their group at the tavern bustles past her, his smile fading.

"Staggnir's scepter, you all look like you've seen the black dog." He turns, giving a cursory glance to Amira before settling his gaze squarely on Taha. "Forgive me, we've not been properly introduced."

Imani gestures at them. "This is Taha, a fellow Shield, and Amira, my sister."

"Well met." Skerric removes his hat and shuts the door. "Imani, Taha: Mister Hardy has arranged for you to meet with armorers tomorrow."

"Tomorrow?" Imani fingers a buckle on her chest. "But we already have armor."

"He says you'll need chainmail. Plate too if you can bear the weight. Helms; you can choose the design."

Taha waves a hand in front of the Harrowlander. "Skerric, is it?"

The young man tilts his face and smiles up at him, blushing. "Yes indeed. Your Harrowtongue is most impressive, by the way."

"Thanks, I've had a lot of practice lately." Taha returns a brief smile. "Maybe now is a good time for you to walk me through what I agreed to tonight?"

# 36

# IMANI

THE NIGHT BEFORE DE WILDE HUNTEN IS RESTLESS. I toss and turn for hours. In my dreams, I confront one bad scenario after another—I die in the Hunten; Glaedric outwits us and steals Qayn's crown; the Sahir is never free again. Shortly before dawn, I become so restless that I abandon any attempt at sleep and run through dagger drills. Someone softly knocks on my door when I'm partway through a stab.

I open it to Qayn. He blinks, his black tresses shifting, and says, "Hello. You're awake."

"You're observant." I step aside. "I was just practicing overhand attacks, if you'd like to keep me company."

He comes in and shuts the door behind him. "Certainly, but it's not even dawn yet. You should be resting."

I slump against the wall. "I *tried,* Qayn. I can't stop thinking that I'm about to die in a few hours. I'm not afraid, I don't want to withdraw; I'm just—"

"Anxious," he says with a concerned frown.

"And restless. I could sprint a loop of the city without needing a break." I perk up slightly. "Interested?"

He smiles. "Thank you, I think I'll pass. It's cold and I never sprint."

I raise a brow. "Never? What if a lion was chasing you?"

"I suppose I'd just have to join him for dinner."

I snort, despite myself. "That is a bad joke, and you know it."

"I know." Grinning, he takes the dagger from my hand and sets it down on the bedside table. "How about a dance instead? You still get to practice your footwork, but we'll be warm."

My heart skips a beat. I pretend to be reluctant about the offer, though I feel exactly the opposite. "Fine." I sigh. "If you insist."

I interlock my fingers with his and very lightly rest my other hand on his shoulder. He wraps an arm around my waist and pulls me against him. My pulse leaps again.

"All we need now is a song," I say, looking up into his face.

"I have one, but you must concentrate. It demands a lot of twirling and dipping."

"Not the dips," I groan. "I swear, Qayn, if you whack my head on the floor trying to be impressive, I will *murder* you."

"I understand that I may not be the most physically imposing individual, but I promise, I won't drop you."

He demonstrates my security by holding me even closer; so close I could rise on the tips of my toes and kiss him. I even feel his heartbeat against mine, racing too.

He begins humming a cheerful, jaunty tune, interrupting it a minute later to sing a chorus with a melody that would put an oasis songbird to shame: " 'We two belong here, you and me, between the date palms and full moon, the desert and the sea.' "

I'm so moved by the beauty of his voice that I don't even

think about where to put my feet next. I just dance, shuffling freely across the small room, safe in his arms. I even survive some twirls and a dip.

"I hate to think you might be feeling left out," I say once he's pulled me straight again. His brows knit until I raise my hand over his head. "Your turn."

I expect him to refuse the twirl, but he dons a devilish smile and rotates gracefully, even adding a flourish at the end with an extended arm before returning to wrap me against him.

"Don't underestimate how much I like to dance, Imani," he warns.

"I'm beginning to realize my error," I say, laughing.

He pauses. And then, "I'm beginning to realize just how much I like you."

I'm so shocked that for a moment, I can only stare at Qayn with a foolish grin plastered on my face. Then I halt him in place. "You do?"

"Yes." He chuckles suddenly, nervous. "I know. It's rather tragic how swiftly you won me over, isn't it?"

I answer his question with a kiss. He smiles against my lips before he returns the kiss with a touch that resembles silk. It's sublime, being this close to him; a gift, to feel his heart galloping in step with mine; to look up at his laughing eyes and see into depths I didn't know were there before. The kiss is lingering, an intensely enjoyable touch of aniseed. But it comes with an undercurrent of guilt that threatens to pull me under.

"Something bothers you," he says when we part. "You don't feel the same way? I was sure you did. All those dreams you have of us together . . ."

"I do," I interrupt self-consciously. "I do like you, Qayn, but . . . I'm afraid that I shouldn't. We're so different."

"Perhaps, but what we share in common is greater than what we don't," he says. "Isn't that the joy of companionship? To seek out and embrace what unites us?" He gathers my hands in his. "You don't have to answer me. And if you send me away after this matter of my magic and the Harrowlanders is done, I will respect your decision. Just know that you and I . . . I think we could find happiness together, if only as companions. Consider it?" He smiles warmly, holding our hands against his chest. Then he glances at the shutters. "I suspect it's nearly time you started getting ready. Go in power, Imani. I'll be with you every step of the way."

He vanishes. I collapse on the edge of my bed, my heart fluttering madly. I wish I could crawl back under my blankets; something tells me I would drift off into a happy slumber and dream only of dancing and Qayn's dimpled smile. Instead, I open the shutters, permitting frigid air to dispel the room's stuffiness. Pale light drifts in too. The sun is rising over Darkcliff, meaning the Bidwell Procession that precedes the tournament is not far off.

I bathe, braid my hair, and dress in a belted green tunic and brown sirwal. The earthy colors are a deliberate choice to help camouflage the parts of my body that won't be covered by armor during the Hunten. Amira, Atheer, and Farida arrive shortly after and help me put on the armor that Mister Hardy sent, which includes a shirt of chainmail and a tunic of thick boiled leather. While Atheer and Farida finish the buckles, Amira asks if she can apply some makeup. "To intimidate your opponents," she explains.

I agree, simply to be in her company a while longer. As she lines my eyes in black kohl, I wonder about her journey through the Sahir. She's told me a few stories, how she and Taha were kept as prisoners, how the settlements were taken over, but I sense that she's omitting the worst details to spare my feelings, and that only distresses me more. These last few days, I've begun noticing changes in Amira. She doesn't laugh as much or as easily. She's content spending hours alone reading in the room that Atheer rented for her, rather than seeking either of us out. I try to convince myself that she's maturing, but I'm afraid she's just withdrawing from the world.

When she's finished my makeup, we go downstairs to the unopened tavern for a tea ceremony. The innkeeper has festooned the dim room with paper decorations in the shapes of stags and suns, and in a show of support for us, she's left a tray of delicious-smelling breads for breakfast.

Skerric is already here, helpfully fetching a teapot off the hearth. He's dressed more like Lord Ashton Hargrave this morning, in a blue-and-gold doublet, a matching cape slung over one shoulder, and a blue hat sporting a very tall white feather. He has even put on some gold earrings.

The tavern is empty aside from him and Taha, who arranges ceremonial tools on the table. Yesterday Amira told me how he protected her during their journey. He lured a giant sand serpent away before it almost killed her; he tied their wrists together during a terrible sea storm so that they wouldn't get separated in the chaos if their ship began to sink. He showed her that he's the hero of the stories I used to hear being passed around the barracks. *It's incredible to me, after all that happened between us, that I now believe Taha is a good person when he's not under his father's influence,* she mused, and she didn't argue or take any offense when I was dubious about her conclusion. *I hope you come to see it too,* she said, oblivious that her words were water upon a vine of twisted longing.

Even with my growing feelings for Qayn, and how hard I've fought to kill that vine, I realized it was reawakening the night Taha returned to us, so I began avoiding him for fear of giving it life. I've barely seen him over the last few days beyond our appointment at the armorers and the meeting we had with Skerric to discuss tournament rules and strategy; we've certainly not spent any time alone. When he isn't pretending to sneak away to meet Glaedric, he's with Amira or Atheer—when Atheer isn't with Farida—or, much to my surprisingly strong jealousy, he's being shown around Darkcliff by a plainly smitten Skerric.

Yet, for all my efforts, my breathing still hitches when he turns to face me. He's wearing his new armor too, a knee-length chainmail tunic held down by a leather vest studded with silver detailing that matches his pauldrons, vambraces, and shin guards. He's slung a dark brown bisht over the top and matched the cloak's green trimming with a green belt. A helm similar to mine, domed and capped with a point like the top of a minaret, rests on the table; tied to its tip, a green ribbon.

"You look like a Sahiran warrior-hero of folklore," Amira compliments him as we approach.

"Doesn't he just? Exactly as Mister Hardy wants," says Skerric. He places the teapot on the table and beams at Taha before finally noticing me. "You look dazzling too, Imani."

Taha sees me staring at him from behind Atheer. I'm quick to act aloof, but rather than giving me that arrogant, goading look he did that time I saw him shirtless, he simply appraises my armor and turns to the mortar on the table, which holds strips of misra.

"The ceremony is ready for you," he says.

I frown at the lone cup on the table and blurt out, "You're not participating?"

Right away, I cringe at my insensitivity. I've heard numerous sad stories about Shields whose mindbeasts die while they're melded. Many never recover their magical aptitude and have to leave active duty. I hope that's not the case with Taha, but now isn't the right time to discuss the matter—nor do I think I'm the right person to broach it.

"Forgive me," I say quickly. "Thank you for arranging the ceremony."

He wordlessly bows his head and joins the others at the hearth.

I place my helm on the table and start grinding the misra. At first, I meditate on the Great Spirit's gift, but later, as I'm sipping the hot tea, I ponder Qayn's approach to magic. It differs totally from the one taken by Auntie and the Order. Qayn doesn't just view the misra differently—as a key or bridge to magic rather than magic itself. He also renounces the foundational tenets of magical practice. The Laws of Adjustment and Essences mean nothing to him. I might accept that, because he's a djinni and his magic comes from another realm with its own set of rules, but he proposes that the Laws should mean nothing to me either. And the longer I keep his company, the more I feel I've spent my relatively short life as a sorcerer engaging not with the truth but with a mural convincingly designed to impersonate it.

After the ceremony, Taha helps me fill flasks with the remaining tea. We work in total silence despite standing side by side. It's a torturous kind of quiet, and more than continuing it, I dread the thought of having to break it during the Hunten.

Outside, the city is awake, and the atmosphere is electric. Thanks to an intense campaign by public street sweepers over the last few days, the streets are noticeably cleaner and the air smells fresher. Even the persistent canopy of smog has cleared from above the city as the factories remain closed. Despite the many coaches occupying the roads, including ours, there isn't enough public transport to go around. Seas of people engulf the sidewalks, hauling stools and other picnic supplies. Closer to Lift Street, musicians play lively ballads among the crowds waving brown-and-maroon pennants, bakers pass out pastries and pies, and vendors distribute wooden weapons, miniature shields, and antler headbands to gaggles of excited children, who spar each other with courageous abandon.

"The House of Brand funds all this from their own coffers," Skerric relates as we gawk out the coach windows. "When the Hunten is over, there'll even be a feast in the streets. It's an old trick, but it works: give the people revelry for a few days and you buy their silence for seven years."

The people of the Dark certainly seem to have set their troubles aside to deal with another day.

At the foot of Lift Street, we step out into the exuberant throb of horns and shouts of city guards marshaling people down the sidewalks. Rows of tables have been set up there, I assume in anticipation of the feast to come, and waist-high wooden fences festooned with flags bar the watching crowd from the Bidwell Procession, moving up the long street to the lifts.

We have to venture through the crowd to reach the guardhouse established behind the cordon. As soon as people notice us, they boo and hurl abuse. I follow Skerric with my head down, trying to ignore the food pelting me. Taha does the same, but his fist is wrapped very tightly around his bow.

Suddenly, a voice rises above the insults: "Ignore the cowards!"

I look up at the group who've pushed through to see us. The encouragement came from a woman at the front, her dress sleeves rolled up as if she means to brawl. She raises a fist to me as we pass, the women and girls behind her cheering. "They fear your power, lady!" she shouts to me. "Kill them with it!"

It's not the reassurance I was looking for, but it's what I need to hold my head high again.

The guards allow us onto Lift Street to meet Everett and Audrey. Everett is dressed as simply as he was at the Filthy Bilge, this time in an austere black doublet slightly detailed in the buttons and around the ruffle of his white collar, with matching breeches and hose. Audrey is in a floor-length brown dress with a cape slung over one shoulder; her only adornment is her belt, with a silver buckle and a green stone at its center. On her fine brown hair, which she has in a single braid, she wears a brown bonnet. Their appearance, particularly that of Everett, seems deliberate in its opposition to decadence.

He shakes our hands without so much as a smile. I wonder why until I remember that we're being watched by thousands of people still weighing up whether to risk gambling on us to win, an outcome Everett *doesn't* want. His apparent anxiety is cunning theater.

As we join the Procession, Everett explains that we'll continue together up to the lifts, after which Amira, Atheer, and Farida must rejoin the crowd. He's rapidly drowned out by a shouting chant rising along the sidewalk ahead.

*"Wulf-syg! Wulf-syg!"*

The famed warrior and two-time Hunten Victor walks farther up the street with a party of courtly-looking men in heavy silk robes. Armed with a poleaxe, Lord Wulfsyg is somehow more imposing than the statue of him that seemed to mockingly watch me perform in the garden for two weeks. His ruddy, bearded face belongs to a man perhaps thirty years old, but his deep-set gray eyes have seen more hardship than they should. He doesn't seem to have been diminished in the slightest by any of it. I suspect he's dealt just as much hardship to others and will be keen to do the same to us.

Yet the smile Wulfsyg directs at the doting crowd is genteel; he even stops to accept roses and kisses from the droves of people trying to throw themselves over the barricades at him. He wears chainmail under leather, though his muscular arms are exposed and painted in swirling blue patterns that match the very dark blue band painted across his eyes. A belt with a large, ornate silver buckle adorns a kind of skirt, constructed in leather strips, worn over dark trousers and fur-trimmed boots. Pieces of white fur have been affixed to the leather armor over his shoulders, and on his back is slung a round shield painted with a stag's head. The outfit lends him a rugged, earthy appeal. I'm certain he's aware of that—this is his own cunning theater, engineered to make the spectators forget that *Lord* Wulfsyg Grim, Baron of Stanfeld, is the king's man and not theirs.

Closer to us is Wilim, an impressively tall fyghtor in a full suit of armor, helm held in the crook of his waist, a longsword as tall as me on his hip; his cropped silvery hair complements his clear blue eyes, which occupy a face of otherwise unexceptional features. He's paired with Col, a stocky younger man in plate armor carrying a wooden flagstaff against each shoulder; one banner boasts the Empire's stag, the other a crest, likely that of the house backing them. Their sponsoring nobles strut alongside them: a man in a puffy bright-red doublet and a woman in a frilled, embroidered red dress so wide in the skirt that she's forced to walk some paces apart from the rest of her party. Wynstan, my opponent in the Proving Round, walks about fifty feet ahead of them with his younger brother, Rodgar, and their sponsoring nobles, including the sour-faced Lord Elmer. But none of the fyghtors are paid even half as much attention by the crowd as Wulfsyg.

"The people adore him," I remark.

Everett leans in. "They adore the *idea* of him more—the commoner ennobled. He was knighted after his first victory; after his second, His Majesty made him a baron. Every person in this crowd wishes that could happen to them."

"It's not wrong to dream of a better life," says Taha. "But Wulfsyg was lucky to be born physically strong with an aptitude for combat."

"Born a Far Northerner too, like His Majesty," Everett points out.

"That certainly helped," Skerric says, noticeably bitter. "It's no secret His Majesty prefers his kith to even his closest allies."

"And Wulfsyg *still* had to win a fight to the death before he was ennobled," Taha says, shaking his head. "I think the only reliable way an average person can improve their life is by holding the people in power accountable, or removing them."

Everett's eyes light up. "Precisely!" he says, while Skerric nods in enthusiastic agreement.

I study Taha out of the corner of my eye, recalling the arguments we had about the state of Sahiran society. I want to admire his commitment to opposing inequality wherever he sees it, but another part of me wants to understand how he can when he murdered three innocent men for opposing his father's election. I suppose I really don't know a thing about Taha after all.

We walk in Lord Wulfsyg's shadow all the way to the Royal Citadel's lift tower. Dozens of the most extravagantly clothed nobles I've ever seen have gathered here to chat, laugh, and drift between the parties, accepting goblets of wine and prim squares of cake from servants. Wulfsyg doesn't glance at us or any other fyghtors when we arrive. In total, I count six pairs, to make twelve of us entering the tournament, although Wulfsyg's partner, the Ent, isn't here, and I don't know if Wulfsyg intends to enter alone this season. The only fyghtors who do look at us are Wynstan and Rodgar. The former waves to get my attention, then points at me before sliding his blue-stained finger across his neck and rolling his eyes into the back of his head. The crowd laughs; Wynstan grins, and Rodgar starts spinning his sword for their entertainment.

Suddenly a roar erupts from the crowd behind us. I turn to see the gigantic Ent looming over everyone as he marches to the gates. As pale as a block of ice with a head of chin-length, stringy brown hair, he must be seven feet tall and wields an even larger poleaxe than Wulfsyg's. The Ent glares at the crowd with contempt, as if he longs for a chance to devour them, but they whoop hysterically, children wave their toy axes, and women toss their bonnets at him.

Our group appreciates the monstrous man's approach in tense silence. Noticing, Wulfsyg smirks at us before returning to his conversation with the nobility collected around him. But it's interrupted only a few moments later by a great trumpeting coming from the boys in tall conical hats flanking the lift tower. The single door in its façade opens, and the gates to the lift grounds swing shut behind us. Guards remove some of the makeshift fences barring the screaming crowd, who sprint to the tower fence and press against it, stopped like a flood meeting a levee.

A silhouette appears in the open tower door. The trumpeting ceases, the crowd quiets, and one of the boys blows a curved horn. A deep bellow issues across the city; even the scree under my boots trembles. I raise a hand to shield my eyes from the morning light as Prince Kendric steps out.

# 37

# IMANI

I DRAW A SHARP BREATH AND HOLD IT. PRINCE KENDric resembles his painting exactly, but rather than a robe, he's donned a heavily patterned dark brown suit of armor. I don't care to look at it. My eye is immediately drawn to the tiara on his brow—and its three jewels radiating light that rivals the morning sun.

"That's them," I whisper.

I know it. I can feel Qayn's magic as I can feel magic emanating from the misra tree, yet somehow this is so much more. Qayn's magic is intense, brimming with potential in a way I've never experienced before.

I drop the wall between our souls; his is already down. He looks through me at the tiara, and as he does, I experience his emotions. It's like having the Serpent Sea thrown over me. Tears well in my eyes. I sway on the spot and struggle to breathe through his raw relief, joy, and gratitude crashing over me, one after the other, wave over wave. I hear his frantic begging, *Please, Imani, you must take them! Let nothing and nobody stand in your way!* And witnessing the jewels and the might burning off of them, I am certain now that his ability to save the Sahir is real. He *did* build the First City; I knew as much, but now I *know* in my heart and soul. Qayn's power is not a lie.

Prince Kendric steps onto the stage erected outside the tower. The nobles and fyghtors crowd in, jostling us to the center behind the podium. As Kendric begins his speech, I identify the one undeniable similarity between him and his older brother: the relaxed, almost apathetic manner in which they speak, as if they never want you to forget how much you bore them.

"I lead as Master of the Hunt in the stead of my brother, His Majesty King Glaedric," declares the prince. "In the season of De Wilde Hunten, the extraordinary Golden Crown stags descend from their mountain refuge above us to battle each other to the death for the right to mate. We too gather to do battle for the right to ensure our great Empire's continued prosperity. Our fyghtors are our Golden Crown stags; our Victors shall earn for us the Ever-King's glory."

The nobles and fyghtors applaud, echoing a refrain of "Glory, glory." There's a delay before the crowd behind us applauds and takes up the refrain. They do it in stages as the prince's speech is passed down through officials standing on raised platforms along the street. Kendric gazes out at the crowd, waiting, but I doubt he's seeing anybody through that foggy gaze. Skerric said there were rumors the prince had a fondness for drink. I think he's already drunk.

It's a few minutes before he picks up again. In that time, I hear Qayn. He's pacing the halls of his palace, whispering incessantly about the jewels, often indecipherably.

Urging me to bring them to him.

He sounds manic.

I tense as Kendric suddenly looks Taha and me over before settling on Wulfsyg and the Ent. "I'm certain you are as impatient as I am to begin this most sacred rite. I will not hold up De Wilde Hunten any longer. May only the best of *our* fyghtors win, and in the glow of their blazing triumph, may we revel for three days and three nights, and another seven years of glory."

He withdraws to the tower, surrounded by his guards. The trumpets sound again, and the audience of fyghtors and sponsors spreads out as last words and supplies are exchanged.

I hug Atheer, Amira, and Farida. "Fight hard for the Sahir and Alqibah," says my brother as he hands me my helm.

I slip it onto my head. "I'll give it everything and then some."

The nobles finish going up the lift to the Citadel, and now it's the turn of the fyghtors and their sponsors. I leave my siblings and Farida with a last nod and follow Taha, Skerric, Everett, and Audrey through the tower door into a long, sconce-lit stone corridor. Our group is the last to enter; two Royal Guards bring the door to a clanging close, muffling the cheering crowd.

We're raised through the lift shaft after the visiting nobility and exit into a vast walled yard containing stables, kennels, an armory, and what appear to be the barracks and servant quarters, among a number of other structures. The Royal Guards lead us through a secondary gate and up a ramp to the imposing keep, though it appears dwarfed in the shadow of the mountain behind it. Rather than entering, we continue along the path. Attached to the keep by a long arcade is a tower ringed in balconies beginning to crowd with nobles and the servants who pamper them with food and wine. They enjoy an uninterrupted view of the harsh mountain and, at its feet, a heavily forested area fenced off by a tall stone wall where the Hunten will take place. From somewhere near the forest's center rises a thin, reddish column of smoke.

We follow the Royal Guards to the fence and gather there while one hands out small fireworks and matchboxes. I recall the ornate letter delivered to Mister Hardy listing the Hunten's rules, which Skerric carefully ran me and Taha through. Each pair of fyghtors will be given a firework, to be kept on one of us at all times. At the end of a battle, the triumphing fyghtors must let off their fallen opponents' firework. After five fireworks have sounded, the winning pair are to blow the horn from Victors' Tower, in the center of the grounds, its location marked by the reddish smoke wafting from its peak.

Taha accepts our firework while I'm shaking hands with Everett. "Good fortunes," he wishes us. "Be pitiless, hmm?"

After Audrey and Skerric wish us well too, the three of them leave with the other sponsors along a hedged path to the observation tower, where nobles are already leaning over the balconies, peering at us through binoculars. A pair of Royal Guards open the gates, and the remaining guards approach to begin escorting us inside.

"Watch your back, Wulfsyg," Taha says in perfectly articulate Harrowtongue.

Wulfsyg strolls over, holding his helm under his arm, and stops so close to Taha that their chests almost meet.

"All bark and no bite, you are. The Hunten is for us, fremde cur. You're here only because the people want blood."

"They'll have it from you," says Taha.

Wulfsyg grins. "Don't count on it."

"Lord Wulfsyg," says the waiting guard.

He puts on his gold-antlered helm, though it stops short of covering his grin. He takes a few steps back, still leering, then turns and marches with the Ent after the guard through the gates.

"Why?" I ask Taha.

"To get in his head. A man in doubt is as good as dead. Something my father taught me."

It's a few minutes before a guard collects us. We enter the grounds last, following a tree-lined path with several concealed paths branching off it. The one we're taken down ends in another gate, which the guard unlocks and swings open. A steep, ancient-looking staircase descending to rugged wilderness has been carved into the cliffside beyond it.

We pass through the gate. The guard shuts and locks it behind us and retreats, the sound of his boots on the gravel gradually diminishing to silence.

I carefully tail Taha down the steps zigzagging to the forest below. At the base of the steps, I stop to stare up at the cliff wall, but I can't see the observation tower from this angle. Now, even more than before, I feel removed from everything and everyone. Alone.

*No,* Qayn says across our souls. *Never alone, Imani.*

A loud whistling interrupts the silence. A raven crossing the sky above swoops away as a firework explodes in a twinkling plume over the grounds with a heart-stopping bang.

I tilt my head back and watch the sparkles fall like rain and die like dusk sun.

"That's it," I say to Taha. "De Wilde Hunten has begun."

# 38

# TAHA

TAHA HASN'T BEEN IN A FIGHT TO THE DEATH BEFORE, but he didn't imagine it would start like this: quiet enough to hear a bird chirping. He studies the shadowy spaces between the tree trunks. The Hunten grounds aren't just quiet; they're still.

Imani moves away from the cliff wall. "We shouldn't linger. Wulfsyg has won the Hunten twice before. He might be familiar with the starting locations of other fyghtors."

Taha follows her across the distinctive, pepper-scented vines carpeting the forest floor. Just like their fabric counterparts that decorated Taeel-Sa, Brooma, and Qalia, the vines are dotted with white flowers. Imani marches ahead, chin tipped to her chest as she surveys for movement. It would be wise for Taha to watch their surroundings too, but he spends more time admiring how cutthroat she looks in her black kohl liner, mail, and leathers. If only she'd turn that gaze on him. It's come back again, the desperate longing and those unspoken words digging like spikes against the inside of his mouth. He should just stop her under the oak ahead and confess his feelings, even if she mocks him for them afterward. That would be all right. Being scorned and hated is the closest Taha ever gets to being seriously acknowledged by Imani. And regardless of her response, at least he'd be alleviated of this burden. The Hunten isn't the most appropriate place to do it, but what better time is there? Things are only going to get harder, more complicated—

Imani stops and draws her dagger, whispering, "I saw something."

Taha snaps out of his shameful reverie. Only a fool would listen more intently to his own thoughts than the forest filled with hunters trying to kill him. He reaches for an arrow in his quiver when the biggest stag he's ever seen bounds past the trees ahead, unleashing an echoing roar. Imani gasps, as astounded as Taha by its size, strong reddish coloring, and radiant gold antlers that end in deadly spikes.

"Look, there's another." She points at a second stag stalking the first, this one with an even larger crown of gold. She and Taha creep over and crouch behind a tree with a closer view of the glade in which the stags are now facing each other.

"They're about to fight," Taha whispers, recalling what Prince Kendric said about why the Gold Crest stags descend from the mountain. "There might be a female nearby."

"There."

He follows Imani's pointed finger and catches a glimpse of a deer, more subdued in coloring, slipping behind a fallen oak. The stags trade a series of grunts and barks before charging each other. They lock antlers in a loud crash, sending up plumes of gold flecks. Imani's eyes widen. The stags wrestle back and forth, coloring the frigid air with gold every time they clash until the glade is swirling with stardust.

"It's beautiful," she murmurs.

*So are you,* he thinks.

After several minutes, the first stag is thrown off balance and impaled in his flank by the stag with the larger antlers. The loser collapses, dead, in the golden glade, and the bloodstained victor lopes off in the direction of the doe. Imani exhales, leaning against the tree.

"That was both awful and amazing."

Taha nods mutely. His heart has started to pound, his palms clammy under his gloves. It has to be done and gotten out of the way. He can't concentrate otherwise.

"Imani, I—"

"Hold on." She straightens, staring over his shoulder.

The unsaid words tumble back down his throat. "What is it?"

"We're not alone." She slowly rises to her feet.

He stands too, frowning. "Another stag?"

"No. People."

Her dagger glows bright blue and lengthens to a shortsword. He turns to where she's looking and nocks his bow. With a careful eye, he inspects the slant of every shadow, the shiver of every fern and bough. Nothing. Yet Imani doesn't waver in her vigilance, so he waits.

"I know you're there," she declares in Harrowtongue. "Hiding won't save you."

Taha is almost surprised when a tall, blond Harrowlander leaves the cover of the trees: the joker Wynstan, wearing a cocky grin and wielding a short axe in one fist and a wooden shield in the other. His brother, Rodgar, appears about twenty feet away, armed with a shortsword. It's either lucky or suspicious how quickly the brothers found them, but Taha sets speculation aside for now and shoots an arrow at the elder brother. Wynstan's shield snaps up, catching the arrow in the patterned wood with a dull *thwack*ing thud. The shield lowers; Wynstan glares over its rim, then the brothers run at them.

"Reposition," Taha says.

Imani pivots and sprints alongside him between the trees. Taha searches his surroundings, hoping for elevation; concealment, too, if he's lucky. An arrow fired from a hidden spot on higher ground will either catch Wynstan in the face by surprise, or force him to raise his shield enough to expose his body to Imani.

The brothers pick up the pursuit, Rodgar shouting "Cowards!" after them. But his jeering is quickly lost behind short bursts from a horn that Wynstan is blowing.

"Why is he doing that?" Imani calls to Taha.

"Don't know," he calls back, leaping over the gnarled trunk of a toppled tree. "Might be trying to scare us."

The horn-blowing goes on for a few more bursts, then ceases. Taha doesn't glance back, even though the pair sound close and the joker's axe was suitable for throwing. He needs to concentrate on where he's stepping—the forest is a mess of mossy rocks, fallen trunks, and roots climbing out of the undergrowth. The brothers maintain a tight chase, navigating the environment with familiarity and ease. But Taha doesn't intend to run forever, only until he finds a better vantage to use his bow.

He gets it in a slope topped with a large boulder.

"Stay down here," he tells Imani, scaling it. "I'll cover you."

# 39

# IMANI

I FACE OUT AT THE BASE OF THE SLOPE WITH MY SWORD. I don't need my iron sense to locate Wynstan; that infernal horn has begun blowing again. Once it quiets, he appears from behind some trees. I look past him for Rodgar, but his brother has vanished, and my iron sense doesn't work with him yet.

Wynstan studies my surroundings too. I've fought only a few battles with Taha, but I've heard that children of the Al-Baz clan are taught to hunt as soon as they can walk. Taha will be hidden, waiting for the perfect moment to send off an arrow that Wynstan doesn't have time to counter with his shield. The Harrowlander vigilantly keeps the circle of wood guarding his chest as he scours the forest. I point my sword at him.

"Come on, then, let's settle our unfinished business."

"Says you, runner. Where's your partner?"

"Find out for yourself," I say.

He maintains a steady but careful approach, watching the crest above me. I glance at his legs. The shield protects him from neck to knees, and he's guarded his shins with greaves.

"What's your plan here?" I ask.

"Isn't it obvious? To be the one who claims your head."

I spin my sword as Rodgar did for the crowd but with much more flair. "Well, if you intend to claim it with that axe, you'll have to expose yourself to arrows first. You have no choice."

"Don't I?" Wynstan stops to watch me spin the blade. It's not immediately clear why; my skill is better but not enough to warrant him halting as if the day's lost all urgency. I disguise my confusion.

"I'd rather this didn't take longer than it must." I catch the sword and point it. "Unless you've had a change of heart and wish to yield. I might accept if you ask politely enough."

He's a pair of angry eyes glaring at me over the shield. "As if I'd ever yield to you."

I can almost perfectly sense the iron in his body now. A little closer and the wiggles will straighten; I'll have complete control, like a sculptor with a heap of willing clay.

"You should reconsider. What I did to you at the Filthy Bilge was only a taste of the pain I can inflict."

The leafy debris suddenly stirs on the crest behind me. Distracted, I half turn. Wynstan sprints at me. There's a grunt behind the boulder; an arrow flies past and lodges in a tree. Two figures drive out of cover, locked in battle: Taha blocking Rodgar's sword with his own.

My iron sense warns me of Wynstan's approach, of the axe slicing through the air. I turn, hand raised, magic electric in my splayed fingers. The axe edge stops an inch from my chest; I suck in a breath and, on a growling exhale, shove the axe back with my magic.

Wynstan stumbles some steps before righting. "I knew it! Witch!" he snarls, and lunges again.

I jump out of the swing; blades clash and clang behind me. Rodgar is proving a match for Taha. I need to intervene; if he's killed, my chances of leaving the Hunten alive drastically diminish.

Wynstan makes a furious push for me. I sidestep his slash and exercise my affinity over his axe. He's unprepared for it, and the weapon slips from his fingers and lands in brush about thirty feet away. I jab at his chest but he dodges me and sprints for the axe. In the same instant that I throw my sword after him, he slings his shield over his back, and my blade lodges in its wood. I draw the sword back to my hand and use the reprieve to focus on Rodgar instead. The younger brother smacks Taha's sword away with his own and boots him in the chest. Taha staggers and falls. As lithe as a spider, Rodgar moves to pounce on him. A spark of panic ignites my magic. I roughly grasp the iron in Rodgar's body, and it's just enough to make him spasm and drop his weapon.

Taha jumps to his feet and points his sword at Rodgar. Wynstan swings his retrieved axe at me, but upon seeing his brother's predicament, halts the blade inches from my neck.

"Don't do it or I'll cut the witch's head off!" he yells up at Taha.

My magic bares its teeth; the axe tugs at Wynstan's fists. He yelps and tugs back. It would be a comical sight, a man fighting his own weapon, but if I don't pry the axe from him now, he'll put its edge in my spine.

"Give it to me!" I demand, mentally hauling on the magical tether between me and his weapon. The axe obeys my call and is ripped from his grasp. I raise my free hand and send the axe flying to rest in the soil perhaps forty or fifty feet away. Wynstan gawks at it, sweat dripping down his flushed face.

I point my sword at his exposed neck. One thrust and he

bleeds out in minutes—well-earned revenge for his attempt at killing me onstage at the Filthy Bilge. I should do it—I've envisioned this victory many times—but I can't bring myself to go through with it. And instead of gloating over his imminent slaughter at my hands, I find myself saying, "You lost. Yield or die."

"What?" Taha glances at me, confused. "They can't yield; it's against the rules."

"Is it?" I ask. "We can't be forced to kill anybody. I imagine if everybody yields to us, we are the Victors."

Wynstan finds that wildly amusing. "Lord Wulfsyg and the Ent would never yield to you, witch!"

"No?" Resentment wields my magic. I release my sword and let it hover over my head. It disappears in a blinding blaze of blue light and reappears as several thrusting daggers with needle-like points. They form a halo around me, all aimed at Wynstan. I raise a hand, ready to command my blades to attack.

"Would you like another demonstration to illustrate my point?"

Wynstan's laugh retreats into an anxious, darting-eyed grin. "You can demand Lord Wulfsyg's surrender right now to illustrate mine."

I follow his gaze to where his axe is in the soil—where it *was.* It's in Wulfsyg's hand now, being turned left and right as he appraises it. Beside him, the towering Ent appraises *me.*

I run cold to the bone. *My store of magic is good,* I remind myself. *It's enough to defend us.* I still can't shake my deep disquiet at this ill-turn of fortunes, and giggling Wynstan isn't helping.

"Stop laughing, fool," I snap heatedly. "He has your axe."

"Don't worry, witch. He's about to give it back."

Wynstan drops to the ground. Rodgar does too, throwing his body back and out of Taha's reach. In my shock, I recoil a step. A second later, something snaps through the air where my head just was: an arrow, spearing the soil behind me.

Taha follows Rodgar with his sword, but I stop him short, shouting, "AMBUSH! RUN!"

I fuse my blades back into my dagger, jogging while sheathing it on my thigh. Taha grabs his bow off the ground and comes sliding down the slope. Wulfsyg and the Ent lope after us. Wynstan scrambles across the ground toward them; Rodgar jumps to his feet and makes to follow his brother. But none of them are armed with a bow, so who fired the arrow? And why is Wulfsyg tossing Wynstan his axe instead of cutting him down with it? This is a battle to the death.

*For us,* Qayn whispers across our souls. *When you're different from them, their rules apply differently.*

Numb terror crashes down my body and threatens to stop my feet in their tracks. More figures appear from the trees on my right: Wilim, the tall fyghtor in the suit of armor and Col, his partner who was bearing the banners. The latter now wields a longbow pulled taut on an arrow that has my name on it. . . .

Taha pulls me forward as the bowstring looses. The arrow cleaves the air across my back and reflects off a beech tree on my left. Suddenly I'm sprinting faster than I've ever done, and the forest becomes a dreamlike blur of greens, browns, and the occasional glint of gold flitting between the ancient oaks, almost half as tall as the trees themselves: gigantic stags, the stamp of their hooves quaking the earth. My speed works against me; I'm liable to catch my boot under a vine or slide off that boulder ahead that needs scaling. Every step must be measured, but I may as well be a spectator, the way I keep glancing over my shoulder out of some gut-sick fascination with what morbid thing comes next. Wulfsyg and the Ent are leading the pursuit, the brothers flanking them, but Wilim and Col are out of sight again. A patch of earth riddled with skull-sized rocks ahead demands my undivided attention, and I glance back only after I've cleared it. In that time, the gap between us and Wulfsyg has halved. *How?* He eclipses Wynstan in size, his body sewn together with hulking muscle, yet he's faster and lighter on his feet than either of the lithe brothers. Moving with the experienced, unflagging determination of a wolf hunting its prey.

Resignation burdens my limbs. *Just get the fight over and done with,* it says, knowing full well that if I do that, I'll lose. I can exercise my affinity on one weapon and one body, not several at once.

And that's what's happening here. Several bodies are *colluding* to kill us.

# 40

# TAHA

THE AIR SUDDENLY BECOMES EASIER TO BREATHE. Glancing behind him, Taha sees something strange: Wulfsyg and the Ent have abandoned the hunt to gather Wynstan and Rodgar and the other pair of fyghtors around them. Another plan is being hatched, but why? Taha doesn't understand, but he sets the puzzle aside and seizes the amnesty he and Imani have been granted.

They run well out of sight until Taha stops at the roots of an enormous tree with a wide spread. "Climb it," he directs Imani. While she does, he goes back to the place where they just came from. He walks in circles over the dirt, crushing twigs and blades of grass and impressing his boot prints in the soil in various directions to obfuscate their trail.

Very carefully, he returns to the tree following the same tracks, scales it, and joins Imani on the widest bough overlooking the forest floor. "We should be safe to rest for a while," he says, hooking his helm on a thinner branch.

Imani does the same with hers. "They're going to come back for us."

"Without a doubt." He takes the water flask off his belt. "Wulfsyg stopped chasing us only to conserve his energy. He's fast and powerful, but if he tires too soon, he's a big, slow target. He probably figured it'd be easier to sniff us out at his own pace."

"The brothers are working with him and the Ent," she says. "Same as Wilim and Col."

"Seems that way." He takes a long swill from his flask.

Imani watches him, chewing the inside of her cheek. "Does that make sense to you? That they're working together in a fight to the death?"

He shrugs, pulling the flask away. "Maybe they have a truce until they eliminate us."

"They hate us that much," she says glumly.

He nearly laughs, despite their situation. It's funny—charming, almost—how much she wants everyone to adore her and how much it upsets her when people don't. He holds out the flask.

"Wynstan called you a witch. What *was* it that you did to Rodgar?"

She takes the flask and fiddles with it. "I found out that I can manipulate the iron in people's bodies." Then she drinks.

He studies her, curious, slightly unsettled. "I didn't know there was metal in our bodies."

She nods, still drinking.

"But wouldn't manipulating it violate the Law of Essences?"

She glances at him as if surprised. Until now, she imagined he had no concept of magical philosophy beyond what he needed to do his duty.

"I suppose it might," she says noncommittally, handing his flask back.

"Did Qayn teach you how to do it?"

She shrugs. "Not really, no. Just sort of came up with it."

Does she really believe that's a convincing answer? That she just "came up" with a way to defy the hard rules that govern their magical practice? It's much easier with a being like Qayn bound to her dagger. But talking about Qayn makes Taha feel out of sorts, so he looks for another topic. "We should've killed Wynstan and Rodgar when we had the chance."

She sighs. "I know. But I couldn't bring myself to do it. And now I don't think I even want to try."

"We don't have a choice," he says, hooking the flask back onto his belt.

"We can make a choice if we're clever about it. We can force the other fyghtors to yield."

"They won't yield to us, Imani," he says with a hint of frustration. "And why should we try something that will have serious consequences if it fails? Trying to best the game only jeopardizes our parents' lives." He sweeps his gaze over the forest floor, glittering with golden flecks. "The safest way to minimize bloodshed is to wait for the other fyghtors to take each other out and then battle the last pair. Wulfsyg and the Ent, most likely. Maybe that pair the gamblers are excited about, Pat and Tenney."

"I think it's wrong, even if they've willingly entered the Hunten," Imani says quietly.

"It's not our place to change their traditions to suit our values," he intones.

"But you saw how afraid Wynstan was when Rodgar's life was in danger. He doesn't want his brother to die."

"He should've thought of that before he entered."

"He clearly didn't."

Taha twists a hand. "So? This is the hyena who nearly killed you onstage."

"You nearly killed me too. Now look at us, fighting on the same side."

Her tone has gained that fanged bite. And somehow Taha finds a way to hate it, dread it, and enjoy it all at once.

"But I suppose it's easier for us to just kill the other fyghtors rather than finding a humane solution, isn't it?" She stares at him, nostrils slightly flared, lips arranged in precise poise; critical gaze seeking any weakness to exploit, no matter how minor, with a falcon's intensity.

Taha knows where this is going, but he can't help himself. She incites the part of him that's always hankering for a fight out of a split-minded desire to conquer and be conquered. He turns his back against the tree trunk to face her.

"Why don't you say what you really want to say, Imani?"

"I *will.* It was easier for you to kill your father's political opponents than to find a peaceful way to object." She points off into the distance. "Amira and Atheer have forgiven you—and I *somewhat* understand your actions in the prison—but I've not forgotten the other things you've done that you should answer for."

"I'll answer for them," he says, eliciting a brow raise from her. "I was barely fifteen when I first killed. Didn't sleep for a long time after it. But I had to do it to protect my father from those men—"

"They have names," she says sharply, inflamed.

He clenches his fist and looks over the bruises and scabs on his knuckles. "Farhat, Sayf, Nasir. Don't worry; I'll never forget. They were pressuring the Elders to revert to their original selection for Grand Zahim, some wealthy bureaucrat with a fraction of my father's experience. Did you know that since his election, admission rates to the Order from clans with few or no sorcerers in their heritage have multiplied fivefold? He's doubled the allocation of taxes to welfare for the needy; he's established the first ever committee dedicated to eliminating corruption involved in the distribution of aid, and he's funded more public healthcare than any Grand Zahim before him. And those *men* wanted to stop him over nothing. What else is that but prejudice? My father read the writing on the wall—they were coming for his position somehow, some way. What else was I supposed to do, Imani?"

It's a question that Taha wishes someone could answer for him, or at least confirm that there was nothing else he could do. Maybe then he could finally oust the guilt that's made a home in his hollowed heart for years.

He braces for Imani to dismiss him with some trivializing, deliberately obtuse comment. Instead, she says, "Honestly, Taha, I didn't really grasp that there was inequality at home until I met you. I assumed that people less fortunate than me were being looked after by the Council and afforded more-or-less the same opportunities that I had. In hindsight, I know that my attitude was grossly ignorant and callous. But at the time . . . I suppose I just didn't think about it." She shakes her head sadly, running a hand along her opposite arm in a gesture of disarming vulnerability. "I don't know what else you could've done except to refuse. Why didn't you say no to your father? Encourage him to some other path? Protests, petitions?"

She isn't blaming him; she sounds despairing on his behalf.

"My father's path is the only path," Taha mutters, wincing at some phantom pain from some beating he can't distinguish from all the others. "I don't think anything else would've worked anyway. We would've needed mass civil disobedience, and that's asking too much of people who have too little to spare. As for me . . ." He shrugs. "I didn't know if I wanted to say no. Felt like if I did, I'd be responsible for my father's removal from office."

"But why did he have to involve you at all?" she asks.

"He was being closely watched—"

"Why didn't he ask someone else?" she presses with more urgency, because Taha hasn't really answered her question.

"My father said it would toughen me up like nothing else could and I needed to be tough to survive against those in power. He was making me a warrior."

Imani whimpers. A small, sad sound, big and deafeningly loud to him. "He made you a murderer, Taha, and you can never take that back. No loving father condemns his son."

Taha stares unblinkingly at the bough above him, the raven perched there, as glossy as black silk.

"I don't think my father knows how to love anymore. When my mother died, his heart died with her. He doesn't even see me most of the time."

Why did he confess such a thing? Loneliness, probably. Nobody left to talk to with Reza and Sinan gone. Nobody left but the girl who doesn't see him most of the time either.

For all Imani's brash confidence, even she can't challenge the silence that falls upon them. But Taha feels so raw and exposed to the elements now that he doesn't think his pain can get any worse. He has nothing left to lose, except, of course, the man who ruined him.

"There's something I want to tell you," he says, dropping his gaze to her. She peeks back at him, round-eyed and rigid on the bough. "I like you, Imani. It's why I kissed you; why I'd kiss you again if you wanted me to, even if for you it's just to prove that I'm like any other fool on the street vying for your attention."

She's quiet. The seconds are crushingly heavy.

"Are you manipulating me?" she finally asks.

He shakes his head.

She stares at him a little longer before scooting across the bough to sit closer. "I don't believe you, Taha. You can't expect me to." With every word, she radiates her familiar, forceful energy. "All you've ever told me is how selfish, ignorant, and entitled I am."

"You can be those things," he says. "I'm sure there are unpleasant things you think about me."

"Plenty!" she agrees, a blush dusting her cheekbones.

"That I'm ignoble, a cruel monster, dishonest—"

"Yes," she interrupts, scooting even closer, "but I'm not the one asking for a kiss, am I?"

"You did kiss me, though. Twice," he reminds her. "Were you manipulating *me*?"

She blinks and scowls, unable to settle on whether she should be taken aback by his question or push him out of the tree for it. Her arms fold, posture becoming proper. Rather than answer, she asks her own question: "What don't you find repulsive about me, then?"

"Your face," Taha blurts out, his breathing quickening.

She rolls her eyes. "You have countless pretty Shields crawling over you at the barracks."

"I only ever cared for you."

Frowning, she glances at his lips and looks away.

"I like your strength," he goes on. "Your bravery and your

loyalty to your family. That you take your Shield duties seriously. And how good you are on a horse, even better with a sword. Much better than me."

Her gaze tentatively finds its way back to him and stays, the light in it softer now. But with her watching him, Taha loses his nerve and falls quiet. It matters, he realizes, how Imani responds to his admission. Earlier he was convinced it would be enough just to tell her how he feels. Now he finds himself desperately hoping she feels the same in some small way. He wishes they could build out common ground between them, with time and patience and mutual understanding. That they could make that ground a garden and not a battlefield.

"I wasn't—" She's interrupted by a loud bang. They look skyward but don't see the firework. "A pair has fallen," she says, adjusting her armor.

"One down, four to go." He glances back at her. "What were you going to say?"

"It has to wait." She points out two shadows slinking along the fringe of distant trees. "Our friends have returned."

# 41

# IMANI

*I WASN'T MANIPULATING YOU.*

That's what I was going to say, but perhaps it's lucky the firework stopped me before I could. Perhaps that's a door I shouldn't open with Taha yet, if ever. I don't know. I'm torn, but I need to concentrate. Survival now, feelings later. Wynstan and Rodgar are stalking through the brush.

"They're alone," Taha whispers.

I confirm as much by searching the trees behind them using my iron sense. No other fyghtors are here yet.

"This is our chance to find out what they're planning with the others," I whisper back.

The brothers creep over our tracks toward this tree. Wynstan walks ahead of Rodgar, axe in one hand, shield raised in the other. There's a distance of several steps between him and his brother, and the gap isn't getting smaller.

"Wait for Rodgar to pass under us," I say in Taha's ear. "He's our target."

We gather our belongings and drop to the bough closest to

the ground. Wynstan crouches to inspect the tracks underneath us. Taha trains the tip of an arrow on him in case he looks up and sees us, but he skulks on after the false tracks. Moments later, Rodgar passes under us. I follow Taha, who's clambering down the trunk with mountain goat reflexes, and leap. Two clanking thuds announce our landing. Rodgar halts a few steps ahead and whips around. I've already lobbed my dagger at him, but just before it can hit, I halt it midair, pointed at his throat. His eyes bug out as Wynstan rounds on us. By then, Taha has aimed an arrow at the younger brother, and Wynstan is forced to stay exactly where he is.

"You know how this goes," I warn him. "Move any closer and your brother dies. Put your axe and shield down, that horn too. You won't be calling for anyone's help this time."

He cautiously obeys, studying me from under his lashes. Though I approach him, my dagger stays trained on Rodgar. "I know you would do anything to save your brother's life. I'll give you an opportunity to do just that if you tell us what you and the other fyghtors are planning."

Wynstan swallows, glancing at his brother. "A few of us have a treaty. Lord Wulfsyg approached us before the Hunten and invited us to work together against you."

"Why would he do that?" I ask. "Why not deal with us alone, just him and the Ent?"

"He didn't want to run the risk of a pair of fremde winning. He was right to be cautious. You're a witch." Wynstan spits in the dirt. "You don't belong in the Hunten or in Harrowland."

"Your laws permit us to enter this tournament," says Taha.

"Doesn't make it right. It should be a Harrowlander who wins—only a Harrowlander can bring glory to the Empire."

"Your Empire wants to include us whether we like it or not," I snap. "How do you think we feel about that? Harrowlanders being in *our* lands, claiming it as their own, raiding and killing our people?"

His nostrils flare. "They're only getting killed because they're violent and refuse to join a proper society."

"Be careful what you say next, Wynstan," I caution, menace lacing my tone.

He only grows more defensive. "King Glaedric is trying to help your people! He's trying to give you peace. If it weren't for his intervention, you lot would keep slaughtering each other in your tribal wars until the end of time."

I'm seeing red now. If the brothers are certain we're violent by nature, I would hate to disappoint them. But Taha must read the murder in my eyes and continues the interrogation before I can end it in a spray of blood.

"You were talking about the treaty," he says.

Wynstan tears his gaze from me. "It's between Lord Wulfsyg and the Ent, us, and Wilim and Col. Lord Wulfsyg isn't friendly with Heath and Linden, and everyone's given Pat and Tenney good odds to win, so he didn't bother asking them." Wynstan sniffs, twitching a shoulder. "We already did Heath and Linden in. The others are hunting Pat and Tenney now."

He relates it too casually. The slain fyghtors are lying somewhere in this chilly forest right now, wearing their shock even in death. What happens to their bodies? Are they left where they fall? Perhaps all the fyghtors who've gone before are part of the debris under my boots, mingled with the gold dust of the stags.

"What's the agreement in exchange for?" Taha asks.

"Survival."

I knit my brows. "You were planning to yield? I thought that was against the rules."

"No, it's just not a favored outcome," he says with a scowl. "People think it's an insult to the gods for a fyghtor to yield, and a greater insult for their opponent to accept."

"So why would you do it?" I ask.

"To protest the greatest insult of letting fremde enter the Hunten," Wynstan says harshly. "It was Lord Wulfsyg's idea. He explained that according to the Old Ways, only even-footed battles are honorable and therefore worthy of Staggnir's blessing. If a fyghtor yields, the battle is no longer even and killing them would be dishonorable, so a fyghtor can accept the surrender of another with no consequence under the old tenet of *gan umber.* Lord Wulfsyg is going to rely on it so the fyghtors in the treaty leave the Hunten alive. He said the punters won't like it, but the people will understand that our defiance is needed to motivate His Majesty into reforming the law."

I mull that for a moment before looking at Taha. "Well. The possibility of surrendering certainly changes things."

He surprises me with a nod and says in Sahiran, "We'll have a tough enough time defeating Wulfsyg and the Ent on their own, let alone with Wilim and Col helping them. We should make our own treaty if we can."

Now he's talking sense. I return to Wynstan. "You don't really believe that Wulfsyg will let you yield, do you?"

"'Course I do. He gave us his word," Wynstan says, folding his long arms. "This protest is what matters to him."

I snort. "You're more naïve than you look. I suppose that goes without saying, though. You entered the Hunten for glory and forgot to factor in the possibility of dying here with your dear brother." He tenses as I step closer. "Wynstan, I would sooner believe that Prince Kendric is going to abandon his chalice and join the Hunten than I would that Wulfsyg is going to let you walk away from this."

"He will," says Wynstan sullenly.

"He won't. He didn't let Pat and Tenney walk away."

Wynstan shades an angry red. "I *told* you why he didn't ask them—"

"He assumed they'd refuse his offer of treaty because everyone thinks they have good odds to win, and they probably think so too."

"Yes—"

"Or perhaps," I say over him, "Wulfsyg just doesn't want to have to face them again in seven years."

"Not true, witch," says Wynstan, shaking his head.

"Listen to reason, Wynstan," I continue calmly. "Wulfsyg has won two seasons before. Do you think he'll throw away an indisputable third victory for a protest that could be interpreted as a bad omen and damage his reputation?"

"Yes—"

"Isn't it more likely that he'll use you to make us easier to deal with, and once we've been dealt with, you'll be next?"

"No!" Wynstan turns his face away like a petulant child. "Unless you have proof of your insulting claims, I'll continue trusting Lord Wulfsyg's word!"

"And if we did have proof? Would you be willing to enter a treaty with us to work together? Unlike Wulfsyg, we'll keep our word to accept your surrender."

"I don't know," he mutters, glancing at me out of the corner of his eye. "What if we refuse?"

I pinch the iron in his body, folding him over. "You'll lose, and your death will be painful. Your brother's will be worse. You have my word on that too."

He hangs on to his knees, glaring up at me. "*Fine*," he snarls. "If you prove that Lord Wulfsyg intends to betray us, we'll join your bloody treaty. As for how you intend to do it—"

I summon his axe off the ground. "Let us worry about that."

It must be an hour before we find a suitable place to execute my plan, and then we have to wait for the pair of enormous stags dueling in it to move their battle elsewhere. But the hillside that drops into the black, rocky gully is the ideal stage for this deception.

Taha reluctantly accepts playing the part of a recently slain fyghtor. "How realistic does this need to look?" he asks, positioning an arrow on a nearby rock.

"Enough that I don't get killed for it," Wynstan grouses from where he stands on the bank with Rodgar, surrounded by my halo of blades. I've had to drink another flask of misra tea to maintain this level of magic use, and I'm beginning to tire. Even the forest's cold is no longer challenging the heat clinging to me.

I watch Taha arrange his bow near a pile of leaves so that when he lies down, it'll look as if he dropped it in the midst of battle. "This will be convincing when viewed from up there," I say, pointing at the hilltop overlooking the gully.

"And if, when he sees it, Lord Wulfsyg upholds his part of the treaty?" asks Wynstan.

I cut a look at him. "For Rodgar's sake, I hope not. Otherwise, there'll be nothing holding me to my offer of truce."

Wynstan returns his gaze to the blades floating around him.

Taha speaks to me in Sahiran: "Are you forgetting that I can't point an arrow at the brother and pretend to be dead at the same time?"

"I've not forgotten. Qayn, will you join us?"

The djinni appears by my side, lips arranged in a menacing sneer. The color drains from Wynstan; Rodgar's eyes bulge. Even Taha is strangely uncomfortable and crosses his arms.

"This is Qayn," I say. "He's a magical being—"

"Something akin to your faeries," he supplies, black eyes as impassive as a dead thing. His statement only serves to heighten the brothers' terror.

"Qayn will be out of sight of the hilltop but somewhere where he can always see you," I say. "Do as we've planned, Rodgar, or you'll have to answer to him."

I fuse my blades back into a dagger and sheathe it, then scramble up the precariously steep hillside with Wynstan. At the top, I return his axe, shield, and horn with a warning: "You know what happens to Rodgar if you deviate from our agreement."

He accepts his gear grudgingly and trots off between the trees. I climb onto a stack of boulders nearby, the top mostly obscured by a half-fallen tree. Down in the gully, Taha lies on the ground and Rodgar sits beside him, holding our firework. Qayn has withdrawn out of sight, but his threat looms nonetheless.

After a few moments, we settle into our positions, and the trap is set.

# 42

# IMANI

THE SUN IS SINKING; THERE'S A TOUCH OF FROST IN the forest air. It's been too long, and I'm worried that Wynstan has deceived us. He cares for his brother, but not more than he cares that the Hunten should be won by a Harrowlander. Perhaps Rodgar is a sacrifice he's willing to make.

But eventually Wynstan's loud voice carries over to me on a chilly breeze. Down in the gully, Taha remains facedown in his pile of leaves, looking very much like a fallen fyghtor, and Rodgar is crouched beside him, seemingly catching his breath after battle.

Up here, Wynstan emerges from between two gnarled trunks, accompanied by Lord Wulfsyg but not the Ent. I shift into a squat as they near the boulders.

"Just down there," Wynstan says, motioning at where the land drops away.

Wulfsyg considers him through the eyeholes of his helm. There's a wolf in the man's gaze—and flecks of blood stain the white fur pieces on his shoulders. "You dealt with them on your own," he says.

I dig my nails into the stone. Wynstan keeps a straight face and recites the lie I taught him: "Wasn't easy. They took us by surprise. The fight was theirs for a good while, but then the archer missed a few arrows, and I pushed on him with my shield. He was no good hand-to-hand. Once we put him down, the girl couldn't contend with both of us."

Wulfsyg goes to the edge of the hillside and peers down at the gully. It would be easy for Wynstan to shove him, if not killing him in the fall then seriously injuring him, but the larger man exhibits no fear, and that makes him even more intimidating. Wynstan whistles at Rodgar, who looks up and waves, before motioning at the firework. Wulfsyg's lips pucker, bristling his blond beard; he runs a thoughtful hand down its braided length. Wynstan is nervous, face locked in a stiff half smile, his temple pulsing every other second.

"Where's the girl?" Wulfsyg asks.

Wynstan gestures ambiguously. "Under those trees. She tried to run. Wasn't so easy with an axe in her back."

He chuckles, but Wulfsyg doesn't join in. He strokes his beard, pondering the scene instead. What about it warrants such intense contemplation? He should be glad that he doesn't have to be the one to face Taha and me; he should clap Wynstan on the shoulder, congratulate the brothers, and—if his intentions are true—proceed with their treaty. But he doesn't do that; he *can't*. He's too busy plotting his next move and trying to find where his stone fits on the board.

"Should we set off the firework?" Wynstan asks quietly.

Wulfsyg opens his hand around his beard in a gesture that

says, *Go on.* Wynstan waves at Rodgar, who sets the rocket in a loose mound of soil and lights the fuse. It shoots up and explodes in a twinkling red cloud, then Rodgar clambers up the hillside using the roots poking out of the soil as handholds. Wulfsyg watches the firework until the very last spark fades.

"The fremde got what they deserve," he says. "Come with me to Victors' Tower."

Wynstan bobs his head. "And Wilim and Col?"

"They'll join us soon. Last I saw, they were finishing off with Pat and—"

Another bang sounds above the forest, not far from here. In the wide silence that follows, I hear the faintest echo of the nobles in the observation tower clapping.

"They're finished." Wulfsyg smiles coldly and walks back in the direction they came from.

Wynstan hurries to keep by his side. "That's it, then. The Hunten is over."

"Aye, season's done and seven years of good things. We'll send off the last of the fireworks, then you can have the honor of blowing the horn."

Wynstan stammers his thanks. I watch them go, sweating nervously under my armor. Have I misjudged Lord Wulfsyg? If I'm wrong, we'll have to battle the treaty of *six* fyghtors. Six fyghtors who are about to join up at Victors' Tower. But there's time yet for betrayal. If Wynstan didn't think the same, *he* would've betrayed *me* already.

I wait until they've walked a decent distance away before I creep down from the boulders and toss a signal rock into the gully. The last I see of Taha is him pushing to his feet. I scurry after Wulfsyg and the brothers, and I have a brief moment of panic when I can't see them. But my iron sense of Wynstan is still strong, and stalking a bit farther reveals them again. I press after them in bursts, keeping low to the ground and halting only in the cover of thick tree trunks. The trio reach a glade where two mighty stags are clashing in a billow of gold dust, at the foot of a thin tower rising out of the redberry shrubs like a gray needle, its entrance steps flanked by very old looking statues of Staggnir as half-man, half-beast. The enormous, curled branches of a bronze horn gleam in the afternoon light on a balcony at the top of the tower, and that signaling pillar of reddish smoke escapes from an urn nearby.

The Ent is alone, striding across the glade to meet them; Wilim and Col haven't returned yet. Wulfsyg gestures at the tower and says something, and Wynstan nods and continues toward it. What does he think he's doing? If the treaty is real, the horn can't be blown yet anyway. Wynstan knows there's still a pair of fyghtors to be dealt with—me and Taha. Unless he's still not convinced of Wulfsyg's intentions. It must be that, and it must have something to do with their conversation.

I spot a wide tree on the glade's edge that should bring me within earshot. I dart for it, praying that Wulfsyg doesn't notice me between the trunks, but the group are still talking on their ambling route around the stags to Victors' Tower. I've almost reached cover when my boot catches on a root. I slam down into something hard, but it's not wood or stone. It's steel. Plate armor. My boot met the splayed armpit of a body lying in a natural depression.

I scramble away from the corpse. It's lying on its back beside its own severed head, which has cropped silvery hair and a pallid face. It's Wilim—and tangled with his body under a smattering of soil is Col, dead from an axe wound at the base of his caved skull. Neither is wearing a helm, neither has sustained any crushing damage to his plate armor, and both have suffered excessively violent yet curiously clean wounds. There's no sign of a struggle. If they'd been killed in honest battle, they'd have their helms on and their injuries might be where their plate armor meets at the joints. This was an unexpected execution when their defenses were down.

A shout fills my chest, sticking its elbows between my ribs as it climbs to my mouth. I clamp my lips together. I predicted this, but it doesn't make the truth any easier to swallow. And if this is what Lord Wulfsyg and the Ent did to Wilim and Col—the brothers are in trouble.

I push to my feet and dash behind the tree trunk. Wynstan is almost at Victors' Tower, flanked by Rodgar on one side and Wulfsyg on the other. But suddenly Wulfsyg cuts his speed to join the Ent, walking behind them. The men exchange a dark look. The Ent shows a skewed grin; Wulfsyg adjusts his fists around the leather-wrapped handle of his poleaxe and nods.

This is where the treaty dies.

I abandon cover and lob my glowing sword across the glade. Wulfsyg swings his axe at Wynstan's back.

*Strike with your heart, Imani!* Qayn urges across our souls.

Magic blazes white-hot in my blood; the sword flies much faster than what gravity, wind, and momentum could ever permit. It halts between the two men as the axe comes down and its head clangs loudly against my blade. Wynstan spins around at the sound. The stags abandon their duel and scatter from the glade, antlers trailing gold dust. Wulfsyg's face warps; he pushes the axe down, the massive muscles of his arms bulging under the blue paint. I grit my teeth; a growl vibrates my chest as my entire body tenses to resist him. My pulse spikes, sweat drips down my temple; I shake from the exertion, magic burning off in my blood.

Wynstan jumps back from the clashing weapons, shouting, "She was right! You were going to betray us all along!"

I summon my sword back, leaving Wulfsyg to fall into the swing of his axe and wound the soil. His furious gaze glides around the glade until it finds me. *"Traitor,"* he spits at Wynstan. "You're in treaty with the fremde." Bizarrely, he doesn't seem in the least bit astonished that he just battled a flying sword.

Wynstan raises his shield. "You gave us a false oath! Did you kill Wilim and Col? Is that why they're not here?"

"Oh, they're here." Wulfsyg drags his axe from the soil. "You're about to join them."

The brothers back away. "Why make the treaty, only to betray us?" Wynstan asks.

Wulfsyg holds out a hand as if he's being very reasonable. "We needed to make it easy for us to eliminate the fremde. Do you see why now? They were plotting to win the Hunten with *magic*. You think this witch is something to fear?" Wulfsyg points at me. "They're *all* like her where she comes from."

Wynstan hesitates, glancing at me. "They are?"

"Witches and warlocks, all of them. Dangerous savages—"

"We've kept to ourselves for a thousand years!" I exclaim angrily.

"Don't believe her lies. This very minute, her people are fighting and killing our soldiers with magic."

"Your king has stolen our homeland!" I shout back.

Wulfsyg ignores me. "Siding with her is siding against *us*, Wynstan. You know what you need to do."

"Yield?" he offers weakly.

"Sacrifice yourself. For the Empire."

"But we had an agreement," Wynstan whines. "You said so yourself, you can accept our surrender and still end the Hunten as Victors! Not even the prince can stop you if you call upon gan umber!"

"Gan umber." Wulfsyg and the Ent share a hearty laugh. "Nobody actually cares about that sort of stuff anymore, Wynnie. Nowadays it's only the warrior who wins that matters, however he does it, and accepting surrender isn't winning. It's an adjourned defeat, a declaration of weakness. We can't show ourselves to be weak, can we? You've got to accept that the Old Ways are dead, and anyone who clings to them is doomed to the same fate."

Tears drip down Wynstan's blanched cheeks. As much as I dislike him, I see myself in his distress. He's realized that his idea of the world is just that—an idea, a romantic view unwittingly seen through a rose-colored lens. But the world beyond that lens is so much more complicated than he's ever imagined.

He blinks away his tears, nodding. "We'll see if that's true, Wulfsyg . . . Rodgar, run!"

His brother breaks into a sprint through the waist-high redberry shrubs past Victors' Tower. There's a pulse of magic as the Ent transforms into an enormous black bear. With a roar, he slams down on all fours and takes off after Rodgar. Wynstan gasps, recoiling.

"Th-the Ent is a *warlock*? You're like the fremde . . ." He returns a fiercer gaze to Wulfsyg and raises his shield. "You shouldn't have sent your partner away. I'm not the only one you need to fight."

Wulfsyg extends a hand at his side, palm open to the ground. "It's all right, Wynnie," he says. "You won't make much trouble."

The grass and redberry shrubs begin to ripple, throwing gold dust into the air. Wynstan hollers at something by his feet. He goes to step back, but one of his boots has become entangled in the vines dotted with white flowers. No, the vines have entangled *him*.

A rope of them shoots up from the rustling shrubbery and snakes around his other leg. He drops his shield and, in his panic, begins hacking at the vines with his axe. He comes so close to mortally wounding himself that I scream at him to stop, but he doesn't hear me. He hacks faster, frantically, yet the vines he cuts through are replaced by more. They race across the ground toward him in an ever-louder hiss, entwining to become thicker; they snake up and around his body and trap his arms, forcing him to drop the axe. Wulfsyg's smile stretches to a wicked grin.

*Magic,* Qayn whispers, breaking my trance.

Yes. Wulfsyg wasn't surprised by my magic because he's a sorcerer with a plant affinity and the Ent is a skin-changer. I've no time to think about the how or why. If I don't act right now, the vines are going to smother Wynstan.

I transform my sword into a spear and throw it at Wulfsyg. He sidesteps, knocking it away with the haft of his axe, and lopes at me. *I'm the Djinni Slayer,* I remind myself as his hulking, blood-splattered figure bears down on me. *I've fought and defeated worse than him.*

I summon my spear and transform it back to a sword. Wulfsyg arrives, swinging his axe with an arc of his powerful torso, the blade angled toward my head. I barely dodge it; a puff of sliced air hits my face, the short *whoosh* of the blade humming in my ears. The poleaxe has worrisome reach, and it'll keep Wulfsyg safely out of mine if I don't press the attack.

I dart in to close the gap between us, but he withdraws with frightening dexterity, grip adjusting on the haft; in a nimble sweep, he brandishes the weapon horizontally and blocks my sword strike with it. I've put so much thrust into my swing that my blade bites the wood, just missing his fingers but locking me in place. He twists in the opposite direction, wrenching my sword—and me—along with him. I immediately release it and hop back a few steps as he finishes slicing. My sword unsticks from the haft and is summoned back to my fist.

A grin appears under Wulfsyg's helm. "Nice trick. I have some too."

He comes at me again, and this time, the forest aids his attack. Vines pulse under my boots, loose leaves and white flowers pluck themselves up to dance in an obfuscating swirl around us. I parry him with my sword, but his axe still glances off my waist. I curse as I'm thrown back several steps. The chainmail may have protected my flesh from being carved open, but the blunt force of the blow has left a throbbing pain in my side. I ignore it and focus on my footing, because if I fall, I'm dead. Wulfsyg chases me, swinging; I deflect, almost putting my wrist under the axe as it rolls off my sword. My heart drums in my ears; my mouth is dust-dry. I hop back as if the ground is a nest of vipers; the vines move like them, meeting and coiling in a sick ritual, birthing new snakes to trap me as they did Wynstan. In my head, I hear a piece of advice that Atheer gave me during one of our earliest sparring sessions: *You can tell someone is losing a fight if they stop answering and only retreat. Then they're just one stumble away from defeat.*

One stumble. I feel it coming.

Qayn's angry voice cuts through the chaos as I dodge another swing. *Seize him by flesh and blood! Strike with your heart!*

The fog of my anxiety clears; strategy returns in sharp relief.

My iron sense latches onto Wulfsyg's body and squeezes. He jolts awkwardly as he finishes a swing and hangs there, allowing me to create another gap between us. But my victory is short-lived. Wulfsyg grits his teeth, raises his poleaxe, and pushes through the pain.

Startled, I thrust magic through me, imagining I'm shoving the iron in Wulfsyg's body. But I'm too scared to test the limits of my newfound power. When his eyes jitter and blood gushes from his nose, I release him in some reflex of mercy. The reprieve is exactly what he needs to come at me again, his mouth twisted in a bloodied snarl. I try to shuffle back, but vines latch onto my boots and drag me to the ground. My sword slips from my hand. Vines curl around my ankles; others spring up and fasten my wrists. Wulfsyg appears over me, poleaxe swinging. I scream, squeezing my eyes shut.

A loud rustling sounds from my right; something weighty crowds my legs. A splintering thud forces my eyes open. Taha is huddled over me with Wynstan's shield on his arm, the poleaxe driven into its face.

Grunting, Wulfsyg drags the axe away. Taha jumps up and crashes the shield into him, driving him back.

I snap out of my shock, but the vines are pinning me to the ground. "Qayn," I yell, "help!"

Qayn appears and saws at the vines with my sword. Behind him, Wulfsyg is thrown to the ground, too distracted by Taha now to fully control his affinity. The vines lose their sentience; the whirling maelstrom of leaves and flowers intensifies with his rage. As Wulfsyg gets back to his feet, Taha trades shield for bow. Wulfsyg tucks his chin in to protect his neck and charges, growling. Taha doesn't hesitate as I did—he looses an arrow and hits Wulfsyg high in the chest. The arrowhead breeches the leather armor and the mail below. It must have an impact; Taha chose the bodkin arrowhead specifically because the armorer suggested it would be good against expensive chainmail like the kind Wulfsyg wears. But Wulfsyg doesn't even blink. His growl becomes a roar; he swings at Taha, who dodges while nocking another arrow.

Qayn frees me and hands me my sword. I push him at Wynstan, still trapped in the vines. "Use his axe to get him out!"

I sprint at Taha and Wulfsyg, locked in a deadly dance. Rather than tiring, the king's fyghtor is swinging his axe with greater power and control each time; Taha ducks, weaves, and jogs back to keep space between them, loosing an arrow any chance he gets. Most hit and defeat the mail to stay lodged, and even if they aren't going deeper than an inch past the padding below, they should be enough collectively to do *something*!

They're not doing anything. Wulfsyg is a roaring, raging, quilled beast perfectly at home with spikes sticking out of his arms and chest. I glimpse Taha's face through the screaming squall. I see his fear at the realization that this man is worse than any monster he has battled. This man might kill us both. It's guaranteed if the Ent returns before we've dealt with him.

I run past Wynstan's shield, discarded in the grass. It's been destroyed by the axe wound that Wulfsyg had meant for me. If Taha hadn't protected me, I'd be dead right now. Taha didn't know what the outcome would be before he stepped between us; he didn't know if the shield would withstand the blow to protect him too, but he took the risk regardless. He gambled his life to save mine.

It is gratitude, not fear or anger, that concentrates the magic in my blood and unburdens my heart of doubt. In the quiet, I sense the poleaxe and summon it to me with no room for protest.

Wulfsyg is midswing when it wrenches from his hands and lands in a shrub out of reach. I throw my dagger and trade my body for its swift steel form. I reemerge beside Wulfsyg and point it at him; Taha aims an arrow from the other side.

"Yield, Lord Wulfsyg," I order.

The cyclone ceases, the leaves and flowers suspending. Wulfsyg pants between us, sweat dripping off his straight nose. His breathing is heavy and wet.

"Yield!" I demand, stepping closer.

He glares at me over his pitching shoulder. "I refuse to yield to you, stranger."

I am desperate for his surrender. I did enough killing while escaping the prison in Taeel-Sa.

"Ask to yield and I will accept!" I yell. "You will die if you don't!"

He grins, showing a stretch of bloodstained gums, and throws the helm off his head. "Better to die than to bow."

Taha readies to shoot, but something flies across the clearing and hits Wulfsyg in the face, knocking him on his back. The suspended leaves and flowers twirl down and blanket the ground around him. I can stomach just one glance at his head: it was an axe that did it. Death dealt in one bloody blow.

I look up at Wynstan, still folded over after throwing. A short, high-pitched horn sounds deeper in the forest; it sounds like the horn Wynstan used earlier.

"Rodgar," he rasps, and runs for the trees. I follow him with Taha; on the way, Qayn gives me a nod from beside the pile of cut vines and vanishes. We sprint in the direction of the horn, but I worry about how we'll deal with the Ent when we find him. It was hard enough stopping Wulfsyg, and he wasn't a gigantic bear.

The horn lures us to a cliff that appears without warning.

Beyond it and far below is the impassable tract of land that protects the Royal Citadel: a barren landscape of sharp boulders and steep crevasses disguised by the shadow of the mountain.

"Help!"

I drop my eyes to see Rodgar peering up at us from the cliffside, strained hands wrapped around some roots poking out of the soil.

"Brother." Wynstan slides to his knees, and Taha joins him in pulling Rodgar up onto solid ground. The brothers hug, clapping each other on the shoulders.

"The Ent—" Wynstan starts.

"Slipped and fell!" Rodgar looks back at the cliff. "Landed hard."

"Died harder," Taha mutters, peering over. I inch to the edge and look too. No longer in his bear skin, the Ent lies motionless at the base of the cliff over a smear of blood, his axe strewn many feet away from him.

Rodgar settles on his haunches, gasping. "Is it finally over?"

"Once we fire off the last firework. Unless—" Wynstan's head turns to me.

I go to him with a hand extended. He tentatively lets me help him to his feet, Taha helping Rodgar to stand.

"You're upholding the treaty." Disbelief hangs over his voice.

"I gave you my word, Wynstan. Gan umber is a noble principle worth upholding—perhaps we can both call upon it."

"Mutual surrender? But that would make us all Victors. . . ." He looks at Rodgar, beaming now, then back to me. "Are you sure? It's never been done before. You might jeopardize your victory, and for there to be no Victor at all is—"

"A bad omen, I've heard." I slide a querying glance at Taha. He sighs but returns a reluctant nod. We both know that Prince

Kendric has to accept us as Victors however we arrive, whether he likes it or not. I return to Wynstan. "I'm sure. Mutual surrender, mutual victory. What do you say?"

Tears dot Wynstan's eyes. "I say that you're both honorable warriors. Yes, let's try. For the Old Ways."

"And for peace," I add. "Whenever you next encounter a stranger, I hope you'll remember how we worked together today."

He puts a hand over his heart. "I won't forget it. Let's blow the horn in Victors' Tower."

# 43

# TAHA

WYNSTAN IS GIVEN THE HONOR OF BLOWING the horn. While the brothers race up the stairwell to the tower's top, Taha takes a break on the steps outside and watches a stag cross the glade, its antlers glimmering in the late light. This is the first moment of peace he's had since dawn, a chance for him to fully internalize their victory against terrible odds. Yet he's still on edge.

"That was a tough fight," says Imani, easing down beside him with an exhausted sigh. "I almost can't believe we won. We *won*!" She laughs out loud.

Taha finishes his long swill of water, humming an agreement. "I understand now why Wulfsyg won the two previous Huntens. He was one of the best warriors I've ever seen."

"More beast than man," she mutters, massaging her flank. "You took a real risk shielding me from him. I would've been killed otherwise." She pauses before adding a gentle "Thank you."

He's too tongue-tied to reply, and glad when he hears the brothers release the firework they pulled from Wulfsyg's body into the sky, followed immediately by blowing the immense horn from the tower's peak above them. Its full-bodied, variegated sound is magnified by its several curling, antler-like branches, producing a declaration so loud it must emanate across the Darkcliff and startle the fish in the Waden. The brothers return to meet them, and they all begin their journey back to the forest's main gate. Wynstan and Rodgar link arms and sing a cheerful song in the Old Tongue. Taha and Imani walk a few paces behind them.

"This next part is going to be much easier than winning the Hunten," she remarks in Sahiran.

Taha worries it's going to be even harder, but he nods. "Kendric knows about your plan to steal the jewels during the celebration. He won't make it difficult."

"That's a relief to hear." Smiling, Imani gazes up at the observation tower, briefly visible between the trees. After a few moments, her smile fades and she becomes pensive. "Kendric also knew that Glaedric wants us to win the Hunten. I'm surprised the prince didn't realize that supplying his fyghtors with misra would make it unnecessarily harder for us. And now that I've thought about it, Wulfsyg seemed to imply that he knew *before* the Hunten that I would be using magic, and that's why he made the treaty." She shakes her head. "None of this seems right to me."

Nor to Taha, and that makes him feel like a hare wandering into a well-concealed trap. Glaedric wasn't exactly pleased when he first learned that they were participating in the Hunten to get to the jewels. The king realized that he couldn't influence the outcome of the tournament. Even if he had Kendric order Wulfsyg and the Ent to surrender to Taha and Imani during the Hunten, assuming the men would obey the order and not their pride, there would still remain the problem of the other fyghtors.

The king eventually accepted that Imani and Taha had to genuinely win. But Imani still has a point here. Kendric could've easily ordered his fyghtors not to use misra in the Hunten without arousing their suspicion. He could've found any reason for the order, that it was too risky given Glaedric is trying to keep the magic a secret for now. Any reason at all, but he didn't. And if Imani is right that Wulfsyg had been forewarned about her magic, Taha can't think of anyone else who would've told him but Kendric.

They begin climbing a steep staircase hewn into the cliff wall between engravings of wolves, ravens, and runes. The brothers stop singing and start practicing their stories about how the Hunten played out. Their group reaches the main gates in the late afternoon, finding them already open, though a brown curtain has been draped over the entrance, and a low drumming is coming from the grounds beyond. The four of them exit together in a line, pushing through the curtain onto a paved path. It's bordered in urns of fire; between them, boys painted in swirls of blue beat large drums.

At the end of the path, a crowd stands under the tall oaks. There's an audible intake of breath as the victorious fyghtors walk up the path. Everett parts from the edge of the crowd, mouth hanging open, but Taha is much more interested in Kendric.

The prince stands on a small podium in the middle, surrounded by guards. He's exchanged his armor for an embroidered brown-and-maroon robe; in one hand, he grips a solid gold scepter, like the one Staggnir is often depicted as holding. Most important, he wears a headpiece with antlers affixed to it. The tiara is nowhere to be seen.

"Stay calm," Taha mutters the instant Imani leans over to him. "Kendric only needs to wear the antlers for the ceremony."

At least, that's what's supposed to happen. But Taha is beginning to fear that Prince Kendric might be one of the only people in the Empire not to exist under Glaedric's thumb.

The nobles are even more outraged than Taha imagined they would be; their powdered, painted faces twist into ugly glowers. Prince Kendric raises a hand, hushing the drums. In the quiet, the echo of celebration rises from the waiting city below.

The fyghtors lower to their knees before the podium, and Wynstan and Imani speak in unison: "For the glory of the Harrowland Empire, we are victorious in De Wilde Hunten."

The nobles whisper heatedly. Kendric's foggy gaze meanders over Imani as if he's confused by her presence, when he's been explicitly ordered to accept her and Taha as Victors.

"Only one pair of fyghtors may triumph," he says.

Imani rises to her feet. "I invoke gan umber, Your Royal Highness. These fyghtors yielded to us. We accept their surrender."

Wynstan stands too. "I also invoke gan umber, Your Royal Highness. These fyghtors yielded to us. We accept their surrender."

Another period of quiet, interrupted by Everett: "Seems we both lucked out on our bets, Lord Elmer."

"They can't do that!" erupts a different nobleman.

Everett restrains a delighted grin. "Gan umber, though ancient, is a perfectly acceptable outcome of the Hunten. There's much literature on it in the epics, isn't there, Audrey?" He turns to his daughter.

"Oh, *yes*," she agrees, nodding. "Staggnir once sent his ravens to peck out the eyes of the famed warrior Odo after Odo slaughtered Eadmund despite his surrender. Odo's repentance was accepted only after he had compensated Eadmund's family with the pelt of the monstrous bear Bayon—"

"I know the epics!" a nobleman snaps from the other side of the podium. "Gan umber applies when one side accepts the surrender of the other, not to this nonsense. This has no merit."

"Why not?" Imani asks. "We were in a deadlock, unable to eliminate the other, and yielded simultaneously. Just because the situation is unusual doesn't mean it has no merit."

The nobles are stumped; Everett smirks openly at their bewilderment.

"The epics aside, we cannot accept this in good faith, Your Royal Highness," a noblewoman mawkishly implores Kendric. "It makes a mockery of well-accepted, *modern,* traditions, and at the hands of whom? *Fremde!*"

Everett faces the group. "My fyghtors are well within their rights to participate in the Hunten if they have a sponsor, which they do. Unless one of you can point me to a King's Law specifying otherwise?" He bows deeply to Kendric. "I would be humbled to hear it, Your Royal Highness."

"This is a disgrace! What about the bloody punters?" someone else complains, inciting another wave of disgruntled arguing.

"Oh, yes, what about them?" Everett sighs.

A nobleman calls to Kendric, "Your Royal Highness—*please!* What will your judgment be?"

Kendric's fingers ripple along the scepter; his lazy gaze drifts to the grass, a gentle wind shifting his long silken hair. Taha tenses, wondering whether Kendric really is going to disregard his brother's orders and not play along. But his fist suddenly clenches, and he bangs the scepter into the platform.

"As the leader of De Wilde Hunten, I accept your invocations of gan umber. To the lift."

The nobles look as if they've suffered a collective slap, but none of them has the boldness to resist their prince's judgment.

Imani, Taha, Wynstan, and Rodgar are ushered after Kendric as he trudges to the lift tower, trailed by the nobles, and they descend the platform to the Dark. They have to wait in the corridor until the trumpet boys signal their arrival, and then Taha can hear the screaming of the crowds through the very stone.

Kendric exits first, to deafening applause, and ascends the stage, joined a moment later by Wynstan and Rodgar, waving. It's only when Taha and Imani reach the stage does the applause ebb. The crowd squints at them; scribes eagerly press against the fence, wielding quills and paper. The rest of the crowd hasn't decided what's happened, but the scribes have sensed very worthy news.

Kendric raises his scepter; it refracts the light of the falling sun, lending him a divine visage. "Victors, recount to us your triumphs and tribulations."

Whispers foam up from the crowd like the hiss of a crashing wave. Wynstan gives his account, omitting the treaty and their united assault on Heath and Linden, relating it instead as if only he and Rodgar defeated them. The scribes' feathered quills flutter frenziedly when Imani takes over the account and explains how she and Taha encountered Lord Wulfsyg and the Ent and a tense battle ensued. Her action-packed tale draws reluctantly thrilled gasps from the crowd and the nobles, who seem to be very slowly forgetting their upset. It doesn't have the same effect on Prince Kendric; bored and dispirited, he might be asleep with his eyes open.

The account is finished jointly by Imani and Wynstan explaining that they fought each other but yielded to protect their partners from harm. Wynstan describes at length how he both offered and accepted surrender out of love for his brother and Staggnir's principles of honest battle, which he then exhorts his people to cling to whether facing kin or stranger. The crowd is surprisingly moved, and many are teary by the conclusion.

Kendric raises his scepter, somewhat roused from his waking nap. "A noble tale of honor and gallant battle that harkens to the Old Ways," he drones. Then he half turns, glancing limply at Taha and Imani. "And though two of our Victors are not Harrowlanders in body, they are in spirit. Some will say their triumph is a bad omen. To those I say it is a sign of prosperity to come. A greater, bigger, more powerful Empire than ever before. I declare this Season of the Hunten ended, for the renewed glory of the Harrowland Empire."

The monotone but eloquent speech is met with fervent applause from the crowd and the refrain "Glory, glory!" echoing down Lift Street and beyond. In the gathering before the stage, Everett practically drowns out the nobility with his gleeful rendition.

"Let us drink and revel in the names of the gods," says Kendric. "Victors and sponsors, your rewards await." He leaves the stage with his guards and disappears inside the lift tower.

Everett arrives onstage with Audrey and Skerric and shakes Imani's and Taha's hands. "Congratulations, you two. *Congratulations!* What an outcome, what a *statement*! Even more powerful than I'd hoped—you cleverly softened the blow of your victory with the mutual gan umber; the people were reluctant at first, but they were swept away by the romance of it by the end! Truly, a tale befitting the epics!"

They take the lift back up to the Citadel, with Wynstan's party chattering loudly on the other end of the platform. Everett leans closer to Imani. "Looking forward to moving into your new estate here in Harrowland?"

"No, actually, we're leaving Darkcliff tonight."

He frowns. "So soon? Before you've been knighted?"

Taha catches Skerric's hopeful eye. "Yes, and our winnings are to go to Skerric," he announces. "Otherwise we'll refuse to accept the winnings at all."

Skerric gives him a small, grateful smile.

Everett's lips curl in his salt-and-pepper beard. "Well, *quite* the generous gift for the Little Master." He nods at their quizzical look. "Skerric's name means 'the littlest amount' in the Old Tongue. Hardly appropriate for a boy born of noble blood, I think."

Skerric considers Everett with catlike caution, but the older man winks, still playful. "Your mannerisms and educated turns of phrase gave you away first. Then that outfit; the pattern and colors of your doublet invoke a certain fallen house of a scandal from some years ago. Am I right?"

Skerric's head rises boldly. "Ashton Hargrave. How do you do?"

Everett trades a quiet laugh with Audrey as the lift nears the top. "Rather meaningful way to avenge one's house, winning the Hunten."

"Cunning," she agrees. "And to win with our Victors—"

"It's a real stick in a certain someone's eye." Everett studies Skerric, continuing in a purr: "I do so like stumbling upon a man after my own heart. Should you not be overly busy with your new tenure, I may have some opportunities for . . . continued enterprise."

They exit the tower, Everett and Skerric shoulder to shoulder, quietly discussing their mutual futures as the House of Brand's antagonists. The guards take their group up to the keep and along a hedged path through several locked gates to a circular hall of black stone, its interior walls lined with built-in glass cabinets. On display are statues, figurines, vessels, rugs, ornamented weapons, musical instruments, headdresses and burial masks, jewelry, finely crafted ceremonial and other garb, and books and parchments—some inked in gold—plus stonework like grave markers and mosaics and entire windows of stained glass. All items from other nations. How did Glaedric describe what happened to the items taken from the temple north of Brooma? *Shipped its artifacts to Darkcliff for academic study and display.* This space is little more than a private, macabre, self-satisfied gallery of the House of Brand's conquests.

Kendric lounges in a throne against the far wall with his chin in his hand, looking toward the center of the hall. There, past a barred gate, is a spiral stairwell that descends underground. Mister Hardy's party and Lord Elmer's are directed to separate corners, and they wait for some time before the gate to the stairwell finally swings open. From it emerges a long procession of uniformed men bearing wooden trunks, which they stack in rows before the two groups. One trunk is opened on each side to display the gold piled inside.

"Sweet Staggnir!" Skerric hisses, his eyes shinier than the coins. Taha is less enthused—their real prize, the tiara, is still out of sight somewhere.

Officials direct them to a table in an alcove on their left, equipped with writing utensils. Skerric walks between Taha and Imani, holding on to Imani's elbow.

"Do you remember what to say?" he whispers.

"Yes. I'm more concerned with what *Prince Kendric* is going to say," she whispers back.

They shuffle behind the table. A monocled man in a brown silk robe puts down a heavy book and a furled scroll.

"On behalf of His Majesty and His Royal Highness and the House of Brand, the Royal Court grants your rewards for triumphing in De Wilde Hunten." The official unfurls the scroll. "For the Victors, Miss . . . er, Im-ay-nigh—"

"Imani. Taha." She points at him. "We accept our gold winnings and grants of tenure and assign them to Ashton Hargrave with no further obligations attached." They step aside for Skerric, who beams at the official. The man's monocle falls and bounces against his chest.

"Hargrave," he mumbles, hurrying to place the monocle over his eye again.

Skerric smirks. "How do you do?"

Taha and Imani sign documents affirming the transfer of their winnings and step out of the alcove, leaving Skerric and the sponsors to their business. It's maybe half an hour before the documents are completed and taken up for Kendric's review, including the ones from Wynstan's side. Skerric tensely watches the prince look over each scroll.

"Ashton Hargrave," Kendric says, his languid voice echoing around the hall. He peers over the scroll at Skerric. "You were there at His Majesty's wedding ceremony." A moment passes, Kendric considering something. Then he says, "Shame, what happened to Duke Attencraw," and returns to the scrolls.

An intense silence occupies the hall, almost everyone casting furtive glances at Skerric who instead stares at the prince with a faraway gaze. During one of their excursions to a museum days ago, Skerric told Taha about how Glaedric framed his father. Taha grasps the significance of Kendric's statement now. It could be dismissed as a poorly worded expression of Kendric's disappointment that Duke Attencraw became involved in a treasonous plot. It could just as easily be interpreted as Kendric's acknowledgment that Duke Attencraw was himself the subject of a treasonous plot.

Kendric finishes reviewing the scrolls and waves the officials away. He plods down the steps of the throne with sunken shoulders, his antler crown askew.

"To the Banquet Hall," he mumbles. "You can have your gold when you leave."

Taha exchanges a glance with Imani and follows the prince.

# 44

# IMANI

WE'RE ESCORTED BACK ALONG THE PATH AFTER Kendric, through the gates and across the front of the keep to the window-lined Banquet Hall. Inside, it's longer than it is wide, with a high ceiling of rib vaults and polished wooden floors covered in maroon rugs. Heavy curtains conceal the stained-glass windows, and between each hangs a gold-framed portrait of a different but equally stern, distinguished-looking Harrowlander. The Hall itself is anything but stern. Down its center runs a table stacked with platters of delicious-smelling food and blazing candelabras. Servants stand against the walls bearing jars of wine, and a troupe of musicians is playing on the stage at the far end, where floor space has been left for dancing.

Taha, Wynstan, Rodgar, and I are shown to washrooms, where more servants wait with warm, wet cloths and steaming pails of water. I clean up in front of a mirror, wiping away dirt and blood and resetting my braid. Back in the Hall, Lord Elmer's party have wasted no time accepting goblets of wine and getting comfortable at the table, but two spaces each have been left on either side of Kendric, who's seated at the head, drinking somberly in the company of his guards. I'm immensely relieved, as is Qayn, to see that he's exchanged his stag antlers for the gleaming tiara; exuding unbridled power, it lures the eye of everyone who passes him.

We sit on Kendric's right, Wynstan and Rodgar taking the seats on his left. We're joined by Everett, Audrey, and Skerric, and then the rest of the nobles are permitted into the Hall from a side waiting room. They've almost entirely shaken off their ill will and are now intent on exploiting the revelry on offer.

"How does this thing go?" I ask Audrey, beside me.

She appraises the Hall with similar apprehension. It must be nerve-racking to sit here, not as a noble but as the daughter of a self-made man of industry—and a clever woman in her own right.

"Apparently there's not much else to it but to drink, feast, and celebrate as debauchedly as one can," she says.

"Sounds like a promising evening," I mutter, glancing back at Kendric. He's face-first in a mug, that glorious tiara beaming upon his yellow hair.

When everyone is seated, wines and juices are poured and great, steaming slabs of meat and fish are cut and served alongside soft vegetables, pickled delicacies, and buttered breads. The feast is heavy and rich, and I'm so famished that not even my ever-increasing anxiety can make me lose my appetite. The nobles dive into the food with even greater enthusiasm; their mouths glisten greasily, their collars loosen, and their sleeves are soon rolled up to the midwrist.

I worry that we'll have to make conversation with Kendric,

but entertainers arrive to fill the void—at least, I think they're entertainers. Their faces are concealed by masks resembling wolf, raven, and hound heads; their outfits are either shapeless shimmering robes or obscenely fitting trousers under multitoned doublets, the toes of their woolen shoes tapering to curved points. The troupe ascend to the stage, lights are put out, and a show begins, accompanied by the musicians.

I can hardly follow the plot at first—the show is silent, and when the actors do speak, it's in an incomprehensible singsong dialect—but the ravens seem to be intently discussing something when suddenly they flee to the side of the stage. The musicians clash metal instruments, and a slender figure in black steps up.

"Who's that?" I whisper to Audrey.

"The Gods' Bane," she answers. "A monster from myth. It's said that a millennium ago, the Bane rampaged across Harrowland with an army of supernatural creatures at its command, until Staggnir descended from his halls and banished it."

"How curious," I murmur, a slow disquiet settling on my shoulders as I contemplate the undeniable parallels between the story of the Gods' Bane and that of the Desert's Bane.

But unlike the Sahir's rampaging monster whose form remains a mystery, the actor playing the Gods' Bane presents with a striking appearance: a red crown sculpted to look like fire; a black mask, blank but for a fanged sneer painted in white; gray shawls stitched along his sleeves, billowing in the manner of smoke, and gloves to give his hands long claws. The audience hisses at him, but he ignores them and meets an older man playing the part of Staggnir, for whom the audience remains respectfully silent. The Bane and Staggnir begin a mesmerizing dance of push and pull. I lean over to Audrey again. "What's happening now?"

"The Gods' Bane threatens the Cataclysm, and Staggnir warns him to retreat or there will be war between them."

The dance finishes with neither triumphing. The Bane makes carving motions with his arms, as if he's cleaving the earth, and summons other actors, who climb up onstage, garbed in monstrous masks and swathes of dark silks. What follows is a cacophony of violence; the monsters destroy everything in their path while the Bane stalks along behind, quietly watching.

"He's a curious figure indeed, the Bane," Audrey whispers, making me flinch. "I traveled recently with my father to a far-off kingdom on business. The people there also spoke of a monster who brought destruction with an army of unearthly creatures and had to be cast out by their gods. Most peculiarly, it's even said to have taken place during the same period of history, and their depictions bore remarkable semblances to ours. I've often wondered if some worldly tragedy struck at the time to produce such a similarity in myths."

The music crescendos victoriously as Staggnir subdues the Gods' Bane and sends him back into the shadows. The lanterns blaze, and when I look again, Audrey is walking to the washroom. By now, the nobles are largely drunk. A painted jester with bells sewn to his doublet and breeches takes to the stage, and everything he says is met with uproarious laughter. He's replaced by jugglers and acrobats, and the only unamused person in the Hall is Kendric. He hasn't said a word the entire evening except when he calls servants over to refill his chalice, which he does often.

The feast is soon supplemented with towering platters of berries and gold trays of glistening, fluffy cakes that are practically inhaled by the nobles. Then their chairs are abandoned and they descend upon the floor in a chattering swarm to dance, drink, and be amused by the entertainers moving through the crowd while the musicians play onstage. Once a dancing, disheveled nobleman tosses aside his doublet and unbuttons his silk shirt, Everett and Audrey take their leave. Skerric, keeping to the plan, decides to depart too and notifies a guard to fetch their gold. We shake hands, and Everett leans his face between me and Taha.

"Best of luck in your future endeavors; I've no doubt I'll hear of them one way or another. Do find us again in the next season."

With a wink, he's gone. Their departure stirs Prince Kendric, as if he's realized he's forgotten to do something. He stumbles upright, chalice glued to his fist, and gestures at me and Taha.

"You two, come with me."

*This is it,* Qayn whispers, his exhilaration coursing into me.

We follow the prince to a set of tall doors. He waves off the guards who attempt to accompany him but orders a servant to fetch more wine. He takes us through an empty adjoining room and out onto a veranda overlooking moonlit gardens, where he all but collapses on an ornately carved bench topped by plush cushions.

Full goblets are placed on the table before us around plates of fruits and pastry, then the servants depart and leave us alone.

Kendric holds his chalice under his nose, staring at our empty hands. "You're to revel with your prince," he intones.

"Forgive me," I say, then collect two goblets and hand one to Taha.

Appeased, Kendric raises his chalice. "Glory, glory."

We echo his refrain and sip. He guzzles his drink and then sits with it cradled in his lap, gazing blearily at the silver-lit, snowy mountain looming over the keep. Minutes pass—I'd estimate more than half an hour—during which Kendric drinks and I force myself to nibble fruit, all endured in the most awkward, tense silence. At one point, I catch Taha's eye. He returns a tiny shake of his head, as if to say, *Wait.* Then Kendric sighs, so suddenly I almost jump off the bench in fright.

"This was the first Hunten I've led," he slurs. "Doubtless my last."

His blatant woe is curious. "Why is that, Your Royal Highness?" I can't help but ask, despite Taha's giving me that headshake again.

"'Tis the king's duty to lead," says Kendric. "Glaedric vowed he won't miss another Season. A long life to him." Kendric raises his chalice and looks inside sadly. "But 'twas only right that I should've won. This, at least." He drains his drink, places the chalice on the table, and sinks into the cushions. His breathing slows; his lids grow heavy. In minutes, he's dozed off.

We stay very still, staring at him, but he only falls into a deeper sleep. We place our goblets on the table.

"What do we do?" I whisper.

"Take the tiara off him?" Taha whispers back.

I wave, signaling that I'll do it. I step around Kendric's knee, inch closer, and bend over him. Qayn watches through my eyes. My hands begin to shake under the weight of his anticipation.

*So close,* he whispers, *after so long, so close, and so beautiful, this gift of mine . . .*

My fingers touch the tiara, and the dark shadow of something colossal moves across me. I sense that I'm standing before greatness, majesty, power. I'm about to change Qayn's life, mine too. Everybody's, including the sleeping young man from whom

I must gently lift the tiara. The future, as big as it is, turns entirely on this moment. On me.

I suck in a breath and pull the tiara free. Kendric doesn't so much as twitch. Taha and I stare at each other, waiting for who knows what, perhaps for the guards to return or one of the servants to stumble upon our theft and scream. Neither happens.

*Go, Imani,* Qayn urges.

I straighten my arched back and slip the tiara inside my tunic. It's time to get back to the ship so Qayn can begin forging his crown.

We return to the Hall, passing a pair of guards marching to the veranda, presumably to check up on Kendric. The chairs at the banquet table are empty; Wynstan and Rodgar are drunkenly dancing in a circle of cheering nobles and drinking guards. Nobody notices us, nobody cares to. We collect our possessions from servants in the foyer and go to the doors. A lone Royal Guard with a skeleton's smile is waiting for us, though he behaves as if he weren't.

"Victors! Might I help you?"

"We have the prince's permission to revel in the city streets," Taha answers.

"Very good!" He opens one of the doors, letting in a gust of frigid air, and takes up a nearby lantern. "I'll escort you to the lift."

He leads us down the shadowy path away from the keep and its echo of merrymaking, smiling behind his lantern. I know Glaedric has arranged for him to help us leave with the jewels, and there's no possibility he'll suddenly decide to search me or turn us back to the keep, but my pulse still races. I watch his every move and that awful, overly polite smile stretching his skin.

Perhaps it's the closeness of the jewels to my heart, or Qayn's bated-breath silence: I'm more nervous and afraid than I've ever been in my life.

We reach the tower and load onto the platform with the liftenboys. The guard stands by the door, still smiling, and gives us a long nod as we descend the cliff face and out of sight.

# 45

# IMANI

MUSIC FLOATS ON THE COLD AIR FROM THE CELebrations happening down the way. We exit the Citadel's lift tower into the gray grounds. Skerric is waiting for us outside with a coach. We exchange nods and mutely pile into the back; the driver turns us around and heads down Lift Street. Red-faced, loose-grinned crowds drift across the street after us, drinking, eating, singing, embracing. I watch the revelry, not a hint of joy in my breast.

The stinking waft of fish and waste declares our arrival at the docks. I don a cloak from my bag and sling the hood over my head; Taha does the same. As we slow, Skerric leans forward on his bench, not more than a faint ghost with gray eyes in the swinging lamplight. "Imani, Taha, I will never forget your friendships or the great gift that you've given me today. Should you ever return to Harrowland, you'll have a warm-hearth waiting for you with the House of Hargrave. A castle next time."

The coach stops and the driver hollers. Skerric reaches to

shake my hand; I hug him instead, and Taha does the same. When they part, Skerric is teary-eyed.

"Safe travels, my friends."

Taha returns a nod. "Safe travels, Ashton."

Atheer is waiting for us at the end of the pier next to a boat manned by two Harrowlander ferryboys and a pilot.

"We have it," I say in Sahiran.

He blinks but shows no emotion. "Ship's ready to leave," he replies in Harrowtongue.

We clamber onto the boat. Using a single sail and oars, it bears us over the icy waters of the lantern-dotted harbor to the *Lion's Prize.* While Farida goes up to the helm with the pilot and the crew gets to work, Taha and I go belowdecks to the shadowy crew quarters, accompanied by Atheer and Amira. I hug my siblings, and then I toss my cloak and begin shedding the heaviest of my armor.

"Are the king's men aboard?" Taha asks quietly. He removes his sword and dagger and places them on a bunk.

Atheer's eyes point to the ceiling. "Six in the captain's cabin, as you said. Assassins. Snuck on when the crew was vacated for an inspection this afternoon. They ordered Farida to keep silent, said the ship's been seized by the king. The crew don't know."

Taha stuffs his bag under a bunk. "Better. They'll act natural. And the *other* king's man? The beastseer I told you about."

"Haven't seen his mindbeast yet." Atheer helps me remove my leather tunic and chainmail. "I thought it was this seagull that'd been hanging around, but after Muhab stuffed it with bread, it flew off and hasn't come back."

Something fat, squeaking, and furry scurries over my boot. I kick my foot, hissing. "The mindbeast could be an accursed rat for all we know! There's already a swarm of them living on this ship."

"Glaedric said it's a bird." Taha lays his vest on the bunk and begins removing his chainmail. "The beastseer will be watching us for signs of betrayal; if he notices that something is wrong, he'll inform Glaedric, and Glaedric will kill our parents. Keep that in mind whenever you're up on deck." He drops the mail in the trunk and pulls his vest back on. "And remember, Glaedric thinks I'm going to take Qayn's crown once it's forged and then signal the men hiding in the captain's cabin to secure our ship until he arrives. He'll be following us on a merchant's ship with our parents aboard. But as soon as that door opens to the captain's cabin, it's war, and I'm killing every man that comes out. Beyond that, it's up to Qayn to stop Glaedric."

"Great Spirit," Amira mutters, her nail-biting intensifying.

I catch her eye as I finish buckling my chest leathers. "Do you remember what you told me back in the Forbidden Wastes, when we still thought Atheer was dead? 'Hold on to hope.' Qayn *will* stop Glaedric, and we *will* free Mama and our people."

Amira nods, but her large eyes avoid me, and her mouth remains puckered in anxiety. My encouraging words weren't enough to make her feel better. I suspect no words could, so I ignore my own unease and concentrate on what remains of the most important mission I've ever undertaken.

We finish getting ready and disperse abovedeck. Just as Taha warned, our ship isn't alone in its cautious journey down the dark River Waden. I can't make out the details of Glaedric's vessel as it sails after us, only the lights of its many lanterns; nor can I look for long or even appear alarmed. If Glaedric has a mindbeast here, the beastseer will be watching me. I ignore the ship and work the rigging as Muhab directs.

We escape the Waden a few hours later. After a short stop for a boat to collect the pilot and the king's dues, we flee into the vast dark where the sky and sea have fused to become one. The course is set, the sails are angled, and we go solemnly into the night with our hunter in pursuit.

"Tell me our troubles have been worth it." Farida descends the gangway to join Atheer, Amira, Taha, and Muhab, gathering with the rest of the crew. I pull the tiara from inside my tunic, scaring the shadows away with its light. It's answer enough for them all; they look upon the jewels as if seeing a vision of their ancestors.

"Qayn, it's time," I say.

He appears on a frosty breeze, black tresses shifting. I hold up the tiara; lantern light dances in the jewels, giving them the quality of sparkling water. A tear rolls down his cheek.

"You've saved me," he says softly. "If you give me some time, I will repay the favor."

He reaches for the tiara with trembling hands; a steadily sprawling light glows from the jewels' mysterious depths. In moments, the light eclipses that of the lanterns, strengthening the closer that Qayn's fingers come to them. The jewels are so impatient to reunite with him that they prize themselves from their oppressive clasps and float before him, their light reflecting like dewdrops in his pupils. His graceful hands move around them, drawing an invisible framework. Slowly he settles onto his knees, and the jewels float down with him to hover between his open palms.

"Qayn?" I say, but he doesn't respond, doesn't blink or react in any way, and neither do I feel his soul stirring. He's been transported elsewhere, here in appearance alone, and the forging of his crown has begun.

I turn to the group. "Now we wait until he's done."

The others nod mutely. There's more that could be said between us, about the Hunten, but nobody ventures there. It doesn't feel right. We watch Qayn in silence, his eyes glowing white, his wavy black locks floating around his face as if he's suspended under water.

Time drifts. Amira goes belowdecks to nap, Atheer gently exercises his healing arm before following her, Muhab smokes in a chair lashed to the mainmast until he dozes off, and between inspections of his bowstring, Taha glances at me. I catch him doing it more than once—or is he catching me? In the light of the jewels, I've become aware of his beauty again: the dazzling emerald hue of his eyes, framed vividly by straight ebony lashes; the prominent cut of his cheekbones and hard jaw; the dangle of hair over his brow, elegantly disheveled. After what happened in the Hunten, I know my desire for him has reawakened, but it doesn't displace the longing I feel whenever I look at Qayn. Somehow those two emotions are coexisting in a delicate state of peace—for now.

At sunrise, ribbons of pulsing light form around the jewels in the shape of a three-pronged crown.

I jump to my feet in the recess under the gangway, shaking off the naplike state I was in for the last hour. "The crown has almost been forged," I say to Taha. "I'll get my brother and sister."

He stands up, collecting his bow. "Imani, before you go, I need to tell you something."

I pause and nervously look back. Taha stops beside me.

"Everything," he says, "that I have ever done—everything I ever *will* do—is to protect our families and the Sahir. I just needed you to know that."

He glances at my lips. I sense his desire to kiss me, but he settles on lightly touching my arm. And something about that is . . . it's like a farewell, the nod you trade with your reluctant adversary before a duel neither of you wants; a gesture to let the other know that what follows won't be easy, but it will be done. An end will be found.

He steps past me, cupping his mouth and calling, "Amira! Atheer! It's almost time!"

An inexplicable dread climbs up my spine as I notice the sea bird perched high between the rigging. I've felt this way before, under the prison in Taeel-Sa. It was too late then too.

Atheer and Amira hurry out of the hatch; Muhab rouses in his chair; Farida appears at the railing above. The group quickly converges around Qayn as the light from the jewels intensifies. I hang back, watching Taha and the bow gripped in his hand. He's hanging back behind Qayn too, but at an angle that gives him a view of the captain's cabin. And although his gaze is keen, Taha suddenly looks so drawn, as if every harrowing thing he's endured since his capture has caught up with him in an instant. He darts his eyes from Qayn to the cabin door to the sea and back. One, two, three. As if our plan—this absence of action—is more complicated than it really is.

I'm suddenly blinded by a bloom of intense light. When it fades moments later, Qayn is rising to his feet between us, his forged crown hovering high above him. It's the most glorious object I have ever seen, an intricate weaving of silver, gold, and light around each jewel. The crown is even more glorious than the one I saw in Qayn's memory, because this one isn't a representation of pure, limitless magic—it *is* pure, limitless magic, simply waiting for its rightful vessel to be channeled through. Even Qayn stares up at it in awe, as if he hasn't fully grasped that this crown is *his.* He is the king for whose return it has been waiting.

As he puts his hands out to catch the slow-falling crown, Makeen shouts from the helm, "Warships off our stern! And forward—portside— They're everywhere, gods' sakes!"

I make out blood-red sails in every direction. Muhab begins clanging the bell on the mainmast, summoning anxious sailors to the deck. Taha slips the bow off his shoulder and reaches up for an arrow. Amira inches closer to Qayn. "Hurry, please," she begs.

I obey instinct and step toward Taha. The crown lands in Qayn's hands and fortifies at his touch, washing the deck in warm light.

"Now!" Taha shouts, swiftly nocking an arrow and pointing it at the captain's cabin. The door swings open at almost the same instant, figures silhouetted in the frame—and Taha drops his aim to Qayn's back.

I tackle him as he releases the bowstring. We hit the deck and roll. Amira shrieks; the bell stops tolling; Atheer cries out, and the Harrowlander men who've been hiding in the captain's cabin order the crew to surrender. I scramble from under Taha onto my knees, searching for the arrow. Atheer appears unharmed, flung against the rail and staring at Amira through weeping eyes. Amira. Standing where Qayn just was, her open cloak wafting around her so that I can't see past her or why she's hunched over. And the arrow, Great Spirit, *where is the arrow!*

"Do not resist!" Glaedric's assassins descend the gangway armed with swords; two archers remain outside the cabin, targeting the deck. "This ship has been seized under His Majesty's authority for harboring insurgents against the Empire!"

"Amira?" I climb to my feet, dizzy and nauseated. *"Amira!"*

Finally she moves. Staggers awkwardly, as if maneuvering around something, and turns to face us. The dark, swirling fabric of her cloak drifts aside, revealing Taha's arrow lodged in the wood by her feet and Taha's dagger in her fist, the blade glistening black. I follow her fiery gaze to Qayn, kneeling on the deck with his hands clutching his chest, black blood seeping between his fingers. . . . Amira steals up the gangway steps; Glaedric's assassins close ranks behind her. It's there, in her other hand: Qayn's crown. . . .

"Amira, what did you do!" I lunge forward. "Qayn, look at me, please!"

He does, right as I slam into the planks and Taha begins dragging me back by my cloak. Qayn lurches to his feet, black blood pouring from him; it streams down his wrists, soaks his tunic, pools on the wood—

*Please don't let me go, Imani,* he whispers across our souls. *I don't want to be alone again.*

He stumbles backward, still gazing at me through shining eyes, one step, two, three, into the railing—and goes overboard.

*"QAYN!"* I scream. "COME BACK! PLEASE, *COME BACK!*"

But he doesn't.

Why doesn't he?

The world suddenly blurs and slows. Sounds bleed together. I stare at the railing, not understanding. Certain I'm seeing things, missing something that'll make this all make sense. But what? Qayn fell overboard. I have to get him back.

I try to summon him to me, but the bond between our souls is tenuous, fading from my perception with every passing second.

I thrash and kick at Taha to go after him, but Taha drops on me, arms locking around my waist, and pins me to the planks.

"Imani, stop!" he growls. "You don't understand what's happening!"

I scream into the wood, rage and misery; he clamps a hand over my mouth so I can only weep. One of Glaedric's assassins points a sword at Farida.

"Order your crew to comply, or you will be sunk."

A strange crackling behind the *Prize* tows the captain's gaze to the sea. The water around the ship is hardening to ice.

"Glaedric's affinity," Taha says in a low voice.

The ship lurches against its new enclosure, swaying everyone onboard. Farida turns back to the assassin. "What must they do?"

"Heave to and have them assemble on their knees."

She relates the order to Muhab, and he grudgingly begins directing the crew. They clamber into the rigging; Farida limps to the helm. Taha pulls me up and walks me to the area between the gangways, past Atheer, who shuffles after us, saying, "Taha, why did you do it, man—"

"Don't try anything, Atheer," Taha warns. "This is for everyone's good."

I stare up at Amira, safe behind the archers with Qayn's crown in her hand. As soon as Taha stops clamping my lips, I twist my head back at him. "This is your doing! You manipulated my sister into this, you dishonest, ruthless—"

"I didn't—"

"DECEIVER!" I scream. *"BACKSTABBING BETRAYER!"*

He puts his hand over my mouth too firmly for me to bite him. But my iron sense of him is good—I could fling him off me without even moving. I can't do the same to Amira, and even if I could wield that mercilessness against my own sister, Glaedric is coming, and our parents' lives depend on the crown's being handed over to him. The only person who could've stopped all this is gone. Qayn is gone. *He's dead!*

I fold over in Taha's arms, sobbing. Glaedric's merchant ship jolts to a stop alongside our ice perimeter, encased by its own. Once our crew finishes adjusting the sails and masts, they kneel on the deck, and the assassins step between them, inspecting for weapons. Satisfied, one nods at the balcony above me. "Go over."

Taha grips me tightly as Amira descends the gangway with the crown, his dagger sheathed in a scabbard on her waist. I struggle in his arms.

"Amira, please don't do this!" I beg. "Whatever Taha has said to convince you, he's *lying*!"

Amira reaches the end of the gangway, sighing. "Taha didn't convince me, Imani. I convinced him."

I falter. "But why? Qayn was going to save our parents. He was going to save us all!"

She hooks the tiara in her belt and gives me a sad look. "No, he wasn't. Qayn is the Desert's Bane."

# 46

# TAHA

IMANI DEADENS IN TAHA'S GRIP, AS LIMP AS A DOLL. She stares at Amira descending the rope ladder off the *Prize* with two of Glaedric's men. "You're lying," she calls hoarsely after her sister.

Taha directs Imani to climb down to the ice and follows her. Amira is already hiking to Glaedric's ship, cutting a dark, determined figure against the freeze. The light of the rising sun has tinted the ice a bloody red.

"Amira, I know you're lying!" Imani yells as Atheer begins his descent above them. "You're making this up because you don't trust Qayn—I know you haven't trusted him since that meeting back in Taeel-Sa—and you refuse to listen to anyone else's opinion!"

Amira's refusal to respond only makes things worse. As they cross the ice, Imani mumbles in disbelief and sobs, wretched with despair. Taha's chest aches for her. She doesn't know the terrible truth about Qayn that they discovered after they left Brooma. Taha could try to reason with her, but Imani wouldn't believe anything he says right now. She'd say he only saved her in the Hunten to earn her trust and make her easier to manipulate. Once again, he's had to sacrifice his reputation with her for an increasingly elusive "greater good." It's an upset he'll have to work through later.

The ice is already softening underfoot when they reach Glaedric's ship, hissing as it melts. Taha boards first and is met by a somber Ser Ulric. Behind him, Glaedric waits between the mainmast and the gangway, oozing self-satisfaction.

"Presuming you fared fine in the Hunten?" Ulric mutters.

Taha freezes as he sees his father for the first time in weeks. Bayek is gagged and roped to the balcony outside the captain's cabin alongside Zahra. Captive like cattle, soldiers pointing swords at them.

Taha turns an enraged glare on Ulric. "Lord Wulfsyg and the Ent tried conspiring with the other fyghtors to kill us, and in the end, Wulfsyg took an axe to the face and the Ent went *splat* over the side of a cliff, so I'd say things went better than fine."

Ulric purses his lips and merely nods. Behind them, Amira, Imani, and Atheer board, Imani crying out when she notices their mother on the balcony.

"Fear not, Imani," Glaedric gloats, drawing her attention. "Your younger sister made the right decision on your behalf." He shifts his leer to Atheer, who leeches of color. "Welcome back, Atheer. I hope you're looking forward to going home and seeing the fruits of your labor." He beckons Amira. "The crown, and your mother and the Grand Zahim go free."

Taha gives Amira a reassuring nod and guides her toward the king.

"Wait!" Imani shouts. She tries to take a step forward, but

one of the assassins holds her back. In her rage, she barely notices. "I want proof, Amira. Tell me something, *anything,* or at least have the decency to admit you're lying in front of your family."

Amira halts, her face flushing. "I am *not* lying. I found a book in Mama's office that was written by Nahla. Do you remember it, Mama? The ancient one with the poems and sketches that you kept in the glass box?"

Zahra's eyes widen and she nods. Imani swallows, glancing at her mother. "Nahla actually signed her name?"

"No, but I deduced from the contents that she was the author," says Amira.

"*Oh,* you *deduced*!" Imani crows harshly. "Show me the book."

"I can't," Amira says through gritted teeth. "It was lost during a storm at sea. That's why I didn't tell you. I was afraid you'd think I was making things up—"

"You are," Imani seethes.

"No! In the book, Nahla described the First City as Qayn's gift to her! She even drew it. She drew a lot of things, including—"

"I am growing impatient," Glaedric warns.

Amira speaks faster: "—including a man-shaped shadow monster with a fiery crown and claws—the *same* monster that Taha saw engraved on a wall in a si'la's den in the Sahir, near an enormous hole in the earth—a *Door* between realms where monsters come out, created by the same being that the si'la pointed to on the wall—she *identified* the monster as the Desert's Bane—"

"Gods' Bane," Imani echoes hollowly.

"And in Nahla's book"—Amira's rises to a shrill pitch—"she wrote that her lover revealed his monstrosity after she defied him! Imani—Qayn *was* the Desert's Bane! We couldn't return his magic to him!"

She marches to Glaedric and thrusts the crown into his hands. Taha instinctively braces as Glaedric lowers it onto his head and exhales an immensely satisfied *"Ahh,"* the crown exuding a bright halo. Threads of light pierce Glaedric's skin and wiggle under it; they flick along his lashes and swirl in his eyes, obscuring the black filaments, then trace the web of veins in his face down into his neck before vanishing under his collar.

"Your Majesty," shouts a sailor from the crow's nest, "there's something in the water!"

Glaedric is heedless in his bubble of bliss; he holds his hands in front of his face and marvels at the light worming its way to his fingertips. Ser Ulric glances at Taha, puzzled. They go to the railing together, trailed by soldiers and sailors crowding the deck. Even the assassins tow Imani and Atheer back so that they can peer overboard.

It's impossible to know where in the vast ocean to look first. The warships have almost reached them from every direction, about eight in the fleet that Taha can see but taller and wider in the hull than any he's familiar with. Opposite Glaedric's ship, the *Lion's Prize* floats free of the ice; everyone aboard it is also crammed against the rails, scouring the water. Taha tips his head forward to look and sees something glide under the ship. Confused waves swing up and flop back against the ice. The sailors grip the rails, their curiosity turning to fear as the disordered simmering ceases and the ocean falls flat. Under the rising sun, the sea is a ribbed sheet of light, glowing brightest where a cobalt crest suddenly breaks the surface behind their stern.

Imani points at it. "There!"

Heads twist; the men gasp. A stony ridge shaped like sharp teeth climbs out of the water. Tall, and taller.

"Staggnir's beard, what is it?" asks a sailor behind Taha.

The ridge moves away from them with incomprehensible speed and sharply submerges. Nobody makes a sound. They wait, apprehensively watching the warships approach. Suddenly the ocean begins to simmer around the closest one.

"Warn them." A sailor down the line cranes his face at the crow's nest. "Selwyn, WARN THEM NOW!"

A horn begins blowing from the nest in a pattern of two short bursts followed by a longer wail, but the warship has already realized that something is wrong. A long line of portholes opens in its hull, and the ends of glinting barrels slide out. Imani leans forward, squinting. "Are they . . ."

"Cannons," Taha realizes aloud.

Her head jerks back to him. "On a *ship*?"

The innovation gets no opportunity to awe. An enormous, serrated tail cleaves the water and seizes the warship. A few cannons fire, to no avail; the tail tightens around the hull and snaps the masts. A series of deafening bangs sound in rapid succession, and then the ship folds in half, as flimsy as paper, and disappears beneath the surface.

Everyone around Taha is silent, staring. The sea is disturbingly serene. And then someone screams, "SEA MONSTER!" and the railings of this ship and the *Prize* are abandoned.

Taha has to raise his voice over the captain bellowing orders from the helm. "A sea monster shouldn't exist beyond the Sahir," he calls out to Imani as she comes closer.

"This isn't a coincidence!" says Amira. She appears between them, her eyes like saucers. "It's *him*."

Imani nods gravely. "Tiamat. Qayn told me about her. He called her his . . . friend."

Amira clutches her sister's arm. "Great Spirit, this monster is Qayn's *ally*? We need to get out of here!"

Yet despite the efforts of the sailors who've ascended the masts, the others towing long ropes from the deck, it's become apparent to the captain and some of the senior men that they aren't going anywhere with ice surrounding the ship. And King Glaedric is standing statue-still, his eyes shut.

"I . . . I think I see it!" Selwyn shouts from the crow's nest.

The sailors curse and whine. The captain hurriedly abandons his post at the helm and comes down to petition his king. "Your Majesty," he says in a gravelly voice, "the ship is still trapped in the ice."

"Aye!" Selwyn shouts again from above. "The beast is coming back!"

The crew's panic amplifies, and some of the sailors have to be shouted at by the quartermaster to keep working. Ulric quiets them all with a whistle and turns back to Glaedric. "Your Majesty," he says evenly, "please, you must free the ship now. We're in grave danger."

But Glaedric either doesn't hear the Marshal or doesn't care to. Jaw ticking, Ulric gestures at two soldiers. "Use your magic; we'll melt the ice."

They run to the port and starboard railings, Ulric to the bow, and direct streams of summoned fire overboard. The ice crackles and creaks, softening; the ship bobs as if shaking off shackles, and the captain orders the men to "Let fall!" the sails.

"The beast is almost upon us!" Selwyn warns from above.

Atheer nudges Taha. "We have to free our parents in case this ship goes down."

They start moving, and the assassins assigned with guarding Imani and Atheer are too distracted to stop them from fleeing toward the gangway. As Taha reaches the steps, he glances over the portside railing. What was a frozen sheet of ice is now a wash of slush and free-floating blocks. Suddenly the ship lurches and almost knocks their group off their feet. Taha grabs the banister with one hand and catches Imani's arm with the other, stopping her fall. They resume hauling up the gangway, only for the ship to lurch again. This time in reverse.

Taha falls knees-down onto the steps, as if the ship has collided with a wall. Canvas and ropes move of their own accord, the sails reef, and Glaedric's booming voice resonates across the deck: "A god does not run from a serpent."

The king parts his barricade of soldiers with wide arms, the crown glowing. The crew gawps at him; even Ser Ulric, who returns from the bow sweaty and confused. A trembling sailor speaks first, wringing his white cap against his chest. "Y-Your Majesty, you didn't see what the monster did to the *Red Gallant.*"

"You dare speak without being addressed first?" Glaedric flicks his fingers, the jewels in his crown pulsing brightly. The sailor flies backward into the nearest mast, and his spine loudly breaks. He drops to the deck, contorted in death. The crew pale, shuffling back. An intense heat loops around Taha's neck. *I made the right decision,* he tells himself. *I chose the lesser evil.*

A sharp swell rocks the ship, and Glaedric smiles. "It's here."

# 47

# IMANI

TIAMAT RISES OVER US, WATER SPITTING OFF HER body.

She's even bigger than Hubaal the Terrible and resembles none of the river or sand serpents I've encountered in the Sahir. From the waist down, she's a scaled monster, but she has two arms and a human torso, albeit molded from smooth, shiny plate; her chin and blue lips resemble a woman's; her nose and eyes are serpentine; her seaweed-and-tentacle hair undulates behind her in myriad blues and greens; and from her shoulders sprout jagged wings, barnacled and draped in strands of flora from the deep. She lowers her arm before the ship, hand opening. Five fingers conjoined by white webbing uncurl, and on her pale-green palm is Qayn, leaning on a gnarled staff of driftwood, one hand pushed against the wound in his chest.

"No, no, no!" Amira rises to her feet. *"How is he still alive?"*

The men cower before Qayn, but Glaedric is mildly curious in his appraisal. "I truly thought a blade to the heart would do it, but perhaps your constitution makes you a little more resilient."

"You think you can kill me?" Qayn says in Harrowtongue.

Glaedric smiles. "I have killed you. We're simply conversing while we wait for your body to hear the news."

"The Invulnerable," Taha murmurs beside me, standing up. "This is what the si'la meant." He tugs my sister's arm. "Amira, Qayn is—"

"You *think* you can *kill me*?" Qayn's hand flutters over the hole in his chest. "Many have tried before, and all failed!"

Glaedric grins. "None were me. I succeeded. Why, I think that makes me the Sahir's savior!"

"I'VE BEEN ALIVE FOR FOUR THOUSAND YEARS; YOU CAN'T KILL ME!" Qayn roars, the vein in his neck straining.

"—immortal," Taha says, finishing his own sentence.

The words swell in my skull: *Qayn is immortal.*

Sailors faint; a few are sick over the railing. Qayn struggles to stay upright on his staff.

"Give me my crown," he demands.

Glaedric bursts into vigorous, insolent laughter. "No! Crowns are reserved for the king! Go off now, goodbye! Go off and die and stop wasting my time! I have a world to conquer."

"Give me my crown," Qayn demands again, his breathing labored, "or I will take it from your body when Tiamat is through."

Glaedric drops the grin; the crown exudes a furious, red-tinted light. "I will feast on the serpent's flesh, and if you survive my punishment today, I will throw you in a cage to punish at my leisure for years to come."

Qayn is wrath personified, barely controlled. "As you wish," he hisses.

"Is it true?" I shout to him, vaulting the side of the gangway.

I push past the sailors to the railing. "Are you really the Desert's Bane?"

He gazes down at me, water cleaving to the ends of his limp locks.

"Qayn," I beg, "Amira and Taha are lying, aren't they? You're not the Desert's Bane. You can't be! The Bane was destroyed a thousand years ago!"

I recite the oft-repeated fact, but I know in my heart that I'm no longer the girl who believed everything the Council told her. I understand now that history is a collection of stories narrated by the people with the loudest voices, the mightiest quills, and the sharpest swords, inked in the blood of the vanquished, just as Qayn said.

"Wasn't the Bane destroyed a thousand years ago?" I ask, tearing up. "Please, tell me, Qayn. Tell me the truth."

"The truth is a thing with many faces—"

*"Tell me!"* I yell.

His breath rattles in his chest. "Yes. Nahla's people—your people—gave me that name long ago."

My pulse drums in my ears. Qayn is the Desert's Bane; he has been this whole time. When he danced with me. When I kissed him. When he talked about our future together. When I risked my life in the Hunten. All the while *knowing* the dark truth of his past. He lied, manipulated me, earned my trust. Made me *care* for him. My head spins as if the world has been deprived of its equilibrium; I grip the railing in case I go over it.

"But I am not the monster of history, Imani, not wholly," Qayn says. "*Please,* trust me. Listen to what I am telling you in your *soul.*"

My soul. I apprehensively lower my defensive wall; he immediately reaches out to me.

*Tiamat will hold Glaedric off for as long as she can. I'm relying on you to do something, Imani . . . on your heart of love. . . .*

Qayn's eyes flutter. He mumbles something to Tiamat before he slides off the driftwood staff to his knees and his head drops forward.

*Qayn?* I try to reach across our souls, but our bond has faded completely, and Qayn isn't moving.

With a roar, Tiamat closes her fingers around him. The ocean churns; her tail spears up. Men scream and dive out of the way. Taha yanks me back as her tail slams into the groaning ship and coils around it. I make for the gangway after him, glimpsing Glaedric and the crown's searing light. The soldiers guarding our parents have fled the balcony, allowing Atheer and Amira to saw at Mama's bindings with Taha's dagger.

Tiamat swipes her free hand at Glaedric, but he shoots off the deck like an arrow, and her hand skims under his feet, slamming into soldiers and the mast. The men are hurled into the ether; the mast snaps, quavering the rigging and tearing the sails.

With how much he's used Qayn's crown already, I expect Glaedric to drop dead. Instead, he floats out over the open water, very much well, his arms held wide in invitation. Tiamat relinquishes the ship, but not before the starboard railing under her tail pops and flings and some part lower down on the hull caves in with a bang. Fizzing water spews across the deck; the ship groans and lists. Tiamat uses her powerful tail to swim after Glaedric, sending waves thumping against the tilting hull.

"Abandon ship!" yells the captain. "Launch the yawls!"

We reach the balcony as Atheer frees Mama. I grip the balcony with one fist and help her stand with the other. "Are you hurt?" I ask.

"I'm all right, my loves!" She pulls me and my brother and sister in for a hug and, sobbing, kisses our cheeks. "My son," she rasps when she reaches Atheer. "My beautiful son is alive!"

I don't even realize I'm crying too until I pull away and find it difficult to see Taha removing his father's gag.

"Are you well, Baba?" he asks in a restrained manner, and begins to saw the ropes binding his father's wrists. Bayek is equally restrained, replying with a simple nod.

The hull gives a death groan, and the ship sinks deeper. The blond man with the fire affinity hauls up the gangway and shouts at Taha: "Quick, boy, get to a yawl before the ship sinks!" Then he goes back down and helps sailors struggling to pull themselves out of the now-slanted stairwell leading to the flooded decks below.

Taha frees his father, and we descend to the main deck. Some soldiers and sailors have already clambered into one of the yawls and launched it into the water half-empty. Before any more can be launched, the ocean thunders off our starboard. Tiamat drags up an immense spear of coral and lobs it at Glaedric in the sky. The crown's light blazes; he raises his hands and halts the spear in midair, then turns it around and shoots it back with excessive force. Tiamat evades it, hissing angrily, and dives below the surface. The spear crashes into the ocean after her, creating gigantic waves that roll toward us.

"Release the yawls!" the captain bellows from farther up the deck.

The two remaining boats are hastily dropped into the ocean.

We grab the railing as the wall of water meets the ship and stumbles over us as if surprised. I see, hear, and taste nothing but freezing seawater. When the wave drains away, it drags the listing ship over with it. The deck pitches sideways and doesn't stop until we're hanging vertically from the railing and several men have gone, wailing, into the depths below.

I hoist over the railing onto the exposed, glistening hull. The Grand Zahim helps me pull Mama up, the gruff blond man lifts Amira over with one arm, and Taha helps Atheer. Then we work together to bring several shivering sailors, all of them about my age, onto the hull. Tiamat still hasn't reappeared; Glaedric hovers alone in the sky above his fleet of warships. Other remaining survivors of this ship huddle on the hull too. Many have already jumped into the water and swum to the safety of the yawls, which are being held fast alongside the ship by long ropes. One of the yawls is almost full, but the other floats empty, and the only people left on the hull other than us are a group of soldiers.

Standing at the back of their group is a slender man, his long face composed in an overly formal expression despite his being sodden from head to heel. He notices us gathered behind his soldiers and addresses the blond man: "Ser Ulric, we'll capsize the yawl if we overload it. The fremde and sailors will have to remain here until the *Stout Heart* can send its own."

Ulric sizes up the warship about half a mile off our bow and the *Lion's Prize* inching along several hundred yards off our portside. His pallid blue eyes would be unremarkable if not for the sickly threads of black surrounding his irises. "The ocean's freezing, Ser Alfred," he says. "They'll drown in minutes."

But of course Alfred isn't surprised by that; he made the

statement knowing there's no hope for us. "We've simply no choice," he says. "The yawl can carry only so many."

"I had an agreement with your king," says Taha, standing at Ulric's side. "The crown for the lives of our parents *and* their safe return to Qalia."

"I am not risking my men's lives for yours," Alfred snaps through a mean-eyed scowl. "His Majesty can judge my actions once we're safe."

Tiamat suddenly breaches, wings beating, and swipes at Glaedric. He slides out of the way, waving his arms. The crown shoots out bolts of light as a brutal gale materializes and sends Tiamat crashing back into the water. The tempest buffets our ship and screams on across the water, driving the waves before it. Now full, the first yawl raises its small sail, and the men begin rowing for the *Stout Heart,* leaving the second, empty yawl bobbing on the swell.

"Get down!" I tell Mama and Amira, lowering myself along with them. The surge off Tiamat's body sprays through the railing and washes over the hull, sweeping one of the screaming sailors out of sight. The ship jolts and sinks a dozen feet before continuing a steady decline to its watery grave.

Ulric rises to his feet. The four surviving sailors bunch around him, teeth chattering, their scared faces as white as sharks' bellies.

"Let them onto the yawl, Alf," says Ulric. "There's room enough for all of us."

"No! The added weight will drown us!" Alf stands brusquely and draws his sword, the other soldiers following suit. "I will be quite clear, Marshal. There is room for you and nobody else. Come along while we have time. I'll stand guard."

"Please, Ser Alfred!" begs a weeping sailor. "Don't leave us. We'll assuredly perish!"

Alf tips his head back sternly. "Chin up, young man. Be brave in the service of His Majesty."

"Glaedric is no king of mine," I say, brandishing my dagger. "Either you let us onto the yawl or we force our way on."

Alf starts, bottom lip jutting out. "Are you threatening to commandeer our vessel? Marshal, are you sanctioning this mutiny?"

Ulric has had enough. He summons handfuls of fire, the skin around his eyes suddenly taut. "One more disrespectful word, Alf, and I'll burn you black and give your ashes to the sea."

Alf's thin lips part in outrage. "You wouldn't attack a fellow knight."

I push Mama and Amira behind me as Ulric holds his hands up. "Yes or no, Ser Alfred. Are you letting us onto the yawl?"

Alf hesitates, cleft chin quivering. "You wouldn't attack a fellow knight," he repeats, weaker.

Ulric cloaks him in fire. It burns so hot that when Alf leaps into the water, the flames extinguish in a loud, steaming *hiss* and leave behind a black, shriveled corpse that rapidly sinks. Some of the soldiers charge Ulric, but a few seem to be surrendering. He burns them all the same, possessed by a wanton rage that even he seems incapable of reining in. He clears the hull of obstacle and folds over, breathless.

"Go, boy," he wheezes to Taha, pointing at the yawl's rope, abandoned on the hull.

Taha uses it to pull the yawl as close to the hull as is safe, and then we all jump into the water. It's even colder than I imagined, and the shock of being immersed in it rips an involuntary gasp from my lungs. It's a moment of anxiously thrashing my limbs before I can control myself and swim. We clamber into the dry base of the yawl, and one of the sailors points at the oars: "Row! Before the ship goes under and takes us with it!"

We form up, oars in hand. The sailor sits at the front and bellows, "Heave-ho," to coordinate our escape.

Half a minute later, the ship sinks in a gurgling whirlpool behind us, sucking the floating remains down to the depths.

# 48

# TAHA

THE *PRIZE* GATHERS SPEED HEADING THIS WAY. AT their backs, Tiamat rises from the water, dragging the wreckage of a sunken ship with her, and hurls it at Glaedric. The warships' masts swivel, hulls turning. Glaedric throws his hands up, freezing the barnacled, seaweed-smothered skeleton of the ship over his head, and flings it back at her. Tiamat narrowly dodges the wreckage crashing into the ocean, but the warships get their angle and open fire. She twists sharply to deflect with her thorny spine, but at least one cannonball finds its mark, staggering her. Glaedric looks to the very distant horizon and seems to scoop something up from the waters there. Several massive objects soar over and swirl around him, raining small, moving things: people.

"Great Spirit, they're *ships*!" Imani exclaims.

Deep-sea Harrowlander merchant vessels, by the look Taha gets before Glaedric begins pelting them at Tiamat.

Ser Ulric grips the gunwale, staring in disbelief and anguish. One ship wounds Tiamat's arm, another tears through her wing.

She tosses her head back and screams. The nightmarish sound triggers two sailors into vomiting over the side of the yawl. Taha clamps his hands over his ears, teeth gritted as bile vaults up his throat. Amira and Imani both duck their heads between their knees, whining.

Ser Ulric, at the front of the yawl, is the first to recover and take up his oar, directing the other oarsmen to the *Stout Heart.* But Imani clambers to him haloed in hovering knives, some pointed at Ulric, some at the sailors.

"I know you didn't save our lives only to return us to captivity, Ser Ulric," she says in Harrowtongue. "We row for our ship, the *Lion's Prize.* You could burn me too for disobeying you, but you'll only ensure that this yawl sinks and we all die."

His cheeks blotch red, but he concedes without a fight, nodding at the sailors. Maybe Imani is right and Ulric saved them out of some stubborn weed of goodness that hasn't been rooted out by years of marauding—the same weed of goodness that saw him take Taha down to the archery range. Or maybe Ulric doesn't want to face the men on the *Stout Heart* after what he did to his fellows. Whatever the reason, the sail is angled to catch the wind blowing toward the *Prize,* affording them respite from rowing. The shivering sailors begin handing out blankets from a supply trunk. Taha collects some and takes them to the others at the back of the yawl, where his father is seated on a bench beside Zahra.

"Tell me everything," she says as Imani accepts a blanket from Taha and drapes it over her mother's shoulders.

Taha wishes he had the courage to do the same for his father. Instead, he mutely hands Bayek a blanket and sits on the opposite bench, fidgeting with the coarse fabric of his own.

Imani kneels before her mother. "It's not what you think—"

"Yes, it is!" Amira interrupts, scrambling over her bench to sit closer too. "Qayn is the Desert's Bane! He admitted it!"

Imani hushes, shoulders rising and falling fast. In her eyes, Taha sees the raging battle between the truth and her refusal to accept it.

Atheer gives his own account without prompting. He relates how he met Qayn in the Sahir and their friendship grew from a shared concern about Alqibah. He describes the injustices he witnessed there, his activities with the rebels, his love for Farida, his captivity and torture at Glaedric's hands. He pauses his speech only as they watch Glaedric and Tiamat trade a volley of ship wreckage. Tears stream down Zahra's otherwise-composed face, and at the conclusion of Atheer's account, she defies the rocking of the yawl to go over and hug him. Taha braces for his father to reprimand Atheer and spoil the reunion, but Bayek remains impassively silent.

"I just can't make sense of it," Imani murmurs to herself, raking a hand through her salt-stiff hair. She looks up as Zahra takes a seat again. "We all genuinely believed that Qayn was a djinni."

"No, Qayn *lied* to us that he's a djinni," Amira clarifies.

"And we had no reason to think otherwise," Imani shoots back.

*So much passion,* Taha thinks. She certainly has deeper feelings for Qayn. Even now that his true identity has been revealed, Imani is still finding ways to defend him. But she turned on Taha in a heartbeat.

He clears his throat. "You mean, apart from the fact that he told us he built the First City and commanded Hubaal the Terrible."

Imani blushes scarlet. "Qayn had a reasonable explanation for everything, and he was only ever helpful to us." She turns back to her mother. "I wouldn't have been able to save Atheer without him, Mama. He is—he *was*—trustworthy."

"And now, instead of repaying him for the kindness, we're running away," Atheer says bitterly, looking over his shoulder at Glaedric.

Zahra recoils, as if learning that her son is deathly ill. "Atheer, *habibi,* what are you saying? You can't help the Desert's Bane! I don't know how the monster is alive, but your friendship with him doesn't change what he was."

"What he *was* is a lie!" Atheer exclaims. "Just like the lie the Council of Old told us about his fate. Ask yourself, Mama, why would they omit certain historical accounts of him? His construction and rule of Al-Medina-Al-Uwla in the Vale of Bones, or the fact that a Sahiran woman *stole* his magic. That he has existed for much longer than a millennium. Why? The Zahim of Old wanted to *hide* something from us, and they used their power and influence to do it."

"Hide what?" Amira asks, hugging herself.

"I don't know. But don't you want to find out? Or would we be happier to go on living the lies of our ancestors? *If* we can."

Taha sees the scholar in Zahra trying to align this information with what she's studied and believed her entire life. Bayek remains emotionless except for the faintest trace of surprise in his dark eyes.

Atheer thrusts a hand toward Glaedric. "Look what the king is doing with Qayn's magic! He destroyed those ships with all souls onboard, his *own people*! Think of the casualties once he reaches land. He will rule every nation, and nobody will be able to resist him." Atheer looks up at the Marshal, tensely observing his king. "Soon Glaedric will realize he doesn't even need his subordinates. They too will be flung away like insects should they upset him."

Taha knows the Marshal understands Sahiran. Ulric pretends that he didn't hear Atheer, but his grip on his stationary oar tightens, and Taha wonders if Ulric is thinking again about how willing Glaedric was to sacrifice him to the giant sand serpent.

Taha looks back at Atheer and says, "It shouldn't matter. Glaedric's already doomed himself by using the crown. He'll die from the consequences, just as Amira and I warned him he would, though he refused to listen."

"Come now, Taha," Atheer says sharply. "If someone survives their initial use of a monster's implement, they can live on for days, even weeks. What if Glaedric is an exception and he lives for months? Or *years*? He'll destroy more in that period than what Qayn did the entire time he was the Desert's Bane. Look at him!"

The king appears to be raising a chunk of the seabed itself from the churning waters.

"That man is the end of the world made flesh," says Atheer.

"But his death *will* come," Taha insists, more for the benefit of his own nerves than anyone else's.

"Qayn's might too, before he has the chance to stop the Harrowland Empire," says Imani, voice heavy with despair.

"*No,* the si'la called him the Invulnerable," says Taha. "I thought the title implied that the Desert's Bane was strong, but the si'la kept referring to the Bane as if he's still alive. When I asked her why she was doing that, she said—"

" 'You cannot kill what doesn't die,' " Amira recites grimly.

"Qayn is immortal and invincible; Glaedric isn't," Taha says.

"If we had given Qayn his crown, there would have been no going back."

"How can you be so sure?" Imani looks between him and Amira. "Nahla defeated Qayn. She didn't kill him, but she incapacitated him for a thousand years. We could do it again if we had to. But if we leave Glaedric, even once he dies, the crown won't be forgotten about. Someone else in the House of Brand will be mad enough to step up and take it. And if we manage to kill Glaedric? We still have to contend with the Empire."

"The Empire's intentions are unequivocal," Atheer agrees. "Qayn's aren't. He promised to help us oust the Harrowlanders if we return his magic. If there's any possibility that he's telling the truth, isn't helping him worth the risk?"

"You've given us no alternative, Atheer." Bayek finally speaks in his characteristic deep-chested rumble. "We're to choose between the certainty of this evil and the possibility of another, worse one."

Atheer pushes his curls away from his eyes. The gaze that's revealed isn't quite steady but attempting to be. "I know how you feel about the decisions I've made, Grand Zahim—"

"Your decisions," Bayek cuts him off, "led to your nation's occupation and the loss of thousands of Sahiran lives, including my nephew's."

Taha's insides tremor. He didn't realize that Bayek had learned of Reza's fate, or that he cared. It's likely he found out through Zahra, who would've learned about it from Amira.

Atheer's eyes fringe with tears. "Yes, I made mistakes, terrible ones, and I should be publicly judged by my peers if we ever free the Sahir. But"—he slides forward on his bench—"I ask of you one concession, my Grand Zahim. Please, let me try to fix the problem that I created. Give me a chance to prove to you that a fairer, freer future for all people is possible."

Taha's hand is slippery on the gunwale, but he thinks it's less from the spray of the ocean and more from his own fear that he made the wrong decision in the worst way possible. Glaedric used his new magic on that hapless sailor without hesitation—one of his *own* men, snapped like a twig against the mast. Which monster really is worse? At least Qayn was theirs.

Bayek's jaw ticks. "I must admit, after I met Glaedric in person and saw for myself the size of his army, I regretted not having dealt with him a long time ago. He isn't the sort of man one should leave unchecked." Bayek exhales through his nose. "We will proceed here on the grounds that the risk is acceptable. What is the Bane's plan?"

Atheer blinks, as if waiting for this illusion to dissipate. The oddity of working with the man who sent Taha to kill him isn't lost on Atheer, nor is it on Taha.

"Qayn has no plan, he's—" Imani is drowned out by the sound of cannon fire and the splintering of a warship being cast aside. "He's relying on *us* to do something!" she yells.

As the yawl nears the *Prize,* the others begin gathering at the front of the boat, preparing to throw a rope to the ship. Taha realizes this might be his only opportunity to finally speak with his father. He steels himself and turns to Bayek: "I owe you a debt for surrendering Qalia and saving my life, Baba."

"It was the Council's decision," Bayek replies, "made based on our assessment of Glaedric's threat and the number of Sahiran captives who would be slaughtered if we refused." Bayek looks him over. "Zahra told me what she learned from her daughter. You should have prioritized your freedom over going back for Reza. You let your heart dictate your actions."

Taha inhales sharply, as if he's been slapped. Before he can stop himself, he says, "Did any part of that decision have to do with your love for me?"

Bayek glowers at him. "That's enough, Taha."

But an old ache has begun troubling Taha in every part of his body. "It's a simple question," he says. "Did you feel any relief or gladness that I was spared? Or was it just disappointment?"

Bayek grabs the front of his tunic and jolts him. "Look around you. Now is not the time for sentiment. Now is the time to have a will as hard as steel."

But Taha is weak in his father's grip, about as strong as candle smoke. He wishes his father would release him. He'd tip and fall overboard and let the sea take him. But he also wishes Baba never lets him go; he hopes Baba holds him forever and keeps him upright as he always has. Baba lifts him up on his shoulders to feel the sun and glimpse the world that was denied to him by everyone blessed with the fortune to stand in front of them.

Bayek surprises Taha by thumbing away the tear that slips down his cheek. "When will you do away with this softness, my son? It slows you down and makes you vulnerable. Softness is what got you caught. Do you understand? Tell me you do."

"I don't," Taha chokes out. He doesn't comprehend why Bayek is intent on stripping him of any concern he has for others, including for his father himself.

Bayek's grip tightens. "You must understand—"

"I love you, Baba."

Bayek's eyes widen, shining. He darts his gaze at the front of the yawl, where the others are surely not unaware of what's unfolding between father and son.

"Stop this, Taha—"

"I won't, and nothing you can say or do to me will ever destroy my devotion," he declares. "I would do anything to honor and protect you."

"I don't *want* you to," Baba says, shaking him with an immature anxiety that reminds Taha of himself.

"Why not!" he demands. "Why can't you love me back? I'm your son! Who else will love me if you don't?"

Bayek's shoulders shift. His rage keeps flashing on his face, only to soften into something despondent. "Because," he rasps, dragging Taha in, "love is a joy in the moment, but the pain of loss stays with you *forever.* And I don't want you to experience that pain." His voice breaks; his grip weakens. "Throw away your heart, Taha, before it's too late. It will only betray you in the end."

Taha dries his face. "You're wrong. You want to spare me the pain of loss, but I've mourned the loss of my father every day since Mama died. *You* are the one who broke my heart. And yet, when you hug me or Taleb or say *one* kind word to either of us, I forget my grief as if it had never existed. Do you see, Baba? It's love, not loss, that endures forever."

Bayek's chin quavers; his mouth opens and closes, brows locked and wobbling over his eyes. "What do you expect me to say to that, Taha?" he asks.

Taha sighs. "Nothing, Baba. There's nothing to be said." He turns and goes to the front of the yawl.

"Taha?" Bayek calls after him. Not angrily, not in a way that demands Taha come back or face punishment. His name escapes his father's lips burdened by despair. Sorrow. Regret.

Taha can't deal with any of it anymore. He joins the others and, out of the corner of his eye, sees Ser Ulric give him a sad look, sad enough to make Taha want to kneel down and cry. But he forces himself to focus on the *Prize* instead.

Muhab secures their yawl alongside, and Farida appears over the rope ladder holding a sword. "Amira and Taha are not permitted on my ship."

Atheer helps his mother up the ladder first. "They meant well."

"I don't. If they try to board, I'll cut them at the knees as I did the assassins we tossed over earlier."

Atheer hoists up after his mother. "Farida, this is my mother, Zahra, and this is Taha's father, Bayek, the Grand Zahim of the Council."

Farida reddens. She tosses the sword out of sight and combs her stringy hair with her fingers. Zahra reaches the deck and nods tersely.

"Hello, Farida. Quite the mess you've gotten my son involved in."

The tall captain looks remarkably small all of a sudden. "Y-yes, I can certainly see why you'd think that—" They pause to look at Glaedric and Tiamat battling with bedrock and coral spears.

"The power of love is inexplicable. I find it's best we don't question it." Zahra's stern gaze eases slightly. "Have you somewhere I can wash?"

Farida bows her head. "Of course. Mina," she calls to her crewmate, "escort Zahra to my cabin. Fetch her fresh water, a washcloth, pail, whatever she needs."

Mina salutes and guides Zahra up the gangway. Farida turns back to the rope ladder, massaging the back of her neck. "Fine, get up here. We need to start putting distance between us and Glaedric, fast."

"No, we need to head back in," says Imani as Taha climbs onto the deck after his father. "Qayn may still be alive. We have to help him."

"*Help* him . . ." Farida drifts off, gazing at Glaedric in the sky.

Atheer squeezes her hand. "Can you get us closer? Those warships have cannons."

She swallows, looking back at him. "I mean, I can try. I saw the warships while we were moored in Darkcliff. They're slow; the cannons take at least a minute to reload."

"And as far as I can tell, their ships don't have captains with water affinities," Atheer adds encouragingly.

Farida stares at him for a little longer and then, with a huff, tilts her head back. "Makeen, take us back in! This fight's not done yet," she adds when some of her crewmates look over in alarm.

"Aye, Captain!" Makeen calls back.

Muhab orders his sailors to work, taking the four meek Harrowlanders with him.

Farida points at Ser Ulric, who's boarding the *Prize* last. "What about this one?"

But Ulric is busy talking to Taha: "I can't permit you to enact a plot against His Majesty under my watch, boy."

Taha folds his arms. "Why not? You said you had to seize the Sahir because we couldn't be trusted with magic. Do you think Glaedric can be trusted with this magic?"

Ser Ulric twists on his heel as Glaedric releases a sky-sundering scream and hurls a chunk of bedrock the size of the Sanctuary at Tiamat. The clouds cleave; somehow even the sunlight flickers unsteadily. Glaedric wavers in the air; the ocean under him rises and falls in tower-sized swells that swallow one of the warships whole.

"Staggnir's justice," Ulric whispers, lines of horror etched around his eyes.

Taha stands beside him. "Why do you really help the king conquer, Marshal?"

"What else am I supposed to do?" Ulric grunts. "The House of Wargen, my house, has served his for generations. That's what's expected of Wargen boys: follow the Brands, to the bloody end if you must, and don't ask questions. I'm no good for anything else."

Maybe they're more alike than Taha wants to admit. "No, you're not a good man, Ser Ulric, but you're too good to be protecting King Glaedric." Taha draws his sword. "I'm getting that crown back and putting things right. Interfere and I'll gut you. Don't force me."

Ser Ulric accepts that with a defeated nod.

# 49

# IMANI

"WE'RE HEADING BACK IN, AS YOU ASKED," Farida says, joining us at the railing to watch the battle. "What now?"

Glaedric floats level again and begins beckoning the ocean. Pillars of seaweed break the surface in a circle around where Tiamat has folded. With every pillar that rises, the light of the jewels intensifies, engulfing the crown's form until it resembles fiery horns on Glaedric's brow. He thrusts his arms out. The pillars wind around Tiamat's wrists and neck; others try to trap her thrashing tail.

I hold fast to the railing as the ship rides the swell. "Saving Tiamat is paramount," I tell the others. "If Glaedric kills her, he turns his attention on us, and we lose."

"He'll turn his attention on us regardless once we're close enough," says Farida. "We need to kill him somehow."

"That's impossible with the crown on his head." I chew the inside of my cheek for a moment. "I need to get close to him while he's distracted fending off another attack; close enough to *physically* remove the crown from him."

"How? He's at least a thousand feet above the ocean."

I tap my finger on the railing, thinking of how I used my magic on Wulfsyg during our battle when Qayn reminded me of my power. *Seize him by flesh and blood! Strike with your heart!* It reminds me of the last thing Qayn said before he collapsed in Tiamat's palm: *I'm relying on you to do something, Imani . . . on your heart of love.* I was too afraid to use my magic fully in the Hunten, but I must now. Every single person alive depends on my ability to strike with my heart.

"I think I know what to do," I say. "I can bring Glaedric down with my magic, but only if he's distracted."

Taha catches my eye from the other end of our gathered group. "Like what you did in the Hunten—"

"Look!" Amira exclaims, interrupting him. "Glaedric's making a storm."

The king has his arms over his head. Above him, the sky is darkening, the clouds are churning, and the winds are rising.

"Lightning," says Bayek, his bisht flapping behind him. "I've killed giant sand serpents with it. He may attempt the same with Tiamat."

She's currently struggling to escape the seaweed entangling her limbs, and the warships are steadily forming a circle around her.

"She's tiring," I say. "He'll succeed if he hits her, and the cannons will finish off what remains."

"I'll divert him using my lightning affinity," says Bayek. "I held him back from Qalia; I can do it again here."

Taha glances at his father, alarmed, and I experience a confusing rush of gratitude for the man I've hated so viscerally these last few months.

"If Tiamat can free herself, the invader will have to fight us both," Bayek continues. "But I don't know what you plan to do with the opportunity."

"Manipulate the iron in Glaedric's body," I tell him, then raise a hand. "I know how that sounds, but Taha has seen me do it. I can bring Glaedric down and get the crown off him—if you can keep him looking this way."

"I'll keep him looking," Bayek says, eyeing the far-off king. The menacing statement isn't even directed at me, and it still sends a shiver down my back.

Taha mutely hands Bayek a flask from his pocket. I overheard bits of their conversation on the yawl, the bitter note it ended on. But Taha meant it when he said that nothing could destroy his devotion to his father. Bayek drinks the misra tea, and Taha watches with the wide eyes of a small boy enthralled to discover that his father is as principled and unafraid as the warrior-heroes of folklore.

I turn to Farida. "The Grand Zahim will give me a distraction, but I need to get as close to Glaedric as possible. The yawl—"

The charcoal sky flashes, thunderbolts carving through it. Farida yells over the rising squall, "No, it needs more hands than I can spare. The *Prize* is small; it won't take many cannonballs to sink us." She points across the deck to the rowboat affixed over the side. "Take the two-oar. Muhab will let you loose in a couple of minutes. The rest of you, look lively! We've a warship taking interest!"

It's the farthest from the grouping around Tiamat but closest to us, and it's slowly turning. We have to act fast.

I turn back to the others and salute Bayek. "Spirits' luck, Grand Commander."

He caps his flask, nodding sternly. "Spirits' luck, Shield."

I never thought I'd live to see the day.

I hug Atheer and Amira and jog across the deck. Mama appears on the balcony outside the captain's cabin, watching me go with tears in her eyes.

"Be safe, my love," she calls to me. "Your father is waiting for us at home."

I sprint up the gangway and embrace her. "We're going back there soon, Mama, I promise."

She reluctantly releases me, crying openly now. I want to hug her again, hug her forever so that she never spills another tear, but I can only kiss her cheek and go back down to the deck.

Muhab is leaning over the side by the rowboat. "Climb in and hold on. It'll be a rough landing once I release you." He claps one hand on my shoulder; the other holds out a spyglass. "Take this with you."

I slide it under my chest armor and drop into the slender boat. A second later, Taha hops in too and grabs the oars, nodding at me.

"I'll row. You save your energy for Glaedric."

I feel another confusing rush of gratitude. We sit on the benches facing each other. The *Prize* crosses an invisible threshold into driving rain and tumultuous ocean swell.

"Ready!" Muhab calls from above.

We brace as the tether is released. The two-oar plummets and slaps the hard ocean, thudding my brain inside my skull. The *Prize* sails past at full speed and leaves us behind in a heartbeat. It was a tumultuous journey aboard the ship, but in this tiny two-oar, we're grains of dust in a sandstorm. A wave carries us to its crest and abandons us in the trough on the other side; my gut cartwheels as we slide down and crash at the bottom in a spray of water. It suddenly occurs to me that what I've offered to do is extremely perilous, and it's wholly too late to turn back. The only comfort is that I'm not facing this alone.

"Which way?" Taha shouts, hands ready on the oars.

I press the spyglass to my eye. Tiamat and Glaedric are on our right, the king with his hands still lifted to the sky, and the *Prize* is sailing in an arc toward them. I point over Taha's shoulder.

"That way! We'll come up behind Glaedric and stop underneath him!"

Taha begins rowing, the thrust of his powerful arms skating us across the water. The waves are taller than I ever thought possible—and dwelling on their height makes me febrile with fear, despite the freezing conditions—but they at least seem to be shielding us from Glaedric and the warships.

The closer we come to the king, the sootier the sky and the heavier the rain. It flattens our hair and clothes against our skin, chills through flesh and bone to my very soul. When I'm not using the two-oar's bucket to bail out the rainwater, I'm consulting the spyglass for the warships and the *Prize,* but my vision is constantly blocked by the waves. I can only reliably see Tiamat, wrestling the seaweed trying to pull her down, and Glaedric, hovering over her, marked by his burning crown.

"Turn now!" I tell Taha.

He adjusts our angle and rows on, panting now from the exertion. Even with the fear and adrenaline coursing through me, I still feel guilty. I turned on Taha too fast when I thought he was betraying us, yet he's come back to help me—not just me, but Qayn, someone who may yet turn out to be our nation's age-old enemy. Taha told me his darkest secrets in the Hunten, confessed feelings that I didn't reciprocate—and he still came back. I suddenly yearn to reach out to him, push his slick hair off his forehead, dry his face, and tell him that I believe in his goodness. I like him too. But that's how it goes, doesn't it? We feel our strongest, truest emotions only when there's a risk that we may stop feeling entirely.

The cracks of lightning become worse. We're still too far away, and no doubt the *Prize* will soon be too close to escape Glaedric's attention. I concentrate on finding the king with my iron sense as we slowly round him, but he's too faint to grasp.

"It's going to happen soon!" Taha shouts to me over the roaring ocean and rain. "We can't let the *Prize* be Glaedric's focus for too long!"

"I know, but I can't sense him yet!" I shout back. "I need to be closer!"

Taha sets his jaw and keeps rowing, pushing himself even harder. The sky discharges a series of ghostly white flashes. I try again to sense Glaedric and finally detect him, stronger this time.

"I almost have it!" I yell. "Just a little—"

The skies open, blazing and booming. A bolt of lightning as thick as a minaret shoots at Tiamat's chest, and she screams. Taha cries out for his father; I grip the edges of the rocking boat and brace for the lightning to land and kill her. But it hits an invisible shield in front of Tiamat instead and gathers there, accumulating wild, pulsating energy; thinner bolts splinter off and sever the seaweed ropes around one of Tiamat's wrists before the entire incredible charge explodes back at Glaedric. He only narrowly swats it away; the bolt cracks into thousands of strikes that spray out and hit the ocean as far as I can see. We fold over in the boat, screaming, as two hit the water near us; the world swims in resounding *boom* after *boom.* When I dare to sit up again, dead fish are floating past the two-oar like disturbed sediment.

Tiamat bites through the rope binding her other wrist, rips the rest away, and dives. A barrage of cannon fire follows her, shaking the already fragile air and making my ears ring. Glaedric turns his head toward the *Prize.*

"ROW!" I shout at Taha.

He snaps out of his trance and takes up the oars. Tiamat comes back up, lobbing pieces of a sunken warship at Glaedric. His head jerks back to her; he flicks the debris away with one hand. One piece goes over our heads and lands somewhere behind us. I swallow my scream and grip the boat. I have to concentrate on my iron sense. Glaedric is high above us but perhaps only one hundred feet away. He looks again at the *Prize;* a moment later, he dodges a bolt of lightning shooting down at him. The light of his crown burns so bright it's painful to look at.

"You should not have meddled in this, Bayek, Grand Zahim," he booms.

Tiamat throws a mast at Glaedric to distract him, but he predicts her attack. The mast has barely left her when he sends it straight back and impales her through the chest with it. She screams and collapses face-first in the water. Glaedric has already turned on the *Prize* again.

"Imani!" Taha shouts. *"PLEASE—"*

My iron sense homes in. I jump up, arms raised, and seize Glaedric's flesh and blood.

*(Strike with your heart. Bend him to your will.)*

I grit my teeth and drag down and in. Glaedric's head rocks forward as I pull him feetfirst toward us. The sky brightens suddenly. The wind and ocean settle. Glaedric writhes in my grip; my magic burns off me; I pinch and pull the iron in his body, eliciting a disturbing scream. The crown's light flares defiantly. I feel Glaedric push back against me. His body flips around; he points his chin down and sees me as he hurtles to the boat. And I see *him,* his red eyes weeping blood, the sickening green veins straining against the ice-white skin pulled taut over his skull. He growls, showing purple gums, and I panic that it's *me* who's done this to him, not Qayn's crown. It's my magic making him into a monster.

I lose my grip. Just for a second, only enough time for Glaedric to wave his arms uselessly. I breathe into my magic and latch onto the iron again, letting go only at the last moment, so that he drops into the ocean and sinks several feet before bobbing back up again, spluttering and thrashing. By then, I've already dived in and scooped Qayn's crown off his head, a shiver racing up my arm. I paddle back to the safety of the two-oar, but for some reason, Taha doesn't help me in. I have to hoist into the boat, paranoid that Glaedric is about to snatch the crown from me, and Taha just keeps staring at something behind me with his mouth open, tears rolling down his cheeks. That's when I hear screaming.

I turn with my dagger in my other fist, expecting a fight. But it's the *Prize.* Not on the ocean, where it's supposed to be—but in the sky, and falling. As if someone's plucked it up by its sails and let go, knowing they don't need to do any more than that. As soon as the *Prize* hits the ocean, it'll disintegrate, killing everyone onboard. And only one person is capable of crafting such cruelty so quickly. Glaedric. In that one instant when I let go of him, he determined the correct path to destroy me. And he chose not to kill me directly but to kill my spirit so that my hollowed body can crawl on through existence, bereft.

I look across the water to see where he's floated. He's upright instead, stooped on a podium of summoned ice, frost clinging to his shock of white-blond hair, stark against the blood in his eyes, the hair-thin fissures splitting every inch of exposed skin, the red of his lips pulled back in a snarl. He looks at the crown in my left hand, the dagger in my right, then wiggles his fingers and freezes a path across the ocean back to his warships.

"Baba," Taha mumbles. "Great Spirit, please save him."

I lower Qayn's crown onto my head.

*This is your gift,* an unfamiliar voice whispers in my ear.

Visions flash over my eyes; places like home—grasslands and rivers, limestone mountains, starlit deserts dotted pink in flowering toughgrass—

*This is my curse,* Qayn whispers in the other.

The visions turn. I see barren deserts, dead places exhausted and dehydrated without end, littered with the skeletons of malnourished cattle and abandoned settlements haunted by the shadows of monsters, and I have the inescapable, gut-wrenching sense that I am responsible for this devastation—

"Imani, what have you done!"

Taha's voice chases the visions away. Now all I see is the falling ship. I raise my hand and catch it. The crown's light flames; the same light works through me, too bright, too brilliant. The ship slows in midair and smoothly floats the rest of the way down to the water. I turn on the warships rotating to confront it, the crown's light burning within me. A different burn to my magic. That one is innocuous, a mere byproduct of use. This has intent. But it's a tolerable burn, enjoyable almost, and why should I let something as small as that distract from the possibilities of what I'm now capable of? With all the ways I could, how should I destroy Glaedric's fleet?

Taha pulls the crown off my head and tosses it in the bottom of the boat. I feel as if I've awakened from a dream, or a nightmare. I drop to my knees and throw up over the side. I see the sick as it goes in the water: ink black. It corrodes my chest and throat and scalds my tongue, and though I feel fractionally better, I sense there is more of it; my veins are thick with it.

Taha drags me back into the boat and starts rowing. "What in Alard do we do now!" He shouts it angrily, but his eyes are wild with worry, his breathing skipping in his chest. He keeps looking at me as if I have a hole in my head.

"I don't know," I mumble. My temples smart; my memories are wavering lines of color and light. "Glaedric . . . where's Glaedric?"

"Gone, didn't you see? He used his own magic to get back to his warships."

I roll my blurry eyes across the water. "Yes, I think I saw that. What of the *Prize*?"

"Safe, but the warships are turning on it."

"And Qayn? Tiamat." I lift my head. "Glaedric killed her, I remember. She was holding Qayn." I stand up, unsteady on my feet; the boat sways, and I almost tip out of it.

Taha holds a hand out. "Imani, *please,* you need to sit down!"

I search the water and spot an immense crumpled form floating on it. "There. Row over there, Taha."

He turns us around. I settle on the bench again, groaning from another wave of nausea.

"How are you feeling?" he asks in a small voice.

I wave a hand. "A little sick, that's all. Must've been the cold of the water." With my peripheral vision, I notice Taha staring at me. Rowing and staring. "What?" I demand. "Why are you looking at me like that?"

"Imani," he murmurs, "you used Qayn's crown."

I falter; my memory drifts. Then I shrug. "Yes, I stopped the *Prize* from crashing. So?"

His eyes shine. "Don't you remember what Qayn said about anyone who uses it?"

"There are unpleasant side-effects—"

"It marks you for death," he cuts me off.

Vertigo grips me; I spin inside my own head. Of course. I remember it as I stare at Tiamat rocking on the waves, glistening a gallery of blues and greens. The oily blood pooled on the surface around her. The quiet indignity of her slaying. I should've acted faster. Been better. Learned as much as I could from Qayn when I had the opportunity. Said yes.

"Imani—"

"I saved my mother." I look at Taha as he stops rowing.

"Yes," he whispers. "And you saved my father."

My breathing steadies; my pulse evens; the vertigo relents for now. "There's no trouble, then. Row us on a bit farther." I lean off the edge to look at Tiamat and see her parting gift, her repayment of the favor she owed an old friend who saved her life once. An open hand, left to float above the surface of the ocean, just out of danger's reach.

And Qayn, curled on his side on her pale-emerald palm, asleep under the sun.

# 50

# IMANI

We lay Qayn in the gap between our benches, and I press my fingers to his clammy neck.

"Qayn can't die," Taha says, giving me an odd look.

"He has no pulse."

"What? That can't be right." He moves my hand away and presses two fingers under Qayn's jaw. I stare at him, my own heart thudding fast and strong. "That doesn't make sense," he murmurs, readjusting his fingers. Then he squeezes between the benches and puts his ear to Qayn's chest.

"He's dead, isn't he?" I say, my head spinning again. "You and Amira were wrong."

Panic flits across Taha's face. "No, it can't be. Qayn is four thousand years old! He doesn't just die because *your sister,* who's never used a sword in her life, stabs him!"

I double over on the bench. "She killed him. Amira killed our only hope of salvation."

Taha's breathing becomes shaky. He fumbles around for the crown. "Here! This'll work; it has to."

He balances the crown over Qayn's hair and pulls his hands away. But Qayn's curled lashes don't flutter, his lips don't part on an inhalation, his pulse doesn't revive. His beautiful face remains serene and undisturbed.

Taha makes an odd sound. He pats Qayn's cheek. "Qayn, wake up. We returned your magic." He gently shakes him by his tunic. "You promised to help us. You asked Imani to trust you, and she did. Wake up and prove that you weren't lying." Taha shakes him harder. "Qayn! Wake up!"

"He's gone, Taha."

But Taha doesn't hear me. He arranges the crown at a slightly different angle, takes it off, tries again; he touches Qayn's cheek, squeezes his hand, hoists him upright, only for Qayn to slide back down, all dead weight robbed of the agile grace that made him appear as if he were floating even when he was barefoot in the earth. At last, Qayn is true to the appearance he chose to charm us: fragile, human. A young man killed too far from home.

Taha is at a loss. "The si'la said you were invincible," he tells Qayn. "How can you be dead? Not even our ancestors could kill you!"

The echo of cannon fire draws my heavy eyes past Glaedric, waiting on his icy pillar to be collected by a warship, to the rest of his fleet, turning on the *Prize.* It weaves between them, a sleek hound between hulking wolves, and it's fast, magically so in moments where the ocean arches its back and propels it on. But the *Prize* lacks Tiamat's specter to distract the warships when its needed most. The ship is outnumbered, its captain skilled with her affinity but lacking the stamina of a practiced water sorcerer with years of training. The *Prize* evades one warship only to cross paths with another's deadly broadside. The cannons thunder. The ocean arcs and hurtles it on; it swings to sail this way, and the warships follow. It has a decent distance on them, but something . . . something in me knows that it's sustained a little too much damage, and the warships have all the ocean to exploit the *Prize*'s weakness without fear. It has nowhere safe to go home to. Neither do we.

A sob shakes my chest. I slide into the bottom of the boat and curl up beside Qayn's cold body.

"I'm sorry," Taha gasps, his fingers interlocking with mine. "Imani, please forgive me. I thought I was doing the right thing, stopping the Desert's Bane. I only wanted to do the right thing."

"I know, Taha." I'm too exhausted to say more. Suddenly I can't even keep my eyes open, and I'm tired of fighting the inevitable. I drift off to sleep before I know it and find myself in the most wonderful dream.

I'm in Qayn's palace, in a vast circular hall with stone floors, long, tapered windows curtained by drops of white silk, a vaulted glass ceiling with a view of a blushing early morning sky, and several corridors branching off like the spokes in a wheel.

"Imani," Qayn whispers. "This way."

His shadow retreats across the stone at the entrance to a corridor. I drift after him, bare feet padding on the cold floor. The corridor extends for a distance I cannot measure; I walk along it for time unknown, blissfully happy to be here again, with him, even if this place is not real and he is not really here.

The white silk curtains flutter around me, rippling like water. I catch glimpses of the windows behind them and a world I know beyond the panes. I stop at a window and reach up to the curtain. Many steps ahead, Qayn's silhouette slows. I tense, waiting for him to stop me, but he doesn't, and across this gap that isn't a gap at all, I grasp his assent. Rather, I wish that he approves, and so in this dream, he does. He finally allows me to learn what I want about him.

I push aside the curtain. Somehow this corridor crosses through a tribe's camp. On the other side of the glass are tents, blazing firepits, pens for horses and camels, and people going about their daily life. A woman in a dark abaya walks barefoot with a tray balanced over the veil on her head; she dodges a group of playing children and an older man in a thobe and keffiyeh riding a donkey laden with bags. Date palms sway behind the tents; in the gaps between them glimmer the life-giving waters of an oasis. The daylight reveals everything, yet nobody notices the corridor cutting through their world. Nobody notices me, marveling at this vision that I've seen before in history books about nomadic life in the ancient Sahir.

Qayn's silhouette moves on. I release the curtain and follow him through the winding corridor to an unadorned cedar door.

"What was that camp?" I ask as I join him.

But this is the Qayn of my dreams. His gaze has lost its cunning; his face isn't dressed in its practiced smirk of supreme confidence. There's something so delicate in the way he looks back up the corridor; distant and longing.

"It was my home," he says. "Before the magic."

His answer swirls in my mind, like smoke upon which I draw a comforting shape. Qayn was once a Sahiran boy, someone I could hold and understand, confident that the whispers about the Desert's Bane are mistakes. "But how?" asks reason, and the shape disintegrates in my hands, the smoke dispersing again to befuddle and elude.

Qayn opens the door and enters first. I tiptoe after him from stone to soft soil, greeted by earthy scents, like that of rain and wind and life. Then I become acquainted with the light, though there's neither sun nor moon in the sky to attribute it to and it is neither day nor night in this wildly overgrown garden. The light simply springs from somewhere and everywhere; it falls upon the garden, yet the garden itself exudes luminance.

I walk beside Qayn along stone pavers almost smothered by the same purple flowers of the First City. Here and there amongst the overgrowth peek waist-high, crumbling mudbrick fences that would fit seamlessly in an ancient Sahiran ruin, but elsewhere, the fences are constructed in perfectly cut blocks of granite. There are lampposts twinkling faintly, but I also spot a campfire in a small clearing that we pass. I'm almost certain there are other people here, though they remain the flimsiest of shadows, fading in and out of recognition between the trees.

The garden is a mosaic of mysterious objects and scenes vaguely plastered together: a black bisht like the kind Baba would wear swings gently from where it's draped over the low bough of a short tree; two long spears skewer the soil a few steps from our path; small, painted clay dolls lie scattered in the grass, a snake slithering away from them; a leatherbound book has been left open atop a fence, the yellowed, stiff pages turning in the breeze; a distinctive black bird with iridescent blue plumage watches us from its perch in a tree; in a distant clearing stands a tent like the kind from the camp, its entrance flap pinned back, a warm, inviting glow emanating from within, where several shadows are painted on the inner wall, laughing and conversing. There's another shadow too stalking between the trees, slender, tall, with a silhouette almost like Qayn's, but it's always just far enough away to avoid being identified any further. It's as if this entire place, this most intimate and sacred of spaces, could be a thoroughfare of what I imagine are Qayn's experiences, the things he might've seen, the people he may have encountered, where echoes splinter off to linger in dreamlike perpetuity.

The path conveys us to a stone gazebo overlooking a stream gleaming silver in the spontaneous light.

"Where are we?" I ask Qayn.

His hand finds mine. "My soul. I brought you here to give you a piece of me."

I'm thrilled, even though this is only a dream. "Why would you do that?" I ask.

"It's something I did with Nahla once," he says. "I didn't even know it was possible before she suggested we try . . . I regret it every day."

I play along with the script out of curiosity, asking, "Then why did you agree?"

"Love," he says. "Loyalty. Lust. She wanted things from me—power, knowledge; insights that I could not give her any other way. To accept the pieces of my soul, she had to—for lack of a better term—*put* them somewhere. We thought the best, most appropriate place was her own soul. She . . . became me, in a way, at least in some part. I still don't know which part that was."

I imagine a droplet of blood landing in a clear pool, the thin red arms rising off the diffusing drop, reaching into the water. Changing its constitution forever.

Qayn's fingers tighten around mine. "A piece of my soul will protect you from the death you earned using my crown. And it will permit you to use it again without being destroyed by its power." His voice moves through me like silk, honey, intoxicating smoke. He leans in, brushing his nose against mine. "But this I will not regret. I want to share my magic with you. I want to be a part of you if you'll let me."

I gaze fondly at our entangled hands, though reason is quick to remind me that I'm not really holding Qayn's hand. I'm holding my own and playing pretend to blunt my grief, and I cannot run from that truth forever.

"This is a beautiful dream, Qayn . . . but it's only a dream," I say.

His brow furrows; his eyes are confused. "No, this is real."

I shake my head sadly. "You died in Tiamat's palm, and now you're on the two-oar with me and Taha, and I'm asleep next to your body."

"It's a temporary death relative to my existence." He speaks faster, more urgently. "But you can hasten the healing process if you use my crown and lay your hands on me."

I keep shaking my head. "This is a dream. Why am I even telling you this? I need to wake up."

"This is not a dream, Imani!" he exclaims. "This is really happening, and I need you to listen!"

His desperation shatters my reverie. I step back from him, my heart pounding. "What are you really?"

"Once, I was a boy." He edges after me, hands raised to placate me. "A human, like you."

I back into the balustrade. "That's not possible. You have magic, and not from the misra tree—"

"Given to me. I was made into this." He gestures at himself. "A being trapped outside time, never to age or change. Unable to die."

My breath stutters. "Taha was right, then. You're invincible."

He grimaces, head inclining. "Yes. I didn't believe it at first, but over the years . . . I've tried to end things and couldn't. Even Nahla made a worthy effort." He pulls the neck of his tunic down to expose his chest. A scar disfigures the skin over his heart; it's interrupted by Amira's bloody black puncture. "When Nahla stole my crown, she also plunged a dagger into my heart to kill me. Funny, isn't it? The wounds of conflict remain long after the blade that created them trades hands." He lets his tunic fall back into place. "We must hurry, Imani. The others are in danger, and so are you."

"But I have so many more questions!" I cry, rushing forward. "Who gave you your magic? Why? How can you be the Desert's Bane?"

"And I have answers, but I can't honestly explain them in the little time left," he says. "Will you accept a piece of my soul? It will save you, and you'll be able to safely use my crown again—but you must use it for one purpose and one purpose only."

"To bring you back to life," I say.

He nods. "Do not deviate from it. You must *trust me* on this, please."

"I do." I look over the lush tangle of the garden. "But which piece do I choose?"

I feel his happiness. It's a sun, shining warm light across the threshold of our souls.

"There are no rules for what we're doing," he says. "Nahla went with the piece that called to her. Perhaps you can do the same."

His answer helps and confounds, opening yet more doors on riddles I long to solve. But I do what he says and go where my heart takes me, down the steps of the gazebo and along the banks of the stream, Qayn softly trailing in my wake. I follow the curve of the crystalline water and pause at a patch of jasmine. Almost enveloped by it is a striking woman seated cross-legged on a mat, working a tray of bulgur wheat. Under the plain veil draped loosely over her head and shoulders, she is perhaps forty, with a wavy fall of glossy black hair and large, dark eyes that stand out in her thin, sharp-featured face, ornamented with dots and dashes in faded ink.

"Who is she?" I ask.

Qayn loiters at my shoulder. "My mother."

A thousand more questions elbow me. "She's beautiful," I say.

"She was," he agrees in barely a whisper.

I sense this is a place I should not dwell. I move on between the trees where no path exists to guide me, following instead the tug of my heart. Occasionally I inspect a plant or stone, contemplating whether this is the piece of Qayn's soul that I will take back with me, but I'm never certain. When a pillar of glowing white limestone appears ahead, made from the same material as the First City, intuition swells in me and I hurry along. One pillar becomes two, flanking an ornate gateway attached to tall walls curtained with purple-flowering vines. I pass under the archway onto a paved path that meanders purposefully through a looked-after garden, in the very center of which stands a tall, mighty tree.

"Is this the misra tree?" I ask, looking over my shoulder at Qayn.

He's some paces behind, half angled away from me, hands dug deep into his sirwal pockets. His lips firm into a sad line, and he ambles away, leaving me alone with this magnificent tree and the wind whispering secrets between its leaves. I climb its trunk, balance on the lowest bough, and, using my dagger, cut off a branch. I jump down from the tree with my chosen piece; the garden around me fades from view, and when the light finds me again, it's sunlight shining strong and unambiguous in a clear blue sky.

I'm in a sandstone courtyard with a fountain and potted

citrus trees, just like the courtyard at home. A gate in the opposite wall leads to another courtyard, that one with rosebushes and lavender, and a gate in that courtyard opens onto a third, from which I can hear bristles on tiles, and I'm almost certain it's Teta, my mother's mother sweeping. I don't know how many courtyards there are here, or what—or *who*—they house, but this one sprouts a fresh garden bed for me to use, complete with a small shovel and a jug of water.

I tentatively approach, Qayn haunting my steps, and kneel before the empty garden bed. He kneels beside me. "Plant the branch. A tree of your own will grow."

But it won't be my own, will it? The tree will be an identical twin of the one in Qayn's soul, except its roots will be in mine.

"What happens once I do this?" I ask.

He flashes a nervous smile. "That's part of the excitement, isn't it? I don't quite know."

"But Nahla—"

"Told me very little," he cuts me off. "It took place at the end of our time together. I've always suspected it was yet another of her thefts."

Concepts previously fickle and fluid solidify. I set the branch down, studying him. "You said that if I have a piece of your soul, I can use your crown to heal you without being destroyed by it."

He nods, watching me carefully. Warily, trying to decipher whether I'm dangerous.

"Nahla had multiple pieces of your soul when she stole your crown. She used it, didn't she? She must have."

"Yes," he admits after a moment, "I believe Nahla used my crown."

"To do what?"

"Ask yourself," he says simply.

It would have been something notable. After seeing Glaedric with the crown, I refuse to believe the consequences of Nahla's use of it have escaped my notice. She would've impacted the course of Sahiran history, but like the book that Amira found, her actions wouldn't have been attributed to her. Or anyone else with a name.

"Nahla was the Unknown Sorcerer," I realize aloud. "I can't believe it never occurred to me! It was *your* crown and the pieces of *your* soul that made it possible for her to cast such complex enchantments. But . . ." My face contorts; my chest aches. "The Unknown Sorcerer is the most significant, respected figure in Sahiran history; they're a hero, and Nahla was a *thief.* She tried to *murder* you!"

He gently touches my arm. "I'm sorry, Imani. I know how deeply it hurts to learn that someone you admired never truly existed."

"But why would she relinquish the jewels in the end?" I ask.

"She was still mortal," he says. "At the end of her life, she would have faced a choice: bestow the crown upon someone else, who would be consumed and destroyed by its power—"

"Or hide the jewels," I murmur, "which she did, in the Temple of Asyratu."

I fall silent, contemplating, but so many details are still missing. I'm viewing a mosaic with chunks removed, and I'm afraid that I can't make an informed decision without seeing the whole picture. If the mosaic depicts two figures facing off in a duel, but what they carry is not shown, who is to say which of them holds the sword and which holds the rose?

"Time is still passing," Qayn says softly.

I look up at him. "Did Nahla create the enchantment to protect the Sahir and the misra tree from outsiders, or was her objective solely to stop you from taking back your magic?" He tries to guide my hand to the shovel, but I pull away. "I want to know everything, Qayn. I want to know why my people called you the Desert's Bane."

Again, he guides my hand. "Plant the branch, Imani. If you are the person I believe you to be, the answers will be yours soon."

I seize the shovel and start to dig. As I hollow a space in the soil, I feel my own reservations scooped away. Too much of my existence is entwined with Qayn's, and there's only one thing now that can truly save me: the truth, as thorned and painful as it may be, because I must understand my nation, my history, the deeds of those who came before me. How else can I honestly participate in the present?

I plant the branch and water it. Qayn helps me to stand.

"What now?" I ask.

He snaps his fingers next to my ear. "Wake up."

# 51

# IMANI

I SIT UP IN THE TWO-OAR, STARTLING TAHA, WHO WAS shaking my shoulder.

"Great Spirit, Imani! I thought you'd—" He swallows and points at the line of warships sailing toward us. The *Prize* is still in front, but barely; it's sitting deeper in the water, and now the warships are on its heels, their cannons at the ready. "The *Prize* will be here in a few minutes, but it can't stop for us. I'm going to try to throw the—" He hesitates, watching me lift the crown from Qayn's head. "What are you doing?"

"You were right, Taha. Qayn is invincible."

He glances at Qayn between us. "He's dead."

"Sort of, temporarily, while his body heals, but I can speed up the process using his crown."

Taha grabs my wrist. "You can't put that back on."

"I can, because Qayn—"

"It'll kill you!" he cries.

I pull my hand away, shaking my head. And perhaps it's the swinging motion after having just roused from sleep—or something else—but I glimpse a vision of dark, wavy hair; the edge of a coy, full-lipped smile; creases of laughter around brown, long-lashed eyes. I hear a woman's throaty voice, as distrustful as it is curious, her question—*How did you do that?*—uttered in the same breath as another—*What are you?* I experience the vision in a heartbeat; it's over so quickly I almost wonder if it happened at all.

"What's wrong?" Taha scoots closer and touches my cheek; then, perhaps deciding that's too familiar, he settles his hand on my shoulder instead.

"N-nothing," I stammer, blinking. I hold up the crown. "Listen to me and don't interrupt. Qayn gave me a way to use the crown without being harmed by it."

Taha stares at me blankly. "When?"

"Just now!" I gesticulate at Qayn. "We're soulbound; I was communicating with him while I was asleep."

Taha's hand leaves my shoulder. "Oh. I thought Qayn was bound to your dagger. When did the arrangement change?"

"I don't know, six or seven weeks ago?" I glance at the ships. "Now's really not the best time to talk about this!"

"Right." Taha sits on his bench and grips the oars. "Be fast, and in case Qayn really is dead, we need to get back on the *Prize* or we're stranded. I'll move us out into open water."

He starts rowing, and for once, I'm grateful he can so easily set aside his emotions to focus on the mission. I kneel beside Qayn and lower the crown onto my head.

*This gift is a curse,* he whispers from somewhere, and a memory is startled to life. I see a familiar doorway with a white linen curtain, parted by a slender brown hand on a garden walled in white stone. A waterfall crashes nearby; I hear that woman with the throaty voice saying, *Is it really ours to keep?*

The memory fades. I push Qayn's tunic off the scar that Nahla gave him and Amira's clean but deep stab wound. Gently I cover them with my hands, shut my eyes, and pray that I can bring Qayn back from the clutches of death. Light flows tenderly through me. My hands warm and tingle around the wound, combating the chill of Qayn's body.

"How much longer do you need?" Taha yells over the roar of the waves.

I ignore him and breathe into my intent. *Return to me, Qayn, please. We need your help.*

I hear Taha ship the oars and take the grappling hook attached to the front of the boat. "Imani!" he shouts. "We're out of time!"

I open my eyes. He's ready to throw the hook to the wounded *Prize,* bearing down on us. A pair of warships have almost pulled alongside it, trailed on the flanks by two more. I look back down. There's more color in Qayn's face, more warmth in his body, but I don't dare remove my hands to check the wound in case that reverses whatever progress I've made.

"Get ready to hold on!" Taha yells.

"I can't!" I yell back. "I need to finish this!"

He darts his eyes between me, Qayn, and the *Prize.* The sun winks in a spyglass near the helm; then Atheer appears on the bow, shouting. Sailors move frantically across the deck behind him.

Taha returns to me. "Just get down as low as you can, all right? This is going to be bumpy."

I nod and fold over Qayn with my hands pressed to his lifeless chest. "Come on," I whisper to him as the warmth around the wound intensifies. "Come back to us, Qayn."

Taha spins the grappling hook, faster and faster. The *Prize* lumbers alongside, lifting us on its swell. He lobs the hook over the railing. I hear it bounce and scrape across the deck and Muhab bellow. The ship moves on, and on—and at last, the rope snaps taut.

We shoot forward under arcing sheets of white water. The force smashes my back against the bench and almost lifts my hands off Qayn. Panicked, I scramble back over him as the two-oar rocks violently and elevates at the bow, forcing Taha to grip the gunwale. I chance a look over it and can't believe what I see: we're being tugged behind the *Prize* in a corridor of water *between* two warships.

Sunlight shines on rows of open portholes, revealing pale, sweaty sailors inside both ships. It burnishes Glaedric's white-blond hair as he staggers to the railing of the ship on our right and sees the crown on my head. He almost falls overboard in his rage, but he's so debilitated by his use of the crown that he can only hang there, screaming at his men. Then the sunlight glints off the cannons swiveling down to aim at us.

"HURRY!" Taha hollers to the *Prize.*

Muhab and several other sailors lean over the railing and grab the rope. "Heave!" the bosun roars. They lean back; the rope shortens. We slide closer to the *Prize,* and yet we're still not safe. The ship itself is losing speed.

The cannons thud and lock into place. Taha twists on his heel, face contorted. "Imani!"

Warmth flares under my hands. "I think I almost have him!"

"We need something *now*!" He bends over the bench and levels his face with mine. "Use the crown to destroy the warships or we're all dead."

Commands are bellowed inside the hulls on either side of us. "MAKE READY THE CANNONS!"

Taha cups my cheek. "Please, Imani, you have to save us again. Our parents . . ."

My hands tremble over Qayn's chest. The crown is already on my head, its power one thought away. There's so much injustice in the world to strike down, wicked actors to remove from the stage, oppressive empires to flatten. I could do it all, and more. I could be glory incarnate, burning with terrible, righteous light. But I would be set on a path that I could never turn back from; I would be driven toward ever greater destruction by an insatiable hunger for control, doomed to be a monster just like Glaedric. And I would be burdened with the inescapable guilt that I betrayed Qayn's trust at his most vulnerable moment. I turned my back on him when he needed me most, and he has never turned his back on me.

"Imani, please!"

Tears sting my eyes. "I *can't*!" I sob. "I'm sorry, Taha, but I have to do this!"

*"FIRE!"*

A thundering curtain of white smoke blots out the mouths of the cannons, parted almost instantly by projectiles. The cannonballs hurtle across the water at us, but Taha's hand doesn't leave my cheek. He gazes at me, and he doesn't blink.

Qayn's chest swells under my hands. His eyes snap open, full of fire. He shoots up, plucking the crown from my head and placing it on his, where it sinks, slightly transparent, and nestles gladly against him. Light blooms from the jewels; he hovers over the boat, as graceful as a black brushstroke, as fast and firm as a whip, and cuts the air with his hands. A blast shoots out from him, so powerful the surface of the water curls away. The cannonballs are flung back at the warships and crash into the hulls;

they bowl through the masts and take sailors with them. Qayn rises higher, hair whipping about his regal face. He looks at the warship on our right and beckons with two fingers. Glaedric lifts off the deck and is carried over to hover before him with teeth bared, shoulders heaving.

"Now you will see why this crown is reserved for me," says Qayn. He draws a steady breath and brings his hands together; at the moment before they meet, he claps, and the two warships and everything and everyone aboard disassemble into millions of fragments that float along for a few seconds before raining into the ocean. Glaedric keens. I cover my gaping mouth. I don't know whether to feel horror or gladness. Whether to rejoice in my victory or fear what I've done.

A smirk bleeds across Qayn's face. "This is the fate that awaits the House of Brand and its great Harrowland Empire." He looks at one warship sailing farther off, then at another, and raises both hands to shoulder height.

Glaedric's head thrashes. "No, don't, please—*DON'T!*"

Qayn snaps his fingers, and the warships crumble to powder. Glaedric howls in agony. The two-oar stops moving, the *Prize* too, despite there being no change in its sails. The ocean flattens like a sheet of silk; the wind doesn't stir.

"Don't kill me!" Glaedric begs. "I'll give you gold, land—kingdoms to rule over however you desire!"

"You have nothing that I want," Qayn replies.

Glaedric wails and desperately tries to reach for Qayn, screeching, "I will be your most loyal servant!"

Qayn gazes at him dispassionately. Glaedric's arms flop by his sides, and he crumples in midair, sobbing. I can't fathom that this is the same man who appeared to me so aloof and impervious that night on his burning ship in the Bay of Glass. That he's been reduced to something this pathetic is deeply unsettling.

"At least have mercy on my sister and brother, and my wife and the innocent babe in her belly!" Glaedric begs. He inhales a wet breath, blinking fast, and then abruptly his gaze stills as it roams the water. "Why did I leave my loving Elfwyn behind?" he murmurs to himself. "She asked me to stop doing this; she said we had enough. She only wanted to go home to her library and the buckthorn tree, the antler moths of winter; her father; and I . . . after all, I don't know for what or why I refused her. . . ." Glaedric falls silent, staring at the ocean, wistfully as if seeing its immense beauty for the first time and recognizing that he will never see it again.

"Go off now," Qayn says with not even a hint of triumph. "Goodbye."

"Goodbye," Glaedric whispers, but he doesn't look at Qayn or any of us. He watches the ocean as he disintegrates to ash, blown away and lost in so many pieces to the indifferent waters below.

# 52

# TAHA

QAYN RAISES TAHA AND IMANI FROM THE TWO-oar and takes them to the *Prize,* setting them down on the deck. Taha's scant relief at having survived vanishes when he sees his father, slumped against the mainmast with his eyes shut. Taha runs over, parting Zahra, Atheer, and Amira, who were kneeling beside Bayek.

"Baba?" he cries, crumpling to his knees. He presses his fingers to Bayek's neck, but no pulse responds.

"He collapsed after the battle with Glaedric," says Atheer quietly. "He asked me to tell you that he's sorry and that he loves you. We couldn't rouse him after that. . . ."

Taha stares at his father, peaceful as if asleep, and seems to forget how to emote. He's overwhelmed, riddled with razor-thin cuts all bleeding—not enough to kill him; just enough to imprison him in this permanent state of unspeakable misery. Suddenly it's as if he's been cleaved in half and everything inside has shattered. He drops his head against his father's chest, sobbing.

"Please, Baba, don't go and leave me behind. I forgive you, do you hear? Wake up, I forgive you. . . ."

The crew gathers around him, ghostlike. He senses their shadows, hears their soft crying, feels them trying to pull him up.

"Hush now, dear," says Zahra. "Your father is with the Great Spirit, and soon, your ancestors."

"But why did he have to be called away?" Taha sobs, clutching Bayek's bisht.

"It is not up to us to know the Great Spirit's will."

Something vile thrashes in him. "But it's not fair!" He sits up and glares at the crew. "Why him? Tell me! Why my father? Why not any of you? Why not your cousins and parents?"

They stare back at him guiltily. Ser Ulric pushes through and jogs over; Taha doesn't know what it is about the red-faced man that makes him burst into tears again. The Marshal puts an arm across his back and pulls him close.

"There, there, boy," he says in his gruff but soothing way—*a little like Baba,* Taha thinks, sending him down another spiral into anguish and panic. "Everyone's got to go someday. But your father went out a warrior, bravely defending this ship until the end. I think that was his way of showing you he cared."

Taha is no longer the Shield who could face danger and difficulty without fear. He's a boy again, tremoring with it as he clings to his father's hand. "This pain is too much," he whispers. "I don't think I'll survive it."

"Felt the same way when my atta passed. I'm still here." Ulric jolts him slightly. "Remember what I said about that sword? This isn't the strike that breaks you."

No, but maybe it's the strike that lays the groundwork for the first cracks, as fine as hair; the ones Taha will ignore until one day, when he least suspects it, they'll destroy him.

"I'm all alone now," he says. "I don't even know where the rest of my family is."

"You've got your friends," says Ulric, gesturing at the others.

But Taha doesn't know whether they're really his friends or just people who are using him.

"And you've got me, if you need me," Ulric adds, more quietly.

"Please, forgive me for interrupting, but this can't wait any longer," Farida says, coming down the gangway, sweating profusely. She looks at Qayn, standing aside. "We took hits on our portside that we can't repair."

He looks toward the hatch. Water begins flooding out of it and overboard. He floats to the portside railing, balances on it, and peers down. Planks bang into place along the hull and after half a minute, the water finishes draining. Suddenly unburdened, the ship rises higher in the water and resumes its journey as if it was never stopped.

Qayn lowers to the deck again. Taha peers up at him, chest swelling with childish hope. "Can you bring my father back?"

Qayn kneels beside Bayek. "No, Taha," he says sadly. "I don't have the power to undo death in others. But I faced the same pain you do now, and I can tell you with certainty that another day follows this one. Permit me to lay your father in the captain's cabin."

"No," Taha clambers to his feet, "don't take him away—"

Ulric squeezes his shoulder. "Just for now."

Qayn raises Bayek and transports him to the captain's cabin. Taha wipes his tears. "How can you have faced the same pain?"

"I'm not who you think I am," Qayn replies.

"You're the single greatest monster to have ever cursed the Sahir with its presence!"

The words come from Amira as she marches over to him. The

same fierce light is in her eyes as when she stabbed him, and it hasn't dimmed.

Qayn's head tilts. "I don't think of myself that way."

"You destroyed the First City and its people! You devastated the Vale and rampaged across the Sahir, murdering tribes of—"

*"Ruthless thieves and co-conspirators,"* he seethes, *"my mortal enemies!"*

She flinches. Zahra hurries over and holds on to her daughter protectively; even Atheer, who has never appeared threatened by Qayn, rushes to her side. Taha is so enervated that he can't even feel uneasy and has to go and sit on the gangway before he passes out.

"Amira," Imani softly warns.

But even while shielded by her mother's arms, Amira remains hostile. "Scholars have debated the motive behind your rampage for a thousand years. None of them could've guessed that the Desert's Bane was just a jilted lover."

"They stole from me," Qayn says with a more controlled fury. "They lied to me and tried to kill me."

"And you wreaked so much havoc in response that the Great Spirit itself had to intervene and grant us magic to defeat you!"

Qayn gives a cold, mean smile. "Speaking of the Great Spirit . . . None of you ever asked what else Nahla stole from me besides my magic."

Amira's shrug has an air of false insouciance about it. "You said it was your fortune, your bounty. Wealth. I assumed you meant gold and other riches."

"So did I," Imani says.

Qayn drags his gaze across them. "Magic."

Amira bobs her head. "*Yes,* you just said that Nahla stole your crown—"

"I gave Nahla magic."

Amira closes her mouth, and they all stare at him. Qayn shuts his eyes briefly, draws a breath of patience. When he speaks, he sounds weary deep in his bones.

"The Great Spirit did not gift your people the misra tree. I did."

# 53

# IMANI

DARKNESS SKULKS ON THE EDGES OF MY VISION. Mama shakes her head, brow and lips crumpled in intellectual anxiety. "No, that—that's not what we know."

"But it is the truth, Zahra," says Qayn. "I built a city in the Vale as a gift for Nahla, the woman I loved, and her tribe. They lived in opulence; no comfort was spared. But Nahla had witnessed the wonders of my power. She became fixated on her dream of her and her people using magic too. I loved her more than anything, so at great cost to myself, I fashioned the misra tree for them as a conduit to my magic, and I planted it in the First City."

" 'A stem of bounty for family,' " Taha murmurs from the gangway, attracting Qayn's curious frown.

Amira slides a hand over her open mouth. "*Nahla's poem.* Mama, do you remember it in the book? 'His gift was a pearl in a green sea; a bed of purple for he and me; a stem of bounty for family—' "

" 'Prosperity guarded by immensity; a secret bought naked in the shade: divinity.' " Mama nods. "I remember."

The vision of earlier commands me—a hand parting a curtain on a garden, a woman's voice—Nahla's—saying, *Is it really ours to keep?*

I wobble on my feet. Qayn notices and nods, wagging a finger. "You know this is the truth. You saw the First City."

Another memory finds me, this of me and Taha riding his horse down a long tunnel painted red by torchlight, its walls etched in familiar landscapes and scenes—and a tree that I pointed out to Taha specifically for its resemblance to the misra tree.

I clutch my head in my hands. The crew backs away as Qayn comes closer. "You saw a burning garden in your dreams, that's why you snuck into the same garden in my memories. You wanted to know what happened on that day that led to the blaze. Imani."

I let my hands fall away and raise my naked gaze to his.

"That garden was *my* garden of the misra tree," he says. "But Nahla and her people made their own garden, and using the magic I gifted them, they made their own city."

"Qalia," I breathe.

"Yes. They uprooted the tree from the First City and planted it in Qalia."

Tears drip down my face. A bitter wind has stirred, drying them where they fall. "Why would her people do that? You freely gave them your magic."

"Doing so had unintended consequences." He enunciates carefully now. "Misra magic, I later discovered, is a kind of beacon. The more intensely that someone uses it, the brighter their beacon burns, and some of the walls between this realm and another are very thin. Imagine them like sheets of paper. Even with only Nahla and her tribe using the misra, the light of their beacons were bright enough to begin luring what you call monsters to the Sahir."

"You didn't invite them, as the accounts say?" Zahra asks.

"Not in the beginning, no." A shadow passes over Qayn's face. "Once I realized there was a problem, I asked Nahla and her people to hold off from spreading the magic until I could investigate the origins of the monsters. In the meantime, I pardoned those willing to live in peace, like Hubaal, and destroyed the rest. Yet, mysteriously, their numbers continued to increase."

A shiver runs through me. "Someone else was using the magic."

He sends me a dark look. "Your people believe the Great Spirit's blessing of magic unified the warring tribes of the Sahir. That's a twisted telling of the truth. The elders of Nahla's tribe used misra to buy the loyalties of rival tribes. Not only was that contrary to my intentions for the magic, but it was a deliberate flouting of the moratorium."

Nahla's voice, tense and pleading, echoes from a memory, startling me: *Please don't fret, Qayn! I can remedy this, I promise. I shall speak with my father.*

"When you found out, you threatened to take the tree away," I say.

"I merely raised the possibility with Nahla. I was growing increasingly concerned about the influx of monsters into the Sahir and the potential consequences that could have for the wider world," says Qayn. "I had no qualms about the magic being shared once I had addressed the issue. Nahla promised me they would stop spreading the Spice. But not long after, the tree was stolen."

"And the people of the First City?" I venture.

"Ready and waiting for me upon my discovery of the theft,"

he says bitterly. "They fought me with my own magic. They called me demon."

"And you killed them," I say.

*"Yes,"* he hisses, striding at me, hair fluttering around his face. "I annihilated them and gave Nahla what she wanted: I opened Doors she couldn't close and invited to the Sahir any monster who would listen—and so very many did."

My heart starts to kick. "You went to Harrowland and did the same there, didn't you? They call you the Gods' Bane."

He retreats at that, a snake that's observed the specter of a falcon on the horizon. "I've borne many names," he says from the corner of his mouth.

"But if you were well aware of Nahla's deceptions, how did she still manage to steal your crown?" Amira demands.

He stops with his back to us. "By using my love for her against me. She invited me to a meeting in the western mountains, where we had first met years earlier, and begged for my forgiveness, claiming she would do anything to right the situation. I didn't see the dagger until it was in my heart and she'd already lifted the crown from me. It went without a fight, I suspect because I had given her pieces of my soul as a marriage gift." He turns sideways and ponders the horizon with a faraway look. "Nahla pushed me off the cliff. I fell at least a hundred feet and landed on stone. Every bone in my body shattered. I felt my organs rupture. Arteries detach. Blood fill cavities where it shouldn't have been.

"Once I had healed the worst of my injuries, I returned to consciousness, but I lay in agony for months while my body repaired. I couldn't fend off new attacks. The healing process had to be frequently restarted. Hyenas found me—"

I press my hands to my face, but I can't bring myself to stop his tale. I must know the truth, even if doing so bleeds away my belief that there is a limit to evil.

"I screamed until I lost my voice and had to endure the horror in silence," he continues. "I will never forget seeing my chest torn open on my still-beating heart, blood gushing with a fountain's vigor." He stops to take a few breaths. Some of the crew walk to the bow and don't return. "A clan of djinn eventually came upon me. We had met once before when I permitted them to dwell in the Sahir. They told me that their realm was deeply troubled, and so they felt they owed me a debt of gratitude for letting them take refuge here. They repaid it by shielding me until I recovered and could shield myself.

"After that, I searched for my crown, but the enchantment of the Sahir's borders had already been cast and I was trapped. Over the years of wandering that followed, I discovered the conspiracy the elders of the now-unified tribes had concocted—I heard the lie that Sahirans were telling their grandchildren about a monster called the Desert's Bane, and the war they had fought against it with magic granted to them by the Great Spirit. I saw the new Council of Al-Zahim, and how covetous they were of the Spice and the prosperity it gave them, such that they indoctrinated every future generation to jealously guard it from outsiders—an outcome that was never my intention when I gave Nahla magic. I learned that, despite her many gifts and sacrifices for the new Sahiran nation, Nahla was condemned to obscurity as the Unknown Sorcerer. Like me, she was written out of history in order to preserve the Council's version of it."

"A history of lies," says Mama, anguished. "I have much work to do in the Archives."

Qayn approaches us again. "I can take you to Qalia. My promise to defend the Sahir was not an idle one."

Mama is cautious. "You don't want retribution?"

Everyone looks at Qayn with palpable apprehension.

"There is no justice in seeking retribution on people who didn't wrong me," he says. "But I cannot permit the privileged few of the Sahiran nation to continue reaping benefits from age-old wrongs. I already sense that simply being reunited with my crown has undone the enchantment over the Swallowing Sands. As for the misra tree, I will allow you to keep it only if the Sahiran people agree to share its magic with others."

Muhab, Makeen, and the other sailors break out in triumphant smiles, while Atheer hugs and kisses Farida. I'm happy for them. When I was confronted by the injustice and poverty in Alqibah, I finally understood why keeping a bounty such as the misra tree to ourselves is wrong. Everyone deserves to have the same things I do that I took for granted for years, and the magic of the misra is a way to do that. But I'm restrained in my joy.

"Sharing the magic is the right thing to do," I say, quieting the others' celebration. "But Qayn, you just told us that the more people who use it, the more that monsters are lured to our realm."

Taha exchanges a mysterious glance with Ser Ulric before standing. "It's already happening," he says. "With all the Harrowlanders using the magic too, the population of monsters in the Sahir has dramatically increased—and some of them are behaving strangely."

"They're attacking major settlements and routes in the daytime," relates Ulric in Sahiran, as my skin tingles with goose bumps. "Not even the presence of soldiers is enough to deter them."

"Spirits," I murmur, looking back at Qayn. "What are we going to do?"

His temple pulses, but he's not shocked by the revelation, let alone surprised. "I was aware of this problem a millennium ago," he says. "I've come up with a few possible solutions in that time. For now, leave the matter to me. I'll deal with it. You can trust me."

"Can we?" Amira asks tartly. "You haven't told us everything, like what you really are—"

"I was a mortal like you once," Qayn cuts her off, "and now I have magic."

"How?" she demands. "Where did you get it from? Are there others like you?"

These are questions I'm eager to have answered too, but so much has been said already that I sense we're now forging into territory that perhaps we're not ready—or even allowed—to enter.

"It draws much from me to look into the past and its tragedies," says Qayn, a faint warning in his tone. "I believe I've given you enough for now and shown you proof of my goodwill. Do you accept my offer of aid, or shall I part ways with you and make good on correcting Nahla's wrongs?"

"We accept," I say quickly, hurrying over to him. "We need your help, Qayn. Glaedric is gone, but the Empire still occupies lands all along the Spice Road, including the Sahir. They must be freed and then, if we can find a way to solve the threat of the monsters, others can finally enjoy the prosperity that your gift gave us for centuries."

Amira skulks to the other end of the deck, unsatisfied.

Thankfully, Qayn doesn't seem to notice. He favors me with a warm, earnest smile. "I'm very glad that you share the same fair vision that I had when I gave Nahla magic. As I said, my promise to deal with the Empire wasn't an idle one. But I must know, how many of their soldiers are in the Sahir?"

"About one hundred thousand, the bulk of them in and

around Qalia," Ser Ulric answers. "Glaedric left his sister, Princess Blaedwyn, in charge of the city. You might try reasoning with her, and not for her sake. . . . Most of the soldiers are only boys, there because they were told to be."

"Very well. I will give Princess Blaedwyn and her forces an opportunity to surrender," says Qayn. "*One* opportunity. Anyone who refuses meets the same fate as Glaedric." He shifts his attention to Farida. "Captain, may I use the *Prize* to convey us to Qalia?"

"The ship's yours, Qayn." Farida points off at our right. "That way will take us straight into the Sahiran coastline. Curve a little around, and we'll hit the Gulf of Fire."

Qayn looks for a long moment, as if he can actually see our destination, and rubs his hands together. "Thank you, Captain. I can look after the journey from here. We'll arrive in the morning."

Farida's jaw drops. *"The morning?"* she echoes as her crew exclaims in disbelief.

Gaze intent, Qayn beckons a tunnel of wind over his shoulders, frightening us into clinging to whatever we can. The masts swivel; the sails strain, their bellies filling. The current shifts favorably behind us, waves fleeing the prow's path and the air ahead softening. The ship sails, unrestrained, across the water.

Even with what I've seen of Qayn's power so far, I'm staggered. A nine-day journey shortened to *one.* A *flying ship.* It's inconceivable, it's miraculous, it's . . . frightening. I should be elated, and I am, but a small part of me can't help but feel anxious. Just yesterday, Qayn was utterly powerless. If not for me, he still would be. I know I made the right decision in returning his magic to him, but that small part of me still wonders. . . .

# 54

# IMANI

WE CLING TO MAST AND RAILS. QAYN WATCHES us, mildly amused by our fright. Like the rest of the crew, I force myself to look over the side of the ship; the *Prize* is barely touching the surface of the ocean. Once the crew realizes that, it's settled that there's nothing more for them to do. They thank Qayn in reverent murmurs and head belowdecks, yawning and rubbing their eyes. Atheer hugs him and descends belowdecks too, holding Mama's and Amira's hands, though it seems more like my brother is dragging our sister away before she decides to have another confrontation with Qayn.

Ulric sees me coming over to Taha, seated on the gangway, and leaves for the bow, where the Harrowlander sailors are huddled. I sit down beside Taha and lightly rest my hand on his knee.

"I know you had a complicated relationship with your father," I say. "Whatever the things he's done wrong, however much of it—he's done right too. None of us would be here if not for his bravery and magical might. He sacrificed himself without hesitation to save us and everyone in the world from Glaedric's oppression. He was a hero, Taha, and he taught you how to be one too."

Taha inhales shakily. After a long moment, he brings my hand up and kisses it. Then silently he goes to the captain's cabin to be with his father.

By now, the deck has largely emptied but for Qayn, who's waiting for me.

"It seems it's just you and me again," I say, joining him at the railing.

He smiles at the water. "I must thank you again for all you've done. I think I must thank you every day from now on."

I can hardly look at Qayn, I'm so nervous. Being around him before could already be nerve-racking. After learning how truly powerful he is, I almost feel that I have no right to share this view of the sea with him.

"I must thank *you* for intervening when you did," I say. "We were seconds from death."

"You trusted me."

I frown. "That was a test?"

"No, I was going to save you regardless," he says. "But I wanted to give you the chance—give *myself* the chance—to prove that you are the person I think you are. Someone I can trust." He turns to face me. "For that reason, I believe there's something else you deserve to know." He reaches over and slides my dagger from its scabbard, flips it so he's holding it by the blade. "Take the hilt and don't let go."

I do, but I'm afraid to handle it properly. He still has the blade pinched between his fingers. He guides it upward; with his other hand, he pulls his tunic away from the pink cross of scars on his chest. I squirm as Qayn rests the blade against them; I try to pull my hand off the hilt as he sinks the blade into his flesh, but he lets go of his tunic and holds my wrist firm. Obsidian blood wells under my dagger. I fight against him.

"Qayn, what are you doing!"

"Watch," he orders.

A memory engulfs my vision. It steals the ship and replaces it with a beautiful green place on a cliffside, high above the world. My hands are no longer my own. I'm holding Qayn's crown in one; I'm stabbing him in the heart with the other, his life flowing over my knuckles and the hilt of my dagger. . . .

I'm expelled from the memory by the strength of my own dismay. I search for Qayn's lifeless body, but he's standing as he was by the railing, lifting the blade away from the tiny nick on his chest.

"What did you see?" he asks, tossing the dagger to me.

I let it fall on the planks at my feet. "I saw Nahla. Killing you with my dagger."

He exhales deeply, as if relieved, and his manner eases. "It's an astounding weapon. Forged by Nahla's father from a flaming star that fell to the Sahir on the night she was born. He called it Bright Blade."

"You're wrong," I protest hastily. "This dagger belonged to my ancestors. It's been in my clan for a thousand—" I dig my teeth into my bottom lip, clamping my hands over my eyes. "Great Spirit, don't let it be."

"It will be, whether you want it or not." Qayn collects the dagger off the deck. "Nahla is your ancestor, Imani. The Beya clan is one of several powerful lineages that descended from her tribe."

"Then we're a poisoned well!" I exclaim in despair, pulling my hands away. "If it weren't for what Nahla and her tribe did to you, the Beya clan wouldn't be so powerful, if at all."

"But it is. Now it's up to you what you do with your power. You decide who you will be and what sort of world you will help create." Qayn flips the dagger again, hilt facing up.

But I don't take it. "I'm so ashamed, Qayn. I've threatened to kill you with the same blade that has already touched your heart before."

"And it's the same blade that aided you in your battles to save me and everybody else. The same blade you may be called upon to use again."

I reluctantly accept the dagger and return it to its place on my thigh. "What made you decide to share your magic with mortals in the first place?"

"Being told I wasn't allowed." Qayn smiles, brief and reserved. "But these are matters for later discussion. You've hardly slept in more than a day, and I need time to meditate before we arrive in Qalia." He pulls me into a hug and holds my head against his chest. "I mean it when I say you're going to need your energy for what's coming. Changing the world isn't without its challenges, you know."

I smile. "I'm sure I can overcome anything with you at my side."

He kisses my forehead. I shut my eyes and linger in the embrace as long as he'll let me. Qayn doesn't go in a hurry. We drift apart in comfortable silence, and I descend belowdecks to finally rest.

# 55

# IMANI

"IMANI, WAKE UP."

I surface with a gasp from the longest, deepest sleep I've had since I left Qalia. But for a few seconds, I wonder if I'm still dreaming. Amira stands over me, face twisted in fear as she frantically shakes me.

I sit up, pressing a hand over my racing heart. "What's going on?"

She stops shaking me but doesn't let go of my arm. "We're flying over the Sahir," she says. "There are monsters *everywhere.*"

I'm on my feet in an instant, stumbling after her through the crew quarters, my head pounding. The first thing I notice when I escape the hatch is the scorched scent tickling the back of my throat, and then the frightened crew lining the railings. Some are looking overboard, but others point at the clouded sky around the soaring ship. I squint, approaching the railing where Qayn is standing. Suddenly a shadow covers the deck. Amira shrieks and grabs my hand as something immense swoops over and past the ship, mind-bending in how dangerously close it is, yet moving so quickly I barely catch a glimpse of scales before it's disappeared into the haze.

Some of the sailors flee for shelter belowdecks. I reach the railing and peer down. We're flying over sweeping Sahiran grasslands scattered with familiar sandstone settlements, threaded together by roads I used to patrol with my squad of Shields. But nothing is as it was.

The land has been draped in a kind of slow-moving, shadowy miasma that shows no response to the sunlight falling onto its surface. It shifts constantly, becoming thicker in some places than others, and where it's thinner, I can make out landmarks—a town burning on the indistinct horizon, the road connecting it to the next settlement piled with crashed wagons. Between them weave giant sand serpents, hungrily searching for a meal. At the sound of screaming, I drop my gaze to the town of Beit Zam, the shadowed road outside it crowded by werehyenas trying to break through the gates and defensive wall to reach the people sheltered inside. I glimpse the burial grounds next to the town, lined with rows of disturbed graves, and a nearby garrison splashed in blood, littered with bodies. Ghouls squat in the yard, feasting on the flesh of dead Harrowlander soldiers, their horses and dogs—

The ship shoots high into the clouds, and the horrors below are concealed from view.

"We have to go back and help those people in Beit Zam," I say to Qayn. He's staring into the clouds with glassy eyes.

"What about Qalia?" Taha asks as he comes to stand beside me. He must've been pulled from his vigil in the captain's cabin by what's happening. "The city must be in trouble too," he says.

"But Beit Zam is about to be overrun," I point out. "Qayn can kill the werehyenas—"

"More will come," Taha cuts me off urgently. "Just from what

I was aware of, Glaedric had already shipped dozens of boxes of misra to Alqibah and *overseas* by the time I left Qalia. There's no telling how much Spice is out there."

"And the more magic that people use, the more monsters that will come," I say in a haunted voice.

The ship breaks through the clouds and halts. Qalia appears far below like a faintly glimmering jewel sinking in a black sea.

The dark haze is thickest here, enveloping the city as if within a death shroud. Qalia is identifiable only because of the lights twinkling along its ramparts. The military camp in the fields outside would be positively incandescent if not for the haze blanketing it. The Harrowlander soldiers are clearly attempting to resist the darkness. They've lit hundreds of torches and concentrated them especially around siege engines, which have been turned to face outward. But in places where there's no source of light, the camp disappears in the murk entirely. And despite the signs that soldiers are present in the camp and on the city's ramparts, everything is quiet in a way I struggle to grasp. It's the deliberate silence before battle. No sounds of trundling carriages and trotting horses, no low hum of chatter or the blow of a horn to direct traffic, no clang of tools, not even birds singing. The city gates are shut; the land is silent. Utterly still until it isn't.

"Look," Amira whispers, as if we're in danger of being heard. "There's something out there."

Yes, there is, standing far out on the road that winds its way to Qalia. Almost impossible to see if you don't look at the right moment, when the miasma drifts and the sunlight manages to fall in just the right place. Enough for me to see some of the gigantic monster: his alabaster skin, like the seamless stone of a monolith; his featureless face, shadows hiding in the hollows of his eyes and cheeks. It's tilted toward the city, from where his focus does not shift.

Then the miasma thickens again, and the giant vanishes from view. But he's still there, and if he is, there may be more surrounding Qalia. Many more. Perhaps that's why the Harrowlanders have faced the siege engines out and placed their soldiers on the ramparts. They're watching and waiting for an attack. . . .

"The clan of djinn that saved me told me about their realm," Qayn says suddenly, breaking the quiet. "They said that it was poisoned at its heart by a spreading darkness."

My eyes widen. "Is that what's happening? The darkness is spreading *into the Sahir.*"

"I fear that may be so," he says. "But I can't be certain from here. I must seek answers in the other realm. Only then will I know how to fix this for good."

I instinctively grab his hand. "Let me come with you."

"You can't go by yourself, Imani. It's dangerous," says Taha from my left. "I'll come too."

Qayn's fingers interlock with mine. The wind tousles his black hair; the miasma steals some of the glory of his crown. Dims it.

"I don't know what will be waiting in there for us," he says.

For some inexplicable reason, I realize that I don't quite believe him, and the small part of me that found Qayn's power frightening becomes just a little bigger.

I look back at the road in time to glimpse the giant's silhouette again. The monster has moved closer to Qalia, only by a step, but closer nonetheless.

"We will find out together."

# ACKNOWLEDGMENTS

I owe the realization of *Serpent Sea* to many excellent people.

My editor, Kelsey Horton at Delacorte Press, helped me precisely uncover the story I wanted to tell. And although she was always thoughtfully guiding me to refine my ideas, to expand the story in some places and simplify in others, she also gave me the most valuable gift that an author can receive: the space to be myself creatively, to explore themes that are personally significant and evolve my characters in ways that are meaningful to me. Thank you, Kelsey—I'm proud of the book we've created, and immensely grateful for your continued faith in the trilogy.

Among many others in the amazing team at Random House Children's Books (who always go above and beyond), my publicist Lili Feinberg, for your enthusiasm in spreading the word about *Serpent Sea*; my copyeditors, Candice Gianetti and Colleen Fellingham, for spotting the illogical prose, typos, and facepalm-worthy plot holes that I couldn't; illustrator Virginia Allyn for transforming my incoherent scribbles into yet another truly magical map; and my designer, Angela Carlino, as well as artist Carlos Quevedo, for creating a powerful, captivating cover that brings this story to life—thank you all.

Deepest thanks to my agent, Peter Knapp, who remains an

unflagging advocate for me and my work—to put it quite simply, I owe you very much. Many thanks to Stuti Telidevara, Kathryn Toolan, and everyone at Park & Fine for working to share my books with readers all over the world. Thanks as well to my agent in the UK, Claire Wilson at RCW, for championing my books across the Commonwealth.

I owe a debt of gratitude to the booksellers at home and abroad who've supported *Serpent Sea* and *Spice Road*—from the bottom of my heart, thank you for seeing something special in my stories and sharing your passion for them with readers.

A special shoutout to Annie McCann, generous and talented friend, colleague, and author. Thank you for supporting my books, and for always making me feel comfortable on panels (no easy feat.)

To my family, thank you for your unwavering love, friendship, and excitement. Nothing quite restores my sanity after a long stint of editing like getting together for a big hearty Arab lunch. I know I can always count on you to help me choose the final cover.

To my husband, thank you for sticking by my side and looking after everything when I was glued to my Word document with no end in sight. Without your loving support, I wouldn't be able to live out this wonderful dream.

And to my precious little one, the sun in my sky: I write for many reasons, but mostly, I write for you. (Thanks for bringing me my hat.)

Last but certainly not least: to my readers, wherever and whoever you are—thank you for giving Imani, Taha, and Qayn their voices.

# ABOUT THE AUTHOR

MAIYA IBRAHIM is the debut author of *Spice Road*, an instant *Sunday Times* bestseller. She graduated with a bachelor of laws from the University of Technology Sydney. When she isn't writing, reading, or spending time with her family, Maiya enjoys playing video games, gardening, and expanding her collection of rare trading cards. She lives in Sydney, Australia.